Orphans of the Storm

Comments from the Press

●

Long after I finished reading the stories, they kept haunting.... *Orphans of the Storm* does what no literary anthology on the Partition has attempted to do so far.... It brings the reader pieces of fiction from both sides of the border, in an attempt to show that no community or individual remained unscorched by the fire of hatred and communalism that the horrific event bred.

Economic Times

Exposes us to the literary wealth of India and Pakistan.

Business Standard

Intensely moving.... One must have strong nerves to suffer with the characters, the terror and the pain which the insensate violence creates in the heart of humane people.

Deccan Chronicle

... an important chapter in the history of literature in the sub-continent.

The Hindustan Times

... a masterpiece that blends humour with pathos with the deftness of a skilled craftsman.... Takes you beyond the brutality of the time and describes its far-reaching effects on the human mind.

The Tribune

UBSPD

UBS Publishers' Distributors Ltd.
New Delhi Bombay Bangalore Madras
Calcutta Patna Kanpur London

– Orphans
of the Storm –

Stories on the Partition of India

Selected and Edited by
Saros Cowasjee
K.S. Duggal

UBS Publishers' Distributors Ltd.
5 Ansari Road, New Delhi-110 002
Bombay Bangalore Madras Calcutta Patna Kanpur London

First Published   1995
First Reprint   1995

Cover Design   : UBS Art Studio
Cover Painting   : Sobha Singh
Back Cover Painting : B.R. Chopra

**This book has been printed on
Recycled Ecological Friendly Paper.**

Lasertypeset in 11 pt. Times Roman at FOLIO, New Delhi
and printed at Pauls Press, New Delhi

Acknowledgements

THANKS ARE DUE to the following authors and/or their publishers for permission to reprint the stories listed:

"A Debt to Pay" and "Revenge" by Khwaja Ahmad Abbas; "The Dark Night" by Aziz Ahmad; "The Avenger" by S. H. Vatsyayan ("Ajneya"); "The Parrot in the Cage" by Mulk Raj Anand; "Aadaab" by Samaresh Basu; "Lajwanti" by Rajinder Singh Bedi; "Peshawar Express" by Krishan Chander; "Another Train to Pakistan" by Saros Cowasjee; "Kulsum", "Pakistan Zindabad" and "A New Home" by Kartar Singh Duggal; "After the Storm" by Attia Hosain; "The Stairway" by Intizar Husain; "How Many Pakistans?" by Kamleshwar; "Toba Tek Singh", "The Reunion", "A Tale of 1947" and "Xuda Ki Qasam" by Saadat Hasan Manto; "The Four-Poster" by Narendra Nath Mitra; "The Broken Shoes" by Giani Gurmukh Singh Musafir; "Where Did She Belong?" by Suraiya Qasim; "The Proprietor of the Debris" by Mohan Rakesh; "Pali" by Bhisham Sahni; "Gods on Trial" by Gulzar Singh Sandhu; "Savage Harvest" by M. S. Sarna; "Ya Khuda" by Qudrat Ullah Shahab; "Defend Yourself Against Me" by

Bapsi Sidhwa; "The Riot" by Khushwant Singh; "Where Is My Mother?" by Krishna Sobti.

Thanks are also due to Professor Faruq Hassan of Dawson College, Montreal, for translating specially for us from Urdu the stories of Aziz Ahmad and Qudrat Ullah Shahab, and to Professor Muhammad Umar Memon of the University of Wisconsin for providing us a copy of his translation of Intizar Husain's "The Stairway".

Contents

Introduction

I$_\text{N THE CONCLUDING}$ pages of Khushwant Singh's *Train to Pakistan* (1956), one of the characters recalls Jawaharlal Nehru's famous words to the Constituent Assembly on the night of August 14, 1947: "Long ago we made a tryst with destiny and now the time comes when we shall redeem our pledge, not wholly or in full measure but very substantially." No doubt revealing Khushwant Singh's own bitter disillusionment, the same character pronounces: "Yes, Mr Prime Minister, you made your tryst. So did many others—on the 15th of August, Independence Day."

Nehru made his tryst with destiny and became India's first Prime Minister. But what of the "others"? This anthology tells something of their tryst—the tryst of the common people caught between the greed of politicians for power and the unseemly haste with which the Labour Government in Britain decided to transfer power. It is on record that Lord Louis Mountbatten, then Viceroy and Governor General of India, got his Reforms Commissioner, Mr V. P. Menon, to draw up the plan for the division of India in just four hours. With this plan he himself flew to London and got Mr Attlee and his Cabinet to accept it in exactly five minutes. "It is all very well," says the historian Leonard Mosley, "to draw up a plan to divide India in four hours and accept it in five minutes. How, in a land consisting of 250,000,000 Hindus, 90,000,000 Muslims, 10,000,000 Christians and—particularly *and*—5,000,000 Sikhs, do you implement it?"

The implementation of the plan with neither foresight nor preparedness led to a holocaust. Overnight, two new states came into existence: a truncated India, and a largely Muslim Pakistan comprising Sind, Baluchistan, North West Frontier Province and parts of the states of Punjab in the West and Bengal in the East. Mahatma Gandhi, Mountbatten's "one man boundary force", kept the peace in Bengal, but indescribable violence broke out in the Punjab. Even by a conservative estimate, ten million people took to the road; a million did not make their destination. Trains packed with Muslim refugees, all of them murdered during the journey, arrived in West Pakistan with messages scribbled on the sides of the carriages reading, "A Gift from India". In turn the Muslims sent back train-loads of butchered Sikhs and Hindus with the message, "A Gift from Pakistan". Foot convoys, some of them 800,000 strong and seventy miles long, moved between the two dominions. Thousands were slaughtered on the way; an equal number fell victim to cholera and other diseases. One Captain Atkins of the British army recalls a road on which a convoy had passed: "Every yard of the way there was a body, some butchered, some dead of cholera. The vultures had become so bloated by their feasts they could fly no longer, and the wild dogs so demanding in their taste they ate only the livers of the corpses littering the road."

The horror accompanying the transfer of population has been a major theme with fiction writers. Some looked on a realistic portrayal of communal violence as the most representative aspect of the Partition experience. Others, chiefly the Progressive writers, who had been a dominant force on the Indian scene since the Thirties, were thrown off balance by the carnage. Having put their faith in human rationality, many of them had no words to express their disillusionment. Faiz Ahmed Faiz summed up their disillusionment and his own in *Subh-i-Azadi*:

> This pock-marked morn,
> This night-stung dawn,
> It is not the dawn we'd longed for.
> It is not the morning in search of which
> We had set out to find it, . . .

Unable to explain the violence, many of the Progressives concentrated solely on painting elaborate scenes of violence in the hope of conveying something of their sense of disgust. In doing so, they consciously avoided taking sides and put the blame equally on both warring factions. The most glaring example of a neutral account is Krishan Chander's "Peshawar Express"—where, in his zeal for impartiality, the author balances the Hindus and Muslims butchered with something of an arithmetical precision. But there is a twist in the story which makes it memorable: it is narrated in the person of the railway engine, the non-human machine which alone, while men kill one another, is capable of human feelings.

Though Partition offered a variety of subject matter, the majority of the writers chose to deal with violence of one kind or another—abduction and rape being particular favourites. The less gifted writers tried to excel in graphic descriptions of women being physically abused and mutilated, and too often succeeded in making the painful nauseating. But in the hands of the masters, the theme of rape resulted in some of the most heart-wrenching stories ever written. Among these are Kartar Singh Duggal's "Kulsum", Khwaja Ahmad Abbas's "Revenge" and Saadat Hasan Manto's "The Reunion".

"Kulsum" illuminates a moment of horror. In this story an old Sikh rapes a Muslim *houri* (whom he has abducted) for failing sexually to oblige his young guest, a schoolmaster. As the old man emerges from the hut tying his *lungi*, we find ourselves as dumfounded as the girl, Kulsum. Her earlier plea to the schoolmaster, "Marry me first . . . I beg of you", repeated many times by the hapless girl, takes on an added poignancy. Abbas's "Revenge" centres on a father's craving for vengeance on seeing his daughter stripped, raped and mutilated in his presence. Nothing less than stabbing a Muslim girl "in her naked breasts" would recompense him. He gets his chance in a brothel. With a dagger poised in the air, he snatches the brassiere off the body of a young girl to find "two horrible round scars" where the breasts should have been. A single word "Daughter" escapes his lips. Melodramatic perhaps, but nonetheless moving.

The most harrowing tale about rape is "The Reunion" by the much publicised Pakistani writer, Saadat Hasan Manto. In it a Muslim girl has been raped so often that her hands involuntarily move to undo her trouser strings even when the doctor asks the girl's father to open the window. The father's exclamation of joy, "She's alive. My daughter is alive", is Swiftian in its irony. The story is, as one critic puts it, "not about guilt but it is powerful enough to make a whole generation feel guilty." Another story, "Xuda Ki Qasam" (I swear by God), in which a mother relentlessly searches for her supposedly dead daughter, comes to very different end. Here, the abducted girl has done well for herself but fears meeting her corpse-like mother. When the mother learns the truth, it is much too painful for her and she collapses on the street. A tragedy like Partition cannot be relegated to statistics alone: there are deaths other than physical which are equally devastating.

But there is much in the fiction of this period that transcends the horror and brutality of Partition by giving a glimpse of the compassion and understanding that suffering generates. Khushwant Singh's *Train to Pakistan*, despite its fearsome portrayal of bloated human bodies floating down the river and the pungent smell of burnt flesh, reveals the selfless love and sacrifice of a Sikh youth for a Muslim girl. It is, in addition, an indictment of politicians, both Hindu and Muslim, who inflame hatred among a simple people to serve their own selfish ends. Chaman Nahal's *Azadi*, which offers the most comprehensive treatment of the partitioning of India, shows the transformation in character possible under the stress of a great moment. The once ridiculous Kanshi Ram, like Major McBride in Yeats' "Easter 1916", is changed utterly. "He, too, has resigned his part / In the casual comedy."

The compassion that one finds in *Train to Pakistan* and *Azadi* has not been easy to capture in the short story. The short story, by the very limitations of length and treatment imposed on it, does not offer the scope for the in-depth psychological study or the gradual transformation in character that the novel does. The short story does, however, offer the writer an opportunity to grasp a vital moment in the lives of his characters and illumine it. Some of the stories in this volume do just that. In Vatsyayan's "The Avenger", a Sikh father and son, having lost all that they once possessed, now keep travelling between two Indian cities to see refugees like themselves safely to their new homes. There is Narendra Mitra's "The Four-Poster"—a story set in East Pakistan after the division of the country. Here, a well-to-do Hindu and a poverty-stricken Muslim are locked in a feud over the ownership of an antique bed which the former has impulsively sold to the latter. Finally, they resolve their differences, not through logic or reasoning, but by a compassionate awareness of each other's sorrows.

Any attempt to categorise stories into groups which depict murder or rape or compassion has its limitations, for most good stories cross boundaries and have more than one theme.

M. S. Sarna's "Savage Harvest", for example, focuses on a Muslim ironmonger who makes axes for a gang of murderers led by his son. He meets his nemesis at the hands of his own tortured conscience when he sees an old, frail woman murdered by an axe he himself had made. The story raises the question of who is more guilty—the doer of evil or the provider of the means of evil? Bapsi Sidhwa in "Defend Yourself Against Me" tells of two young Sikhs who beg forgiveness of an old woman for violence to her person by their elders. The old woman forgives them, saying, "How else could I live?" Forgiveness is all very well, the author seems to say, but one must not forget. And she quotes a Bolivian poet at the close of the story to underscore her warning: "Defend yourself against me / against my father and the father of my father / still living in me". Sidhwa, like most Pakistani writers, considers the Sikhs the chief adversaries in the Partition riots. It would be well to remember that the Sikhs, as the main losers in the division of the Punjab, were, as Collins and Lapierre say in *Freedom at Midnight* (1976), the "most vicious killers of all."

Among both communities, the Hindu and Muslim, there were those who accepted conversion to the other's faith to save their lives. Not that such conversions always worked. In Gulzar Singh Sandhu's "Gods on Trial", the recent Muslim converts to Sikhism are easily singled out by their symbols of conversion—new yellow scarves and bright steel bangles—and are mercilessly put to death by a gang of marauding Sikhs. In Bhisham Sahni's "Pali", a lost Hindu child is adopted by a Muslim couple and forcibly circumcised and pronounced a Muslim. Some years later, the boy is discovered by his real parents and taken back to India where he is rebaptised as a Hindu. Behind this grim comedy lies the traumatic experience of the boy which allows the author implicitly to suggest: To whom does a child belong? Does he belong to the parents who give him birth or does he belong to those who succour him? Does the child have a choice in this matter? Above all, the story contrasts the innocence of the child with the bigotry of the adults.

Almost all the fiction on Partition by Indian writers ignores Mohammad Ali Jinnah's two-nation theory—one to which even Nehru and Sardar Vallabbhai Patel silently acquiesced in the days preceding the birth of Pakistan. Is such an omission a failure on the part of writers to keep pace with the ever-changing face of politics or is it because the two-nation theory appeared too parochial a subject? Whatever be the reason, many Indian writers and a good few Pakistani writers did show Hindus and Muslims as one people.* Ennobling as the subject seemed, its execution often ended in a stereotyped plot in which a Hindu or a Muslim rises defiantly above communal and group feelings to embrace his opposite number in everlasting brotherhood. As Muhammad Umar Memon says in his study of Intizar Husain, "The treatment remains superficial and artificial due perhaps to the desire to appear impartial. The hero is forced to react not according to the dictates of his personality and nature, but according to an ideal superimposed upon his personality." However, in the hands of ingenious writers, the notion that Hindus and Muslims are one people and that Partition was a grievous mistake, occasioned stories of the first order. Among them are Manto's "Toba Tek Singh", Khushwant Singh's "The Riot", and Samaresh Basu's "Aadaab".

The most imaginative of Manto's Partition stories, "Toba Tek Singh", is at the same time a very personal document. Fearful of communal tensions prevailing at that time, and persuaded by his wife and family, Manto left Bombay for Lahore in January 1948 and always regretted having done so.

---

* That Hindus and Muslims are not necessarily one people in matters of religion, culture, traditions and sense of values has been argued by historians such as Percival Spear, Sir Hugh MacPherson and Sir Theodore Morison.

He had looked on the partition of the country as an act of insanity, and he takes this theme of insanity to its culminating point in the story by having the governments of India and Pakistan agree to an exchange of lunatics. Humour and pathos are deftly mingled throughout the story as in the medley that takes place on the border of the two states:

> Getting the lunatics out of the buses and handing over custody to officers of the other side proved to be a very difficult task. Some refused to come off the bus; those that came out were difficult to control; a few broke loose and had to be recaptured. Those that were naked had to be clothed. No sooner were the clothes put on them than they tore them off their bodies. Some came out with vile abuse, others began to sing at the top of their voices. Some squabbled; others cried or roared with laughter. They created such a racket that one could not hear a word. The female lunatics added to the noise.

Among the group is an old Sikh, Bishen Singh, who wants to be neither in India nor Pakistan but in the village—Toba Tek Singh—to which he belongs. And it is through his "weird cry" and death that Manto speaks of the pain and grief of the millions who were forced to leave their homes.

The riots were a natural corollary to Partition and Khushwant Singh, with incisive irony, presents the genesis of one such riot in a story called simply "The Riot". Tension ran high in the two communities, but the real culprit of the day was the bitch, Rani. A stone thrown at her by the Hindu shopkeeper, Ram Jawaya, catches a Muslim grocer, Ramzan, in the solar plexus. And soon, "what had once been a busy town was a heap of charred masonry." The threadbare, matter-of-fact account of the happenings, without comment or aside from the narrator, exposes the hideous face of riots. Samaresh Basu's "Aadaab" makes clear that not only do riots fester in fear and suspicion, but that they are the real enemy of the common man. In the riot-torn city of Dacca, a Hindu and a Muslim confront each other in a dark alleyway with extreme suspicion Fearful of each other's motives, they probe into each other's lives and discover their common humanity. As their hearts go out to one another, a bullet from the dark fells one of them.

In any internecine war or hostility, it is the innocent non-partisan who pays the highest price. The stories by women writers in this volume look at the tragedy strictly from the non-partisan point of view—of children and women struggling to keep alive in a hell let loose by their menfolk. Though few in number, the stories are significantly rich in feeling and craftsmanship and exhibit a refinement and sensibility which are essentially feminine. The best of them is Attia Hosain's "After the Storm". Bibi, "a child with serious anxious eyes", is led to speak about her past. Her account, given in snatches and with several digressions, is a curious blending of fact and fiction. Nonetheless, the alert reader is able to piece together enough facts to see that Bibi is an orphan without a soul she can call her own. The real horror of the story comes through, not from what the child says, but from what she leaves unsaid.

Bibi was able to cope with her circumstances because of the make-believe world she had created for herself. But the little girl in Krishna Sobti's "Where Is My Mother?" has no such recourse. Her repeated pleas to the Baluchi, "I want my mother. Where is my mother?" hint at the unspeakable horrors imprinted on the child's mind, horrors which no promises of help can now erase. Suraiya Qasim's "Where Did She Belong?" also deals with non-partisans—in this case, courtesans—caught in the mass hatred. Just as for a child there is no country but only a mother, so for a courtesan there is no caste but only her customer. Munni Bai knows this and remains true to her profession; it is her lovers (both a Hindu and a Muslim) who desert her when she most needs them.

Since Partition was as much a Pakistani as an Indian experience, five Pakistani writers are presented in this anthology. Of these, Saadat Hasan Manto and Bapsi Sidhwa have already been mentioned. Manto is Pakistani simply by an accident of history. His stories, like himself, belong to neither India nor Pakistan; they are about people, lost and confused, as he himself was for a time. Bapsi Sidhwa's situation, on the other hand, is quite different. A Parsi herself, she was at the time of Partition about the same age as her narrator Lenny in *Ice-Candy-Man* (published in the US as *Cracking India* in 1990)—a premier Partition novel. Through Lenny, Sidhwa voices many of her adult perceptions on the creation of Pakistan and the nature of violence. As we have already seen, her story "Defend Yourself Against Me" ends on a stern note of warning that the lessons of history must not be forgotten. The other three writers who have distinguished themselves in Urdu Partition literature are Qudrat Ullah Shahab, Aziz Ahmad and Intizar Husain.

Qudrat Ullah Shahab's "Ya Khuda" (O God), skilfully translated into English by Faruq Hassan, is a powerful tale of what befell Muslim women during Partition. Dilshad, a Muslim girl awaiting transportation to Pakistan, suffers every imaginable abuse at the hands of her Sikh captors in India. At last, she boards a train to her new home—with new hopes. These are quickly shattered when she discovers that her countrymen look upon her as merely an item of sexual pleasure. The story, free from puerile sentimentality and marked with genuine anger, makes much better reading than others of its kind. When we finally put it aside, the title "Ya Khuda" reverberates in our mind and sums up our total experience as no other words can.

Aziz Ahmad's "Kali Raat" (Black Night), a rhapsodic tale, focuses on something other than the cross-border migration of people. It deals with the plight of a well-to-do Muslim family within India trying to get to Secunderabad (Deccan), a place of relative safety, from Delhi, a city in turmoil in the days immediately following Partition. The enemy, however, is powerful and numerous, and the entire family is brutally murdered in an ambush on the train. But it is not just the Muslims in India who face sectarian anger; a Sikh family undergoes a similar fate in Pakistan. The story includes a number of juxtaposed episodes involving Hindus, Sikhs and Muslims, as both perpetrators and victims of violence and savagery. Aziz Ahmad is fair in assessing blame. He weighs human behaviour which is grossly wanting in tolerance, decency and charity with the potential for goodness which has been asserted by thinkers, philosophers and heroes of ancient myths.

Intizar Husain, who has equated the migration of the Muslims to Pakistan with the *hijrat* of the Prophet, feels that Partition as a creative experience has failed. In "The Stairway", the central character, Saiyid, finds himself exhausted and bereft of memory at the end of his journey. What is unique about this story is that Partition, from which the main action stems, is kept totally in the background. Only the word "migrated", used but once, establishes that this is a Partition story; there is no violence in it of any kind, and even the principal communities such as the Hindus, Sikhs and Muslims are not mentioned by name. Husain's story takes us beyond the immediate bloodcurdling consequences of Partition to explore quietly its far-ranging effects on the human mind. In doing so, it opens up new vistas for writers, both in India and Pakistan, on a subject whose potentiality is far from exhausted.

Saros Cowasjee

University of Regina
Regina, Canada
1994

KHWAJA AHMAD ABBAS

A Debt to Pay

My NAME IS Sheikh Burhanuddin.

When violence and murder became the order of the day in Delhi and the blood of Muslims flowed in the streets, I cursed my fate for having a Sikh for a neighbour. Far from expecting him to come to my rescue in times of trouble, as a good neighbour should, I could not tell when he would thrust his *kirpan* into my belly. The truth is that till then I used to find the Sikhs somewhat laughable. But I also disliked them and was somewhat scared of them.

My hatred for the Sikhs began on the day when I first set my eyes on one. I could not have been more than six years old when I saw a Sikh sitting out in the sun combing his long hair. "Look!" I yelled with revulsion, "a woman with a long beard!" As I got older, this dislike developed into hatred for the entire race.

It was a custom amongst old women of our household to heap all afflictions on our enemies. Thus, for example if a child got pneumonia or broke its leg, they would say "a long time ago a Sikh, (or an Englishman), got pneumonia: or a long time ago a Sikh, (or an Englishman), broke his leg." When I was older I discovered that this referred to the year

-1-

1857 when the Sikh princes helped the *ferringhee*—foreigner—
to defeat the Hindus and Muslims in the war of independence.
I do not wish to propound a historical thesis but to explain
the obsession, the suspicion and hatred which I bore towards
the English and the Sikhs. I was more frightened of the
English than of the Sikhs.

When I was ten years old, I happened to be travelling
from Delhi to Aligarh. I used to travel third class, or at the
most in the intermediate class. That day I said to myself, "Let
me for once travel second class and see what it feels like." I
bought my ticket and found an empty second class
compartment. I jumped on the well-sprung seats; I went into
the bathroom and leapt up to see my face in the mirror; I
switched on all the fans. I played with the light switches.
There were only a couple of minutes for the train to leave
when four red-faced "tommies" burst into the compartment,
mouthing obscenities: everything was either "bloody" or
"damn". I had one look at them and my desire to travel
second class evaporated.

I picked up my suitcase and ran out. I only stopped for
breath when I got into a third class compartment crammed
with natives. But as luck would have it, it was full of Sikhs—
their beards hanging down to their navels and dressed in
nothing more than their underpants. I could not escape from
them, but I kept my distance.

Although I feared the white man more than the Sikhs, I
felt that he was more civilised: he wore the same kind of
clothes as I did. I also wanted to be able to say "damn" and
"bloody fool" the way he did. And like him I wanted to
belong to the ruling class. The Englishman ate his food with
forks and knives; I also wanted to learn to eat with forks and
knives so that natives would look upon me as advanced and
as civilised as the white man.

My Sikh-phobia was of a different kind. I had contempt
for the Sikh. I was amazed at the stupidity of men who

imitated women and grew their hair long. I must confess I did not like my hair cut too short; despite my father's instructions to the contrary, I did not allow the barber to clip off more than a little when I went to him on Fridays. I grew a mop of hair so that when I played hockey or football it would blow about in the breeze like those of English sportsmen. My father often asked me, "Why do you let your hair grow like a woman's?" My father had primitive ideas and I took no notice of his views. If he had had his way he would have had all heads razored bald, and stuck artificial beards on people's chins. . . . That reminds me that the second reason for hating the Sikhs was their beards which made them look like savages.

There are beards and beards. There was my father's beard, neatly trimmed in the French style; or my uncle's which went into a sharp point under his chin. But what could you do with a beard to which no scissor was ever applied and which was allowed to grow like a wild bush—fed with a compost of oil, curd and goodness knows what! And, after it had grown a few feet, combed like hair on a woman's head. My grandfather also had a very long beard which he combed . . . but then my grandfather was my grandfather and a Sikh is just a Sikh.

After I had passed my matriculation examination I was sent to the Muslim University at Aligarh. We boys who came from Delhi, or the United Provinces, looked down upon boys from the Punjab; they were crude rustics who did not know how to converse, how to behave at table, or to deport themselves in polite company. All they could do was drink large tumblers of buttermilk. Delicacies such as vermicelli with essence of *kewra* sprinkled on it, or the aroma of Lipton's tea was alien to them. Their language was unsophisticated to the extreme; whenever they spoke to each other it seemed as if they were quarrelling. It was full of "*ussi, tussi, saadey, twhaadey*",—Heaven forbid! I kept my distance from the Punjabis.

But the warden of our hostel (God forgive him), gave me

a Punjabi as a room mate. When I realised that there was no escape, I decided to make the best of a bad bargain and be civil to the chap. After a few days we became quite friendly. This man was called Ghulam Rasul and he was from Rawalpindi. He was full of amusing anecdotes and was a good companion.

You might well ask how Mr Ghulam Rasul gate-crashed into a story about the Sikhs. The fact of the matter is that Ghulam Rasul's anecdotes were usually about the Sikhs. It is through these anecdotes that I got to know the racial characteristics, the habits and customs of this strange community. According to Ghulam Rasul the chief characteristics of the Sikhs were the following:

All Sikhs were stupid and idiotic. At noon-time they lost their senses altogether. There were many instances to prove this. For example, one day at 12 noon, a Sikh was cycling along Hall Bazaar in Amritsar when a constable, also a Sikh, stopped him and demanded, "Where is your light?" The cyclist replied nervously, "*Jemadar Sahib*, I lit it when I left my home; it must have gone out just now." The constable threatened to run him in. A passer-by, yet another Sikh with a long white beard, intervened, "Brothers, there is no point in quarrelling over little things. If the light has gone out it can be lit again."

Ghulam Rasul knew hundreds of anecdotes of this kind. When he told them in his Punjabi accent his audience was left helpless with laughter. One really enjoyed them best in Punjabi because the strange and incomprehensible behaviour of the uncouth Sikh is best told in his rustic lingo.

The Sikhs were not only stupid but incredibly filthy as well. Ghulam Rasul, who had known hundreds of them, told us how they never have a hair cut. And whereas we Muslims washed our hair thoroughly at least every Friday, the Sikhs, who made a public exhibition of bathing in their underpants, poured all kinds of filth, like curd into their hair. I rub lime-juice and glycerine in my scalp. Although the glycerine is white and thick like curd, it is an altogether different thing—made by a well-known firm of perfumers of Europe. My glycerine came in a lovely bottle whereas the Sikh's curd came from the shop of a dirty sweetmeat seller.

I would not have concerned myself with the manner of living of these people except that they were so haughty and ill-bred as to consider themselves as good warriors as the Muslims. It is known over the world that one Muslim can get the better of ten Hindus or Sikhs. But these Sikhs would not accept the superiority of the Muslim and would strut about like bantam cocks, twirling their moustaches and stroking their beards. Ghulam Rasul used to say that one day we Muslims would teach the Sikhs a lesson that they would never forget.

Years went by.

I left college. I ceased to be a student and became a clerk; then a head clerk. I left Aligarh and came to live in New Delhi. I was allotted government quarters. I got married. I had children.

The quarters next to mine were occupied by a Sikh who had been displaced from Rawalpindi. Despite the passage of years, I remembered what Ghulam Rasul had told me. As Ghulam Rasul had prophesied, the Sikhs had been taught a bitter lesson in humility at least, in the district of Rawalpindi. The Muslims had virtually wiped them out. The Sikhs boasted that they were great heroes; they flaunted their long *kirpans*. But they could not withstand the brave Muslims. The Sikhs' beards were forcibly shaved. They were circumcised. They were converted to Islam. The Hindu press, as was its custom, vilified the Muslims. It reported that the Muslims had murdered Sikh women and children. This was wholly contrary to Islamic tradition. No Muslim warrior was ever known to raise his hand against a woman or a child. The pictures of the corpses of women and children published in Hindu newspapers were obviously faked. I wouldn't have put it beyond the Sikhs to murder their own women and children in order to vilify the Muslims.

The Muslims were also accused of abducting Hindu and Sikh women. The truth of the matter is that such was the impact of the heroism of Muslims on the minds of Hindu and Sikh girls, that they fell in love with young Muslims and insisted on going with them. These noble-minded young men had no option but to give them shelter and thus bring them to the true path of Islam. The bubble of Sikh bravery had burst. It did not matter how their leaders threatened the Muslims with their *kirpans*, the sight of the Sikhs who had fled from Rawalpindi filled my heart with pride in the greatness of Islam.

The Sikh who was my neighbour was about sixty years old. His beard had gone completely grey. Although he had barely escaped from the jaws of death, he was always laughing, displaying his teeth in the most vulgar fashion. It was evident that he was quite stupid. In the beginning he tried to draw me into his net by professions of friendship. Whenever I passed him he insisted on talking to me. I do not remember what kind of Sikh festival it was, when he sent me some sweet butter. My wife promptly gave it away to the sweeper woman. I did my best to have as little to do with him as I could. I snubbed him whenever I could. I knew that if I spoke a few words to him, he would be hard to shake off. Civil talk would encourage him to become familiar. I knew that Sikhs drew their sustenance from foul language. Why should I soil my lips by associating with such people!

One Sunday afternoon, I was narrating to my wife some anecdotes about the stupidity of the Sikhs. To prove my point, exactly at 12 o'clock, I sent my servant across to my Sikh neighbour to ask him the time. He sent back the reply, "two minutes after twelve!' I remarked to my wife, "You see, they are scared of even mentioning 12 o'clock!" We both had a hearty laugh. After this, many a time when I wanted to make an ass of my Sikh neighbour, I would ask him "Well, *Sardarji*, has it struck twelve?" The shameless creature would grin, baring all his teeth and answer, "Sir, for us it is always striking twelve." He would roar with laughter as if it were a great joke.

I was concerned about the safety of my children. One could never trust a Sikh. And this man had fled from Rawalpindi. He was sure to have a grudge against Muslims and to be on the look out for an opportunity to avenge himself. I had told my wife never to allow the children to go near the Sikh's quarters. But children are children. After a few days I saw my children playing with little Mohini, and the Sikh's other grandchildren. This child, who was barely ten years old, was really as beautiful as her name indicated; she was fair and beautifully formed. These wretches have beautiful women. I recall Ghulam Rasul telling me that if all the Sikh men were to leave their women behind and clear out of the Punjab, there would be no need for Muslims to go to paradise in search of houris.

The truth about the Sikhs soon became evident. After the thrashing in Rawalpindi, they fled like cowards to East Punjab. Here they found the Muslims weak and unprepared. So they began to kill them. Hundreds of thousands of Muslims were massacred; the blood of the faithful ran in streams. Thousands of women were stripped naked and made to parade through the streets. When Sikhs, fleeing from Western Punjab, came in large numbers to Delhi, it was evident that there would be trouble in the capital. I could not leave for Pakistan immediately. Consequently, I sent away my wife and children by air, with my elder brother, and entrusted my own fate to God. I could not send much luggage by air. I booked an entire railway wagon to take my furniture and belongings. But on the day I was to load the wagon, I got information that trains bound for Pakistan were being attacked by Sikh bands. Consequently my luggage stayed in my quarters in Delhi.

On the 15th of August, India celebrated its independence. What interest could I have in the independence of India! I spent the day lying in bed reading *Dawn* and the *Pakistan Times*. Both the papers had strong words to say about the manner in which India had gained its freedom, which proved conclusively how the Hindus and the British had conspired to destroy the Muslims. It was only our leader, the great Mohammed Ali Jinnah, who was able to thwart their evil designs and win Pakistan for the Muslims. The English had knuckled down under Hindu and Sikh pressure and handed over Amritsar to India. Amritsar, as the world knows, is a purely Muslim city. Its famous Golden Mosque—or am I mixing it up with the Golden Temple!—yes of course, the Golden Mosque is in Delhi. And in Delhi, besides the Golden Mosque there are the Jama Masjid, the Red Fort, the mausoleums of Nizamuddin and Emperor Humayun, the tomb and school of Safdar Jang—just everything worthwhile bears imprints of Islamic rule. Even so this Delhi (which should really be called after its Muslim builder Shah Jahan as Shahjahanabad) was to suffer the indignity of having the flag of Hindu imperialism unfurled on its ramparts.

My heart seemed torn asunder. I could have shed tears of blood. My cup of sorrow was full to the brim when I realised that Delhi, which was once the very foundation of the Muslim Empire, the centre of Islamic culture and civilisation, had been snatched out of our hands. Instead we were to have the desert wastes of Western Punjab, Sindh and Baluchistan inhabited by an uncouth and uncultured people. We were to go to a land where people did not know how to talk in civilised Urdu; where men wore baggy *salwars* like their womenfolk, where they ate thick bread four pounds in weight instead of the delicate wafers we eat at home!

I steeled myself. I would have to make this sacrifice for my great leader, Jinnah, and for my new country, Pakistan.

Nevertheless, the thought of having to leave Delhi was most depressing.

When I emerged from my room in the evening, my Sikh neighbour bared his fangs and asked, "Brother, did you not go out to see the celebrations?" I felt like setting fire to his beard.

One morning, the news spread of a general massacre in old Delhi. Muslim homes were burnt in Karol Bagh. Muslim shops in Chandni Chowk were looted. This then was a sample of Hindu rule! I said to myself, "New Delhi is really an English city; Lord Mountbatten lives here as well as the Commander-in-Chief. At least in New Delhi no hand will be raised against Muslims." Reassuring myself in this way, I started towards my office. I had to settle the business of my provident fund; I had delayed going to Pakistan in order to do so. I had only got as far as Gole Market when I ran into a Hindu colleague from the office. He said, "What on earth are you up to? Go back at once and do not come out of your house. The rioters are killing Muslims in Connaught Circus." I hurried back home.

I had barely got to my quarters when I ran into my Sikh neighbour. He began to reassure me. "*Sheikhji*, do not worry! As long as I am alive no one will raise a hand against you." I said to myself: "How much fraud is hidden behind this man's beard! He is obviously pleased that the Muslims are being massacred, but expresses sympathy to win my confidence; or is he trying to taunt me?" I was the only Muslim living in the block, perhaps I was the only one on the road.

I did not want these people's kindness or sympathy. I went inside my quarters and said to myself, "If I have to die, I will kill at least ten or twenty men before they get me." I went to my room where beneath my bed I kept my double-barrelled gun. I had also collected quite a hoard of cartridges.

I searched the house, but could not find the gun.

"What is *huzoor* looking for?" asked my faithful servant, Mohammed.

"What happened to my gun?"

He did not answer. But I could tell from the way he looked that he had either hidden it or stolen it.

"Why don't you answer?" I asked him angrily.

Then he came out with the truth. He had stolen my gun and given it to some of his friends who were collecting arms to defend the Muslims in Daryaganj.

"We have hundreds of guns, several machine guns, ten revolvers and a cannon. We will slaughter these infidels; we will roast them alive."

"No doubt with my gun you will roast the infidels in Daryaganj, but who will defend me here? I am the only Mussalman amongst these savages. If I am murdered, who will answer for it?"

I persuaded him to steal his way to Daryaganj to bring back my gun and a couple of hundred cartridges. When he left I was convinced that I would never see him again. I was all alone. On the mantelpiece was a family photograph. My wife and children stared silently at me. My eyes filled with tears at the thought that I would never see them again. I was comforted with the thought that they were safe in Pakistan. Why had I been tempted by my paltry provident fund and not gone with them? I heard the crowd yelling:

"*Sat Sri Akal . . .*"
"*Har Har Mahadev.*"

The yelling came closer and closer. They were rioters— the bearers of my death warrant. I was like a wounded deer, running hither and thither, with the hunters' hounds in full pursuit. There was no escape. The door was made of very thin wood and glass panes. The rioters would smash their way in

"Sat Sri Akal . . ."
"Har Har Mahadev."

They were coming closer and closer; death was coming closer and closer. Suddenly, there was a knock at the door. My Sikh neighbour walked in. *"Sheikhji*, come into my quarters at once." Without a second thought I ran into the Sikh's verandah and hid behind the columns. A shot hit the wall above my head. A truck drew up and about a dozen young men climbed down. Their leader had a list in his hand— "Quarter No. 8—Sheikh Burhanuddin." He read my name and ordered his gang to go ahead. They invaded my quarters and before my very eyes proceeded to destroy my home. My furniture, boxes, pictures, books, druggets and carpets, even the dirty linen was carried into the truck. Robbers! Thugs! Cut-throats!

As for the Sikh, who had pretended to sympathise with me, he was no less a robber than they! He was pleading with the rioters: "Gentlemen, stop! We have prior claim over our neighbour's property. We must get our share of the loot." He beckoned to his sons and daughters. All of them gathered to pick up whatever they could lay their hands on. One took my trousers; another a suitcase.

They even grabbed the family photograph. They took the loot to their quarters.

You bloody Sikh! If God grants me life I will settle my score with you. At this moment I cannot even protest. The rioters are armed and only a few yards away from me. If they get to know of my presence . . . .

"Please come in."

My eyes fell on the unsheathed *kirpan* in the hands of the Sikh. He was inviting me to come in. The bearded monster looked more frightful after he had soiled his hands with my property. There was the glittering blade of his *kirpan* inviting me to my doom. There was no time to argue. The only choice was between the guns of the rioters and the sabre of the Sikh. I decided: rather the *kirpan* of the old man than ten armed gangsters. I went into the room hesitantly, silently.

"Not here, come in further." I went into the inner room like a goat following a butcher. The glint of the blade of the *kirpan* was almost blinding.

"Here you are, take your things," said the Sikh.

He and his children put all the stuff they had pretended to loot, in front of me. His old woman said, "Son, I am sorry we were not able to save more."

I was dumbfounded.

The gangsters had dragged out my steel almirah and were trying to smash it open. "It would be simpler if we could find the keys," said someone.

"The keys can only be found in Pakistan. That cowardly son of a filthy Muslim has decamped," replied another.

Little Mohini answered back: "*Sheikhji* is not a coward. He has not run off to Pakistan."

"Where is he blackening his face?"

"Why should he be blackening his face? He is in . . . ." Mohini realised her mistake and stopped mid-sentence. Blood mounted in her father's face. He locked me in the inside room, gave his *kirpan* to his son and went out to face the mob.

I do not know what exactly took place outside. I heard the sound of blows; then Mohini crying; then the Sikh yelling full-blooded abuses in Punjabi. And then a shot and the Sikh's cry of pain—*hai*.

I heard a truck engine starting up; and then there was a petrified silence.

When I was taken out of my prison my Sikh neighbour was lying on a *charpoy*. Beside him lay a torn and blood-stained shirt. His new shirt also was stained with blood. His son had gone to telephone for the doctor.

"*Sardarji*, what have you done?" I do not know how

these words came out of my lips. The world of hate in which I had lived all these years lay in ruins about me.

"*Sardarji*, why did you do this?" I asked him again.

"Son, I had a debt to pay."

"What kind of a debt?"

"In Rawalpindi there was a Muslim like you who sacrificed his life to save mine and the honour of my family."

"What was his name, *Sardarji*?"

"Ghulam Rasul."

Fate had played a cruel trick on me. The clock on the wall started to strike . . . 1 . . . 2 . . . 3 . . . 4 . . . 5 . . . The Sikh turned towards the clock and smiled. He reminded me of my grandfather with his twelve-inch beard. How closely the two resembled each other!

. . . 6 . . . 7 . . . 8 . . . 9 . . . . We counted in silence.

He smiled again. His white beard and long white hair were like a halo, effulgent with a divine light . . . 10 . . . 11 . . . 12 . . . . The clock stopped striking.

I could almost hear him say: "For us Sikhs, it is always 12 o'clock!"

But the bearded lips, still smiling, were silent. And I knew he was already in some distant world, where the striking of clocks counted for nothing, where violence and mockery were powerless to hurt him.

(Translated from the original in Urdu by Khushwant Singh)

2

Khwaja Ahmad Abbas

Revenge

Red and yellow, yellow and red—these two colours haunted him day and night.

Red—like fresh human blood!

Yellow—like the pallor on a dead man's face!

Red and yellow, yellow and red, bubbles floated about in the air all the time.

Yellow and red, red and yellow, rays from some strange, unholy sun struck his eyes and penetrated right into his brain; they pierced his whole body like unseen needles of red and yellow light.

Day and night, awake or asleep, walking or sitting, he saw red and yellow, yellow and red, flames dancing before his eyes—like the myriad fiery tongues of a creature of hell. A devil's camp-fire in which dead bodies were burnt instead of wood. A thousand funeral pyres in one, and round it a million ghosts danced a weird dance, yelling and shouting:

Revenge!

Revenge!!

Revenge!!!

Red and yellow, yellow and red—these two flaming colours permeated his entire being—his body and mind and soul. In the pinkish glow of dawn, in the dying glory of the setting sun, he saw flames everywhere. A fiery fluid, instead of blood, coursed through his veins. His very breath had the acrid smell of smoke. He sometimes felt that he was no longer a human being but had been transformed into some fiery phantom out of hell.

Everyone said Hari Das had lost his reason. He did not care to meet or talk to anyone, not even his relations and friends. And because he kept to himself and never talked, they were convinced of his insanity. Else, why didn't he talk? Whatever topic was being discussed in his presence, his face registered no reaction whatever. As if he was made of stone. As if he was dead. Or, perhaps, blind as well as deaf and dumb. But if, by chance, the conversation turned to the riots and the massacres, his eyes became aflame with hate and fury, and though he spoke not a word his eyes proclaimed the battle-cry:

"Revenge! Revenge!! Revenge!!!"

It was known, of course, that Hari Das was a prominent lawyer in Lyallpur when the Punjab was split into two and thrown into the blazing furnace of a horrible civil war. The refugees from Lyallpur said that he had lost his entire family in the massacres. But ten months had passed since then and Time, the great healer, was slowly healing the wounds of painful memory. Moreover, no one knew for certain in what circumstances his wife and daughter had lost their lives. Had they drowned themselves in the river as so many others had done to save their honour, or had they been burnt in their house or were they the victims of an assassin's knife? Hari Das had revealed nothing, taken no one into his confidence.

Hari Das was not mad, though sometimes he wished he was. Then he could forget. Now he remembered everything—how his house was looted and set on fire, how his wife had thrown herself into the river, how his neighbours and friends were massacred. But whenever he thought of his daughter

Janki, something snapped in his brain. Some horrible episodes flashed on the screen of his memory, but without continuity, like a cinema projector gone wrong.

Pictures. Beautiful pictures. Horrible pictures.

Janki. The seventeen-year-old Janki. The darling of her mother, the apple of her father's eye!

Janki who had a rose-petal complexion, whose eyes put *nargis* flowers to shame, who was so delicate and fragile that one feared she might break at the merest touch! The most beautiful and the most intelligent girl in Lyallpur.

The fair and innocent face of Janki.

And then some ugly and frightful faces, with animal lust in their eyes, a devilish smile in the curl of their lips.

The razor-sharp blades of the knives, flashing in the sun. The black, unseeing eyes of the rifles.

Those horrible faces slowly, deliberately, advancing towards Janki.

Even after ten months Hari Das could still hear the echo of his own cry for mercy: "Kill me. But spare my daughter."

Again those horrible faces advancing towards Janki.

"I am ready to become a Muslim. My daughter, too, will adopt your faith. Please do not harm her."

Not a trace of pity on those cruel, grim faces. The lustful eyes continued to advance towards her—like a cobra approaching its hypnotised victim.

"My daughter is young. She is beautiful, as you can see. Let one of you convert her and then marry her. But spare her life."

The most frightful of all the frightful faces. Yellow, dirty teeth, eyes full of sadistic lust, a bristly beard quivering with devilish excitement. And only a few inches away—the delicate, flower-like beauty of Janki. Then he could not see her. A dark, ugly, evil cloud covered the moon. But before her innocence was crushed by untamed barbarism, Hari Das saw in the eyes of his daughter a strange and frightening expression in which fear, hate, helplessness and despair, an appeal for mercy and the knowledge that it was futile, were all mixed. The helpless father, bound to a tree and purposely kept alive so that he could see his daughter's dishonour, could bear the sight no longer and had closed his eyes. Whenever that moment returned to torture his memory he involuntarily closed his eyes.

He had wished he could have closed his ears, too, and had not heard those sounds, more horrifying than anything one could see—the merciless tearing and ripping of the clothes, the heavy lustful breathing of that monster, and Janki's screams, moans, sobs and sighs—that still haunted his ears.

Even with eyes closed, one frightful face after another passed across the screen of memory. One. Two. Three. Four. Five . . . till even those helpless sobs died away into a silence that was more frightful than those blood-curdling screams. And he opened his eyes.

Janki's flower-like face. Like a flower trampled in the dust. Without colour, without fragrance, without life. Dust in the dishevelled hair. The marks of cruel teeth on the cheeks. Blood oozing out of the fresh wounds—rouge for the pale, dead face! The marks of sharp, cruel teeth that had bitten into the skin, not only on the cheeks but also on the ears, the nose, the throat—and on the naked breasts. For ever and ever this picture—painted in blood by the devil himself—had been branded on the mind of Hari Das. Never to be forgotten. Never to be forgiven!

With his own hands he had built the funeral pyre for the body of his daughter. The fire-god soon devoured that delicate body—devoured Janki with her innocence, her wounds, her dishonour and humiliation. He could still see the flames of that pyre, they still danced before his eyes— those red and yellow flames! He had felt that it was not Janki but the honour of India that was being cremated, it was humanity that was going up in flames, decency and kindness and pity that were being reduced to ashes.

The flames of the funeral pyre had at last died down. But not the fire of revenge that they had set ablaze in the mind and heart of Hari Das. That fire could never be extinguished. It would never be extinguished. Never . . . Never . . . . At least not until he was able to take revenge by stabbing a Muslim girl *in her naked breasts*. It was only for that that he was living. Once he had wreaked his vengeance, he did not wish to live a moment longer.

Revenge!

Retaliation!

He kept a sharp knife hidden in his coat for the purpose. But where was he to find a Muslim girl on whom to wreak his vengeance? Of the Muslims of Delhi some had been killed, others had been frightened into running away to Pakistan, and the few that remained never dared to venture out of the purely Muslim localities. Damn cowards!

Then fate played a strange trick with Hari Das. He received three hundred rupees from the Refugee Rehabilitation Fund. But what was he to do with so much money? He had neither a home nor a family, he was not interested in food or clothes—why should he be when he was not interested in living? What was he to do with this money? Pondering this question, he roamed all over New Delhi and Old Delhi.

From Connaught Place to Chandni Chowk, from Chandni Chowk to the Jama Masjid whose slim minarets and white domes reminded him of the revenge he had to take against the Muslims—*all the Muslims!* From Jama Masjid to Daryaganj. Raj Ghat, where even the sight of Mahatma Gandhi's *samadhi* could not extinguish the fire of revenge that burnt in his heart. He thought: "Gandhiji was a Mahatma, a saint. I am an ordinary human being. He could forgive his enemies. But I cannot." Back from there to Edward Park where the stone king rode a stone horse. "*Wah*, Your Majesty, *wah*. You have gone and left us in this miserable plight."

It was night now. He had drifted to some unfamiliar

place. To the right, many homeless refugees like him were sleeping on the pavement. In the air there was a heavy, pungent, mixed aroma of scent, perspiration, wet earth, urine, flowers, phenyl and petrol. To the left, there was a row of shops—sweets shops, milk shops, eating houses, some still open while the others were closed. But every passer-by had his eye turned upwards, towards the first-floor balconies where lights were twinkling invitingly. There was music in the air. What *was* this place?

"*Babuji!*"

An oily-looking man with a vicious leer across his face accosted Hari Das. "*Babuji*, want me to show you something?"

Hari Das did not understand what he meant and continued on his way. But that man was not to be got rid of so easily. He blocked the way. "*Babuji*, don't pay me a pie unless you are really satisfied." More than his words, the expression on his face revealed his meaning.

"I am a refugee, brother," said Hari Das.

"I am myself a refugee, *Babuji*. And if you are a refugee, you come with me and I will show you a Muslim girl we have got here. After all that you suffered in Pakistan, here is your chance to enjoy a Pakistani *hoor* (houri)."

Muslim girl! Pakistani *hoor*!!

The red and yellow flames of revenge began their weird dance before his eyes.

On the way the pimp volunteered further information. "She is a rare chicken, *Babuji*. Just about seventeen or eighteen." And then in a lower voice, looking furtively to the right and left. "We brought her from Jullundar. Daughter of some prominent man. It has taken us ten months to tame her and to put her into this business."

Wasn't Janki, too, of the same age? Wasn't she too, the daughter of a prominent citizen? And yet those horrible faces had shown not a trace of pity. One. Two. Three. Four. Five . . . . till that innocent flower had been trampled in the dust!

"Then why should I show any mercy?" thought Hari Das, feeling the knife in the folds of his coat.

The usual atmosphere of a courtesan's parlour. A dirty white sheet on the ground, a chandelier hanging from the ceiling. Two life-size mirrors. A fat, ugly, pock-marked, middle-aged woman, sat in one corner preparing a *paan* and keeping a shrewd watch on the proceedings. And, surrounded by the musical instruments and their players, sat that Pakistan *hoor*, singing a song.

Hari Das had never seen a *hoor*, but he had heard descriptions. This girl was really a *hoor*. Her complexion was even fairer than Janki's, but it had a touch of anaemic paleness. Very slim and delicately built. Big black eyes but lacking the life and gaiety of Janki; instead one could see in them the dark, grim shadow of despair.

Hari Das saw that she was singing, but his ears heard nothing of what she was singing. He saw a crowd seated all round the room, but he did not see who they were or what they looked like, rich or poor, gentlemen or loafers. Huddled in a corner, he continued to stare at this Pakistani *hoor*. But there was no lust in his eyes. Only red and yellow flames of revenge.

The pimp had told him that he would have to wait till midnight for all the others to leave. The "price" settled was two hundred for the night. What would be do with the remaining hundred rupees? They were of no use to him, for he had no intention of living on the next day. Tonight was the last night of his life. Tomorrow he would be free of everything—free of money, free of revenge, free of life itself. So, a ten-rupee note at a time, he gave away all of the hundred rupees to the singer. Every time that Pakistani *hoor salaamed* him while picking the ten-rupee note from near his feet, it gave great satisfaction to his embittered soul. He felt that by humiliating that one Muslim girl he was avenging the humiliation of his daughter.

But this was only a very minor aspect of his total plan of revenge.

With fixed, unblinking eyes, he watched every little movement and expression of the girl. He could see that she was no "professional". Though she simulated all the "tricks of the trade"—moving her bare arms and wiggling her eyes as she sang—she did it mechanically, without feeling. Like a clockwork doll! And Hari Das had the uncanny feeling that he was watching not a living human being but a corpse which somehow had been animated by a magician.

Another thing he noticed. Whenever anyone tried to touch her, on the pretext of giving her money, she quickly withdrew her hand, recoiling as if stung by a live electric wire. She did not like being touched. And yet her face registered no reaction whatever, neither anger nor disgust. It was as if all emotions had been squeezed out of her face. However, every time someone gave her a rupee or a note she carelessly tossed it to the fat, black woman in the corner. Even then there was no expression on her face, but there was infinite contempt in the movement of her wrist with which she threw the money. As if she said: "Take it, the money for which you are selling me in this market. Take it and be done with it. Take it . . . take it . . . ."

Somehow this manifestation of the girl's outraged innocence appealed to Hari Das. It clearly proved that she belonged to some respectable, well-to-do family. Her intonation and pronunciation showed that she must be educated, too. In every way, she was an ideal choice to pay the price for Janki's dishonour and humiliation.

At midnight the rest of the crowd left. The girl, without even glancing at Hari Das, her would-be customer, went into the bedroom. Hari Das handed over the two hundred-rupee notes to the pimp who passed them on to the fat, black woman. She scrutinised them closely, rubbing them, holding them against the light. Satisfied, she took out a ten-rupee note and gave it to the pimp who *salaamed* and disappeared. Exhibiting her dirty, pyorrhoea-infected teeth, she winked at Hari Das. "Go in, *Babuji*, but be a bit careful. She is quite new to this game, you know." The next moment he was inside the bedroom.

Carefully, deliberately, he bolted the door. Then he advanced towards the girl who was sitting on the four-poster bed, facing the wall, thinking he knew not what thoughts. Seeing Hari Das, she stood up respectfully, her eyes downcast. Then she sat down to unlace his shoes. Perhaps those were her orders.

"Leave it," he said harshly, but how gratified he felt to see a Muslim girl cowering at his feet.

"Take off your clothes," he ordered.

With hands that were slightly trembling, she unwrapped the *sari*. Only the petticoat and the blouse remained.

"These, too."

For shame she turned her face towards the wall. The petticoat fell to the ground. Hari Das felt the knife in his pocket.

"I want to see you completely naked, do you understand? It's not free. I have paid two hundred rupees."

The girl turned round, with an unspoken appeal in her eyes, hoping to melt the heart of her middle-aged customer. Maybe he would take pity on her and not insist on her total nudity.

"Hurry up," he shouted, unrelenting, "I have no time." Inside the pocket his hand was feeling the sharp edge of the knife.

The girl made a slight movement towards the electric switch.

"No." He blocked her way. "I don't want it in the dark." Wasn't his Janki dishonoured in the daylight on a public road?

The girl took off the blouse. Only the brassiere remained to cover the youthful curves of her full breasts.

"This, too," he commanded indicating the brassiere. The knife was ready for action.

Once again the girl looked at him with an appeal for mercy in her eyes. Thus had his Janki looked at those heartless beasts, and they had shown her no mercy. Nor would he!

The girl covered her face with her hands and started sobbing. A few tear-drops fell on her brassiere.

The knife-blade flashed in Hari Das's right hand as it went up, poised for the fatal plunge. With the other hand, he roughly pulled at her hands. He wanted her to see what he was going to do, as Janki had seen what had been done to her. This was the moment for which he had waited for ten long months. The red and yellow flames danced in glee.

When she saw one hand holding the dagger and the other advancing towards her brassiere, the girl gave a shriek, and a look of stark terror came into her eyes. Hari Das recognised more than terror in the look—there was fear and hate and a plea for mercy and complete hopelessness. It was the exact look that he had seen in his Janki's eyes.

But that look had not saved Janki.

With a lightning stroke his left hand snatched the brassiere. In that split second it seemed heavier than it should have been . . . as he pulled it away. And along with it . . . .

The dagger remained poised in the air. He averted his eyes with shame.

One single word escaped his lips: "Daughter!"

Beneath the brassiere where he was going to stab her, there were no breasts . . . there was nothing—nothing but two horrible round scars!

3

Aziz Ahmad

*Kali Raat**

The Grand Trunk Express train was late by ten hours. The anxiety of those waiting at the Secunderabad station was mounting. Their hearts beat faster when, finally, the signal fell. At last the train, with the two compartments that had been detached from the Grand Trunk Express and were bound for Hyderabad, arrived. The three brothers leaped towards the compartment which had the sign Hyderabad displayed on it. Its windows were shut. Something was not right. They didn't see anyone's face peeping out. When the train stopped with a jolt, the compartment door which hadn't been securely shut fell open.

The youngest of the three brothers rushed into the compartment through the open door. A broken wicker basket lay inside the wire-net above. There was no other baggage. There wasn't any human being inside either; only blood-stains, on the floor, the seats, the wooden walls, everywhere. It was thick, black, clotted blood, overlaid by dust and soot that had settled on it along the way.

By now the other two brothers had also looked in and

---

* Dark Night.

seen the sight. Keeping up their fight against hopelessness, they thought maybe their family had missed the train at Delhi. They started reading the names of the passengers who had travelled in that compartment. The names were legible on the dust-covered card outside:

Mr Baqar Ali Khan
Mrs Baqar Ali Khan
Miss Baqar Ali Khan
Mr Sikandar Ali Khan

And nearby, on the first class coupe, the card clearly showed the names of the bride and the groom: Mr and Mrs Tahawwar Ali Khan. Some railway officer had mercifully locked the coupe door.

The guard arrived and explained that there had been an attack on the Grand Trunk Express between Delhi and Mathura. The hearts of the three brothers sank. Sometimes when the shock is too great, its effect is not felt immediately. At first the senses are dulled and the brain registers nothing. Hope wants to keep its tiny lamp lit against the certainty of hopelessness. The brothers thought, perhaps their names went up on the cards but they never boarded the train.

Having sent wires to a few friends in Delhi, and return telegrams to the High Commissioner of Pakistan and to a high official in the Indian government, they decided that the youngest of the brothers, Ghazanfar, should fly to Delhi to look for whatever clues could be found.

While they were inside the station telegraph office sending telegrams, a Sikh was inquiring from a clerk: "*Babuji*, from which platform does the train for Bangalore leave?"

The clerk mumbled something to him in a hurry. The Sikh's clothes were soiled, his turban and hair full of dust. He wore a *salwar-kameez*, loose baggy clothes, and had a cotton band tied around his middle; a scimitar hung from it.

Going at a leisurely pace, he walked up to another Sikh who looked much like him and said something to him in

Punjabi. Then the two of them picked up their cloth pouches and nudged the two veiled and bent female forms who stood close by. They began moving.

Two secret service men had been watching them for some time. Now, accompanied by two railway policemen, they approached them.

"*Sardarji*, you're Sikhs. Why do you have these veiled women with you?" one policeman asked.

One Sikh answered rudely, in Punjabi, "Our women observe *purdah*."

The secret service men were not satisfied. They had already got in touch with their Inspector and told the Sikhs: "We want to have a word with these women."

This time the Sikh answered in Urdu, "Our women speak Punjabi. They don't know Urdu."

This started an argument. One secret service man went and brought the Assistant Station Master, a Punjabi, who questioned the women in Punjabi, but they didn't respond.

The Inspector arrived and ordered the women sent to the ladies' waiting room. There, when their veils were removed, two beautiful young girls emerged who had been gagged, and had had their hands tied in the back. One of them swooned right there; the other looked at the other women in the waiting room through eyes dazzled by light and asked for water.

Then the two girls told their woeful tale. They were from a *zamindar*—land-owning—family in Ferozepur. One evening there were rumours of trouble brewing. At night, shouts of "*Sat Sri Akal*" were heard. Swords and daggers were brandished. There was noise of fighting. Their father and all the brothers were killed. These two girls became the booty. After that the Sikhs had been dragging them from city to city, all over the place.

Because of the use of force by the police, the two Sikhs also confessed. They were brothers, both cabinet-makers from near Chaklala, Rawalpindi. They were friends with the Muslims. Then the disturbances began. Those who were their friends looted their house, dishonoured their women. Amid sobs, one Sikh said that they hacked off his wife's breasts right before his eyes. Then their journey, and that of the rest of the Sikhs, all of them hurting and wounded, began, a journey spread over thousands of miles, a journey of hunger, want and death. They crossed the borders of independent Pakistan and entered independent India. There, the plundering and pillaging was going on in full swing near Ferozepur. They too joined in and walked away with the spoils, these two girls. They had heard that Bangalore was known for its good furniture-making. So, they were headed that way.

None of the three brothers ate or slept that night. The little sleep they did have was no different from being awake. Everything seemed vague and uncertain. The Indian newspapers had treated the trouble in Delhi as a minor disturbance. Pakistan Radio was being circumspect. Only the BBC was giving the full story in all its terrifying details, but the Indians were bewailing the perfidy of the BBC; it had turned an ordinary incident in Delhi into a catastrophe. Be that as it may, the three brothers were unable to deal with the events in Delhi dispassionately. This time their blood circulation, their pulse and their nerves had been affected. Earlier that year, there were disturbances in Calcutta and in Bombay. Actually, Ghazanfar was in Bombay when the riots broke out. He was coming out of a cinema hall when the stones started flying from all directions—Hindu stones, Muslim stones, stones from the atheists' camp, stones from the believers' corner. One flew past him, about half-an-inch away from the windscreen. He pressed hard on the accelerator, actually feeling more afraid of soda-water and acid bottles than stones, and invoked the name of the Caliph Ali to help him, as Muslims often do in times of trouble and difficulty. In any case, the worst that happened at that time was that some of the buses were made to take an alternate route;

the "B" route buses went via the Marine Drive. The passengers felt some sea breeze on their faces. That was it. The riots were limited to the back streets.

Then there were disturbances in the Punjab. Till that time they were five, not three brothers. How happy they were that Muslims had beaten the daylights out of the Sikhs and Hindus. What a fine performance! It was all the doing of the Punjab Muslim League, of Nawab Iftikhar Hussain Khan Mamdot. Well, if not his, then of Mian Iftikhar-ud-Din, or of Begum Shah Nawaz and of Sir Feroz Khan Noon's English wife. Oh, what a courageous woman she had turned out to be! It was not her doing? All right, then, of Major Khurshid Anwar! In any case, it was the doing of the Punjabi Muslims. As the poet Mohammad Iqbal had said in his poem . . . , and so on and so forth.

When Ghazanfar was in Lahore in April, the Muslims seemed awesome, but the Hindus and Sikhs were not sitting passively either. They were preparing for a counter-attack. He went to visit Saroop Shori's film studio on Multan Road, about seven miles out of Lahore. He was not really interested in the studio as much as he was in that girl, Kuljeet Kaur, who had replaced Manorama in the movies. Poor Shori's older studio had burnt down, and he had built a new one. Some appreciation of his efforts was certainly in order. Was his wife still as jealous of the film actresses as she had been earlier on? Anyway, Saroop invited him to dinner the next day, in a small restaurant, what was its name, on the Mall. That was where Ghazanfar had met that extraordinary couple, Saeed and, that Sikh girl Sheila whom he had married fifteen years ago.

Whatever Sheila's claim to fame—her hysteria, her Girton education, her Cambridge veneer, her inter-faith marriage, her married life—the previous few weeks' fighting in which her husband's tribesmen, the Muslims, had scored a temporary victory over her father's, the Sikhs—had played havoc with it. She knew that Ghazanfar was a Muslim, though perhaps only in name, but she insisted on ordering pork. Then she asked Ghazanfar what kind of a Muslim he was, one who only believed in or one who also practised his faith. At one point she said that for her holidays that year she was going to Kulu valley where there was a boarding house in which, "Thank Heaven," only the upper class Hindu and Sikh families were allowed to stay. She also said, "Sometimes I suspect Saeed to be a Muslim Leaguer, even though, you know we do not believe in any religion. We had a civil marriage." Later on, when they were talking about a well-known Muslim girl, she said, "Do you know she wanted to marry Saeed? But I took him away. The Sikhs always get what they're after!"

It was also at that dinner that Ghazanfar met Romesh Chandar—("I'm not the Romesh Chandar who writes articles for *People's Age*; he's the one in Bombay. But I'm also a Party Member. Come to our office some day.") Saroop's wife was asking: "Brother, what do you think of non-violence? If one party perpetrates violence, should the other reciprocate or remain non-violent?"—poor woman, eternally jealous of the vulgar attractions of Saroop's disgruntled actresses! Conversing with his graduate wife, Romesh Chandar suddenly turned to Ghazanfar and said, "Today, some people came to see me. They said they wanted to take revenge on the Muslims; they were asking for contributions—anything, even four annas. At first I tried to reason with them, but when they refused to understand, I told them, my salary was thirty rupees a month. What did they think I could give them out of that?"

During their talk someone used the word *Nihang*. Ghazanfar inquired what that was. Romesh told him: "That's a sect among the Sikhs, a little more extremist than the others. Do you know what they say about the Amritsar disturbances? They claim that when the Muslims attacked, they were busy with one of their festivals, or they would have taught the Muslims a lesson."

Romesh laughed at the cumulative stupidity of India.

Mrs Saeed, the Sikh lady, said, "And now we have to listen to the claim that even Muslims can be brave!"

"Violence or non-violence?"

"You know, I heard it with my own ears in the *Pakistan Times* office; Sardar Shaukat Hayat Khan was telling Mian Iftikhar-ud-Din, the owner of the paper, that the Sikhs had purchased jeeps and lorries worth over a million rupees."

"Patiala . . . "

"Bahawalpur . . . "

"We had decided never to hire a *tonga*—all *tonga*-drivers in Lahore are Muslims."

"Kuljeet Kaur . . . "

"No coffee. Nothing for me, thank you."

And when he was travelling by train to Simla, Ghazanfar had used a fictitious name, DeSilva; that was why Lalaji, the other passenger, had casually talked to him about all their preparations: "We'll only fight a defensive battle in Lahore, but from Amritsar to Delhi, that's where we'll teach them a lesson they won't forget for centuries to come."

In Simla, everyone knew Ghazanfar's real name, but *Lalaji* kept on addressing him as Mr DeSilva. It was lucky that no one called Ghazanfar by his real name, or poor *Lalaji* would have had a fit. He had revealed all of his party's plans to an enemy.

Like his brothers, Ghazanfar too couldn't sleep that night. The compartment of the Grand Trunk Express was coated with the blood of his parents and brothers, yet he was thinking about Saroop Shori's party and the stories he had heard about the preparations for the second wave of disturbances in the Punjab. How meaningless and absurd all this was! But his mind went on thinking irrelevant and ambiguous thoughts. He thought of Amjad, the nationalist, who called himself a "free Muslim". (Once, when somebody had asked Ghazanfar what a free Muslim was, he answered:

one who is free of all family ties.) In the last days of August, when the same Amjad had said, "What do you say now to the way the Hindus and Sikhs are butchering your Muslim brothers in East Punjab?" Ghazanfar's blood began to boil. He became Amjad's sworn enemy. The thought of his parents and brothers stared at him again; again there was the train compartment, the bloodstains, the dust that had settled on the stains, on the cards, on their names. . . . "

Of all the trains in India, there's none as hopeless as the Grand Trunk Express. Just as Turkey is known as the sick man of Europe, this Great Indian Peninsula Express can be known as the sick woman of all the Indian trains. Whenever there is any trouble or political crisis, this train is most affected. It owes its existence to Sir Akbar Haidari, as do a number of other stupid things in the State of Deccan. For some time after the tracks were laid, it did wend its slow way from Mangalore to Peshawar via Madras. But then the companies in the far north and south got tired of its crawling pace, and its run was limited to between Madras and Delhi. But every step of the way, it still moved like a sick person; whenever and wherever there was a train crossing, it would be made to wait like a beggar for the other train on some small, unknown station. Don't even mention what happened to it during the turmoil of 1942. At times it was late by as much as twenty-four hours. Was it even conceivable that mother India was in the grip of the independence fever, and the Grand Trunk Express was not affected by it?

Reaching Old Delhi railway station, Meer Baqar Ali Khan and his family heaved a sigh of relief. Now there was hope of getting out of Delhi alive. Their train to the Deccan was waiting at platform 9. The station was, no doubt, affected by the happenings in the city, but not too much. There were lots of policemen on the station; their presence was heartening.

Cheap novels and journals were, as usual displayed on the Wheeler bookstall. The coolies were pushing baggage carts as they had always done. Soldiers from the Madras regiment were eating their lentils and rice on leaf-plates. The platform was, as always, stained with spit and vomit and other such compounds. Looking at the green compartments of the E.I.R., and the air-conditioned coaches of the B.B. & C.I., one could sense that civilisation was on its last legs here as well. The seats for the whole family were reserved. They had had nothing to eat or drink for the past couple of days; at the station at least they found something to eat. No doubt a few Sikhs and some blackguards, probably of the Rashtriya Sevak Sangh, were hanging about the train, but they would not be able to do anything now. In a few minutes the train would move, and they would be out of their reach.

It was a miracle that they had escaped. In the last couple of days they had heard and seen a lot, each incident more brutal and outrageous than the other. Each one of them had chosen one of the dozens or so stories they had heard as the culminating point of the nightmare they were going through.

Soldiers of the Baluch Regiment, who had pulled them out of the claws of death, had told innumerable stories. Sakina had been shaken and horrified. She was the Miss Baqar Ali Khan of the compartment card, twenty years old— six years older than the conventional beloved of Urdu classical poetry. In those six years she had done her B.A., and was now preparing for a degree in teaching. She would often wonder, during the time of disturbances, if it was fun being abducted, as it was in Ibsen's *Helgeland*. But then she heard additional details of the abductions and all thought of fun vanished. For example, one soldier was telling her father, in her presence, that the abductors after raping women often cut off their breasts, or slit open their stomachs with scimitars.

Sometimes it also happened that a woman's husband, father or brother was killed in front of her; then, some of his organs were hacked off and shoved into the woman's mouth. How decent the Vikings in Ibsen's *Helgeland* were, in contrast! They would abduct women and, then take them in small peacock-like boats for a tour of America—, from where Hollywood movies, syphilis germs and American tourists hadn't yet come to the old world.

Sikandar had been particularly affected by one incident. Two sisters were left by themselves in a small house on Meer Daad Road. Abeda's husband was killed just outside the door of his house. She was pregnant, so she couldn't escape quickly. But, Zaheda, the younger one, ran up to the roof and crouching behind a parapet kept watching what was going on below. A few of the attackers were busy ransacking the house, while seven or eight wilder ones, all with beards and turbans, crowded about Abeda. They tore off her clothes on the terrace. She was pregnant, but one after the other, they disgraced themselves with her. She cried and screamed until she couldn't anymore. Her tears dried up and her eyes became still. She lay there senseless and motionless. Zaheda couldn't bear to watch what they were doing to her sister, yet she kept on watching. And when at last all seven or eight of them were through with her, one of them took out his scimitar and in one gash cut her open from her genitals to her neck, even though one or two of the others kept dissuading him. The world reeled before Zaheda's eyes. As soon as she was able to recover, she made up her mind that she wouldn't let those murderers take her alive. But how to fall so as not to stay alive? She looked at Abeda. Even though she was her sister, her own dear sister, how disgusting she looked lying there, all drenched in blood! Zaheda made another quick decision. The terrace was made of concrete; if she jumped down headlong, her head would smash, but none of those beasts would be able to touch her. And that was what she did. Her head

smashed in the fall. One of the victors said something to the
other about that "pretty girl." The other swore at him and said
her face wasn't even recognisable; how the hell did he know
she was pretty? When the Baluchi soldiers came to evacuate
the two sisters, it was already too late. Sikander had named
those two unknown girls, Abeda and Zaheda. They could have
had any other names: Asghari, Akbari, Jamal Ara, Husn Ara,
Naheed Jehan, Khurshid Jehan—any would have done. The
important thing was that they be kept alive in human memory.

The train stopped between Delhi and Mathura. Actually it
was forced to. But trains had stopped many times before:
sometimes because the signal hadn't been given, sometimes
because of the water-buffaloes crossing the tracks, sometimes
even because of someone having pulled the emergency cord.
What had happened? Was it a festival? It seemed like one.
Hundreds of men, who looked like highwaymen, were
brandishing their shiny scimitars. The Rashtriya Sevak Sangh
people were working as the train crew. Their most important
duty was to pull the Muslims off the train. It looked as if
thousands of insects had come out of the bushes and had been
transformed into human beings. Shouts of *"Jai Hind & Sat
Sri Akal, Jai Bali Dev"*; noises of the game hunt; calls of the
beaters, the hunters, the butchers, the goats; cries of those
who refused to get off the train, of those who were being
lanced or stabbed—all were mixed up.

Tahawwar had locked the coupe door from inside. There
were knocks and curses! His new bride, married only a week
ago, clung to him. It was like the wedding on the battlefield
of Karbala; dozens of elegies by the poets Anees and Dabeer
came to mind. "Islam is reborn after every Karbala," a poet
had said, but this time there were no signs of any rebirth, nor
even any hope of it. The glass of the window broke with a
loud clink. The tinsel dust in the parting of the bride's hair
was now mixed with big beads of perspiration. She was
shuddering with fear. Now only the venetian window remained

between the wild animals outside and Tahawwar and his bride.

Tahawwar took out his revolver from his bag. "Even as I die, I'll take a few of them with me. Can't bring dishonour to the name of Nizam-ul-Mulk Asaf Jah's army, can I?" he said wryly. There were only four bullets left. With what difficulty had he saved that revolver in Delhi! In the next assault the venetian window came down. A person looked inside and commanded Tahawwar to get down from the train. Tahawwar rebuffed him insolently. Another Sikh attacked; his scimitar grazed Tahawwar's left hand. Tahawwar fired twice, one after the other. Two persons fell, but two bullets were gone too. Some other people rushed towards his compartment. From the open window he saw a few people dragging his sister away. He lurched forward and pulled the venetian shut. The attackers outside once again got busy trying to bring the venetian down.

"Batool," he called his wife.

She looked at him. She was shivering all over. A week ago her shivers were of love and passion; today they were of fear of death.

"You're not afraid of dying, are you? These people won't let you live anyway," he said.

"I'm only afraid for my honour," was all she said.

"There are still two bullets left."

She nodded. The attack on the venetian window became more intense. He applied the entire weight of his body to the venetian and opened his arms. His bride came in his embrace. He brushed his lips against hers and said gently, "I give you in the care of the Prince of the Nobles, peace be upon him."

"God look after you."

"God look after you."

He placed the muzzle on her temple and pulled the trigger. Her arms that had circled his neck suddenly fell. Blood mixed with bits of brain tissue shot out. He couldn't bear to watch. How beautiful she had been only a few moments ago. I loved her, and I destroyed her. At the same time, despite all the weight he had put on the venetian, it fell and a scimitar went through his ribs from behind. The attacking Sikh swore at him; he leaned inside the window and undid the bolt from inside. The vandalising of the baggage began. The last bullet in Tahawwar's revolver remained unused.

His father's compartment fared worse. When the Sikhs entered it, they first attacked Sikandar. He fell down wounded. Then they killed Meer Baqar Ali Khan's wife, and then him. When a Sikh raised his scimitar to kill Sakina, a valiant Rashtriya Sevak Sangh warrior said, "Don't, brother. She is such a pretty girl. We shall purify her. Hey, girl, want to come with us?"

The girl was clinging to her mother's body and crying. Her clothes were drenched with the mother's blood. The Rashtriya Sevak Sangh warrior and his companion dragged her away to the bushes.

Was he dead or alive? His consciousness of being alive was so faint that he couldn't be sure. Lying near the doorway of the compartment, his body was obstructing the looters. So someone had dragged him out and left him for dead near the tracks. His consciousness was so faint that he barely felt alive. He tried moving his right arm. It wouldn't. Perhaps he'd never be able to use it again. A continuous hammering went on inside his head, and there was nothing but darkness before his eyes. In that dark night he could discern the outlines of shrubs and thickets standing around like midget-sized demons. Despairing of the right arm, he tried moving the left. With his will power he was able to raise it and keep it raised for a while, but soon it fell down lifeless. It fell on something that felt like fibre strings. It was the beard of some corpse. Involuntarily, he moved his hand on the corpse's face,

eyes and lips. At that very moment he heard the howl of the
jackals. So now man's guests had also arrived. What a grand
feast had been laid for them! For the first time he felt a wave
of fear travel from one end of the spine to the other. When
your right arm has revolted against you, your left is not fully
in your control, and your legs are perhaps entangled in some
dead woman's hair, how are you going to fight the sharp
teeth of the jackals? The scimitars would have been better!

There were four or five stars in the sky and the dark
night was beautiful, infernally beautiful like a wanton woman.
Her black aspect had overshadowed the entire blood-soaked
scene. He began thinking. How had the rest of his family
fared? The hammering going on in his head became more
intense. There was so much anguish, so much sorrow. But
this pain and suffering did reach a limit, after which all
consciousness was dulled. And what became of all of them?
Of his brother, sister, sister-in-law, parents? So many dead
bodies lay about in that dark night. Which one was whose?
He tried to move his head to look. The pain was excruciating,
as if someone had twisted his neck. And then he heard a
rumble, heavier than the howls of the jackals. Perhaps it was
another train. Perhaps there were going to be new murderers
and fresh victims . . . . No, it wasn't that. It was a small
army train that had come to remove the wounded and the
dead. He saw the headlight of the engine. The engine seemed
to be driving on tracks inside his head. There was an explosion
in his head, and the wave of consciousness disappeared again.

Two lanterns stopped near him. He was unconscious. The
doctor said he wasn't dead. Unbeknown to him, he was taken
away from there on a stretcher.

The dark night, the wayward, wanton night, laid out in its
blood-soaked beauty, spread all the way from Peshawar to
Saharanpur. On such dark nights, the sons of enslaved India

used to visit the upper-storey flats of the prostitutes. Now, from Peshawar to Saharanpur, no one needed to go to a prostitute's flat any longer; the woman who was bought with money could now be had with the sword. And you could have hundreds, thousands, tens of thousands, to make love to, to hate, to show your humanity to, to terrorise—to do whatever you wished. One cannot do without a woman, but no one needed her children any longer; they had been put to eternal sleep with spears, bayonets, daggers and swords.

And suddenly the dark, wanton, errant night moved, showing the tinsel dust of stars in the parting of her hair. It stretched itself in a yawn. The breeze blew; there was a rustle in the leaves of the shrubs. The night introduced herself to the dead bodies. Do you recognise me? I have been around since the middle ages and even before. You were conceived in my womb. Then you were born; you crawled on all fours. Playing and reading and writing, you grew up and became adults. You married. You told many lies, cheated your companions and yourself. And tonight, you lie in my lap, in a sleep from which you will never wake up.

Not just because I am ancient, historical or eternal; because I am also Walpurgis night, when ghosts and goblins dance and witches ride the broomsticks and go on a tour of the upper regions of the sky. I am Walpurgis night, still in her prime. You haven't seen much yet. You all perished in a common wayside accident. I am the magical night; I am the black tresses of an Indian beloved, the iris of her eyes; I am the pitch dark night of the eastern poets; I am the night of parting, of separation. I cannot even begin to describe what I have seen with my thousand eyes—in Multan, Rawalpindi, Lahore, Amritsar, Jullundar, Gurgaon, Delhi and Dehra Dun, and what more is still there for me to see.

In the hospital, Sikandar's neck wound was bandaged. He had a 105 degree fever. His subconscious began climbing the ladder of that dark night, going from one planet to another, from one darkness to another, until he reached the final rung of the ladder. But the sky was still far.

Humbly and earnestly, he repeated a line from a German Christmas carol to the Walpurgis night: Heilige Nacht, Schön Nacht—Holy Night, Beautiful Night. A ray of light shone brightly on the hospital wall. Perhaps that ray had emanated from his own brain. He stood at the top rung of the ladder which was swinging in the air. Then the night handed him the witch's broom. He saw many corpses astride witches' broomsticks flying towards the blueness of the sky. But he did not want to follow them. No, he had to go the other way, towards the earth.

He was wrapped all around in a plaster cast. He couldn't turn in bed. He did so in his imagination and went to sleep pressing a pillow between his knees and holding on to the bed-frame. His subconscious took leave of his sick body for a while, and, like the dark night, stretching itself in a yawn, merged in the subconscious of the common man.

Now, once again, he stood on the top rung of the ladder swinging in the air, afraid that the ladder might give way any minute. The witches' broomsticks were nowhere in sight. The corpses riding them seemed to have reached their destination. All birds sat within their dovecotes, cooing peacefully; only he hung on to the ladder, swinging and fearful of falling.

And the common man's subconscious sent his sick subconscious back to him in the hospital, and alone began swinging on the ladder. How many centuries, how much effort had it taken him to get to the top of the ladder! How many implements had he devised, how many incarnations he had gone through, but now this ladder was swinging, about to fall down, anywhere between Peshawar and Hiroshima.

In that dreaded moment, when the ladder was about to give way, the common man made the confession: "I am human; I am the one who has climbed the ladder of evolution and reached so high. Millions of life forms emanated from the core of life, each to reach a limit and stop; I alone was able to go on moving, going beyond limits, leaving instinct behind and following the road of reason, sloughing off my thick skin, making clothes, worshipping snakes and killing them, taming bulls, horses, steam, electricity and the atom. But in the process I made myself my own slave. I achieved so much, yet I am so helpless. Right now, a special train full of Hindu and Sikh refugees is coming from Gujranwala. I am travelling on that train, moving towards freedom, self-will and security. Yet I am also the one firing on that train with my sten guns and machine guns. My will engenders all postulates, all calculations, all actions, which enable me to harness nature; yet it is also my will which makes the sword descend, which creates darkness, and reduces everything to nothingness in an instant."

And then man's volition, his action, strength and imagination spread their roots all through the universe. "Not only light but all kinds of energy—from heat, electricity, magnetism—has mass. But more important, matter and energy are equivalent and interchangeable;" having said this, Einstein's student became silent.

What energy? Which matter? A train full of Muslim refugees was moving from one dark corridor to another. The army officer guarding the train told his Subedar-Major that there was a girl in the next compartment whom he found very beautiful. At the next station, the Subedar-Major, with the help of a few soldiers, brought over that twenty-year-old girl for his boss and another girl, a tawny 17-18 year-old, for himself. Their families could do nothing but swear at them and cry. And when the train had reached its destination across the border, the doctors on duty who examined the girls found that their bodies were sore all over.

Beware! Some day these jointed creatures—these ants, these bees, these spiders—will overcome man!

"Moral virtues are produced in us neither *by* Nature nor *against* Nature. (If they were produced by Nature, their reception would have posed no difficulty; and if they were contrary to Nature, their reception would have been impossible.) Nature, indeed, prepares in us the ground for their reception (moral goodness being a potential faculty), but their complete formation is the product of habit (not teaching or knowledge)."

Oh, so that's what it is! And who are you? Ah! Aristotle. All right. Come with me. Let us make a round of man's moral virtues. This is a street in India's capital, Delhi. Do you see those? Those are soldiers, and ten, twelve or fifteen naked Muslim girls are walking behind them. Their lips are parched, their hair tangled, their bare feet scalded. Some among them are those who hadn't ever stepped outside of their houses. Let alone their bodies, no stranger had even seen their faces before. Their bodies are graceful, well-formed and full of youth. They were called the daughters of the nobility. They were kept cooped up like hens so that they could produce more children of the nobility. Do you see them now, Aristotle? What is this? Why have you covered your eyes with your hands? And one quick-witted girl, who must have been pert even before, turned towards Aristotle and said, "Look! Take a good look at us. Hundreds have defiled us. Come, why don't you do it too?"

In the field of Kurukshetra, Krishna taught Arjuna the way of action. He told him: "I am the One source of all: the evolution of all comes from me. The wise think this and they worship me in adoration of love. Their thoughts are on me, their life is in me, and they give light to each other. For ever they speak of my glory; and they find peace and joy. To those who are ever in harmony, and who worship me with their love, I give the Yoga of vision. . . . "

Hundreds of thousands of Hindu refugees were gathered in the same field of Kurukshetra, like ants or termites. Cholera and other diseases were rampant there. It was a flood of people that had gathered together from various streams and rills. And here its flow had been stopped as if by means of a dyke. These people had walked all the way. During the day as they walked, they were attacked; at night while they rested, they were attacked. Their children were slaughtered, their young men butchered, their women taken away from them. Then they crossed the border. Now, they were in the jurisdiction of Sardar Patel and the Maharaja of Patiala. Now, they walked during the day and attacked and ambushed others, slaughtered their children, butchered their young men, and abducted their women. As the locusts devastate thousands of miles of land, these people had destroyed the humanity, morality and civilisation of India.

These people had starved. Bread was dropped for them from the sky. Now, in this temporary city of theirs—the battlefield of the *Kauravas* and *Pandavas*—their souls were starving amidst filth, stench and putrefaction. One camp officer said to an old friend, an army man, "I've had it with these people. Someone's daughter was going to the toilet when somebody fondled her breasts. He came with a complaint. Somebody raped another's wife, and he brought a complaint. Somebody overturned the cart owned by someone of his own sect; so there was the hassle with the police."

The night, the wanton, errant night, once again stretched itself in a yawn, and the stars in the parting of her hair began disappearing one by one. And then man's subconscious lowered the ladder, on which he was swinging, into a well stuffed with corpses. Some corpse might want to climb up the rungs of the ladder and go to the top. Then, man's subconscious merged once again in Sikandar's; he lay on the hospital bed, all plastered and burning with 105 degree fever, imagining himself turning in the magnificent vastness of the bed.

Hoping against hope, Ghazanfar left the very next day for Delhi in the Deccan Airways plane. This conflagration had been set by our national leaders. What did we get from this independence, this partition, this Pakistan, this India? Acharya—what a great name! Go ahead, incite more people. Didn't even bother to think that Genghis Khan and Halaku Khan were not Muslims. They were murderers of Muslims. What sense did it make to threaten to follow in their footsteps? And the other day, Mian Bashir Ahmad was sitting exasperated, resting his forehead on his hand, for there was an argument going on between the President and the Organiser of the Punjab League, about who should contribute more towards the fund to counter the riots. Consequently, no one had contributed anything.

Remembering this and other incidents, he smiled at times, and the pain of the memory of his parents and brother and sister, lessened a little.

While nodding off in the plane, Ghazanfar thought: did those millions die so that the politicians might rule these countries—Pakistan and India? That they should have fun while human beings were massacred; my own parents, my brother and sister. . . . The plane began its descent. Below, the Narmada flowed peacefully like an open sewer. A mountain appeared under the plane and shot out of sight. Then the pond in Bhopal showed itself like a large sapphire. Then came Gwalior, and then Delhi.

Ghazanfar didn't waste a minute after arriving in Delhi. He had many friends in the Government of India. He stayed with a Hindu friend. He visited the site of the carnage where he identified the dead bodies of his father, mother, Tahawwar and Batool. Mangled and rotting bodies. Sakina could not be found. About 200 yards from the tracks, under a bush lay the abused and bruised body of a young woman. Before finishing with her, as she lay unconscious, the beasts had smashed her head and face with a huge stone. She was unrecognisable.

Ghazanfar, who for the past fifteen years had always seen his sister in silks, could not have recognised that naked girl.

Then months later, when Khwaja Shahab-ud-din's statement about a graduate girl living as a servant and a mistress in an illiterate potter's house appeared in the newspapers, the hearts of the three brothers beat fast for a moment. But then they realised that the girl was in Kapurthala. She was surely a Punjabi girl who must have been repatriated to Pakistan.

Then Ghazanfar went to the hospital where he saw his brother who was unconscious, suffering from delirium because of the injury to his head and neck.

Alexander the Great! Aristotle's student. Seeing the naked girls in the soldiers' wake, Aristotle had covered his eyes. Thousands of years ago, he had bred Great Alexander to subdue the world. Aristotle; Alexander; Nietzsche's Overman.

Dark night arrived again, wanton, gorgeous, devilishly beautiful; tinsel glitter of stars in the parting of her hair; the pendant of the moon on her forehead! Man, standing on the top rung of the ladder, lifted his hands towards the sky and proclaimed the Overman. Let it be known that in himself the Overman challenges all of reality. In his spiritual self, he challenges divine reality; in his physical self, the reality of the senses. In his creative self, he is face to face with the heavens.

From the ladder of evolution, man was looking skyward. Look at me, he said. I am the message of the lightning. I am the big raindrop fallen from the clouds. The lightning is the herald of the Overman.

In a place of worship, about which one couldn't be sure whether it was a mosque, a Hindu temple, a *gurdwara,* or a church, a woman's corpse lay rotting. And in that part of her anatomy from where human beings are born, and from where Overman himself is born, someone had, after brutalising and murdering her, shoved a page torn from a book. Call the Prime Ministers of India and Pakistan over here. In this dark night, they might be able to decipher the writing on that page and tell us whether it is a leaf from the Quran or the holy *Vedas*, or the *Granth Sahib,* or the Bible, or the Communist Manifesto or Bergson's Creative Evolution.

Embarrassed, the Overman again lowered the ladder into the well which had been stuffed with rotting corpses, and started climbing down the rungs to where the beasts ruled, where insects lived, and where the worms crawled in the corpses. And then the Overman was no more.

Having buried the bodies of his parents and of that unknown girl, when Ghazanfar returned to the hospital, he discovered that his brother had died in his delirium. The doctor said: "We're really sorry. We tried our best to save his life."

(Translated from the original in Urdu by Faruq Hassan)

4

S. H. Vatsyayan   Ajneya

The Avenger

Having managed to shove her baggage in, dump the boy in her lap on to the empty seat, push her daughter up the footboard and scramble in herself as the train started to move, Suraiya heaved a deep sigh in the name of Allah, the Protector, and looked round the dark compartment. She realised that the two shadowy figures, all wrapped up in their *chaddars* in the deep gloom at the other end of the compartment, were not Muslims, brothers of the faith, but Sikhs. In the streaks of light from the station glow-lamps, as the train picked up speed, it seemed to her that she could see something inhuman in their unblinking eyes. It was as if their eyes stared at her without seeing her; their aloofness had something fearful and intangible in them. She could not see distinctly in the inadequate light, but with a vision sharpened by imagination she saw that those eyes were bloodshot. And she shivered with fear. But it was too late to change the compartment, the train was already moving. She could have jumped from the moving train, but being thrown out by another traveller would not be much worse than jumping from the train herself with her children! Her eyes wandered to the handle of the alarm chain dangling above her head. As she sagged uncertainly into her seat, she thought she would get down at the next station. It was a short run and there shouldn't be any danger. In any case, nothing had happened on this run so far.

"How far are you going?"

Suraiya started! It was the older Sikh. How heavy his voice sounded! She was suddenly struck by the irony of someone being polite to her who might a couple of stations later knife her, throw her body out of the running train.

She did not answer. The Sikh asked again:

"How far would you be travelling?"

Suraiya had turned her *burqa* back. She now pulled it over her face and answered, "I'm going to Etawah."

The Sikh thought for a moment before he spoke, "No one with you?"

Suraiya noted the moment's pause. He must have been calculating how much time he would have to kill her, she thought. And though she knew it meant no protection unless one's companions were in the same compartment, she took courage and lied.

"My brother is in the next compartment," she said, looking out of the window.

Her boy, who was lying on the seat, suddenly sat up.

"Where, Mother? Uncle is in Lahore."

Suraiya rebuked him in a fierce undertone, "Shut up, Abid."

There followed an uneasy silence. The Sikh spoke again, "Do you have your own people in Etawah?"

"Yes."

The Sikh was silent again for a while. Then he continued, "Your brother should have sat with you. Whoever sits apart from one's womenfolk in these times?"

Has the old fox guessed I am unaccompanied? thought Suraiya, shivering with fear.

The Sikh said slowly as if to himself, "But in misfortune there never is anyone to stand by you . . . . . All are alone."

The train was slowing down. A wayside station. Suraiya was undecided. Should she stick it out or leave? Two other passengers got in. "Hindus", registered Suraiya's mind quickly. She grew frightened and unconsciously her hand reached towards her bundles.

"Are you getting down?" asked the Sikh.

"I might as well go and join my brother," said Suraiya, standing up.

"Please stay seated," said the Sikh. "There is nothing to fear here. I look on you as my sister and these kids of yours as my own. I will see you safely to Aligarh and beyond Aligarh there is no danger. From there many of your own brethren will be on the train."

One of the Hindus said, "Let her go if she wants to, *Sardarji.* Why should you bother?"

It would have been difficult for Suraiya to decide how to take the Sikh's words or the Hindu's comment. But the train decided things for her by moving. She sat down.

The Hindu spoke, "Are you coming from Punjab, *Sardarji?*"

"Yes, sir."

"Where is your home?"

"Home was in Shekhupura. Now—now it is here!"

"What do you mean—here?"

"Home is where I am now. In this corner of the railway compartment."

The Hindu seemed to measure his words. It was as if someone had poured out a little pity into a cup and held it forth. He said, "So you are refugees."

And the Sikh, almost as if pushing the cup aside with a "No thank you—I don't drink," said with a dry laugh, "Yes, sir."

There was a resonance in that laugh, the meaning of which the Hindu could not catch. He spoke with feigned passion, "You people must have gone through unspeakable suffering." For a fraction of a moment the Sikh's eyes smouldered, but he did not rise to the bait. He kept silent.

The Hindu continued, his gaze now fixed on Suraiya. "People in Delhi tell of the atrocities they have committed there on Hindus and Sikhs. The things they tell—one is ashamed to put them into words. Women were stripped and . . . ."

Just then the Sikh turned to the other wrapped up figure beside him and said, "Son, go and stretch yourself on the upper berth." It was obvious that they were father and son, and when the lad stood up obediently and surveyed the bunk, his eyes glowed the same amber glow that had smouldered in the older Sikh's eyes. He climbed up and stretched himself; on the lower seat the Sikh straightened his legs and looked out of the window.

The Hindu resumed his speech: "Sisters and daughters were stripped before their brothers and fathers . . . ."

"*Babu Sahib*, how wise you are! But is there a need to put in words what we all have seen with our eyes?" said the Sikh.

The Hindu gentleman, however, missed the irony in the Sikh's tone, and feeling encouraged, continued: "You are right. We cannot understand your suffering. We can sympathise, but after all sympathy does not mean very much if we do not know the magnitude of the suffering. How can we understand how those Sikhs must have felt who saw their own daughters and daughters-in-law stripped before their eyes and . . . ."

The Sikh's voice quivered as he intervened, "All people have daughters and daughters-in-law, *Babu Sahib*."

The Hindu gentleman felt a little abashed at not being able to understand the precise meaning of the Sardar's words. But he was not to be deterred for long. "Now at last Hindus and Sikhs are also hitting back," he said. "Vengeance is not a good thing, but how much can one endure? Now in Delhi there have been pitched battles and in some places they have applied the law of an eye for an eye. In truth, that is the only thing that works. They say in Karol Bagh a Muslim doctor's daughter . . . ."

This time there was no veiled sarcasm in the Sikh's voice but an explicit harshness as he pronounced, "*Babu Sahib*, a woman's shame is everybody's shame." And turning to Suraiya he entreated, "Sister, I seek forgiveness that you should have to listen to all this."

The Hindu gentleman, taken aback, said: "What? . . . what? I have said nothing to her." Then restraining himself, but with some insolence, he asked: "Is she—is the lady with you?"

The Sikh replied with a marked severity in his voice, "Yes, I am seeing her to Aligarh."

Something within Suraiya said: This old gentleman is going to Aligarh—this poor man . . . . She gathered courage to say, "Are you getting down at Aligarh?"

"Yes."

"Do you have relations there?"

"I have no relations anywhere. My son is with me."

"Why are you going to Aligarh? To stay?"

"No, I'll be back tomorrow."

"Then you are going for pleasure?"

"For pleasure!" answered the Sikh, repeating the word "pleasure" in a lost voice. Then pulling himself together he said, "No, we are not going anywhere. We are only looking for somewhere to go. Meanwhile, one can stay on a moving train."

Something in Suraiya's mind again prodded her. But Aligarh? Aligarh . . . poor old man . . . . She then said, aloud, "Aligarh is not a nice place. Do you have to go there?"

The Hindu, with the air of a man taking pity on a lunatic, shook his head confusedly.

"Good or bad, all places are the same to me," said the Sikh.

"But aren't you afraid? Someone could stab you in the night!"

The Sikh smiled wryly. "That might even be a release, you know."

"Oh, please don't say such things," she exhorted.

"But really! And who would stab me?" asked the Sikh. "He would be either a Muslim or a Hindu. If he should be a Muslim, I shall go and join the rest of my family wherever they have gone. And if he should be a Hindu, I would consider that that was all that was needed—that the killing sickness has now reached its peak and that the road to hell lies before us."

"But why would a Hindu kill? A Hindu may be very wicked, but he would do no such thing," contended the Hindu gentleman.

The Sardar shook with anger. "You do talk, *Babu Sahib*," he said, looking at the Hindu fiercely. "A moment ago you were narrating those gruesome details about Delhi with such relish. If you had a knife and had no fear for yourself, wouldn't you have . . . ? Would you have spared your co-passengers? They? Or me, if I had intervened?"

Seeing that the Hindu gentleman was about to protest, the Sikh shut him up with an imperious gesture. "You show me compassion because I am your refugee. Compassion is a great thing and I would consider myself blessed if you were fit to give compassion. But how can you understand my suffering if in the same breath you can talk of happenings in Delhi in this callous fashion? If you could really share my grief—if you had heart enough for it—then the things you wanted to tell me would have cut you to the core and turned you dumb with despair. A woman's shame is a woman's shame; it is not the shame of a Hindu or a Muslim, it is the shame of the mother of man. I know what happened with us in Shekhupura—but I cannot avenge it because for that there can be no revenge. I can only make reparations: offer penance, and not let what happened to me happen to anyone else. It is for this reason that I keep shuttling back and forth between Delhi and

Aligarh, escorting people from one city to another. It helps me pass my days and also to make amends. If during these journeys someone should kill me, my penance would be complete—whether the killer is a Muslim or a Hindu. What I strive for is that no one should have to see what I have seen, whether he is a Hindu or a Sikh or a Muslim."

After this there was total silence in the compartment. When the train slowed down for Aligarh, Suraiya tried very hard to say a few words of gratitude to the *Sardar*, but she seemed to have lost her voice.

At Aligarh, the *Sardar* half-rose and called the boy on the upper berth, "Come down, son, this is Aligarh." Then standing up, he turned towards the Hindu gentleman and said, "*Babu Sahib*, I seek forgiveness for any harsh words I might have uttered. You are our refuge."

The Hindu gentleman's expression clearly showed that if the Sikh had not been getting down there, he himself would have moved to another compartment.

5

MULK RAJ ANAND

The Parrot in the Cage

"*RUKMANIAI NI RUKMANIAI*", the parrot in the cage called in the way Rukmani's friends used to call her when they entered the alleyway in Kucha Chabuk Swaran in Lahore. And he repeated the call even before she could answer him as she was wont to do when she wanted to humour the bird. She did not answer but sat crouching on the fringe of the road about half a furlong away from the Amritsar court.

"*Rukmaniai ni Rukmaniai!*" the parrot called again.

She was peering through the little clouds of dust raised by the passing motors and *tongas* and *yekkas* in the direction from which, she had been told by the roasted gram-stall keeper, the "Dipty Collator" was to come and so she remained heedless of the parrot's cry.

"*Rukmaniai ni Rukmaniai!*" the parrot called shrilly and went on repeating the cry with the sure mocking bird's instinct that if he kept on calling her she would answer.

"*Han, bete, han . . .*" the old woman said after all, wearily. There had been a dull ache behind the small knot of hair on the back of her head and, now, with the mounting heat of the September morning, it seemed to her like the rumblings of that dreadful night when murder and fire had raged in her lane.

Little rivulets of sweat trickled through the deep fissures of old age which lined her face and she shaded her eyes, with the inverted palm of her hand, to probe the sunlight more surely for a sight of the Deputy Commissioner. Her contracted, toothless mouth was open and a couple of flies came from the direction in which she looked and settled on the corners of her lips.

She waved her left hand gingerly to chase away the flies. But they persisted and set up an irritation in her soul through which she felt a panic seize her belly.

"Ni tun kithe hain?" the parrot tried out another cry which he had learnt from the old woman's friends who invariably asked on entering the lane, "Where are you?" For she used to be away earning her living as a maid of all work, cleaning utensils for the people in the bigger houses in the lane, or was mostly hidden from view in the inner sanctum of the dark ground floor room by the wall in the *gully*.

"Son, I don't know where I am . . . ." she said listlessly, in an effort to keep the parrot quiet by assuring him she was taking notice of him. "I only know that if Fato had not given me her *burqa* to escape with, I should not be here . . . ."

"Ni tun ki karni hain?" the parrot persisted with the third call which Rukmani's friends used to utter.

"Nothing, son, I am doing nothing . . . only waiting . . ." the old woman said tiredly, as though now she was holding a metaphorical conversation with her pet to keep her mind occupied. For, from her entrails arose a confusion which was like the panic she had felt at the mad mob bursting with shouts of *"Allah-ho-Akbar!"* *"Har Har Mahadev!"* *"Sat Sri Akal!"* on the night of terror when she had fled from the lane.

There had been flashes of blazing light; cracking of burning housebeams; smoke, smoke, choking smoke . . . . And she had thought that her last days had come, that the earth itself was troubled through the misdeeds of the *Kaliyug* and that soon the *dharti* would open up and swallow everything. And then Fato had come and told her she would be murdered if she did not leave.

"*Ni tun ki karni hain?*" the parrot repeated. "*Ni tun kithe hain . . . ?*"

"Nothing son, nothing," Rukmani answered. "And I don't know where I am . . . ." And as she looked steadily towards the junction of the Mall Road and Kutchery Road and saw no sign of the Deputy Commissioner, her last phrase seemed to get meaning.

"*Rukmaniai ni Rukmaniai!*" the parrot called again.

Her answers to his metallic, shrill nasal cries did not irritate her anymore, but relieved the heavy pressure of the demons of the dreadful night on her head and her chest and her bowels.

"*Ni tun ki karni hain?*" the parrot persisted.

"Son, I am waiting for the Sahib, so that he can give me some money to buy bread with. . . . They say that the Congress Sarkar will give back what we have lost, son, they say—I heard at the station, son, at the station! . . . Are you hungry, my son—you must be hungry. . . . I shall buy you some gram from that stall keeper when the Sahib gives me money. . . ."

"*Mai*, you are dreaming! You have gone mad!" the gram-stall keeper said. "Go, go your way to the town, you may get some food at the Durbar Sahib temple. You won't get anything from the *Dipty Collator* ."

"*Vay jaja*, eater of your masters!" she shouted bitterly. Such common sense as that of the complacent gram-seller seemed to break the pitcher of her hopes. And in defiance she mooed like a cow, at the end of her speech.

"*Achha*, don't abuse me. I only said this for your own good," the stall keeper answered as he whisked the flies off his stall with the end of a dirty apron.

"Oh, why did I leave home to wander like this from door to door!" old Rukmani whined almost under her breath. "Oh why did you have to turn me out of my room in my old age, God . . . Oh why . . . ? Why didn't I tie the rupees I had earned in a knot on my *dupatta*! . . . *Hai Rabba!* . . ."

She moaned to herself, and tremors of tenderness went swirling through her flesh. And tears filled her eyes. And in the hazy dust before her the violent sequence of the terrors of falling houses and dying, groaning men and heavy, shouting men, danced in macabre trembling waves of sunlight, dim and unsubstantial like the ghosts on a cremation ground before whom she had always cowered every time she had attended a funeral.

"*Rukmaniai ni Rukmaniai!*" the parrot called and brought her to herself.

Crackling flames of heat now assailed her. And she sweated more profusely. And yet she crouched where she was, only shuffling like a hen sitting over her eggs.

"At least go and sit under the shade of the tree," the gram-seller said.

The pupils of her eyes were blistering with the glare. She wiped her face with the end of her *dupatta* and heaved as though she was lifting the weight of a century's miseries up with her. Then she took the handle of the iron cage in which her pet parrot sat and, bent-backed but staring ahead, ambled up to a spot where the precarious shadow of a *kikar* tree lay on the rutted earth.

"*Ni tun kithe hain? ni . . .*" the parrot's monologue continued. So did her self-communion, aroused by the monotonous, meaningless, repetitive calls: "Nowhere, son, nothing, nothing . . . ."

She had hardly settled down when suddenly a motor whirred past, with a motor cyclist ahead and some policemen in a jeep behind, scattering much dust on the fringe of the roadside.

"There goes your 'Dipty Collator'," said the gram-stall keeper.

"*Hai hai!* Come, my son!" she screamed, as she shot up

with great alacrity and picked up the cage in her hand. "Come, I will join my hands to the Sahib and fall at his feet."

"Mad woman!" the gram-seller said cynically.

She heeded him not, but penetrated the clouds of dust.

Behind her, and on all sides, she could hear the sound of rushing feet storming towards the gloomy gates of the *kutchery*. And their cries whirled in the air, "*Hujoor, Mai-Bap*, hear us! *Sarkar! Dipty Sahib!* . . . We have come on foot all the way from Lahore . . . . You . . . ." She nearly fell as the more powerful men among the crowd brushed past her and their own women.

"*Rukmaniai! Tun kithe hain?*" the parrot in the cage cried even as he fluttered his wings in panic at the voices and the hurtling feet.

The old woman did not answer but sped grimly on. Only, in a moment, the dust storm which was proceeding towards the court was turned back by a furious whirlwind from the opposite direction. A posse of policemen charged the refugees with *lathis* and angry shouts which drowned the chorus of voices of which Rukmani's sighs and her parrot's cries had been a part.

In the delirium of motion which was set afoot by the *lathi* charge of the police, all valour was held at bay and turned back.

Rukmani was brushed aside by some desperate arm and she reeled and fell not far from where she had sat waiting for the Sahib. But she clung to the handle of the cage in which her parrot sat as she lay moaning in suppressed, helpless whispers.

The parrot fluttering furiously as though he was being strangled, called out shrilly:

"*Rukmaniai! Ni Rukmaniai! Ni tun kithe hain! . . . Ni tun ki karni hain!*"

But the old woman, though concerned for him, had turned in upon herself with a sudden dimness that seemed to be creeping upon her.

After the crowd had been cleared, and the dust had settled, the gram-seller was irritated by the parrot's constant cries from his perch. He was afraid that the old woman had expired. But as he came near her, the parrot called her more shrilly and she answered faintly, "*Han, han* son, *han*," and the man knew that she was still alive. He lifted her up and found that her hands and arms were slightly grazed.

"Come and sit in the shade, mother!" he said.

"*Achha*, son, *achha*!" she moaned.

And she lifted the cage and proceeded towards the shade. The parrot was a little reassured as he saw the gram-seller helping his mistress and he shrieked less shrilly.

"Come, my little winged one, I shall give you some gram to eat," the gram-seller said to him.

"May you live long, son!" the old woman blessed the gram-seller in a feeble, strained, moanful voice.

"*Rukmaniai ni Rukmaniai! Tun kithe hain? Tun ki karni hain?* . . ." the parrot called now in a slow measured voice.

"*Han han,* son, *han* my son, . . . I don't know where I am! I don't know. . . ."

6

SAMARESH BASU

*Aadaab**

THE MUFFLED STILLNESS of the night was broken by the roar
of a mobile military van on duty. It swung round Victoria
Park and was gone.

The city was in the grip of a riot between the Hindus and
Muslims. In spite of the curfew and the enforcing of Section
144, clashes continued—open encounters with sticks and
daggers. Secret assassins lurked in the dark alleyways, ready
to strike.

In the wake of the fighting came the marauders, filling the
dark and horrible night with their fiendish yells. Slums and
hutments were set ablaze, screaming of women and children
completed the hell-like atmosphere. In no time the armed cars
were on the scene, shooting at sight. Law and order had to be
kept at all costs.

At the intersection of two lanes, from behind an overturned
dustbin, a man crawled out on all fours. Too frightened to lift
his head, he lay very still, straining to recognise the war
cry—was it *Allah-ho-Akbar* or *Bande Mataram*—the Muslims
or the Hindus?

* Farewell

The dustbin moved. The man was instantly on the alert, terror coursing through his veins; he clenched his teeth, and waited for something terrible to happen. Some time passed— no sound came, nothing stirred.

It could have been a dog. The man pushed the dustbin in a feeble effort to chase it away. Nothing happened, then the dustbin moved again. The man was now curious, he lifted his head very slowly to meet another head emerging from the other side. So it was a man after all! With the dustbin between them, the two men stared at each other, with fear and distrust in their eyes, their hearts pounding. Each was expecting the other to pounce, each thought the other was a murderer. They waited, but neither made the first move. Both of them began to wonder if the other fellow was a Hindu or a Muslim. This was the crucial issue; it would decide their future. Yet neither could get round to asking the terrible question. They crouched, petrified; they could not get up and run for each was afraid the other would get him first.

They grew uncomfortable and suspicious—their patience being taxed to the limit. At long last one of them spoke.

"Are you a Hindu or a Muslim?"

"Suppose you tell me first."

Neither seemed willing to reveal his identity. Each regarded the other with suspicion. Then they tactfully changed the subject.

"Where are you from?"

"From across the Buriganga, a place called Subaida, and you?"

"Chashada—near Narayanganj. What do you do for a living?"

"I ply a ferry boat, I'm a boatman. How about you?"

"I work in the cotton mill at Narayanganj."

There was another pause, during which each tried to make out what kind of dress the other had on, what he looked like. But the darkness and the dustbin came between them. Suddenly from close at hand, shouts from two hostile crowds went up. The boatman and the mill worker began to fidget.

"Seems quite close," remarked the mill worker in a panic-stricken voice.

"Let's get out of here," the boatman was scared.

"Are you mad? Do you want to get killed or what? Don't budge," the mill worker observed wisely.

The boatman looked at him suspiciously, wondering about his motive. Their eyes met. The mill worker insisted, "Sit down, stay where you are."

Why is the man so insistent? The boatman grew apprehensive. "Why must I?" he asked with distrust.

"You ask me why? You seem to be real keen to meet your death," the mill worker whispered.

The boatman did not like the way he talked. He grew desperate. "Am I going to stay in this dark lane forever?" Why was he being so stubborn? The mill worker began to wonder. "What is in your mind? You didn't tell me what your religion is. Are you going to call your people and murder me?"

"I like that!" The boatman could have shouted in desperation forgetting the situation they were in.

"I am talking sense; don't you realise what a man feels?"

Something in his voice reassured the boatman.

"I don't want to be alone here."

The yelling died down. Again a death-like stillness descended on the scene. Every moment was agony. In the dark lane, from their vantage positions the two men thought of their immediate danger, of their homes, of mother, wife and children. Were they ever going to see them? They grew confused as they thought of how suddenly out of the blue the riot had erupted all around them, upsetting their normal pattern of living. Wasn't everybody living happily, chatting and laughing in the streets and market-places? The very next moment they were at each other's neck, out for blood. How could they be so heartless! What a cursed race! The mill worker heaved a sigh. The boatman sighed too.

"Care for a smoke?" The mill worker offered him a *bidi*. The boatman took it, felt it, as was his habit, and put it between his lips. The mill worker was trying to light a match, but it was soaked. He tried in vain a couple of times, a blue spark was all he could get out of the match. He threw down the stick in disgust.

"Blast the matchstick! Wet as my shirt." He tried another.

The boatman crept closer. "Let me light it for you." He snatched the stick and produced a flame.

"*Sobhan Allah*. Be quick now."

The mill worker froze as if he had seen a ghost. The *bidi* dropped from his lips.

"You mean you are . . . ."

The flame went out. The two pairs of eyes stared at each other in horror.

"Of course I am a Muslim. So what?" the boatman declared boldly.

"No, nothing—but," the mill worker fumbled. "What have you got there?" he pointed to the bundle the other carried.

"Clothes for the children. Tomorrow we have the *Id* festival, don't you know?"

"What else do you have in there?" The mill worker was not convinced.

"You think I'm lying? Have a look?" He pushed the bundle towards the other man.

"That's all right, brother. But you know in these days one can't trust anyone—don't you agree?"

"True. But are you sure you haven't got anything hidden away?"

"I swear by the name of God—I don't have as much as a needle with me. I only wish I could go back home all in one piece." The mill worker let the other man feel his clothes.

They quietly smoked away for a while. Then the boatman said, "Well, could you tell me what all this fighting is for?" He spoke very intimately, as though he was talking to a blood relation.

The mill worker was a well-informed man. He was familiar with newspapers. He said heatedly, "Your Muslim League people are the ones who started it—a struggle to achieve some nonsense."

The boatman uttered a foul word. "What do I understand about those things. I ask you, who gains by fighting. Some of our people would be killed, some of your people would be killed. So what's the point?"

"Well, I say the same thing. Fat lot do they gain." He made a gesture with his thumb. "We die and our children go begging and that's all we gain. Why, in the riot last year they butchered my brother-in-law. I have to support my widowed sister and her family. The leaders are comfortable in their fine seventh floor flats. They just order you about—and we face the music."

The boatman clutched his knees in futile anger. "We have turned into dogs, haven't we, brother—fighting each other?"

"That's right, brother."

"Does anybody care for us? There is a riot—which of those blasted fellows is going to lift a finger to help you get something to eat? You know, they sunk my boat at the *ghat* of Badamtali. The manager of the village landlord used to cross the river in my boat every year. What a generous man he was! He would pay me five rupees as fare and five as a tip—it used to keep me going for the whole month. I doubt if the Hindu *Babu* is ever going to step into my boat again."

The mill worker was going to say something, but the sound of approaching boots stopped him. The steps were coming towards them from the direction of the main road—it was unmistakable. They looked at each other in apprehension.

"What are we going to do now?" The boatman clutched his bundle tightly.

"Let's get away from here, but where? We don't know the city."

"It does not matter. I am not going to be beaten up by the police. I don't trust those fellows."

"Right, brother, which way do we go?—they are almost here."

"This way."

The boatman pointed to the southern end of the lane. "If we can reach the *ghat* of Badamtali we are safe."

They ducked and ran till they reached Patuatuli Road. The empty road stretched before them, bright with the electric lights. Was anybody lurking around? But there was no time to lose—they scanned both the crossings and fled westward. Presently they heard horse hooves following them. To be sure a mounted soldier was coming their way. Quickly they slipped into a narrow wayside lane, meant only for sweepers. The Englishman rode past, holding a revolver; the clattering of the hooves sent a shiver through their hearts. When the sound died at last, they came out of hiding.

"Let's keep to the side," suggested the mill worker.

They kept to the edge of the road. "Wait a minute," ordered the boatman. "Come here, have a look." He dragged him behind a *paan* shop.

About a hundred yards ahead an English officer was talking to a dozen armed policemen, who stood stiff as statues on the verandah of a room from which light was streaming out. The officer was smoking a pipe and gesticulating. Down on the ground another policeman stood holding the reins of a restless horse.

"That's the Islampur police station. We have to cross it, and take the lane to the left. Then we reach the *ghat* of Badamtali."

The information frightened the mill worker.

"That's why you should stay here. This is the Hindu

stronghold—and Islampur belongs to the Muslims. You can go home tomorrow morning."

"What about you?"

"I have to go." The boatman broke down, "I can't stay here, brother. How can I? I haven't heard from home for one whole week. Allah only knows what has become of them. If I can reach the lane by any means—the rest is easy. I can swim across the Buriganga in case I can't get a boat."

"Are you out of your mind, *Mian*?" The mill worker held on to the shirt of the boatman. "How can you possibly go?" His voice shook with emotion.

"Please let me go, brother. Don't you understand, tomorrow is *Eid*—the children must have seen the moon tonight. How they would be looking forward to meeting their father—they are dreaming of climbing on my shoulder, wearing new clothes. The wife would be weeping her heart out. I'm homesick, brother, I can't stay away," his voice was choked. The mill worker's heart grew heavy, he let go of his grip.

"But supposing they spot you?"

"You needn't worry. They won't."

"But promise, you will wait here. Farewell, brother. I shall always remember this night. Perhaps we may meet again if destiny wills so—*Aadaab*."

"Neither will I forget you, brother. *Aadaab* to you too." The boatman left, walking on tiptoe.

Anxiety gnawed at the breast of the mill worker who waited, straining his ears, praying for his friend's safe journey home. After some breathless moments he began to feel optimistic. He was happy for the children who would see their father, rejoice in the new clothes. How could a father's heart bear to be away on such a day! The mill worker tried to visualise the wife clinging to her own *Mian Sahib*, sobbing. A faint smile twisted the lips of the worker as he thought how the boatman would respond to her caress.

"Halt."

His heart seemed to stand still as he heard shouts and the sound of boots.

"Watch out—the ruffian is getting away."

The officer sprang with his revolver, shots rang out, tearing the stillness of the night.

Bang! Crash! A couple of blue flashes. The mill worker bit his finger hard. He saw the officer leap on the horse and rush to the spot—he had heard the ruffian scream in mortal agony.

A scene swam into the dazed vision of the mill worker, the blood oozing from the chest of the boatman and seeping into the bundle, containing new clothes for the kids, a *sari* for his wife. All he could hear was the last words of the boatman, "I couldn't make it, brother. They didn't let me—the sons of the enemies. My children and the *Bibi* would have to spend the festival in tears."

(Translated from the original in Bengali by Enakshi Chatterji)

7

RAJINDER SINGH BEDI

Lajwanti

The leaves of Lajwanti wither at the touch of human hands.
—Punjabi folk song

AFTER THE GREAT holocaust, when people had washed away the blood from their bodies, they turned their attention to those whose hearts had been torn by the partition.

In every street and by-lane they set up a rehabilitation committee. In the beginning people worked with great enthusiasm to rehabilitate refugees in work camps, on the land and in homes. But there still remained the task of rehabilitating abducted women, those that were recovered and brought back home, and over this they ran into difficulties. The slogan of the supporters was "Rehabilitate them in your hearts". It was strongly opposed by people living in the vicinity of the temple of Narain Bawa.

The campaign was started by the residents of Mohalla Shakoor. They set up a "rehabilitation of hearts" committee. A local lawyer was elected president. But the more important post of secretary went to Babu Sunder Lal who got a majority of eleven votes over his rival. It was the opinion of the old petition writer and many other respectable citizens of the locality that no one would work more zealously than Sunder Lal, because amongst the women abducted during the riots, and not recovered, was Sunder Lal's wife, Lajwanti.

The Rehabilitation of Hearts Committee daily took out a procession through the streets in the early hours of the morning. They sang as they went along. Whenever his friends Rasalu and Neki Ram started singing "the leaves of *Lajwanti* wither with the touch of human hands", Sunder Lal would fall silent. He would walk as if in a daze. Where in the name of God was Lajwanti? Was she thinking of him? Would she ever come back?—and his steps would falter on the even surface of the brick-paved road.

Sunder Lal had abandoned all hope of finding Lajwanti. He had made his loss a part of the general loss. He had drowned his personal sorrow by plunging into social service. Even so, whenever he raised his voice to join the chorus, he could not avoid thinking—"how fragile is the human heart" . . . exactly like the *Lajwanti* . . . one only has to bring a finger close to it and its leaves curl up.

He had behaved very badly towards his Lajwanti; he had allowed himself to be irritated with everything she did—even with the way she stood up or sat down, the way she cooked and the way she served his food; he had thrashed her at every pretext.

His poor Lajo who was as slender as the cypress! Life in the open air and sunshine had tanned her skin and filled her with an animal vitality. She ran about the lanes in her village with the mercurial grace of dew drops on a leaf. Her slim figure was full of robust health. When he first saw her, Sunder Lal was a little dismayed. But when he saw that Lajwanti took in her stride every adversity including the chastisement he gave her, he increased the dose of thrashing. He was unaware of the limit of human endurance. And

Lajwanti's reactions were of little help; even after the most violent beating all Sunder Lal had to do was to smile and the girl would break into giggles: "If you beat me again, I'll never speak to you."

Lajo forgot everything about the thrashing as soon as it was over; all men beat their wives. If they did not and let them have their way, women were the first to start talking: "What kind of man is he! He can't manage a chit of a girl like her!"

They made up songs about the beatings men gave their wives. Lajo herself sang a couplet which ran somewhat as follows:

> *I will not marry a city lad*
> *City lads wear boots*
> *And I have such a small bottom.*

Nevertheless, the first time Lajo met a boy from the city, she fell in love with him; it happened to be Sunder Lal. He had come with the bridegroom's party at Lajwanti's sister's wedding. His eyes had fallen on Lajwanti and he had whispered in the bridegroom's ear, "Your sister-in-law is quite a saucy morsel; your bride's likely to be a dainty dish, old chap!" Lajo had overheard Sunder Lal. The words went to her head. She did not notice the enormous boots Sunder Lal was wearing; she also forgot that her behind was small.

Such were the thoughts that coursed through Sunder Lal's head when he went out singing in the morning procession. He would say to himself, "If I get another chance, just one more chance, I would really rehabilitate her in my heart. I could set an example to the people and tell them—these poor women are not to blame, they were victimised by lecherous hooligans. A society which refuses to accept these helpless women is rotten beyond redemption and deserves to be liquidated." He agitated for the rehabilitation of abducted women and for according them the respect due to a wife, mother, daughter and sister in any home. He exhorted the men never to remind these women of their past experiences because they had become as sensitive as *Lajwanti* and would, like the leaves of the plant, wither when a finger was pointed towards them.

In order to propagate the cause of Rehabilitation of Hearts, the Mohalla Shakoor Committee organised morning processions. The early hours of dawn were blissfully peaceful—no hubbub of people, no noise of traffic. Even street dogs, who had kept an all-night vigil, were fast asleep beside the *tandoors*. People who were roused from their slumbers by the singing would simply mutter, "Oh, the dawn chorus" and go back to their dreams.

People listened to Babu Sunder Lal's exhortations sometimes with patience, sometimes with irritation. Women who had had no trouble in coming across from Pakistan were utterly complacent. Their menfolk were indifferent and grumbled; their children treated the songs on rehabilitation like lullabies to make them sleep again.

Words which assail one's ears in the early hours of dawn have a habit of going round in the head with insidious intent. Often a person who has not understood their meaning will find himself humming them while he is about his business.

When Miss Mridula Sarabhai arranged for the exchange of abducted women between India and Pakistan, some men of Mohalla Shakoor expressed their readiness to take them back. Their relatives went to receive them in the market-place. For some time the abducted women and their menfolk faced each other in awkward silence. Then they swallowed their pride, took their women and re-built their domestic lives. Rasalu, Neki Ram and Sunder Lal joined the throng and encouraged the rehabilitators with slogans like "Long Live Mahinder Singh . . . . Long Live Sohan Lal." They yelled till their throats were parched.

There were some people who refused to have anything to

do with the abducted women who came back. "Why couldn't they have killed themselves? Why didn't they take poison and preserve their virtue and their honour? Why didn't they jump into a well? They are cowards, they clung to life. . . ."

Hundreds of thousands of women had in fact killed themselves rather than be dishonoured. How could the dead know what courage it needed to face the cold, hostile world of the living—a hard-hearted world in which husbands refused to acknowledge their wives. And some of these women would think sadly of their names and the joyful meanings they had: "Suhagwanti . . . of marital bliss"—or they would turn to a younger brother and say "Oi Bihari, my own little darling brother, when you were a baby I looked after you as if you were my own son." And Bihari would want to slip away into a corner, but his feet would remain rooted to the ground and he would stare helplessly at his parents. The parents steeled their hearts and looked fearfully at Narain Bawa; and Narain Bawa looked equally helplessly at heaven—the heaven that has no substance but is merely an optical illusion, a boundary line beyond which we cannot see!

Miss Sarabhai brought a truck-load of Hindu women from Pakistan to be exchanged with Muslim women abducted by Indians. Lajwanti was not amongst them. Sunder Lal watched with hope and expectancy till the last of the Hindu women had got down from the truck, and then with patient resignation plunged himself in the committee's activities. The committee redoubled its work and began taking out processions and singing both morning and evening, as well as organising meetings. The aged lawyer, Kalka Prasad, addressed the meetings in his wheezy, asthmatic voice (Rasalu kept a spittoon in readiness beside him). Strange noises came over the microphone when Kalka Prasad was speaking.

Neki Ram also said his few words. But whatever he said or quoted from the scriptures seemed to go against his point of view. Whenever the tide of battle seemed to be going against them, Babu Sunder Lal would rise and stem the retreat. He was never able to complete more than a couple of sentences. His throat went dry and tears streamed down his cheeks. His heart was always too full for words and he had to sit down without making his speech. An embarrassed silence would descend on the audience. But the two sentences that Sunder Lal spoke came from the bottom of his anguished heart and had a greater impact than all the clever verbosity of the lawyer, Kalka Prasad. The men shed a few tears and lightened the burden on their hearts; then they went home without a thought in their empty heads.

One day the Rehabilitation of Hearts Committee was out early in the afternoon. It trespassed into an area near the temple which was looked upon as the citadel of orthodox reaction. The faithful were seated on a cement platform under the *peepal* tree and were listening to a commentary on the *Ramayana*. By sheer coincidence, Narain Bawa happened to be narrating the incident about Rama overhearing a washerman say to his errant wife: "I am not Sri Rama Chandra to take back a woman who has spent many years with another man." And being overcome by the implied rebuke, Rama Chandra had ordered his own wife Sita, who was at the time far gone with child, to leave his palace.

"Can one find a better example of the high standard of morality?" asked Narain Bawa of his audience. "Such was the sense of equality in the Kingdom of Rama that even the remark of a poor washerman was given full consideration. This was true *Ram Rajya*—the Kingdom of God on earth."

The procession halted near the temple to listen to the discourse. Sunder Lal heard the last sentence and spoke up: "We do not want a *Ram Rajya* of this sort."

"Be quiet! . . . Who is this man? . . . Silence,!" came the cries from the audience.

Sunder Lal made his way through the crowd and said loudly, "No one can stop me from speaking."

Another volley of protests came from the crowd. "Silence! . . . We will not let you say a word." And someone shouted from a corner, "We'll kill you!"

Narain Bawa spoke gently, "My dear Sunder Lal, you do not understand the sacred traditions of the *Vedas*."

Sunder Lal was ready with his retort: "I understand at least one thing: in *Ram Rajya* the voice of a washerman was heard, but the present-day protagonists of the same *Ram Rajya* cannot bear to hear the voice of Sunder Lal."

The people who had threatened to beat up Sunder Lal were put to shame.

"Let him speak," yelled Rasalu and Neki Ram. "Silence! Let us hear him."

And Sunder Lal began to speak: "Sri Rama was our hero. But what kind of justice was this, that he accepted the word of a washerman and refused to take the word of so great a Maharani as his wife!"

Narain Bawa answered, "Sita was his own wife; Sunder Lal, you have not realised that very important fact."

"Bawaji, there are many things in this world which are beyond my comprehension. I believe that the only true *Ram Rajya* is a state where a person neither does wrong to anyone nor suffers anyone to do him any wrong."

Sunder Lal's words caught everyone's attention. He continued his oration. "Injustice to oneself is as great a wrong as inflicting it on others. Even today, Lord Rama has thrown out Sita from his home—only because she was compelled to live with her abductor, Ravana. What sin had Sita committed? Wasn't she the victim of a ruse and then of violence, like our own mothers and sisters are today? Was it a question of Sita's rightness and wrongness, or the wickedness of Ravana? Ravana had ten heads, the donkey has only one large one. Today our innocent Sitas have been thrown out of their homes. Sita— Lajwanti"—Sunder Lal broke down and wept.

Rasalu and Neki Ram raised aloft the banners the schoolchildren had cut out and on which they had pasted slogans for them. They yelled, "Long Live Sunder Lal Babu." Somebody in the crowd shouted "Long Live Sita—the queen of virtue." And somebody else cried "Sri Ram Chandra . . . ."

Many voices shouted "Silence!" Many people left the congregation and joined the procession. Narain Bawa's months of preaching was undone in a few moments. The lawyer, Kalka Prasad, and the petition writer, Hukam Singh, led the procession towards the great square, beating a sort of victory tattoo with their decrepit walking sticks. Sunder Lal had not yet dried his tears. The processionists sang with great gusto:

"The leaves of Lajwanti wither at the touch . . . ."

The dawn had not yet greyed the eastern horizon when the song of the processionists assailed the ears of the residents of Mohalla Shakoor. The widow in house 414 stretched her limbs and, being still heavy with sleep, went back to her dreams. Lal Chand who was from Sunder Lal's village, came running. He stuck his arms out of his shawl and said breathlessly: "Congratulations, Sunder Lal." Sunder Lal prodded the embers in his *chillum* and asked, "What for, Lal Chand?"

"I saw sister-in-law Lajo."

The *chillum* fell from Sunder Lal's hands; the sweetened tobacco scattered on the floor. "Where did you see her?" he asked, taking Lal Chand by the shoulder.

"On the border at Wagah."

Sunder Lal let go of Lal Chand. "It must have been someone else," he said quickly and sat down on his haunches.

"No, brother Sunder Lal, it was sister-in-law Lajo," repeated Lal Chand with reassurance. "The same Lajo."

"Could you recognise her?" asked Sunder Lal gathering bits of the tobacco and mashing them in his palm. He took Rasalu's *chillum* and continued: "All right, tell me, what are her distinguishing marks?"

-74-

"You are a strange one to think that I wouldn't recognise her! She has a tattoo mark on her chin, another on her right cheek and . . . ."

"Yes, yes, yes," exploded Sunder Lal and completed his wife's description: "the third one is on her forehead."

He sat up on his knees. He wanted to remove all doubt. He recalled the marks Lajwanti had had tattooed on her body as a child; they were like the green spots on the leaves of the *Lajwanti*, which disappear when the leaves curl up. His Lajwanti behaved exactly in the same way; whenever he pointed out her tattoo marks she used to curl up in embarrassment as if in a shell—almost as if she were stripped and her nakedness was being exposed. A strange longing as well as fear racked Sunder Lal's body. He took Lal Chand by the arm and asked, "How did Lajo get to the border?"

"There was an exchange of abducted women between India and Pakistan."

"What happened?" Sunder Lal stood up suddenly and repeated impatiently. "Tell me, what happened then?"

Rasalu rose from the *charpoy* and in his smoker's wheezy voice asked, "Is it really true that sister-in-law Lajo is back?"

Lal Chand continued his story: "At the border the Pakistanis returned sixteen of our women and took back sixteen of theirs. There was some argument—our chaps said that the women they were handing over were old or middle-aged . . . and of little use. A large crowd gathered and hot words were exchanged. Then one of their fellows got Lajo to stand up on top of the truck, snatched away her *dupatta* and spoke: "Would you describe her as an old woman? . . . Take a good look at her . . . is there one amongst those you have given us who could measure up to her?" and Lajo *Bhabi* was overcome with embarrassment and began hiding her tattoo marks. The argument got very heated and both parties threatened to take back their "goods". I cried out "Lajo! . . . sister-in-law Lajo!" There was an uproar—our police cracked down upon us."

Lal Chand bared his elbow to show the mark of a *lathi* blow. Rasalu and Neki Ram remained silent. Sunder Lal stared vacantly into space.

Sunder Lal was getting ready to go to the border at Wagah when he heard of Lajo's return. He became nervous and couldn't make up his mind whether to go to meet her or wait for her at home. He wanted to run away; to spread out all the banners and placards he had carried, sit in their midst and cry to his heart's content. But, like other men, all he did was to proceed to the police station as if nothing untoward had happened. And suddenly he found Lajo standing in front of him. She looked scared and shook like a *peepal* leaf in the wind.

Sunder Lal looked up. His Lajwanti carried a *dupatta* worn by Muslim women, and she had wrapped it round her head in the Muslim style. Sunder Lal was also upset by the fact that Lajo looked healthier than before; her complexion was clearer and she had put on weight. He had sworn to say nothing to his wife but he could not understand why, if she was happy, had she come back! Had the government compelled her to come against her will?

There were many men at the police station. Some were refusing to take back their women. "We will not take these sluts, left over by the Muslims," they said. Sunder Lal overcame his revulsion. He had thrown himself body and soul into this movement. And there were his colleagues Neki Ram, the old clerk, and the lawyer, Kalka Prasad, with their raucous voices yelling slogans over the microphone. Through this babel of speeches and slogans, Sunder Lal and Lajo proceeded to their home. The scene of a thousand years ago was being re-enacted; Sri Rama Chandra and Sita returning to Ayodhya after their long exile. Some people were lighting lamps of joy to welcome them and at the same time repenting their sins which had forced an innocent couple to suffer such hardship.

Sunder Lal continued to work with the Rehabilitation of Hearts Committee with the same zeal. He fulfilled his pledge in the spirit in which it was taken and even those who had suspected him to be an armchair theorist were converted to his point of view. But there were many who were angry with the turn of events. The widow in number 414 wasn't the only one to keep away from Lajwanti's house.

Sunder Lal had nothing but contempt for these people. The queen of his heart was back home; his once silent temple now resounded with laughter; he had installed a living idol in his innermost sanctum and sat outside the gate like a sentry. Sunder Lal did not call Lajo by her name; he addressed her as a goddess—*Devi*. Lajo responded to the affection and began to open up, as her namesake unfurls its leaves. She was deliriously happy. She wanted to tell Sunder Lal of her experiences, and by her tears wash away her sins. But Sunder Lal would not let her broach the subject. At night she would stare at his face. When she was caught doing so she could offer no explanation. And the tired Sunder Lal would fall asleep again.

Only on the first day of her return had Sunder Lal asked Lajwanti about her "black days": Who was he? Lajwanti had lowered her eyes and replied, "Jumma." Then she looked Sunder Lal full in the face as if she wanted to say something. But Sunder Lal had a queer look in his eyes and he started playing with her hair. Lajo dropped her eyes once more. Sunder Lal asked, "Was he good to you?"

"Yes."

"Didn't beat you, did he?"

Lajwanti leant back and rested her head on Sunder Lal's chest. "No—he never said a thing to me. He did not beat me, but I was terrified of him. You beat me but I was never afraid of you. You won't beat me again, will you?"

Sunder Lal's eyes brimmed with tears. In a voice full of remorse and shame he said, "No, *Devi*, never . . . I shall never beat you again."

"*Devi!*" Lajo pondered over the word for a while and

then began to sob. She wanted to tell him everything, but Sunder Lal stopped her. "Let's forget the past; you did not commit any sin. What is evil is the social system which refuses to give an honoured place to virtuous women like you. That doesn't harm you, it only harms society."

Lajwanti's secret remained locked in her breast. She looked at her own body which had, since the partition, become the body of a goddess. It no longer belonged to her. She was blissfully happy; but her happiness was tinged with disbelief and a superstitious fear that it would not last.

Many days passed in this way. Suspicion took the place of joy: not because Sunder Lal had resumed ill-treating her, but because he was treating her too well. Lajo never expected him to be so considerate. She wanted him to be the same old Sunder Lal with whom she quarrelled over a carrot and who appeased her with a radish. Now there was no chance of a quarrel. Sunder Lal made her feel like something fragile, like glass which would splinter at the slightest touch. Lajo took to gazing at herself in the mirror. And in the end she could no longer recognise the Lajo she had known. She had been rehabilitated but not accepted. Sunder Lal did not want his eyes to see her tears, nor ears to hear her wailing.

And still, every morning, Sunder Lal went out with the morning procession. Lajo, dragging her tired body to the window, would hear the song whose words no one understood—

The leaves of Lajwanti wither at the touch of human hands.

(Translated from the original in Urdu by Jai Rattan)

8

KRISHAN CHANDER

Peshawar Express

Wʜᴇɴ I ʟᴇꜰᴛ Peshawar, I heaved a sigh of relief. All my bogies were occupied mainly by Hindus. They came from Peshawar itself and from Mardan, Kohat and Char Sadda, from Khyber and Landi Kotal, Bannu and Naushehra. Finding themselves unsafe in Pakistan, they were fleeing their home towns. There were strict security measures at the railway station: the army personnel appeared quite fastidious. Every compartment had two fully armed Baluchi soldiers to ensure their safety. The soldiers with their peacock *turrahs* at the back of their turbans gazed at the well-preserved womenfolk of the evacuees and made rude comments.

The passengers in the train were shedding tears of blood in their heart of hearts. They were leaving the land of their birth, the land that had made them hardy. They had drunk deep at its salubrious springs. And today they had become strangers to it. It had shut its doors on them.

They were proceeding to an unknown country. When they thought of its parched plains and its scorching sun their hearts sank. But they must go to save themselves, to protect the honour of their wives and daughters.

Still, their eyes were riveted on the ancient plateau—their

own. They wanted to know why they were being thrown out, why the land of their birth no longer belonged to them. As I gathered speed, the passengers occupying the various compartments were trying to cling to the familiar sights of hills and meadows, valleys and orchards. Seeing them feel so forlorn, my spirits sank and I felt weak in the knees. I feared I might collapse any minute.

I reached Hasan Abdal. The passengers continued to be morose and depressed. At Hasan Abdal—also known as Panja Sahib, the Temple of Guru's Palm—they were joined by Sikhs with their swords. It appeared they had been decimated with their own weapons. Rather than bring relief, they only added to the gloom. The moment they entered, they started exchanging notes with the old passengers. It was the same story. Their houses had been burnt and property looted; they could escape just in the clothes they were wearing. They told their tales of misery to fellow-passengers and won their sympathy. The Baluchi soldiers guarding the compartments with loaded guns heard it too and felt merely amused.

At Taxila railway station, the halt was unusually long. I could not understand the reason. Maybe they were waiting for the non-Muslim evacuees to arrive from the surrounding villages. When the train guard asked the station-master again and again, the latter replied in desperation: "The train won't go any further." Another hour passed in uncertainty. The people pulled out their tiffin boxes and began eating. The children stopped crying, the young girls began peering out of the windows, the *hookahs* of the old started an uninterrupted hubble-bubble. Suddenly a noise and beating of drums was heard in the air.

I thought it must be the non-Muslim evacuees anxious to escape Pakistan. The passengers craned their necks out of the windows to see them approach. As they came close, there was a firing of guns. The passengers quickly pulled themselves in. They were indeed Hindus, being brought by Muslims from the nearby villages. But they were now mere corpses of *kafirs* on the backs of their Muslim neighbours. Their crime? They had tried to flee their villages!

The Muslims nonchalantly handed over the dead bodies to the Baluchi soldiers for safe conveyance to India. The Baluchis took their charge dutifully, and the corpses were evenly distributed to the various compartments: fifteen corpses to every compartment. Having done the job, the Muslims fired a volley of shots in the air and signalled the station-master to let me proceed. I had hardly moved when I was stopped again. It occurred to the leader of the mob that with two hundred Hindus lost to their villages, they would be left desolate. Moreover, they would incur economic losses, having lost so many hands. He must have two hundred passengers detrained to replace them. Accordingly, two hundred passengers, not one more nor one less, were detrained and handed over to the leader by the Baluchi soldiers.

The leader of the mob then roared, "Fall into line, you *kafirs*." He was the biggest *jagirdar* of the region. He heard the echoes of the holy crusade in the flow of the blood in his veins.

The *kafirs* stood still, fear-stricken. They couldn't move. They were physically lifted and made to stand in a row. They were like living corpses with their frozen faces and stony looks swimming in the air.

The Baluchis this time gave the lead. Fifteen people were brought down at the first volley.

It was Taxila.

Then another twenty fell.

It was Asia's biggest university where thousands of students studied and benefited from it.

Fifty more were gunned down.

The Taxila museum has the most wonderful specimens of sculpture reflecting the glory of this ancient land.

Yet another fifty were slaughtered now.

In the background are the ruins of the palaces of Sircopo and an extensive sports stadium in a town sprawling for miles and miles.

Thirty more joined the dead.

Kanishka ruled over this land and taught people to live in peace and amity.

Another twenty-five were shot dead.

It was here that the Buddha's call for compassion echoed and re-echoed and his followers carried his message far and near.

The remainder were finished.

It was at Taxila that the Muslim flag of brotherhood and love was hoisted for the first time on the soil of India.

All two hundred were dead. The entire platform was smeared with blood. There was blood on the railway tracks. When I moved, my wheels started wobbling. I feared I might tumble down any minute and also finish those left in the compartment.

Death was hovering in every compartment. The living corpses sat around the dead bodies. The Baluchi soldiers saw all this and smiled. At times, a child would start whimpering, or an old woman would articulate a wail. Or, maybe, a widowed young girl would curse her fate. I moved on hooting and whistling and arrived at Rawalpindi station.

No one entrained here except fifteen *burqa*-clad women escorted by two armed young men. However, a lot of firearms, including machine guns and revolvers, were loaded in a luggage van.

I was made to stop between Gujar Khan and Jhelum. The Muslim men escorting the *burqa*-clad ladies stepped down from the train. Just then one of the women tore open her veil and began shouting: "We are Hindus and Sikhs. We are being kidnapped." The other women joined in the cry and pleaded for help, but none was forthcoming. The Muslim escort just laughed and pulled them out and drove them away.

A Hindu boy from the Frontier jumped out of the train and tried to escape. He was instantly gunned down by the Baluchi soldiers. Some fifteen Hindus made a vain attempt to run away while the train was stationary. They, in turn, were surrounded by armed Muslim *goondas* and killed. The kidnapped girls were prodded with rifles and forced into a jungle. I shut my eyes and ran as fast as I could, belching black smoke that looked like clouds of doom hovering on the horizon. I felt that I was going to lose my breath soon and the red flames of fire raging in my belly would in a twinkling of an eye burn to ashes the entire jungle that had devoured the fifteen girls.

When I reached Lala Musa the dead bodies had started putrefying. The foul stink was becoming oppressive. The Baluchi soldiers would order a passenger to pick up a corpse and take it to the door of the compartment. They would then push the passenger along with the dead body from the running train. Before long, all the corpses were disposed of and along with them an equal number of passengers. There was now room in the train for the remaining passengers to stretch themselves a little.

After Lal Musa I arrived at Wazirabad Junction. Wazirabad town is known for manufacturing knives and daggers. It was here that Hindus and Muslims celebrated the festival of *Baisakhi* every year and feasted each other. The platform was literally littered with dead bodies. Maybe they had assembled there to participate in the *Baisakhi* celebrations. It had turned out to be a festival of corpses. Thick smoke continued to spiral from the town towards the sky. Then a band was heard being played near the railway station. It was followed by a cheering crowd. A little later the procession entered the railway platform. It was led by folk dancers. They were followed by a host of naked women, old and young, married and unmarried, mothers and daughters, virgins and those pregnant. They were all Hindus and Sikhs. The men following and jeering at them were Muslims. Evidently, this is how they had celebrated *Baisakhi* this year. The women had bruises on their naked bodies. With hair falling loosely on their shoulders, they walked straight as if they had wrapped themselves in thousands of folds. The anguish in their eyes reminded one of Draupadi.

Someone from the crowd shouted "Pakistan *Zindabad,* Islam *Zindabad, Qaid-i-Azam Zindabad."*

The procession came close to the compartments. The passengers started pulling down the shutters of their windows. The womenfolk began to cover their faces with their *dupattas.*

The Baluchi soldiers forbade the passengers from bringing down the shutters—it was getting stuffy in the compartments. But no one would listen to them. So they began firing their rifles. Nevertheless, all the shutters were pulled down, though some of the evacuees lost their lives. The naked women were forced to sit with the passengers.

And then amidst the slogans of Pakistan *Zindabad* and *Qaid-i-Azam Zindabad,* I pulled out of the station.

A child in one of the compartments went over to an old woman and staring at her naked body, asked: "You had your bath?"

"Yes, child, I was given a bath today by the sons of my motherland." And tears gushed into her eyes.

"But where are your clothes?"

"They were stained with the *sindoor* of a wedded wife, they have taken them away to wash them."

In the meanwhile, two naked young girls jumped out of the running train. I did not stop: whistling and hooting I reached Lahore.

I was diverted to Platform 1. There was another train stationed at Platform 2. It had arrived from Amritsar with Muslim refugees. A little while later, a band of Muslim *mujahids* started searching my compartments. They collected all the jewellery, cash and other valuables they could find with the evacuees. They picked out four hundred of them and made them stand on the platform. They were to be slaughtered because the train that had just steamed in from Amritsar had arrived minus four hundred Muslim refugees. And no less than fifty women had also been kidnapped. It was therefore decided to detrain fifty Hindu women so that the balance in the population of both India and Pakistan could be maintained.

The Muslim volunteers surrounded the four hundred Hindu evacuees standing on the platform and started stabbing them. Before long they finished the whole lot.

I was now allowed to leave the station. Every bit of my body was stinking. I felt unclean all over. I felt as if I had been thrown out of hell and despatched straight to Punjab. When I reached Atari, the whole atmosphere changed. The Baluchi guards had already been replaced at Mughalpura by the Dogra and the Sikh soldiers. At Atari, there were so many dead bodies of Muslim evacuees that the Hindu refugees now felt exhilarated. I was now entering Independent India. Where else could one find such an air of freedom? As I reached Amritsar, my ears were splitting with the slogans shouted by the Sikhs and the Hindus. Here, too, there were piles of corpses, but of Muslim evacuees. The Sikh *jats* wielding swords came and peeped into every compartment in search of *shikar*.

A little while later, four persons looking like Hindu brahmins entered a compartment. They sported proper Hindu *chotis*, each one of them. And they wore their *dhotis* in the typical caste Hindu fashion. They said they were going to Hardwar.

At Amritsar, a number of Sikh *jats* had fanned themselves out into the compartments in search of *shikar*. One of them got a bit suspicious and asked one of the four brahmins where he was going.

"To Hardwar on pilgrimage."

"Is it Hardwar or Pakistan you are going to?"

"Allah forbid," blurted the man.

The Sikh laughed and then pounced on him with his axe. The Sikh's companions overpowered the other three "brahmins".

"You all must be medically examined before you are allowed to go to Hardwar," said the Sikh.

The four "brahmins" were stripped of their clothes, found to be circumcised Muslims, and done to death.

I left Amritsar and was proceeding at top speed when I was stopped in a thick jungle. The moment I came to a halt, the Sikh *jats* and Hindus got out and pounced upon Muslim evacuees hiding behind trees and bushes. Shouting slogans of *Sat Sri Akal* and *Har Har Mahadev*, they surrounded the helpless men and women and murdered them brutally. A Sikh *jat* held a baby on the point of his spear and shouted: "*Ai Baisakhi oh jat, Ai Baisakhi*".

Before entering Jullundar there was a Pathan village. I was stopped here again and everyone in the train, the refugees and the local *jats*, came out and attacked the village. The Pathans put up a brave resistance, but to no avail. Men and children were killed, and it was now the turn of their womenfolk. They were assembled in the open *maidan* outside the village. Here they harvested their crop. Here they assembled on festival days and sang and danced, and made merry. Here fifty Pathan beauties found themselves in the clutches of five hundred ruffians. Fifty sheep and five hundred wolves. Having completed their task they carried some of the dead bodies to their compartments. When we passed over a canal, the bodies were thrown into it. One by one, as the compartments came over the canal bridge, they would hurl the dead bodies into the water. Having got rid of the corpses, the Sikh *jats* started drinking country liquor. I moved on puffing the smoke of blood and hatred.

Reaching Ludhiana, the refugees and their escorts traced out Muslim localities and began looting and massacring. They returned to the train about four hours later, duly laden with booty. This was repeated several times before I reached

Ambala. At every wayside station they slaughtered as many Muslims as they could lay their hands on and relieved them of their few possessions.

I had wounds all over my body. My soul was bruised. I badly needed a bath. But I knew it was not in my lot to get one during the current journey.

At Ambala, a Muslim Deputy Commissioner and his family entered and occupied a first class compartment. After midnight when the train left Ambala, it was stopped at a distance of about ten miles from the city. Sikhs and Hindus broke into the Deputy Commissioner's compartment and massacred the entire family save his charming young daughter. They carried the girl and her jewellery box to a nearby jungle. She was so captivating that they did not know what to do with her.

The girl pleaded: "Why must you kill me? You may convert me to Hinduism. One of you can even marry me. What good will it do you to kill me?"

"She is right," said one.

Another stepped forward and stabbing the girl in the stomach, remarked: "What is this sentimental nonsense? We have work to do; let us go back to the train."

The girl lay dying on the grass. In her hand she was clutching a book on socialism, its theory and practice.

She must have been an intelligent girl with dreams of serving her people and her country. She must have wanted to belong to someone, to be a mother and to rear children. She was a young girl. She was a darling. She was a mother, the creator, carrying the secret of the universe in her bosom. And here she was lying in a desolate jungle—her virginal body a feast for the vultures and wild animals.

I moved on. People were drinking and shouting the slogan—"Long live Mahatma Gandhi!" And then, finally, I arrived at Bombay.

I have since been given a thorough bath and parked in a

shed. Occasionally, I am reminded of the harrowing time I have had, and I tremble all over. I would now like to get out and make a journey to the Punjab only when there are rich crops and its people are singing the songs of love and good neighbourliness.

I am made of wood and steel. There is no life in me. And yet, rather than witness bloodshed and be burdened with dead bodies, I want to carry grain to the famine stricken areas. I want to visit coal mines, steel mills and fertiliser plants. And transport in my compartments happy and carefree peasants. Women with their eyes longing for their menfolk. Children with smiles on their faces. People who would salute the brave new world where there would be no Hindu and no Muslim. They would be all peasants and workers. Just human beings.

(Translated from the original in Urdu by K. S. Duggal)

9

Saros Cowasjee

Another Train to Pakistan

1947 WAS NOT like other years. It affected the life of almost everybody on the sub-continent, because it was such an eventful year. It touched millions directly: hundreds of thousands lost their lives in the great stampede across the border and many more were left homeless. New governments in the saddle at Delhi and Karachi were fast undoing the past and, for better or worse, had to bring in changes.

In spite of the magnitude of the occasion, the transfer of populations, the widespread massacre and looting, the common man should have remained unaffected in a population of 400,000,000 people. But the common man no longer thought himself common after such a fight for freedom. The present did not trouble him—he just could not do anything about it. And so he thought of the future. What will happen to us in the future? This was the question people everywhere were asking each other.

Leslie, a young Anglo-Indian, had a fairly lucrative job in one of the automobile workshops in Amritsar. He was hardworking and all his friends thought that one day he would become the boss of the workshop. But it was 1947 and Leslie thought differently. The future was troubling him. He depended on newspapers for his information, and the news that he gathered from them seemed plainly to threaten his future.

One day he came home late from the workshop and said to his wife, "Irene, we should be in Pakistan."

"But why?" she asked, surprised.

"Because we have nothing before us here. These Hindus, once they have settled with the Muslims, will drive us out of India. They hate us like anything, because we are so superior to them."

"But the Pakistanis won't be any better. Our home is England, and we are here for work. In Pakistan you may not have even this little job," argued Irene.

The job was the thing, and Leslie could not just throw it up. And England, he had quite forgotten! He must always keep it in mind that England was his home and that these Hindus and Muslims were mad dogs snapping at each other.

A few days later, Leslie had forgotten all about England. He could not go on pretending to love an island home some 5,000 miles away which he had never visited. The present was a reality and the future . . . .

It was not long before he broached the topic again: "Irene, I'll have to chuck up this job."

"Why, what's wrong?" she asked.

"Why, what's right?" he retorted. "We have no future in this city and still less in the country. These bearded Sikhs are criminals, talking of nothing else but how to wipe out the Muslims. They've sacked the mechanic Rafi, and I feel I'm going to be their next target. The workshop will sink, I tell you. They can lift up a truck with their brawn, but not all the Sikhs of Amritsar can make it go."

Irene was not impressed by her husband's arguments.

"Leslie, we are happy here. Nobody troubles us. Not one of our people has been killed so far. They will leave us alone. It is a Hindu-Muslim feud; it does not concern us."

"It does concern us," Leslie said emphatically. "It concerns us deeply. We have nothing in common with these filthy cow-worshippers. They hate the English, and they hate us because we have English blood flowing through our veins. The bastards! They wouldn't pay me my salary if they could help it."

"I am not so sure of that," snapped Irene.

"I am," said Leslie. "I know their type. The Muslims are better; their religion is more akin to ours and their approach more western."

Such discussions between the two soon became a regular feature. Leslie did his best to conjure up the worst possible future in India, while Irene did her best to show that things in Pakistan wouldn't be any better.

One evening Leslie turned up a little early. He was very excited. No sooner did Irene see him than she was sure that his job was over.

"Darling, I have resigned!" he said. "It was no good working with those heathens. We leave for Pakistan tomorrow. See, here's the reservation ticket for the through Express to Lahore."

"But what will we do there?" asked Irene in tears. "Let's not leave this place."

Leslie, seeing his wife disturbed, placed his arm round her waist and drew her near. "Irene, Pakistan needs trained mechanics, too. I shall find a job, and a better one than this, somewhere. They will pay me better. We will no longer be stared at, hooted at, looked upon as half-breeds."

"I don't want to leave India," sobbed Irene. "All our people are here."

"Some of our people are there, too," Leslie tried to comfort her. "My own brother, Robert, a Captain in the army, is posted at Lahore. A good soldier, mind you. He always said that I could get a Commission in the army whenever I wanted. I think the time has come. I'll join the Pakistan army and skin these Hindu bastards. I tell you we shall conquer India."

All this did not convince poor Irene, but there was nothing she could do now. Next morning they were at Amritsar railway station with all their trunks and suitcases.

"Only eight annas, Sahib, for all this luggage?" pleaded the coolie, after he had arranged the things in a Class II compartment.

"Get off, you son of a pig," shouted Leslie. "You'll cheat us even as we leave your damn country."

"No cheating, Sahib. Give me my due," protested the coolie.

"Your due? Aye, turn round and take your due," said Leslie, landing a hard kick on the coolie's bottom.

The coolie shrieked, cursed, and ran and stood a few yards away where a number of coolies, who had witnessed the scene, had gathered. Leslie looked at them straight. A conspiracy—they were discussing him, the bastards.

Leslie walked up and down the platform, asking every ticket collector the time when the train was due to leave.

"Five minutes more," said the last man he asked.

He thought he could make one more round of the platform, when there—to his astonishment—stood his brother Robert!

"What, Robert! You here, old boy!" exclaimed Leslie, clasping his brother's hands.

"Me? I have had myself transferred to the Indian Army. I am off to Jullundar by the next train."

"But why?"

"Oh, Pakistan is an awful place. They've a scrap of an army there, and God knows where that will be in a year's time. It's all rotten there . . . I . . . I thought of my future . . . of you, Irene, I wanted to be with you both. How are you getting on with your job? By God, you have a steady one."

Leslie stood stunned. He turned pale, there was not a trace of blood in his face.

"What's wrong Leslie?" asked Robert.

"We are on our way to Pakistan," muttered Leslie. "I thought India was no good . . . I have left my job—resigned. We are in the train. I thought . . . I . . . I . . . ."

"You fool, what are you doing?" gasped Robert, wiping the sweat off his forehead.

A shrill, sharp whistle pierced the din on the platform.

"Good heavens! The train is starting!" panted Leslie.

Both Leslie and Robert ran down to the compartment in which Irene sat.

"Get down, Irene," shouted Leslie, "Get down. We are not going."

"Why?" she asked.

"Get down, Irene. For God's sake, hurry." And he called to the coolies, "Coolie! Coolie!"

But the coolies stood at a distance and watched. Leslie swore and protested, but not a coolie would come forward. He tugged at the trunks himself, but they were too heavy for him to lift.

"I will give you whatever you want," he promised.

But no coolie would step forward to help him. They were all laughing at him now.

There was a second whistle. A green flag fluttered from the rear and the train moved forward. Leslie jumped into the compartment and pulled the alarm chain. Alas, it had been disconnected so as to prevent miscreants from stopping the train on its journey. He hung on to the chain for some time, but as the train gathered speed he slowly loosened his grip. He craned his neck out of the window to look for the last time at the land he refused to call his own. Quietly he came and sat down beside Irene.

The train rushed on to Pakistan.

10

KARTAR SINGH DUGGAL

Kulsum

WHAT GIFT DID the old man bring for him?

The restless footsteps of the young schoolmaster faded into silence inside the hut. On one side he saw a pile of pots and pans. On the other lay the old man's little prayer-mat neatly spread with a disarranged rosary on it. He peered further inside. It was utterly dark. The sun had not set, but this portion of the hut was always benighted. The schoolmaster stared hard, trying to pierce the darkness.

What could it be that the old man brought for him from the city?

Suddenly, his eyes fell on a young girl standing against a pillar. Tall, fair, with hair cascading down, as if a jasmine creeper had snaked up to the roof in the full glory of its youth. The schoolmaster stared.

Before the pillar, in a pool of darkness, was a *charpoy*. The linen was fresh and sparkling white.

"My name is Kulsum."

The schoolmaster's gaze flicked from the *charpoy* to the girl's face, to and fro, again and again.

"My name is Kulsum. What's yours?" The lips opened like blossoming rose-buds.

The young schoolmaster sat limp on the *charpoy*. He felt as if he had been walking endlessly, all the twenty-five years of his young life.

He understood now why the old man had been so impatient. Why he had sent word so many times. Why he had wanted him to come straightaway. This was the "gift" awaiting him. But he could not come any sooner. He had to wait till the school closed for the day.

The gift was fit to be swallowed whole. He would put his lips to hers and drain her into himself. The young schoolmaster felt his body stiffen all over. His eyes were ablaze with a strange inebriation.

This, perhaps, was the awaited Independence. The substance of it. It was only yesterday that the country had won its freedom, the young schoolmaster repeated to himself. The songs and the slogans were still ringing in his ears. And today—only a day later—right before him, a Muslim *houri*!

Kulsum.

The gentlest touch would soil her.

"My name is Kulsum."

The young schoolmaster thought. Yesterday, in that very village, no Hindu or Sikh girl could come out of her home, even by day. Muslim *goondas* with their smutty hisses roamed the lanes. No one could deter the ruffians. They had ruled over the entire Punjab—hurling insults at the people in broad daylight, setting thugs on them, abducting their women in the open streets—no infamy was beyond them. No one could arraign a Muslim neighbour. That was yesterday.

And today, a Muslim fairy was standing before him, awaiting his pleasure. As though someone had snatched her out from behind the seven veils. A peerless pearl. The young schoolmaster's body ached with impatience. Gnawing hunger swam in his eyes. An obscene smile crept up his lips. He lunged at the girl and tried to pull her towards the *charpoy*.

The girl did not move. The young schoolmaster pulled at her again. The girl remained stuck to the pillar.

"Speak to me first, please," she pleaded.

The young schoolmaster's mind was drained of thought; insane obduracy filled it. He pulled at her again and again.

"Marry me. Marry me first. How can I sit on a *charpoy* with a stranger?" the girl begged.

The young schoolmaster's face was dark with brute desire. Cruel hunger burned in his eyes. He did not speak a word. He pulled her time and again towards the *charpoy*.

"Don't do it. I beg of you. Don't do it. Marry me first. You are young. I was betrothed to a man of your age. Tall like you, broad-shouldered like you, teeth like yours, bright as pomegranate seeds. The rioters hacked him to pieces. My father and mother, my brother and all my relations have been killed. I don't know how I escaped—I alone. I ran on and on like a mad person when this old man caught me and brought me here. On the way, he made me a promise. He said he would seek a husband for me. Marry me, please."

The schoolmaster could hear nothing. Every inch of his being was intoxicated. He pulled at her with all his strength. But the girl did not let go of the pillar. She stood her ground, steadfast.

"Marry me. I beg of you on bended knees. Marry me first. Did ever a young girl plead thus for love? Did ever a maid shed her shyness and beg as I do? Marry me. I shall be your slave for all time."

The young schoolmaster could hear nothing. He jumped up in a rage of desire and pulled at the girl with both his hands. Helpless and at bay, the girl changed for a moment into a young lioness. She pushed him away from her with all her might. The young schoolmaster tripped and fell on the *charpoy*.

"I beseech you," the girl said in a rush of tears. "I beg of you. Marry me first, please. You are young. Marry me and I shall be the mother of your children. The mother of your pearly children. We shall have our own home and our courtyard. . . ."

As the girl wept and begged, the young schoolmaster rose in a towering frenzy and strode out of the hut.

The old man was sitting under the *neem* tree coiling strands of jute into a rope. On hearing the young schoolmaster's story, he put down the spindle. "The bitch," he spat out, "she asks to be married." And he rushed into the hut, banging the door shut behind him.

Hardly had three minutes ticked by when the door opened. The old man came out knotting his *lungi*. "Go *masterji*, go in without fear," he said, picking up the water jug that stood near the door. He walked briskly to the *neem* tree and going behind it, began washing himself.

Walking slowly, the young schoolmaster entered the dark hut. He espied the girl sitting on the edge of the *charpoy* with her back to him. Her silk trousers were rumpled. The *dupatta* had slipped from her head. A lock of dishevelled hair stuck to her cheek. Streams of sweat flowed down her neck. The young schoolmaster sat by her side. The girl did not rise from the *charpoy*. The young schoolmaster put his hand on her shoulders. She sat motionless.

"Kulsum," the young schoolmaster called softly. The girl who had begged and pleaded three minutes ago said nothing. She sat silent, her head averted to one side, her vacant gaze resting on the *charpoy*.

"Kulsum," the young schoolmaster called again.

A wave of darkness rose in the hut, perhaps it was night outside.

11

Kartar Singh Duggal

Pakistan Zindabad*

Her real name was Ram Rakhi, though she had now been given the name of Allah Rakhi. But she was called Rakhi before and she was called Rakhi now.

That dreadful night when the drums were beaten, the slogans shouted, the spears flashed, the heavens thundered, the earth rocked, Rakhi jumped out of bed and, half-asleep as she was, she leapt over the boundary wall, crossed the fields and fell into a ditch outside the village.

She lay there the whole night. The bullets fired in the village deafened her ears. She heard her dear ones cry for help; she heard her near ones wail in despair.

And then there was silence. The silence of death.

The next morning the entire village started humming with activity as usual. The strings of tiny bells tied around the cows' necks were chiming. The cattle jostled one another on their way for grazing. The grinding of the Persian wheels filled the air with its crazy music. There were flocks of birds of all kinds in the sky once again. The *muezzin* gave his call. The smoke rose from the kitchens. Curd was heard being churned to make buttermilk.

---

* Long Live Pakistan

Soon after dawn, Rakhi crept out of her hiding place and walked up to her Muslim neighbours. They were laughing and talking, but the moment they saw Rakhi each one of them looked stunned. The womenfolk thought that she had, perhaps, risen from the dead. The menfolk believed that they had been duped. The young Sher Baz was furious. His eyes were bloodshot, his nerves taut with anger. He pulled his hatchet from beneath his *charpoy* and pounced upon Rakhi. But, to his surprise, Sher Baz found his mother and sister covering Rakhi, the *kafir*. Helpless, he withdrew.

Ever since then, Sher Baz had wondered how he could have thought of harming Rakhi. His hatchet reminded him of his heartlessness. Every time he felt ashamed, he thought he would throw away the hatchet into the nearest well. And Rakhi would, at times, put her bridal *peera* on the spot where Sher Baz had rushed to slaughter her and lounge there for hours, the way her mother-in-law did, and her mother-in-law's mother-in-law had done in her youth.

One day he had rushed out to slaughter Rakhi in his mad fury, and the next day he had taken her as his wife, pledging to love her in life and in death. He had always admired her. They had played together as little children in their lane. And when she grew up, Sher Baz had sung many a song for her. She had haunted his dreams for years. How he would hide himself in the thick mango grove and watch her go to the well to fetch water morning and evening!

After her marriage to Sher Baz, Rakhi endeared herself to everyone. She was a great favourite of her mother-in-law. She swept the house every morning, fed the cattle, milked the cows, fetched water from the well and cooked for the whole family. And, in the afternoon when everybody relaxed, she was busy teaching the neighbouring girls how to knit and embroider, read and write. She kept her house clean and tidy, never allowed her mother-in-law to bother about household chores, and took over all the big and small responsibilities.

Everyone in the village marvelled at her. She had made friends everywhere. She sang and danced as no one else could.

If someone had sore eyes, Rakhi would apply a pinch of collyrium and the person was cured. If someone had fever, Rakhi would suggest a broth and it brought relief. Her cooking recipes were popular throughout the village. The young girls who had secrets to share found in Rakhi the most reliable confidante.

Rakhi sat on the swing under the *peepal* tree and wondered how her people could leave their village where they had been born and brought up. Rakhi splashed the clear water of the village lake on her face and wondered how her people could forget their own hearth and home. Rakhi walked in the green fields and wondered if any place on earth could be as fertile as their village fields. And she felt as if the fully grown village trees were waiting for those who had gone away. The fruits seemed to be awaiting their return to ripen. The streets were lonely in their absence. The deities called their devotees to come back and pay their homage to them.

One day a political leader of Pakistan had to pass through their village. Rakhi organised a memorable welcome for him. They smothered him with garlands and paved his way through the village with rose-buds. And their throats went hoarse shouting the slogan—"Pakistan *Zindabad.*"

Rakhi was happy, very happy. Days, weeks and months passed by in bliss, when suddenly, one day while going to visit a friend, she heard someone shout for her—"Oh Rakhi!" And the next moment, she was in the arms of her brother.

Rakhi couldn't believe her eyes. Both of them shed tears of joy and hugged each other for a long time. Rakhi wept like a child, having met her only brother after so long. She hadn't even noticed a stranger standing beside them. He looked like a police officer.

Before Rakhi could ask them to her house, her brother told the stranger: "She is my sister Rakhi; she has to be taken along with us."

"But where?" Rakhi's reaction was a little delayed but sharp. She was not prepared to leave her own village. She would not go to an unknown place.

How could she leave the streets where she had played and grown up? How could she leave the fields in which she had roamed and sung songs of love and joy? How could she leave her *trinjan* where she had made friends and shared with them the secrets of their hearts?

In the evening after milking the buffalo, she promised her that she would not leave her and go away. While watering the grapevine, she gave it her word that she would be there to enjoy its first crop. She whispered into the ears of her cow that she would see her calf in the spring. She went into her room and cried out, "This is my own home. I shall never leave it."

As night fell, the westerly winds started to blow. She sat on her terrace and admired the moon. She remembered all the saints and *darveshes* she had ever met and prayed to them for their help. She looked at the ditch in which she had jumped during the Partition riots, where no one had been able to find her. But how could she do it now? With Sher Baz's precious gift treasured in her womb, how could she jump into a ditch now?

"Sher Baz, what has happened to your hatchet now?" Rakhi asked him again and again.

Ever since he came back from the *lumbardar's* house, Sher Baz was lying bewildered on his bed. He had not uttered a word. He had not eaten a morsel of food.

"Sher Baz, I can sacrifice a hundred brothers to be with you," Rakhi repeated.

But Sher Baz lay silent, his eyes brimful with tears. "Sher Baz, let us run away," Rakhi suggested at last.

It seemed Sher Baz had developed high fever. He was lying almost unconscious. He didn't utter a word.

And what could he say? The *lumbardar* had told him in no uncertain terms that Rakhi being born a Hindu, must be restored to her parents who had been evacuated to Hindustan. All the conversions that had taken place during the Partition riots were null and void. Rakhi must be sent away so that an abducted Muslim girl could be brought back from India to Pakistan in exchange. This was the decision of the country's government. One has to make every sacrifice for Pakistan.

Sher Baz didn't know what to do. He would regain consciousness only to fall unconscious again.

The next morning, hardly had the day dawned, when a jeep drove right into their courtyard. Finding armed police in the jeep, Rakhi started screaming, "I am not going. I'll never leave my village. What if the name has since changed, this is our own country. This courtyard is mine. I have swept it day and night. These plants are mine. I have watered them morning and evening. These streets are mine. I have played in them since my childhood." Her eyes were swimming with tears. "Sher Baz, why don't you speak?" She then exhorted her husband. "Why don't you utter a word? What do I do with your progeny lying in my womb?" And Rakhi fell down in a swoon.

Sher Baz and Rakhi were closeted in the room. The *lumbardar* thought about it again. The village elders were consulted. The police officer was spoken to. But nothing could be done. It was a decision of the government and it must be carried out. No sacrifice was too big for Pakistan— their beloved country.

Then the door opened. There was Rakhi followed by Sher Baz Khan. Rakhi was dressed in a rich bridal suit. She had put on all the jewellery she had. Everyone was stunned to see her. She had hardly come and sat down in the jeep when Sher Baz Khan brought the trunk full of clothes and other articles that belonged to her. He then went into his room and fetched a bowl on which his name, Sher Baz Khan was etched. The last time Sher Baz went in, he brought her a hand fan made of jute on which Rakhi with her own hands had embroidered— "Pakistan *Zindabad*."

12

KARTAR SINGH DUGGAL

A New Home

THE DEPUTY COMMISSIONER told us that houses for high officials had been set apart—that all spacious bungalows had been locked and sealed as soon as the Muslim evacuees left. That is why, perhaps, I got the allotment order in about ten minutes.

Outside in the car were my mother, who had come from our village in Pakistan, a servant whose loyalty had stood the severest tests of time, a box or two and a bed that we had succeeded in salvaging from Lahore.

My wife and I thanked the Deputy Commissioner and came out. We were told our bungalow was on a strip off the Mall.

The main entrance had been sealed. We scanned the seal closely, snapped it open and went in.

The moment my mother set foot in the house, she drew a deep, heavy sigh which seemed steeped in her long and painful experiences.

Mother had never cherished any particular attachment for bungalows, nor had she a predilection for cars or a desire for a retinue of servants. She had lived a simple, peaceful life. Not all our persuasion could induce her to leave our native village. Even for occasional meetings, it was we who went to her.

When riots broke out, she disregarded our letters urging her to come and stay with us. She saw no reason to desert her own hearth and home. And then one day the rioters walked into the village. I have it from our neighbours, my mother sat unconcerned in the courtyard of our *haveli*. The rioters were no strangers! They were none other than the peasants and farmers from the countryside around. They used to come to our house almost every day for buttermilk. My mother would distribute old woollen clothes among them every winter.

Now eight to ten hefty brutes crashed in, armed with man-size *lathis*. Jumma, the oil presser, was among them and Sharfu, the sweeper, Jehana, the professional jester, Meero, the ironsmith, Madu, the water carrier, Dulla, the cobbler, and the three sons of Sayden, the tailor, from the nearby village.

"*Chaudhrani*, we offer *salaams* to you," they greeted my mother in the courtyard and entered the house giggling. Mother got up and, standing on the verandah, watched them take away the household effects. But as they were about to remove our nuptial bed, she remonstrated, "Jehana, my son, this bed is from my daughter-in-law's dowry."

Jehana wouldn't listen.

"Shameless Jehana, don't take it away."

"*Chaudhrani*, let it be," rejoined Jehana with a snigger, "don't be sentimental."

And my mother kept tugging at the mirror-set *newar* bed even as they carried it to the lane outside.

And as the sons of Sayden, the tailor, were straining to lift the heavy boxes in the dingy store-room, my mother ran towards them with a hurricane lamp: "Oh, you good-for-nothings! It is the season of snakes and scorpions. Take care lest you come to grief." She herself advised Meero, the ironsmith, to place the glassware in a separate basket and put metal vessels in a gunny bag. The fool was shoving all utensils into the same sack.

And thus the rioters entered the *haveli* laughing and left it exultant, *salaaming* my mother.

This is what happened in almost all the other houses in the village. Not a single person received any injury, not one cry went up to the skies. The rioters kept pillaging the village all day long, encountering no resistance whatsoever.

That evening the Hindus and Sikhs shifted to the neighbouring Muslim village and passed the night there.

Rawalpindi had been the scene of disturbances long before Lahore. My mother, therefore, could not but join us at Lahore. Then the trouble started sizzling in Lahore as well. In August it was ablaze. The residents of Model Town, we thought, were safe. Besides, I was staying on in Pakistan at the behest of the Government of India. We reasoned, that Model Town at least was beyond danger as only educated and cultured people lived there.

The 15th of August passed by in a spate of bloodshed. Panic persisted for a few days. But when putrescent corpses began to be removed from the streets, one hoped peace would return.

We, however, did not step out for full seven days. One evening, I had almost decided to resume attending office from the next day, when a neighbour brought me news that *goondas* of the vicinity were getting out of hand and that we had better leave the place within an hour.

I tried to expostulate with my Muslim friend, but with folded hands he entreated me to agree to his suggestion. He could not take on so heavy a responsibility with the rabble breaking out of control. This friend of ours was a police officer. Finding him so panicky, we walked out of our bungalow leaving everything behind. We drove to the Pakistan border accompanied by a Muslim constable whom our friend had deputed to go with us.

My mother was stunned at the way we were forced to leave with just our clothes on, the Muslim constable guarding us with his gun against the menacing looks of those who stared at us.

My mother sat still throughout the journey. She saw endless lines of refugees trail along and uttered not a word.

Now, as we broke the seal and entered a Muslim evacuee's house, my mother heaved a sigh.

A walking-stick hung by the hat-stand, its handle rubbed black by greasy palms. Some seven caps occupied other pegs. On the floor lay a few letters slipped inside from under the door, letters addressed to Khan Bahadur Sheikh Mirajuddin, Miss Zubeida, M.A. and Begum Mirajuddin. Some of them were wedding invitations. One letter was a call for a peace committee meeting to be held at the Commissioner's residence. An anonymous threatening letter addressed to Khan Bahadur warned him to leave the place within twenty-four hours or face the consequences.

Dust lay thick everywhere on the floor. Cobwebs quivered in the corners of the ceiling. Deck chairs were set on the verandah. A table stood by them. A white, *dhobi*-washed table-cloth covered it. On the table was a flower vase. It contained withered stalks of flowers whose petals lay scattered around the vase, looking like wilted peelings of onions.

In the thickly-carpeted drawing-room, sofa sets were lying undisturbed; *The Dawn* of August 15, 1947 lay open on a chair. The ceiling fan was whirling—it had been on day and night for the last ten days.

The table was set in the dining-room, with *shami kebabs, korma, dopiaza, pilau* and other dishes. There was a plate of rice in front of the folding chair of a child; curd and a spoonful of rice lay uneaten in the quarter plate beside it. The clock on the mantelpiece had stopped at ten minutes past twelve. The radio set was burnt out and the wall had blackened a trifle with the smoke emitted by it.

A prayer mat was spread in the bedroom with a rosary over it. A corner of the prayer mat was turned up. Many gilded volumes of the Holy Quran were arranged on the shelf.

In the kitchen a *chapati* had burnt to cinder on the baking disc. The vessel lying under the water tap had spilled over with the long and weary drippings. Five *lotas* of various shapes and metals nestled close to the wall.

In the servants" quarters a chained dog had dropped lifeless, his muzzle resting on the threshold. A *bulbul* lay dead in a cage suspended from the lemon tree.

Mother saw all this but did not speak.

We looked long at the *malta* tree in the garden. My wife and I tried to work the Persian wheel. We then started counting the broken *lotas* on the chain and those that were missing. My wife said the *maltas* would ripen in October. I held that they would be juicy enough to be eaten only in November. She kept on chomping the parrot-nibbled guavas.

In the hen-coop, hens had laid eggs everywhere. And this fact helped overcome my wife's initial disgust at the excreta-spattered courtyard.

When we returned to the bungalow after about an hour, the driver had swept it clean. Smoke was curling up from the kitchen. The water was running out of the courtyard tap vigorously.

My wife with an apron full of lady's fingers plucked in the garden, walked to the colourful string seat.

My sobbing mother stretched herself on a *charpoy* on the verandah.

And I switched on the radio set in the dining-room, hoping that no other part besides the transformer had been damaged.

13

ATTIA HOSAIN

After the Storm

THE FLOWERS WERE awkwardly crowded into the small-necked bottle. Its paper label had not been successfully washed away and triumphantly survived in its scratched mutilation.

On and around the bottle there was dust. There was a film of dust on everything. It crept in with the hot wind that found its way into the room in spite of closed doors and windows. Green paper on the glass panes shut out the glare that burned away colour from earth and sky and all things that provided sensual delight of vision to the eyes.

The heavy, sweet scent of the flowers reached out into the skin-drying air with a cooling touch. The flowers were white and wax-petalled among thick deep green leaves. Their buds were tightly wrapped in slender pale green sepals. They were allies in the battle against the cruel summer—lying cool on hot pillows—around earthenware water pots—strung in garlands sold in scented streets by singing men—adorning women when gold and silver grew heavy with heat and sweat.

This summer the battle was lost before it began. The desolation it brought was a visible reflection of desolate hearts. The tainted wind blew hot from blazing homes, and carried the dust of devastated fields, and the dead. . . .

She tore me out of the shroud of my thoughts, a child small and thin with serious, anxious eyes and a smile on her face, a garland in her hand. She looked at the bottle and the flowers.

"Do you like them? I put them there. This is for you too." I bent my head and she slipped the garland over with a faint smile and stepped back.

"I knew you were coming today and I cleaned your room."

"Who are you?"

"Your servant. I've been put in charge of this part of the house," she said with proud responsibility.

"What is your name?"

"Bibi."

"How long have you been here?"

"A long time. Just before I left home there was the fair at Shahji's tomb." She sounded uninterested, then said brightly: "Do you need anything? The others are all sleeping. You rest and then I shall bring you some tea. I have put cold water for your bath in the buckets."

"Weren't the buckets heavy?"

"Oh no—I have always brought water from the well."

I could not tell her age. Her assured manner made me feel younger than she was. Her eyes had no memories of a childhood. Her body was of a child of nine or ten, but its undernourished thinness was deceptive; she could have been eleven or twelve. There was no telling how many years of childhood life had robbed her of.

She came every morning with flowers no one else cared to pick, and every evening with garlands no one else cared to thread.

"Aren't they pretty? In my home we had two big bushes near the well. I made garlands for my mother and aunt."

The nails of her peasant hands were worn with work. By now I knew her story, but knew she had to tell it herself how and when she willed.

"Had you any brothers and sisters?"

"After my sister was married she went to live far away; a whole day's journey by bullock cart. My brother was older than me. He could read and write. He was clever. You will teach me, won't you?"

She kept her clothes very clean—old discarded clothes which were cut down for her and hung loosely on her. She wore tight pyjamas that were easier to clean than loose ones, and she kept her head covered like the older women, with *dupattas* that were made from torn cotton *saris*. She used to dye them herself and was fond of bright colours. Her hair was combed back smoothly from a centre parting, oiled and plaited with a rag. The pigtail was short and stood out stiffly. She was not a pretty child, and one would not have noticed her. But she was now a symbol and around her hovered the ghosts of all one feared.

Sometimes she threaded buds into the pierced lobes of her ears.

"I had gold earrings," she said proudly, but with no reproach. "My mother said after the next harvest she would buy me gold bangles. When we had feasts I was sorry I had no bangles."

I had bought her glass ones.

When she brought me tea she said:

"Do you like these English cakes? My mother made such lovely *halwa*—you would have loved it."

"Do you remember your father?"

"He died long ago. We lived with my uncle and aunt. He kept labourers to help in the fields."

One day she suddenly put her head on my lap—"I like you. Will you always keep me with you?"

Then I asked her: "Bibi—how did you come here?"

I wanted to allay my ghosts of imagined horror, and hear her tell me what actually happened.

"The police brought me. I was at the railway station.

Then they took me to a place where there were lots of
women and children. I ran away from them.".

"Why?"

"I don't know. I got up at night and ran away. Then I
came here."

"Who brought you?"

"The police."

Her mind refused to fill the gap between the refugee
camp and her adoption.

"What happened to your mother?"

Her voice was detached—a child telling a fairy story. "I
don't know. I was with Chand Bibi. I had gone to visit her."

"Who was she?"

"Oh, she was brave. She had a big house where I played.
She fought and fought and killed so many of them—then her
arm was cut off."

"Where was your mother?"

"At home. They said the house was full of blood. They
said Chand Bibi kept on fighting until her arm was cut off."

"Who said?"

"Some people—I ran into the fields and a man said,
"Come this way," and he carried me, we hid in the
sugar- cane—then he put me on a train, and I came here. See
how long this garland is. You can put it twice round your
neck."

In the bottle she had put fresh flowers.

14

INTIZAR HUSAIN

The Stairway

Bashir Bhai drifted into silence for a minute or two. This made Akhtar restless, even a bit worried. Finally when Bashir Bhai heaved a sigh and stirred, Akhtar felt relieved, but still apprehensive of what Bashir Bhai might say next.

"What time was it?"

"Time?" Akhtar fell into thought, "I just can't seem to remember."

"One ought to though. One must always keep track of the time," observed Bashir Bhai in the same reflective vein. "Without knowing what time it was, it just won't make much sense. No worry if it occurs in the earlier part of the night, for then one can dismiss it as the devil's whispering; but not if that happens towards the end of the night. Then, one must give alms."

Akhtar's heart started to race. But Razi still sat silent; only the wonder in his eyes became a shade stronger.

"It is my habit," began Bashir Bhai in his now awakened voice, "to mind the time—always. Then again, as it goes with me, I'm allowed a vision of things before they actually happen—and that is usually a little before dawn. My eyes snap open and I feel I've just seen something wide awake . . . now take this one time: after arriving here I kept tramping around everywhere for months looking for a job. Oh, was I worried! It seemed all doors to betterment had been slammed shut. Anyway, I had this dream one night. And what did I see? My late grandfather. He seemed to have just stepped out of the mosque, holding a basket made of fresh green leaves. He picked up a *pera* from the basket and held it out to me . . . just then I woke up . . . the call for the dawn prayer came sailing in. I got up, did my ablutions and stood up to perform the prayer . . . three days later I got a job."

Both Razi and Akhtar were listening with rapt attention, but Saiyid, who had his back turned toward the cots on which the rest of them were stretched out, was trying hard to fall asleep. His eyes were closed tight.

"Bashir Bhai," said Akhtar, "I just keep seeing these corpses, a lot of them. What do you make of this?"

"It's a blessing to see a corpse. It means one who saw it is going to live long."

"But . . . but this one . . . ?" Akhtar stopped short.

"Yes, I suppose you could say it's a bit unusual," replied Bashir Bhai, his voice suggesting that the matter was not too serious after all. "But if you see a corpse eating with you—now that, for sure, I wouldn't call a good omen . . . it may mean there is going to be a famine." He was about to leave it at that but decided otherwise, saying in a louder voice, "But you don't even remember the time. One mustn't trust *untimely* dreams anyway. Give alms—just to be on the safe side."

Irritated, Saiyid turned over in his bed and sat up. "Damn it, you're incredible, all of you! And you, Akhtar, in particular. I guess you never go to sleep, do you? You keep telling us your dreams till midnight, then start dreaming all over again. Do you ever get time to sleep?"

That irked Akhtar. He snapped, "You're a strange man. You take everything as a joke."

"You're a strange man yourself. You have dreams every night. How about me—why don't I have dreams?"

"It's man's nature to dream," said Bashir Bhai. "Everybody does, only some dream more than others."

"Where has my nature taken off to then? I don't dream at all."

"Not at all?" asked Akhtar, confused.

"At least not since I've set foot in this place. I don't recall having ever dreamt here."

"Then there is something the matter with you . . . did you hear that, Bashir Bhai?"

"On the contrary, something is the matter with *you*," said Saiyid. "I just can't imagine how anyone can possibly see so many dreams sleeping on this tiny roof. And what a roof! Four cots and the damn thing is jammed from end to end. Every time I get out of bed at night I feel I'm going to fall into the alley below . . . but the roof of our house," he stopped midway, then continued slowly, "why mourn the lost. There wouldn't be anything left of it now—not even burnt bricks."

Saiyid walked over to the low wall at the edge, and poured himself some water from the earthen flask. "The water is warm," he remarked. "When was this pot filled?"

"Why, in the afternoon, of course. But it's too old," answered Bashir Bhai. "We'll get a new one tomorrow."

"Shall I lower the wick in the lantern?" asked Saiyid. "The light's bothering my eyes."

"Go ahead and then set it down over in the corner. The moon will be out in a little while anyway," answered Bashir Bhai.

Saiyid shook the lantern as he lowered the wick, then muttered to himself, "Only a little kerosene left—it might not last the whole night." He raised the flickering wick a little and set the lantern on the ground by the low wall. The weak, dim light of the lantern pooled in the small corner, leaving most of the roof in darkness.

Though the cots of Razi and Akhtar boasted of regular bedding, it was Saiyid's that shone like silver in the moonlight. Bashir Bhai only had a lightweight sheet which, for the time being, he had rolled up and stuck under his head as a pillow. Earlier in the evening, while sprinkling water on the scorched roof to cool it off, he had also thrown a tumblerful on the coarse, grassy matting of his own cot, so that now not only was his bare back kept cool and moist but also the fragrance, like fresh raw soil, rising from the wet fibre inundated his sense of smell.

Razi, who had been sitting mute for a while suddenly coughed, cleared his throat and began, "Bashir Bhai, what would you say if one dreamt of the big *alam*?"

"An auspicious sign—I would say," remarked Bashir Bhai reflectively. "But describe your dream first."

Akhtar turned his attention to Razi. Saiyid rolled over and turned his face away from them. He had closed his eyes and was once again trying to fall asleep.

"Do you remember the morning, Bashir Bhai, when you had just gotten up to perform the prayer and asked me why I was up so early?—well, that night I just couldn't fall asleep. God knows what happened. The whole night I kept tossing and turning. All kinds of thoughts went through my head. But I must have dozed off a bit just before dawn. And I dreamt . . . . " Razi's voice quaked, so did his body. "I dreamt of our *imam-bara* and saw the big *alam* rising from it . . . the big *alam*, the same *alam*, with the same waving green sash and the swaying silvery *panja*. . . which shone forth so intensely it nearly blinded me. Just then I woke up."

Bashir Bhai sat up with a start and closed his eyes. Akhtar was so overawed his body was motionless. And there was still a trace of a shiver lingering on in Razi. Saiyid too turned in his bed and faced them. His eyes were fully open, a tiny aperture slowly forming in the darkness of his mind. A streak of light filtered in through the aperture. In the fragrant darkness of the mourning chamber he could see arrays of glittering *alams*, silver and gold *panjas* that gave off streams of light, green and red sashes of brocade with their lustrous silver borders, and the crystal chandelier that hung from the ceiling in the centre of the chamber with its countless shimmering glass pendants. God knows how, he himself had come to possess one of these glass lustres—it was broken though, almost completely colourless on the outside, but like a rainbow inside if you looked through it with one eye closed.

"A very strange dream," mumbled Akhtar.

"No, I wouldn't call it a dream," Bashir Bhai said slowly.

Both Akhtar and Razi stared at him.

"Were you asleep or . . . ?" asked Bashir Bhai.

"No, not completely. I just dozed off."

Bashir Bhai fell into thinking, then said in a low but decisive voice, "It wasn't a dream. Instead, you have received good tidings."

Razi kept staring at him in silence. The wonder in his eyes changed into a bright wave of joy. But it subsided soon, giving way to a sense of deep anxiety.

"That year," he began in a low, solicitous voice, "the big *alam* was not carried out of our *imam-bara* in the procession."

"Why not?"

Both Akhtar and Bashir Bhai became anxious.

"Well, all the members of our family had already migrated here; only mother stayed behind. She vowed that she'd never abandon the *imam-bara* as long as she lived. Every year she herself made all the arrangements for the celebration of *Muharram* and personally saw to it that the big *alam* was borne out in a procession with great pomp and ceremony, just as it had always been."

"Then?"

"She'd grown very old and weak. No matter how hard I tried, I still couldn't get there in time. . . ." Razi's voice became hoarse and tears rolled down from his brimming eyes.

Bashir Bhai's head dropped, so did Akhtar's. Saiyid had in the meantime sat up straight. Bashir Bhai heaved a sigh, and after a brief and uneasy silence Akhtar remarked, "You have been living here with us for quite some time now but you never told us that before. How strange."

"What was there to tell?"

Bashir Bhai and Akhtar again felt stupefied, their heads strangely empty of thought. But a peephole had suddenly opened up in Saiyid's memory through which a meandring ray of light made its way down in the darkness. . . .

The mourning chamber remained locked throughout the year, except during the ten days of *Muharram* and a few days on the occasion of *Chihlam*. When the desire to unravel the unknown proved irresistible, young Saiyid would steal his way toward the door and peek through the cracks in it. Seeing nothing, he would step on the door-joints and hoist himself up holding on tight to the iron fastenings and peek in through the grating above the door. He would strain his eyes until they became accustomed to darkness and could travel unhindered inside. Peering inside, the crystal chandelier would flash. He would stare for a long time but seeing nothing, his heart, overawed, would begin to pound nervously. Then he would climb down and leave.

Darker still was the underground vault. One of its windows opened into the black stairway. The darkness of the vault never overwhelmed him, though it did frighten him. Even though, as mother used to say, the spotted snake that lived there never bothered anyone unless provoked—on one occasion her own hand accidentally fell on something slippery as she was climbing up the stairway one night but it simply slithered by, disappearing behind the window without hissing at her once—he could never muster enough courage to climb up to the window and let his eyes probe the darkness beyond. He never caught a glimpse of the spotted snake, but Bundi would swear she saw it with her own eyes.

"You're a liar."

"All right, I'm a liar. Don't believe me."

"I will, if you swear to it."

"By God. It's true."

But he still would not believe her. "Tell me, what did it look like?"

"Jet-black, dotted all over with white spots . . . when I peeked in, it was crawling on the wall. Right away I slammed the window shut."

His heart sank. They both stared at each other. With fear in their eyes and hearts pounding, they suddenly got up from where they had been sitting huddled together on the stairs and rushed down all the way to the courtyard where they perched themselves on the edge of the well.

Soon they were looking down into the well where the light slowly dimmed to a faint shade which little by little thickened and finally became altogether dark. At the bottom of the darkness water rose first in tiny ripples, sending sudden flashes—like lightning—to the surface then fell to a darker hue. Two images fast disintegrating on the lustrous, black, ripply surface.

"Genies!"

"Don't be crazy. Whoever heard of genies inhabiting wells."

"Then who are these?"

"Nobody," he said, sounding like an experienced old man. "You're absolutely crazy. Okay, watch; I'll call out." He stuck his head into the well and shouted. "Who's there?" The darkness echoed back, "Who's there?" A wave of fear ran down their spines. Scared, they instantaneously pulled back their heads.

"Is there somebody down there?" Bundi's heart froze.

"No one—I told you," he replied, absolutely unaffected, as if fear could never enter his heart.

They just sat there in inviolate silence. Slowly the fear began to dissipate. Still perched on the rim of the well, Bundi asked a question: "Saiyid, tell me, where does all this water in the well come from?"

He laughed at her ignorance. "Don't you know even that? Well, there's nothing but water below the ground. That's why the well never dries up."

"If there's nothing except water," she began, thinking hard, "then where do snakes live?"

Yes, where do snakes live?—now he too fell to thinking. The snake, he speculated, is not the king of water, that's for sure; it is the earth he rules over. But if there is just water below the earth, then where does he live? And how did Raja Basath's palace ever got built?

Saiyid had not quite figured that out when Bundi asked another question: "Saiyid," she said, "is it true that the snake first lived in paradise?"

"Yes, that's true."

"If he lived in paradise, then how did he get down here on earth?"

"He sinned. So God punished him. His legs were broken off and that's why he's down here on the earth."

Sin. Fear flashed in Bundi's eyes, and their hearts began to pound.

Bundi got up with a start. "I'm thirsty," she announced, "I'm going home."

With a quick movement of his hand, he grabbed the big water bucket that lay at the rim of the well. "Let's drink from the well," he said. "The water's very refreshing and cool." He quickly lowered the bucket down into the well. The rope raced through his hands, rubbing against his palms and almost burning them. Then came the gentle sound of the bucket hitting the water, a sound which sent a sweet ripple of sensation through his body. Together they began to pull the rope up, aware of a mysterious pleasure slowly emerging in their hearts. When the bucket bearing the delightfully cool water emerged, Bundi first held it while Saiyid cupped his hands and drank his fill. Then he held it and poured the water into the delicate cup of Bundi's hands. The gradually deepening cup of fair hands, pearl-like water, thin, gentle lips—he let the water stream down with such force that it not only splashed on her clothes but also made her choke. . . .

"Actually," Razi was saying, "it was a votive *alam*. You see, my mother hadn't been able to bear children. So she went to Karbala-e-Mu'alla. Just about anybody can go and petition at the tomb of the Imam—he is known to be patient, after all—but . . . but my mother used to say that such radiance, such grandeur fell on the grave of the Younger Hazrat that as soon as you entered the chamber, you were overwhelmed by reverential awe and began to shake. Not a day passed without a new miracle. When my mother had just arrived there, something strange happened. A man was stepping out of the sanctuary when, all of sudden, the door grabbed him. He tried, but he just wasn't able to break himself loose from the clutches of the door—unable to go out or in. His body burned red, as if it had just been struck by lightning . . . the man's mother kept crying. Finally, after a long time, one of the keepers of the sanctuary came and said to the woman, 'Lady, your son seems to have offended His Younger Eminence by his rudeness. Now, go to the sanctuary of the Imam and beg him to do something about it, for only he can appease His Younger Eminence.' So the poor woman, wailing and weeping, went all the way to the Imam's tomb and clung to his grave . . . " Razi's voice sunk to a whisper. "All of a sudden, a radiance broke out everywhere in the sanctuary and the suffering man returned to normal."

"That's really something!" exclaimed Akhtar under his breath.

Bashir Bhai yawned, then drifted off into silence once again.

"What really happened is that the man had taken a false oath," Razi added slowly. Taking advantage of Bashir Bhai and Akhtar's silence, he continued: "At any rate, my mother said, 'Come what may, I am not going to budge an inch from here without the promise of a child.' The whole night she kept weeping and entreating the Imam, her hands touching his grave all this time. At dawn, she dozed off and saw a lion entering the sanctuary. She woke up with a start. Her eyes fell directly on the *alam*, the *panja* emitting flaming rays. Just then a fresh jasmine flower dropped right into her lap. . . ."

"Yes," exclaimed Bashir Bhai in a somewhat raised voice, "there can be no doubt about his greatness!"

"That *alam*," a strange dreamy grandeur came over Razi's voice as he began, "is the true *alam*. It's the one that emerged from the Euphrates and still stands at the head of the grave, all wrapped in a green sash, in all its awe-inspiring majesty, so brilliant you can hardly look at it . . . just like the sun."

Saiyid actually felt the strong rays blinding his eyes and filtering wavily through them into the dark interior of the cellar of his mind. The cellar suddenly lit up as the rays penetrated its every nook and corner. Lustrous darkness, bright dreams, a glowing face, the radiant *alam*, and flaming kites—the kite which, when it swooped, suddenly severed from its string in mid-air, brought with it the memory of Bundi drifting farther and farther away from him after a moment of unhappiness. . . the dream that kept climbing an endless flight of stairs, the bed tapes that rolled out into infinity, the loose end of the kite string which a gentle breeze had blown almost into the hand, but which bobbed and fell out of reach just the instant the hand tried to close on it. He kept climbing the stairs that once led through a tunnel and next rose high into the air . . . higher and higher he rose, amid his heart's mad throbbing, his fear mounting that he might trip and fall, feeling at times that he was actually falling in a dark, bottomless pit, ever so slowly; he would try to balance himself, to rise as he fell, only to wake up with a start, filled with horror and shaking all over.

"*Ammanji*," he would say, "I dreamt I was climbing a flight of stairs."

"A prophetic dream, son. It means you will go far—you *will* become an officer."

"*Ammanji*," what would you say if one saw a flying kite in a dream?"

"Oh, no, son. No. One mustn't dream such dreams. It is not a good omen to see a kite. It can only be a premonition of vagrancy and homelessness."

"*Ammanji*, I dreamt that there was this staircase I was climbing. I kept climbing up and up. Finally a roof appeared and the staircase vanished . . . and I found myself standing all alone on top of that roof, and a kite . . . ."

"No, son, no," his mother cut him short. "It is not a dream. All day long you keep hopping from roof to roof, and that's what you saw in your sleep . . . you mustn't dream such dreams."

"*Ammanji*, I dreamt about our roof and a monkey was perched on one of its walls . . . ."

His mother again cut him mid-sentence, a little sternly this time. "That's enough, son. Now go back to sleep."

"I will, but first you must finish the story."

"All right. God bless you, where did we stop?"

"The princess asked, 'Who are you'?"

"Oh, yes. The princess kept insisting that he must reveal his identity, but he tried hard to talk her out of it, saying, 'O lucky one! Don't ask me that or you will have to endure great suffering.' But the princess would not give in. 'You must tell me who you are,' she insisted, 'and until you tell me that, I won't talk to you.' So the man reluctantly gave in. 'All right, if that's what you want. Let's go to the river and I will tell you about myself there.' So they both started out for the river. Once there, he again begged her, 'Please don't ask that.' But she just wouldn't listen to him. 'On the contrary,' she said, 'I insist that you tell me that.' The man walked into the water.

When the water reached up to his chest, he implored her again, 'Please don't ask.' But she remained adamant. 'I *will*,' she said firmly. And when the water rose up to his neck, he begged her once again and she once again refused. The water reached all the way up to his face and he beseeched her the last time, 'Listen, there is still time; give up the idea or you will be sorry for the rest of your life.' But she said, 'I *will* ask you!' So the man immersed himself completely. A black serpent's hood emerged from the water and dived back to be lost forever. . . ."

"So she had an *alam* made from some silver which had been blessed by a touch from that jasmine flower. And you know what? I was born the same year."

"One must consider that auspicious," observed Bashir Bhai.

"But . . ." Razi's voice trailed off and his body shivered. "But . . . ."

"But what?" asked Bashir Bhai.

"It disappeared!"

"It disappeared—how?" Both Bashir Bhai and Akhtar were mystified.

"It's like this," began Razi, his body still shaking. "The procession did not take place that year . . . we had a neighbour. He used to say that no one kindled even a single lamp that night in the *imam-bara*, but when he woke up the next morning to offer the prayer, he saw that the whole *imam-bara* was so brightly lit up that for a moment he thought all the light came from gas lamps . . . anyway, when he went there in the morning he saw this strange sight: all the other *alams* were intact, but somehow the big *alam* had vanished. . . ."

The darkness that was deepening and had obsecured everything suddenly changed into brightness. Still sitting on the rim of the well they saw a shadow glide by in the bright sunshine. "A kite!" Like a bullet both shot forward, chasing after it. They went into the stairway, frantically climbing up the flight of stairs and out on to the open roof.

"Where did it go?" he gave a searching look all around.

"I saw it fall right here on this roof," Bundi said with certainty.

"But if it did, then, where has it disappeared to now?"

All of a sudden Bundi's hand grabbed his sleeve, and then her grip tightened around his arm. "Saiyid . . ." she whispered, scared stiff, "look . . . a monkey."

He too was scared stiff. "Wh . . . where?" he managed with difficulty.

"There!" She pointed toward the wall with her eyes.

A big, fat monkey sat dozing serenely on the wall. When it saw them it got up abruptly and the hair on its body stood erect like so many quills of a porcupine. They both froze. The monkey stood there for a while, screeched at them menacingly, then walking leisurely along the wall, climbed down into the alley and disappeared.

When they finally made it to the stairway, their hearts were still pounding, their bodies dripping with sweat. Bundi rubbed her face dry with her shirt, wiped her neck, and rearranged her dishevelled hair. Then they sat down on the stairs. He looked at Bundi with fright in his eyes, seeing that her own terror-stricken eyes appeared even more horrified in the half-light of the stairway. By now he was totally overcome by fear. "Let's get out of here," he said, standing up. They began to bolt down the stairs, and he, on their way down, stopped briefly at the first bend to look through the ventilator shaft behind which the field and the trees beyond the field appeared like an altogether different world.

"Don't ever look there," Bundi cautioned him.

"Why not?"

"Because a sorceress lives there," she replied, her terror-filled eyes gleaming. "And she has a mirror. Anyone who looks into that mirror is bewitched and follows her along timidly."

"You're just making that up."

"I swear it's true."

Full of dread he again sneaked a look through the ventilator shaft. "I don't see her anywhere," he said.

"Really?" She couldn't believe it. "Let me have a look." She walked up to the shaft.

She tried hard but was unable to hoist herself up far enough. She implored, "Saiyid, please, please help me see through the shaft!"

He raised her to where her face came level with the shaft . . . and he had the pleasant feeling of holding a bucket of sweet, refreshing water . . .

The ray of light descending in the darkness got entangled and broke. He rolled over in bed and sat up. Akhtar, Bashir Bhai, Razi—all three seemed to be sound asleep; Bashir Bhai was even snoring. The moon was slowly climbing up and by now the moonlight had reached all the way to the foot of his bed. He got out of bed and walked to the small drainage pipe at the base of the low wall, which was enveloped in utter darkness. During the rains the pipe served as an outlet for excess water and through the rest of the year as a convenient urinal. After a while he got up and poured a glass of water from the flask and downed it in one big, hurried gulp. The water had now become quite cool. He glanced at the lantern that sat in the corner. It had gone out. As he was lying down again his eyes fell on Razi and he had the feeling that Razi was not yet quite asleep.

"Razi!"

"Yes," Razi replied, opening his eyes wide.

"You're still awake?"

"No. I was just falling asleep, but the noise of your shuffling around woke me up."

They fell silent. Razi's groggy eyes once again began to

close. Akhtar and Bashir Bhai were still sound asleep. Now Akhtar too had started snoring.

Saiyid yawned, turned over in the bed, patted Razi on the shoulder, and asked, "Are you asleep, Razi?"

Razi threw open his eyes again. "No, I'm awake," he replied in a voice heavy with sleep.

"Razi, why is it that I don't ever have any dreams at all?" he asked in a voice which blended innocence with a trace of profound suffering.

Razi laughed. "But why should everyone have to have a dream every night?"

Both of them fell silent again. Sleep was afloat in Razi's eyes and he desperately wanted to turn over in the bed and close his eyes, but Saiyid spoke up again, "When I was a child I once had a dream that . . . that I was climbing up a landing chasing after a loose kite and the stairs just . . . ."

"You call it a *dream*, eh?" Razi gave out a laugh. "Those are just vagrant thoughts that cross the mind during sleep."

Saiyid began thinking: Was it not a dream then? And must he therefore assume that his whole life is devoid of dreams? And that he has never in his life seen a real dream? His imagination tried to close in on many a shimmering snowflake adrift in the expanse of memory, only to wake up to the painful realisation that these were not dreams but actual events. He cast a probing look at his past life, the whole of it, and saw a dreamy quality in each event, in each corner, and yet he could not find a single dream. He felt that dreams had somehow become inextricably fused with his past so that it was impossible to isolate dream from reality, very much like the *gulal* mixed with mica—shimmering, but from which those sparkling particles could not be neatly separated; or one of those pendants hanging from the crystal chandelier in the *imam-bara*—almost entirely colourless on the outside but full of rainbow colours trapped inside, colours which it was impossible to extricate; or water in the depth of the well—at once bright and dark, one could not tell them apart.

"Are you awake, Razi?"

"Yeah." Razi's voice was drowsy.

"After such a long dream," he muttered to himself, "what's left for anyone to dream about? To me even our old house looks like a dream. Climbing up in the half-lit landing you had this strange sensation of walking in a tunnel: one bend leading to another, the second to a third, as if all your life you would be zig-zagging along a never-ending series of twists and turns, with stairs unfolding into infinity, but then, unexpectedly, the bright open roof appeared and you felt you were entering an altogether unknown country . . . and there were times when our roof was invaded by a strange desolation: a monkey, snug and comfortably settled on the wall of the tallest roof, lolled, then fell asleep—inert, you felt it would never wake up again, but then it perked up, shook its body, got up, hopped down onto the roof below, and walked leisurely toward the landing . . . both our hearts cringed with fright. It started descending the stairs, taking all its time to stop on this stair or that. We were afraid of it, and we hid ourselves behind one of the columns in the outer hall. It walked languidly toward the well and settled on the rim . . . it sat there for a while . . . then vanished . . . or maybe went down into the well, who knows. . . ."

Sleep began to drift away from Razi's tired eyelids. He gave Saiyid a deep, probing look. Saiyid rambled on undaunted: "We peeked down into the well, then we shouted, 'Who's there?' The well was filled with an immense resonance and an undulating beam of light rising from the water and spiraling upward in the dark, poured out everywhere in the courtyard, as if someone had set the heart of darkness ablaze with sudden fireworks. A shadow was floating on the bright surface of the water. 'It's a kite!' I cried out, pulling myself back and throwing my face up toward the sky. A huge black-and-white kite was loose in the sky, the bit of string still attached to it sparkling against a bright sun. From the wall it swooped down and tumbled into the courtyard where it hovered above my head. I reached for it but it slipped away. I dashed into the dark stairway . . . as I came close to the window of the underground vault my heart skipped a beat. I closed my eyes and threw myself forward, climbing the stairs, cutting one corner, then another, then stairs, more stairs, still more stairs . . . a whole century passed and I was still climbing, up and up . . . finally I emerged onto the open roof, but then I was once again trapped in a never-ending maze of stairs . . . ."

"Friend," said Razi, giving him a look full of wonder, "you're talking dreams."

Saiyid fell silent.

The moon had in the meantime climbed higher and the moonlight which had been at the foot of his cot was now touching the side of the wall in front. The glass sitting next to the clay flask was sparkling in places, as if a few beams of light had been trapped inside it. Bashir Bhai and Akhtar were still sound asleep. Because of the cold, Bashir Bhai had removed the lightweight sheet from under his pillow and thrown it over his body, while the quilted blanket that was earlier lying on Akhtar's legs now lay all crumpled and bunched up on his chest.

For a few minutes Razi lay with his eyes closed but soon got bored and threw them wide open.

"Saiyid!"

"Yes." Saiyid's voice was drowsy.

"Are you sleeping? My sleep's gone."

He opened his sleep-laden eyes and looking toward Razi he said in a mysterious voice, "My heart's pounding. It seems I'm going to see a dream after all."

His eyes began to close again.

(Translated from the original in Urdu by Muhammad Umar Memon)

15

KAMLESHWAR

How Many Pakistans?

WHAT A LONG journey! And I fail to understand why Pakistan comes in my way again and again. Salima, have I been unfair to you? Then why are you so unkind to yourself? You are laughing. But I am sure your laughter has poison-laden salvos in it. These are no buds of the queen-of-the-night that blossom in the moonlight.

It amuses me to be reminded of the moon. You used to say—I am moonstruck. Do you remember it, Salima?

You do remember all. The womenfolk never forget anything. They only pretend to forget. If they didn't pretend, life would become difficult for them. I feel odd addressing you, Salima. I would like to call you Bano. Bano, who collected blossoms of the queen-of-the-night—the fragrance of which mingled with your breath.

I would feel intoxicated, Bano. I hate to address you by this name. I wonder if you care for it yourself any more. In any case, what's there in a name?

And I felt like going up the stairs that night again and remind you of something. But what was there you needed to be reminded about?

God knows, how many more Pakistans have been created

along with the birth of one Pakistan. Everything is mixed up. Nothing seems to have any meaning—nothing seems to be what it is.

That night too was similar. God knows whether it was the *peepal* tree or Badru in the neighbourhood who said—"Kadir Mian! Pakistan has come into being, the accursed one is born. . . ."

There were three main stages in this journey. The first, when the fragrance of the queen-of-the-night intoxicated me. The second, when I saw you, Bano, naked for the first time in the moonlight. The third, when you stood on the other side of the door and asked, "Is there anyone else?"

Yes there was. There was one . . . .

B ano, why did you laugh after that wavering, blind moment? What harm had I done you? On whom were you trying to take revenge? On me? On Muneer? Or was it on Pakistan? Whom were you trying to humiliate—me? Muneer? Or . . . ?

Why must this Pakistan come between us? For you and me, it is no country. It is a name given to an unfortunate reality—something which separates us when we are together. It makes the members of your family, your relatives, and your community insensitive. Perhaps it is this insensitivity that has come to be known as Pakistan. It is like having flowers without blossoms, blossoms without colour, colour without smell, smell without wind to carry it. Pakistan is the name given to the stillness of the breeze of warm feelings.

Listen, had it not been so, why would I have left Chinar and become a stranger? I can never forget the evening when Compounder Zamin Ali came and told my father, "Though there is no truth in it, yet it will be difficult to convince people. Let Mangal leave the town for a few days. If he remains here, everyone will continue to talk about his affair with Bano. Marriage is out of the question. It may lead to a communal riot."

You can have no idea what happened to me when I heard this. How could I leave Chinar? But then, I had to leave. The intoxicating Chinar nights! The water of the Ganga! The boats carrying passengers to Kashi! The ruins of Bhartrahari's castle! The octroi post where I used to sit and listen to your blandishments! The narrow streets torn with drains from which, Bano, you planned many an attempt to escape!

We didn't even know we were no longer treated as children. We had grown up. Our innocent meetings suddenly came to be looked upon with suspicion.

That our love for one another could lead to communal tension never occurred to us. How could it happen, Bano?

How would you know about it? We crossed all the three stages, unawares. At none did we pause and talk to each other. Neither when the blossoms of the queen-of-the-night intoxicated us, nor when I saw you naked in the moonlit night for the first time, nor when standing behind the door you said, "Is there anyone else?"

Blossoms of the queen-of-the-night

Chinar! Where you and I lived. A lane from my house led to the main bazaar and then on to the banks of the Ganga and terminated at the main gate of Bhartrahari's castle.

The octroi post was situated where the road turned towards the castle. Close to the octroi post, the road bifurcated: one branch led to the citadel, the other to a *kutcha* path which was a virtual web of drains. This path ended in the lane where, Bano, you belonged.

Beyond your lane was another cobblestone road which led to the mission school. It was here that there were plants of the queen-of-the-night and belladonna. The belladonna had been a source of grave anxiety to me. When there was tension in the town on account of our affair, you once managed to come up to the octroi post and said, "If the *Maulvi* and his folks misbehave, I'll swallow belladonna and go to sleep. Don't you leave the town. If you do, remember that the Ganga flows nearby."

We couldn't talk much, and you left. I couldn't tell you what unpleasantness it had created in our house, how strangers threatened my father. They feared that I would be assassinated one of these days. Or the Muslims might just raid the house.

Pakistan had come into being and yet your father, the drill master, continued to write the story of the Hindu saint—Raja Bhartrahari. His people thought he had gone crazy: a Muslim writing in praise of a Hindu ruler! "He is no Turk—he is a low-caste Hindu converted to Islam," they vouched. And they were up in arms when they heard of your feelings for me.

I am aware the drill master, your father, did not object to our involvement with one another. But he felt that whatever the *Maulvi* said or did was right. He never thought out things for himself. Once he came to my father on the quiet and cried bitterly. After that, though he continued to write Bhartrahari's story, he never let anyone get wind of it. That he continued to write the story, I came to know when the octroi clerk slipped a paper into my sweating hand as I was leaving the city.

It was a frightfully dark night. Everyone was terror-stricken, nobody knew what might happen the next moment. Shouts of *"Ya Ali, Ya Ali"* could start any minute and there would be bloodshed all over. Even the holy Ganga was trembling that evening. The *peepal* tree on the bank was restless. The wind was fierce—it whistled through the ruins of the castle. My father brought me to the railway station with half a dozen Hindu youths so that I could entrain safely. It was first suggested that I should go to Jaunpur. Then I don't know how it was decided that I should proceed to Bombay and seek a job in the railway workshop where an uncle of mine was employed.

Bano, what a dreadful night it was! And how I was being humiliated having to leave my own home town. There was a fierce conflict in my mind. At times I thought I should go back, pick up a hatchet and put all your so-called Muslims to death. Wreak havoc and win you over. If I failed, I could always drown myself in the Ganga.

Yes, I was escorted to the station by half a dozen Hindus. We avoided the main bazaar and took the desolate Fort Street. The octroi clerk came with a lantern in his hand and managed to pass on to me that slip of paper. There was no light on the road. Then at the platform there were people around us. I got into a parcel train that would take me to Mughal Serai; it was the only train left. My father was extremely uneasy. He was scared, too, and felt humiliated. It seemed communal riots would break out the moment I left the town—the Hindus returning from the railway station would start it. They would fall upon the Muslims in the last hours of the night.

The parting that night was unbearable. There was a nip in the air. The Vindhya hills and pine trees across the railway station looked on at us coldly.

What should I tell you? To tell you the truth, for me it was only then that Pakistan came into existence. Like a dagger it pierced through my heart. The breeze in the town had ceased blowing, and it seemed a siege had been laid on my Bano.

Travelling in the parcel train that night, I read that slip of paper handed over to me. You had no words of comfort for me; you spoke of your father and how he continued to write the story of Bhartrahari.

The train gathered speed. I became a stranger. Never again have I thought of returning.

I was aware that the drill master must be feeling suffocated in Chinar. I was not so sure about you. I knew that you couldn't have drowned yourself in the Ganga. You must live. You would be there—maybe with someone. Happy or unhappy, you must be somewhere there. Warming someone's bed at night. Giving someone your love. Maybe someone beats you— beats you and rapes you. Nevertheless, like a devoted wife you pray for your man's welfare. You must be applying *henna* to your palms. Bringing up his children. You may be happy. You may be regretting it all.

Well, Bano! What had to happen had already happened. From Mughal Serai I went to Allahabad and from there to Bombay. My uncle found work for me at the Kurla Railway Workshop, but after a few weeks I moved to Poona. I was employed in a hospital workshop where they manufactured artificial limbs. I was convinced that no one would be able to live in Chinar, neither my people nor yours. But I could never imagine that my father would migrate so soon along with several other families.

The fact of the matter is that there was hardly anything left in Chinar. When something like Pakistan comes into existence, a part of man dies. The crops are destroyed. The streets are narrowed. The skies weep. The clouds dry up. The wind ceases to blow.

After some time my father wrote to me that along with several other families he had moved to Bhiwandi in search of unravaged crops, open streets, blue skies and rain-laden clouds. I was not aware that he had taken your people along with him. What was the drill master doing in Bhiwandi? My father opting for Bhiwandi made sense—he traded in cotton. But the drill master?

Bano! I came to know about you from my father when he visited me in Poona. He mentioned to me casually, "The drill master had also come with me to Bhiwandi. He has been absorbed in a school. Bano is married. The drill master's son-in-law works a handloom. He has a good finger for silk cloth."

From the way my father spoke I could see he was deliberately making it sound casual. However, I was not aware that my father and you people lived in the same house: you on the ground floor and my father upstairs.

In my weaker moments I felt like visiting Bhiwandi and meeting you all. But I desisted. Maybe because you were married. And also because my father had indicated in a subtle manner that it would not be advisable for me to come. He had a lot of regard for the drill master. He knew that what had happened was through no fault of your father. He did not wish to embarrass him with my presence. What an awkward situation! How could I come and live in the same house?

Bhiwandi, too, got caught in the communal riots. Not because of you and me but because of the virus of distrust which was spreading everywhere. When I heard about it I was shocked. Who could have been responsible for it? Five years ago I could be accused. But now I was not there? I had never visited Bhiwandi, fearing how I would react if I saw you. When I saw you. When I did see you, did I know what was in store for me?

It was a moonlit night and Bano was naked

I arrived in Bhiwandi soon after the communal riots. As I entered the town I noticed heaps of debris and burnt down buildings. The havoc of incendiarism was everywhere. The air smelt of smoke and ashes. It pricked my nostrils—the pungent smell of roasted earth.

You too must have smelt it. Is there anyone in this country who does not recognise the smell of ashes? When I alighted at the bus stand, it was getting late in the evening. There were stray policemen here and there. Most of the buses were empty—even the Shirdi bus was without any passengers.

What is it like walking through a riot-torn town? You may have known it. I did not. A queer, uncanny quiet.

Desolate streets. An obvious absence of people. One ceases to see. Even if one tries one sees nothing.

It is difficult to locate a house in such conditions. And when I found the street and the house, it was all quiet. What had the Hindus done to this town? Could there be any life possible in such dreadful quiet?

Bano! I knew that the drill master, your husband, Muneer, and my people would all be there. Since it had grown dark, I was a little scared.

It was an open courtyard of a sort. There were two water pitchers lying in a corner. Next to them there were two grey shadows. Of two women. One of them was naked to her waist. The other sat close to her. Her hand would again and again move to the neck of the naked woman and then slip down to her waist. I failed to understand what she was doing, but I could distinctly see the naked form of a woman. I took fright and stepped out.

In the street, I found the drill master. He didn't greet me—he didn't know how to receive me. Wherefrom to pick up the thread of dialogue? What to say? Before he could open his mouth, I took the initiative and asked about my father.

"He left for Chinar the day before yesterday," the drill master told me.

"Day before yesterday?"

"Yes, he would not stay back. A few of the families also accompanied him."

I could understand why, in spite of all that had happened, my father could return to Chinar but not the drill master. The reasons for the drill master leaving Chinar were not the same as those for my father and me. The drill master had been exiled with the tide of time. And it is difficult for time to recall anyone. I had been exiled only by a handful of people.

Since my people were not there, I didn't know what to do. Where could I find shelter in a riot-torn city. It was not possible for the drill master to put me up for the night. Bano,

you would be there. How could you treat me as a stranger?
Things had not come to such a pass yet.

"Has father taken the household effects along with him?"
I asked.

"No, most of his things are still here," he replied.

"Has he locked the house?"

"Yes, but I have a duplicate key."

"I would like to stay here for the night. I have to return
tomorrow evening." I inflicted myself on the drill master. I
had no choice, I was a stranger in the city.

He went into the house and brought the key along with a
candle. He led me to the first floor, up a staircase on one side
of the house. He opened the door and asked, "Have you had
something to eat?"

"Yes," I said and went into the room.

"Do tell us if you need anything." Saying this he descended
the stairs. The author of Bhartrahari was shrewd enough to
say "tell us" and not "ask for it."

Bano! What a strange night it was! You were not aware
that I was there. The drill master could not have told you
about it. If the police had not raided the house early next
morning, you would have never known whose shadow it was
that hovered on the terrace the whole night.

It was a moonlit night. The air was still. I decided to put
the *charpoy* on the terrace and sleep in the open. Maybe I
was awaiting you in my heart of hearts.

The tree in the neighbourhood was bathed in moonlight. I
had put my *charpoy* at a place from where I could see the
courtyard below. But what I saw was horrendous.

There were two *charpoys* in the courtyard. One was
occupied by you and the other by your mother. I felt a tug at
my heart seeing you lying there.

The moonlight was spreading all over. And you were
lying there with your breasts uncovered. You had also pulled
your petticoat up to your waist. Your breasts were like

full-blown balloons. You lay there like a half-dead fish. You were moaning.

"*Hai Allah!*" I heard you call out.

"Try to sleep, Bano," I heard your mother plead.

"They are bursting," you wailed and then held your breasts in both your hands as if you were trying to crush them.

Your mother got up and came over to you. "Let me milk them." Saying this she started squeezing them gently. Jets of milk started shooting out. You continued to moan. At times the milk stopped as if there was some constriction. But it would start shooting out again. Your naked body was drenched with it; there were pearly milk drops all over you.

Bano! what was it that I was seeing? I was stunned. I was sweating all over. Your sobbing and moaning and a pair of breasts as if hanging from heaven. I was getting wild. A storm was raging within me. It was perhaps remorse for having seen what I ought not to have seen.

I lay restless on the terrace till late in the night. When I found that it was all quiet down below and you had covered your breasts with your *sari*, I, too, went to sleep. I saw youthful breasts hanging all over the sky.

I had hardly slept when there was a wailing in the neighbourhood. Someone was shouting: "Kadir Mian! Your Pakistan has come into being. The accursed one is born."

Had there not been the sacred *peepal* tree in the neighbourhood, I would have imagined it was a ghost and made good my escape. But now even with my eyes open I was witnessing weird scenes: blood raining from the sky, dead bodies running helter-skelter in the dark, headless trunks standing in the midst of the bazaar and the slashed gory necks piled on the roadside.

I had a heavy head the next morning. Some two hours before sunrise I had to leave my bed. The drill master woke me up and said, "There are policemen who are asking for you."

"Why?" I wanted to know.

"They verify particulars of every visitor to the town."

The moment I heard it I was beside myself with anger. Did anyone ask my particulars when I was made to leave my town in the dead of the night?

The police started their investigation. They asked all sorts of questions. Why was I visiting the town? What could I tell them? Why does one travel or go to another place? They would have harassed me a great deal had not the drill master turned up and given them all the answers. The drill master being a Muslim, proved handy. What better proof of a Hindu's credentials than that a Muslim should vouch for him?

Released by the police, the drill master and I sat down on a log lying nearby. But neither of us knew what to say to the other. The silence was becoming irksome when the drill master spoke:

"Badru has gone crazy. He has been sitting under the *peepal* tree ever since the riots broke out. He has burnt his forty handlooms. Did you hear his call to Kadir *Mian*?"

A little later he told me about you—"Bano is not too well. She gave birth to a baby three days before the riots started. She was admitted to Dr Sarang's Nursing Home. The rioters set fire to the nursing home and the mothers with their new-born babies had to jump from the first floor to escape. Two mothers and five babies were killed. Bano too lost her baby. Bano is all right now, but the milk in her breasts is making her life unbearable."

"It's time I started for Poona." I wanted to find an excuse to get up.

"If you can make it, why not go to Chinar? You will be able to meet your father," said the drill master.

"Why? Is he unwell?"

"One of his arms has been slashed. The rioters came to attack us. Had he not been there, we wouldn't have survived. He rushed out into the street to prevent the *goondas* from harming us. In the skirmish, he lost his arm. But he did not lose his nerves. He put up a heroic fight and at last fell down unconscious."

"What happened to his arm?" I asked in consternation.

"It is no longer there, but your father is all right. God is merciful. I suggest you go and look him up."

I came and lay down on the bed in my room. The drill master returned to his quarters. After a little while there was a noise in the courtyard below. Bano, you, your husband Muneer, your mother and your father, everyone was there. There was an argument.

"Why must you insist on continuing to live here alone?" Muneer shouted.

"You'll never understand it," you railed back. "I must get my baby from this very soil and only then will I move from here. I'll go, then, wherever you will take me."

I peeped through the railing. A thin, lean Muneer was shivering in rage. "Then you may do what you like. You may sleep with anyone you please."

I was taken aback. Maybe it had a reference to me. No, I was wrong. The next moment I heard you shout back, "How could you be father of a child anymore? You go and sell your blood to the blood bank people in Bombay so that you can drink every evening."

Hearing this, Muneer went into a rage and slapped you. There was more shouting.

"Don't I know?" you continued to insult him. "Every time you go to Bombay you sell your blood. And then you lie in your bed shivering the whole night."

What was I hearing? A Pakistan seemed to be shedding tears within me. Everyone had his own Pakistan to nag him. Crippled limbs? Half-dead folks!

What a dreadful day it was. I left Bhiwandi very much the way I stole out of Chinar. I found a taxi going to Thana and bought a seat. From Thana I took a bus to Bombay and from there I returned to Poona. I was in Poona for several days.

Bano! I wanted to forget everything. I wanted to withdraw within myself. Man is a queer creature. He lives and walks about even if he is crippled, his limbs decapitated one after the other.

And if in such days of loneliness one hears someone say, "Is there anyone else?" what should happen to him? You can't imagine it Bano.

Is there anyone else?

About five months had elapsed when I learned from my father that he had returned to Bhiwandi. Because of the Sindhis and Marwaris entering into the trade, he was not doing too well. A number of handlooms were out of action. Since he had lost one of his arms the balance of his body had been impaired and people had started calling him *tonta*.

He didn't have much to say except that Muneer had gone away to Bombay with you. Nobody knew whether you were still in Bombay or had migrated to Pakistan. The drill master had gone crazy. He practised drill at home and wrote the story of Bhartrahari in the school.

If I had not come to Bombay that day, maybe I would never have met you. What a painful meeting it was! I have regretted it ever since. I wish I had been in place of my friend. You must be imagining that I, too, indulged in all that, Bano. To tell you the truth, I do all that, but because of you.

I was in Bombay only for a day. I had broken my journey on the way to Bhiwandi. At the station I met Kedar, an old Bombay friend, quite by chance. Kedar suggested that we spend the evening together. We had a few drinks in a pub in Colaba. Then we walked till we came to the Handloom House. Close to it there is a lane. We entered the lane and some five minutes later we stood before a tall building.

The building had a lift—one of those open kinds. The staircase was quite clean. Kedar and I decided to go up the stairs. We were quite out of breath when we reached the sixth floor. Kedar pressed the call bell.

As the door opened we found ourselves standing before a Sindhi, breathing heavily like a hippopotamus. He directed us to a room. It was sparsely furnished. The man continued to breathe heavily as he inquired if we cared for a drink or something.

I was feeling restless. I went and stood at the window for fresh air. I could see dirty rooftops of various dimensions. Kedar had told me that I could wait in that room while he visited her. The Sindhi brought a Coca-Cola for me and then took Kedar into a corner. He was showing him someone in a dark veil.

The two disappeared, and I came and sat down on the only chair in the room. The Sindhi reappeared after a little while and asked me if I would like to have a glass of beer.

"I wouldn't mind one," I said.

The Sindhi got me a beer, but would not join me.

"You don't seem to belong to Bombay?" he began.

"I am from Poona," I replied.

"A pleasure trip, is it?"

"No, I had some work here."

"Are you in business?"

"No, it was something personal. I am on my way to Bhiwandi."

The Sindhi continued to breathe heavily. Then Kedar reappeared. The moment the Sindhi saw him he got up clumsily. I was feeling quite disconcerted. I gulped down the remaining beer and went up to Kedar. As Kedar was paying for my beer, the door of the adjacent room opened and someone handed him a bunch of keys and a comb. Finding me standing alongside the Sindhi, she asked: "Is there anyone else?"

I turned around. With your hands on the frame of the door, it was you, Bano, in a petticoat and a blouse.

Yes! There—there was another.

And you, too, had recognised him after a faltering, blind moment. And there was a venomous smile on your face, full of deadly poison and contempt. Or is it my imagination?

I do not know against whom you were taking revenge—me, Muneer, Pakistan?

I came down the stairs. Kedar followed me.

Where should I go now? Which town must I leave to escape Pakistan? Where can I live with all my love and all my longings?

Bano! I find Pakistan at every step. It keeps stabbing me. I am bleeding—I am humiliated.

(Translated from the original in Hindi by K. S. Duggal)

16

SAADAT HASAN MANTO

Toba Tek Singh

A COUPLE OF years or so after the partition of the subcontinent,
the governments of Pakistan and India felt that just as they
had exchanged their hardened criminals, they should exchange
their lunatics. In other words, Muslims in the lunatic asylums
of India be sent across to Pakistan; and mad Hindus and
Sikhs in Pakistani asylums be handed over to India.

Whether or not this was a sane decision, we will never
know. But people in knowledgeable circles say that there were
many conferences at the highest level between bureaucrats of
the two countries before the final agreement was signed and
a date fixed for the exchange.

The news of the impending exchange created a novel
situation in the Lahore lunatic asylum. A Muslim patient who
was a regular reader of the *Zamindar* was asked by a friend,
"*Maulvi Sahib*, what is this thing they call Pakistan?" After
much thought he replied, "It's a place in India where they
manufacture razor blades." A Sikh lunatic asked another,
"*Sardarji*, why are we being sent to India? We cannot speak
their language." The *Sardarji* smiled and replied "I know the
lingo of the Hindustanis." He illustrated his linguistic prowess
by reciting a doggerel:

Hindustanis are full of *shaitani*
They strut about like bantam cocks.

One morning, an insane Mussalman yelled the slogan "*Pakistan Zindabad*" with such vigour that he slipped on the floor and knocked himself senseless.

Some inmates of the asylum were not really insane. They were murderers whose relatives had been able to have them certified and thus save them from the hangman's noose. These people had vague notions of why India had been divided and what was Pakistan. But even they knew very little of the complete truth. The papers were not very informative and the guards were so stupid that it was difficult to make any sense out of what they said. All one could gather from their talk was that there was a man with the name of Mohammed Ali Jinnah who was also known as the *Qaid-i-Azam*. And that this Mohammed Ali Jinnah alias *Qaid-i-Azam* had made a separate country for the Mussalmans which he called Pakistan.

No one knew where this Pakistan was or how far it extended. This was the chief reason why inmates who were not totally insane were in a worse dilemma than those utterly mad—they did not know whether they were in India or Pakistan. If they were in India, where exactly was Pakistan? And if they were in Pakistan, how was it that the very same place had till recently been known as India?

A poor Muslim inmate got so baffled with the talk about India and Pakistan, Pakistan and India, that he got madder than before. One day while he was sweeping the floor, he was suddenly overcome by an insane impulse. He threw away his brush and clambered up a tree. And for two hours he orated from the branch of this tree on Indo-Pakistan problems. When the guards tried to get him down, he climbed still higher. When they threatened him he replied, "I do not wish to live either in India or Pakistan; I want to stay where I am, on top of this tree."

After a while the fit of lunacy subsided and the man was persuaded to come down. As soon as he was on the ground he began to embrace his Hindu and Sikh friends and shed bitter tears. He was overcome by the thought that they would leave him and go away to India.

Another Muslim inmate had a Master of Science degree in radio-engineering and considered himself a cut above the others. He used to spend his days strolling in a secluded corner of the garden. Suddenly, a change came over him. He took off all his clothes and handed them over to the head-constable. He resumed his perambulation without a stitch of clothing on his person.

And there was yet another lunatic, a fat Mussalman who had been a leader of the Muslim League in Chiniot. He was given to bathing fifteen to sixteen times during the day. He suddenly gave up bathing altogether.

The name of this fat Mussalman was Mohammed Ali. But one day he proclaimed from his cell that he was Mohammed Ali Jinnah. Not to be outdone, his cell-mate who was a Sikh, proclaimed himself to be Master Tara Singh. The two began to abuse each other. They were declared "dangerous" and put in separate cages.

There was a young Hindu lawyer from Lahore. He was said to have become mentally unhinged when his lady-love jilted him. When he heard that Amritsar had gone to India, he was very depressed: his sweetheart lived in Amritsar. Although the girl had spurned his affection, he did not forget her even in his lunacy. He spent his time cursing all leaders, Hindu as well as Muslim, because they had split India into two, and made his beloved an Indian and him a Pakistani.

When the talk of exchanging lunatics was in the air, other inmates consoled the Hindu lawyer with the hope that he would soon be sent to India—the country where his sweetheart lived. But the lawyer refused to be reassured. He did not want to leave Lahore because he was convinced that he would not be able to set up legal practice in Amritsar.

There were a couple of Anglo-Indians in the European ward. They were very saddened to learn that the English had liberated India and returned home. They met secretly to deliberate on problems of their future status in the asylum: would the asylum continue to have a separate ward for Europeans? Would they be served breakfast as before? Would they be deprived of toast and be forced to eat *chapatis?*

Then there was a Sikh who had been in the asylum for fifteen years. And in the fifteen years he said little besides the following sentence: "*O, pardi, good good di, anekas di, bedhyana di, moong di dal of di lantern.*"

The Sikh never slept, either at night or in the day. The warders said that they had not known him to blink his eyes in fifteen years. He did not so much as lie down. Only on rare occasions he leant against the wall to rest. His legs were swollen down to the ankles.

Whenever there was talk of India and Pakistan, or the exchange of lunatics, this Sikh would become very attentive. If anyone invited him to express his views, he would answer with great solemnity: "*O, pardi, good good di, anekas di, bedhyana di, moong di dal of the Pakistan Government.*"

Some time later he changed the end of his litany from "of the Pakistan Government" to "of the Toba Tek Singh government."

He began to question his fellow inmates whether the village of Toba Tek Singh was in India or Pakistan. No one knew the answer. Those who tried, got tied up in knots explaining how Sialkot was at first in India and was now in Pakistan. How could one guarantee that a similar fate would not befall Lahore and from being Pakistani today it would not become Indian tomorrow? For that matter, how could one be sure that the whole of India would not become a part of Pakistan? All said and done, who could put his hand on his heart and say with conviction that there was no danger of both India and Pakistan vanishing from the face of the globe one day!

The Sikh had lost most of his long hair. Since he seldom took a bath, the hair on the head had matted and joined with his beard. This gave the Sikh a very fierce look. But he was a harmless fellow. In the fifteen years he had been in the asylum, he had never been known to argue or quarrel with anyone. All that the older inmates knew about him was that he owned land in village Toba Tek Singh and was once a prosperous farmer. When he lost his mind, his relatives had brought him to the asylum in iron fetters. Once a month, some relatives came to Lahore to find out how he was faring. With the eruption of Indo-Pakistan troubles these visits had ceased.

The Sikh's name was Bishen Singh, but everyone called him Toba Tek Singh. Bishen Singh had no concept of time—neither of days, nor weeks, or of months. He had no idea how long he had been in the lunatic asylum. But when his relatives and friends came to see him, he knew that a month must have gone by. He would inform the head warder that "Miss Interview" was due to visit him. He would wash himself with great care; he would soap his body and oil his long hair and beard before combing them. He would dress up before he went to meet his visitors. If they asked him any questions, he either remained silent or answered, "*O, pardi, anekas di, bedhyana di, moong di dal of di lantern.*"

Bishen Singh had a daughter who had grown into a full-bosomed lass of fifteen. But he showed no comprehension of his child. The girl wept bitterly whenever she met her father.

When talk of India and Pakistan came up, Bishen Singh began to question other lunatics about the location of Toba Tek Singh. No one could give him a satisfactory answer. His irritation mounted day by day. And now even "Miss Interview" did not come to see him. There was a time when something within had told him that his relatives were due. Now that inner voice had been silenced. And he was more anxious than ever to meet his relatives and find out whether Toba Tek Singh was in India or Pakistan. But no relatives came. Bishen Singh turned to other sources of information.

There was a lunatic in the asylum who believed he was God. Bishen Singh asked him whether Toba Tek Singh was in India or Pakistan. As was his wont, "God" adopted a grave mien and replied "We have not yet issued our orders on the subject."

Bishen Singh got the same answer many times. He pleaded with "God" to issue instructions so that the matter could be settled once and for all. His pleadings were in vain; "God" had many pressing matters awaiting "His" orders. Bishen Singh's patience ran out and one day he let "God" have a bit of his mind "*O, pardi, good good di, anekas di, bedhyana di, moong di dal of Wahi-i-Guru ji ka Khalsa and Wahi-i-Guru di Fateh! Jo boley so nihal, Sat Sri Akal.*"

This was meant to put "God" in his place—as God only of the Mussalmans. Surely if He had been God of the Sikhs, He would have heard the pleadings of a Sikh!

A few days before the day fixed for the exchange of lunatics, a Muslim from Toba Tek Singh came to visit Bishen Singh. This man had never been to the asylum before. When Bishen Singh saw him he turned away. The warders stopped him: "He's come to see you; he's your friend, Fazal Din," they said.

Bishen Singh gazed at Fazal Din and began to mumble. Fazal Din put his hand on Bishen Singh's shoulder. "I have been intending to see you for the last many days but could never find the time. All your family have safely crossed over to India. I did the best I could for them. Your daughter, Roop Kaur. . . ."

Fazal Din continued somewhat haltingly, "Yes . . . she too is well. She went along with the rest."

Bishen Singh stood where he was without saying a word. Fazal Din started again, "They asked me to keep in touch with you. I am told that you are to leave for India. Convey my *salaams* to brother Balbir Singh and to brother Wadhawa Singh . . . and also to sister Amrit Kaur . . . tell brother Balbir Singh that Fazal Din is well and happy. Both the grey buffaloes that they left behind have calved—one is a male, the other a female . . . the female died six days later. And if there is anything I can do for them, I am always willing. I have brought you a little sweet corn."

Bishen Singh took the bag of sweet corn and handed it over to a warder. He asked Fazal Din, "Where is Toba Tek Singh?"

Fazal Din looked somewhat puzzled and replied, "Where could it be? It's in the same place where it always was."

Bishen Singh asked again: "In Pakistan or India?"

"No, not in India; it's in Pakistan," replied Fazal Din.

Bishen Singh turned away mumbling, "*O, pardi, good good di, anekas di, bedhyana di, moong di dal of the Pakistan and Hindustan of dur phittey moonh.*"

Arrangements for the exchange of lunatics were completed. Lists with names of lunatics of either side had been exchanged and information sent to the people concerned. The date was fixed.

It was a bitterly cold morning. Bus-loads of Sikh and Hindu lunatics left the Lahore asylum under heavy police escort. At the border at Wagah, the Superintendents of the two countries met and settled the details of the operation.

Getting the lunatics out of the buses and handing over custody to officers of the other side proved to be a very difficult task. Some refused to come off the bus; those that came out were difficult to control: a few broke loose and had to be recaptured. Those that were naked had to be clothed. No sooner were the clothes put on them than they tore them off their bodies. Some came out with vile abuse, others began to

sing at the top of their voices. Some squabbled; others cried
or roared with laughter. They created such a racket that one
could not hear a word. The female lunatics added to the
noise. And all this in the bitterest of cold when people's teeth
chattered like the scales of rattlesnakes.

Most of the lunatics resisted the exchange because they
could not understand why they were being uprooted from one
place and flung into another. Those of a gloomier disposition
were yelling slogans, "Long Live Pakistan" or "Death to
Pakistan." Some lost their tempers and were prevented from
coming to blows in the very nick of time.

At last came the turn of Bishen Singh. As the Indian
officer began to enter his name in the register, Bishen Singh
asked him, "Where is Toba Tek Singh? In India or Pakistan?"

"In Pakistan."

That was all that Bishen Singh wanted to know.
He turned and ran back to Pakistan. Pakistani soldiers
apprehended him and tried to push him back towards India.
Bishen Singh refused to budge. Toba Tek Singh is on this
side he cried, and began to yell at the top of his voice "*O,
pardi, good good di, anekas di, bedhyana di, moong di dal of
Toba Tek Singh and Pakistan.*" They did their best to
soothe him, to explain to him that Toba Tek Singh must have
left for India; and that if any of that name was found in
Pakistan he would be dispatched to India at once. Bishen
Singh refused to be persuaded. They tried to use force. Bishen
Singh planted himself on the dividing line and dug his
swollen feet into the ground with such firmness that no one
could move him.

They let him be. He was soft in the head. There was no
point using force; he would come round of his own—yes.
They left him standing where he was and resumed the exchange
of the other lunatics.

Shortly before sunrise, a weird cry rose from Bishen
Singh's throat. The man who had spent all the nights and

days of the last fifteen years standing on his feet, now sprawled on the ground, face down. The barbed wire fence on one side marked the territory of India; another fence marked the territory of Pakistan. In the no man's land between the two barbed-wire fences lay the body of Bishen Singh of village Toba Tek Singh.

(Translated from the original in Urdu by Khushwant Singh)

17

SAADAT HASAN MANTO

The Reunion

THE SPECIAL TRAIN left Amritsar at two in the afternoon, arriving at Mughalpura, Lahore, eight hours later. Many had been killed on the way, a lot more injured and countless lost.

It was at 10 o'clock the next morning that Sirajuddin regained consciousness. He was lying on bare ground, surrounded by screaming men, women and children. It did not make sense.

He lay very still, gazing at the dusty sky. He appeared not to notice the confusion or the noise. To a stranger, he might have looked like an old man in deep thought, though this was not the case. He was in shock, suspended, as it were, over a bottomless pit.

Then his eyes moved and, suddenly, caught the sun. The shock brought him back to the world of living men and women. A succession of images raced through his mind. Attack . . . fire . . . escape . . . railway station . . . night . . . Sakina. He rose abruptly and began searching through the milling crowd in the refugee camp.

He spent hours looking, all the time shouting his daughter's name . . . Sakina, Sakina . . . but she was nowhere to be found.

Total confusion prevailed, with people looking for lost sons, daughters, mothers, wives. In the end, Sirajuddin gave up. He sat down, away from the crowd, and tried to think clearly. Where did he part from Sakina and her mother? Then it came to him in a flash—the dead body of his wife, her stomach ripped open. It was an image that wouldn't go away.

Sakina's mother was dead. That much was certain. She had died in front of his eyes. He coud hear her voice: "Leave me where I am. Take the girl away."

The two of them had begun to run. Sakina's *dupatta* had slipped to the ground and he had stopped to pick it up and she had said: "Father, leave it."

He could feel a bulge in his pocket. It was a length of cloth. Yes, he recognised it. It was Sakina's *dupatta,* but where was she?

Other details were missing. Had he brought her as far as the railway station? Had she got into the carriage with him? When the rioters had stopped the train, had they taken her with them?

All questions. There were no answers. He wished he could weep, but tears would not come. He knew then that he needed help.

A few days later, he got a break. There were eight of them, young men armed with guns. They also had a truck. They said they brought back women and children left behind on the other side.

He gave them a description of his daughter. "She is fair, very pretty. No, she doesn't look like me, but like her mother. About seventeen. Big eyes, black hair, a mole on the left cheek. Find my daughter. May God bless you."

The young men had said to Sirajuddin: "If your daughter is alive, we will find her."

And they had tried. At the risk of their lives, they had

driven to Amritsar, recovered many women and children and brought them back to the camp, but they had not found Sakina.

On their next trip out, they had found a girl on the roadside. They seemed to have scared her and she had started running. They had stopped the truck, jumped out and run after her. Finally, they had caught up with her in a field. She was very pretty and she had a mole on her left cheek. One of the men had said to her: "Don't be frightened. Is your name Sakina?" Her face had gone pale, but when they had told her who they were, she had confessed that she was Sakina, daughter of Sirajuddin.

The young men were very kind to her. They had fed her, given her milk to drink and put her in their truck. One of them had given her his jacket so that she could cover herself. It was obvious that she was ill-at-ease without her *dupatta*, trying nervously to cover her breasts with her arms.

Many days had gone by and Sirajuddin had still not had any news of his daughter. All his time was spent running from camp to camp, looking for her. At night, he would pray for the success of the young men who were looking for his daughter. Their words would ring in his ears: "If your daughter is alive, we will find her."

Then one day he saw them in the camp. They were about to drive away. "Son," he shouted after one of them, "have you found Sakina, my daughter?"

"We will, we will," they replied all together.

The old man again prayed for them. It made him feel better.

That evening, there was sudden activity in the camp. He saw four men carrying the body of a young girl found unconscious near the railway tracks. They were taking her to the camp hospital. He began to follow them.

He stood outside the hospital for some time, then went in.

In one of the rooms, he found a stretcher with someone lying on it.

A light was switched on. It was a young woman with a mole on her left cheek. "Sakina," Sirajuddin screamed.

The doctor, who had switched on the light, stared at Sirajuddin.

"I am her father," he stammered.

The doctor looked at the prostrate body and felt for the pulse. Then he said to the old man: "Open the window."

The young woman on the stretcher moved slightly. Her hands groped for the cord which kept her *salwar* tied round her waist. With painful slowness, she unfastened it, pulled the garment down and opened her thighs.

"She is alive. My daughter is alive," Sirajuddin shouted with joy.

The doctor broke into a cold sweat.

(Translated from the original in Urdu by Khalid Hasan)

18

SAADAT HASAN MANTO

A Tale of 1947

MUMTAZ WAS SPEAKING with great passion: "Don't tell me a hundred thousand Hindus and the same number of Muslims have been massacred. The great tragedy is not that two hundred thousand people have been killed, but that this enormous loss of life has been futile. The Muslims who killed a hundred thousand Hindus must have believed that they had exterminated the Hindu religion. But the Hindu religion is alive and well and will remain alive and well. And after putting away a hundred thousand Muslims, the Hindus must have celebrated the liquidation of Islam; but the fact is that Islam has not been affected in the least. Only the naive can believe that religion can be eliminated with a gun. Why can't they understand that faith, belief, devotion, call it what you will, is a thing of the spirit; it is not physical. Guns and knives are powerless to destroy it."

Mumtaz was very emotional that day. The three of us had come to see him off. He was sailing for Pakistan, a country we knew nothing about. All three of us were Hindus. He had relatives in West Punjab, now Pakistan, some of whom had lost their lives in anti-Hindu riots. Was this why Mumtaz was leaving us?

One day Jugal had received a letter which said that his uncle who lived in Lahore had been killed. He just couldn't believe it. He had told Mumtaz, "If Hindu-Muslim killings start here, I don't know what I'll do."

"What will you do?" Mumtaz had asked.

"I don't know. Maybe I'll kill you," he had replied darkly.

Mumtaz kept quiet and for the next eight days he didn't speak to anyone; on the ninth day he announced that he was sailing for Karachi that afternoon.

We had said nothing to him nor spoken about it. Jugal was intensely conscious of the fact that Mumtaz was leaving because of what he had said, "Maybe I'll kill you." He wasn't even sure if the heat of religious frenzy could actually bring him to kill Mumtaz, his best friend. That afternoon, Jugal was very quiet; it was only Mumtaz who didn't seem to want to stop talking, especially as the hour of departure drew close.

Mumtaz had started drinking almost from the moment he climbed out of bed. He was packing his things as if it was a picnic he was going to, telling jokes and then laughing at them himself. Had a stranger seen him that morning, he would have come to the conclusion that his departure from Bombay was the best thing that had ever happened to him. However, none of us were fooled by his boisterousness; we knew he was trying to hide his feelings, even deceive himself.

I tried a couple of times to talk about his sudden decision to leave Bombay, but he didn't give me an opportunity.

Jugal fell into an even deeper silence after three or four drinks and, in fact, left us to lie down in the next room. Brij Mohan and I stayed with Mumtaz. There was much to do. Mumtaz wanted to pay his doctor's bill; his clothes were still at the laundry, etc. He went through all these chores with the utmost aplomb. However, when we went to buy cigarettes from our regular shop in the corner, he put his hand on Brij Mohan's shoulder and said, "Do you remember, Brij . . . ten years ago when we were all starving, this shopkeeper, Gobind, lent us money?" His eyes were moist.

He didn't speak again till we got home—and then it was another marathon, an unending monologue on everything under the sun. Not much of what he was saying made a great deal of sense, but he was talking with such utter sincerity that both Brij Mohan and I had no option but to let him go on, getting in a word edgeways when we could. When it was time to leave, Jugal came in, but as we got into the taxi to go to the port, everyone became very quiet.

Mumtaz was looking out of the window, silently saying goodbye to Bombay, its wide avenues, its magnificent buildings. The port was crowded with refugees, mostly poor, trying to leave for Pakistan. But as far as I was concerned, only one man was leaving today, going to a country where no matter how long he lived he would always be a stranger.

After his baggage was checked in, Mumtaz asked us to come to the deck. Taking Jugal's hand, he said, "Can you see where sea and sky meet? It is only an illusion because they can't really meet but isn't it beautiful, this union which isn't really there?"

Jugal kept quiet. Perhaps he was thinking, "If it came to that, I may really kill you."

Mumtaz ordered cognac from the bar because that was what he had been drinking since morning. We stood there, all four of us, our glasses in our hands. The refugees had started to board. Jugal suddenly drank his glass down and said to Mumtaz, "Forgive me. I think I hurt you very deeply that day."

After a long pause, Mumtaz asked, "That day when you had said, 'It is possible I may kill you,' did you really mean that? I want to know."

Jugal nodded, "Yes, I am sorry."

"If you had killed me, you would have been even sorrier," Mumtaz said philosophically. "You would have realised that it wasn't Mumtaz, a Muslim, a friend of yours, but a human being you had killed. I mean, if he was a bastard, by killing him you wouldn't have killed the bastard in him; similarly, assuming that he was a Muslim, you wouldn't have killed his Muslimness, but him. If his dead body had fallen into the hands of Muslims, another grave would have sprung up in the graveyard, but the world would have been diminished by one human being."

He paused for breath, then continued, "It is possible that after you had killed me, my fellow Muslims may have called me a martyr. But had that happened, I swear to God, I would have leapt out of my grave and begun to scream, "I do not want this degree you are conferring on me because I never even took the examination. In Lahore, a Muslim murdered your uncle. You heard the news in Bombay and killed me. Tell me, what medals would that have entitled you to? And what about your uncle and his killer in Lahore? What honour would be conferred on them? I would say those who died were killed like dogs and those who killed, killed in vain."

"You are right," I said.

"No, not at all," he said in a tense voice. "I am probably right, but what I really wanted to say, I have not expressed very well. When I say religion or faith, I do not mean this infection which afflicts ninety-nine per cent of us. To me, faith is what makes a human being special, distinguishes him from the herd, proves his humanity."

Then a strange light came into his eyes. "Let me tell you about this man. He was a die-hard Hindu of the most disreputable profession, but he had a resplendent soul."

"Who are you talking about?" I asked.

"A pimp," Mumtaz said.

We were startled. "Did you say a pimp?" I asked.

He nodded. "Yes, but what a man, though to the world he

was a pimp, a procurer of women!" Then Mumtaz began his story.

"I don't remember his full name. It was something Sehai. He came from Madras and was a man of extremely fastidious habits. Although his flat was very small, everything was in its right place, neatly arranged. There were no beds, but lots of floor cushions, all spotlessly clean. A servant was around, but Sehai did most things himself, especially cleaning and dusting. He was very straight, never cheated and never told you anything which was not entirely true. For instance, if it was very late and the liquor had run out, he would say, 'Sahib, don't waste your money because in this neighbourhood they will only sell you rubbish at this hour.' If he had any doubts about a particular girl, he would tell you about them. He told me once that he had already saved up twenty thousand rupees. It had taken him three years, operating at twenty-five per cent. 'I need to make only another ten thousand and then I'll return to Benaras and start my own retail cloth business.' Why he wanted to earn no more than that I didn't know, nor did I have any idea what he found so attractive about the retail cloth trade."

"A strange man," I said.

Mumtaz continued: "First I thought, he cannot really be what he appears to be. Maybe he is nothing but a big fraud. After all, it was hard to believe that he considered and treated all the girls that he supplied to his customers as he would his own daughters. I also found it strange that he had opened a postal savings account for each of them and insisted that they should put their earnings there. There were some whose personal expenses he subsidised. All this was unreal to me because in the real world these things do not happen. One day when I went to see him, he said to me, 'Both Ameena and Sakeena have their weekly day off. You see, being Muslims, they like to eat meat once in a while, but none is cooked in this house because the rest of us are all strictly vegetarian.' One day he told me that the Hindu girl from Ahmedabad, whose marriage he had arranged with a Muslim client of his, had written from Lahore, 'I went to the shrine of the great saint Data Sahib and made a wish which has come true. I am going again to make another wish, which is that you should quickly make thirty thousand so that you can go to Benaras and start that retail cloth business of yours.' I had laughed, thinking that he was telling me this story about the popular Muslim saint only because I was Muslim."

"Were you wrong?" I asked Mumtaz.

"Yes—he really was what he appeared to be. I am sure he had his faults but he was a wonderful man."

"How did you find out that he wasn't a fraud?" Jugal, who hadn't spoken until now, asked.

"Through his death," Mumtaz replied. "The Hindu-Muslim killings had started. Early one morning, I was hurriedly walking through Bhindi Bazar, which was still deserted because of the night curfew. There were no trams running and taxis were out of the question. In front of the J. J. Hospital, I saw a man lying in a heap on the footpath. I first thought it was a *patiwala*, who was still sleeping, but then I saw blood and I stopped. I detected slight movement and bent down to look at the man's face. It was Sehai, I realised with a shock. I sat down on the bare footpath. The starched and spotless twill shirt that he habitually wore was drenched with blood. He was moaning. I shook him gently by the shoulder and called his name a couple of times. At first, there was no response but then he opened his eyes; they were expressionless. Suddenly, his whole body shook and I knew he had recognised me, 'It's you,' he whispered."

"I plied him with questions. What had brought him to this preponderantly Muslim locality at a time when people preferred to stay in their own neighbourhoods? Who had stabbed him? How long had he been lying here? But all he said was, 'My day is done; this was *Bhagwan's* will.'"

"I do not know what *Bhagwan's* will was, but I knew

mine. I was a Muslim. This was a Muslim neighbourhood. I
simply could not bear the thought that I, a Muslim, should
stand here and watch a man, whom I knew to be a Hindu, lie
there dying at the hands of an assassin who must have been
a Muslim. I, who was watching Sehai die, was a Muslim like
his killer. The thought did cross my mind that if the police
arrived on the scene I'd be picked up, if not on a murder
charge, certainly for questioning. And what if I took him to
the hospital? Would he, by way of revenge against the Muslims,
name me as his killer? He was dying anyway. I had an
irresistible urge to run, to save my own skin, and I might have
done that except he called me by my name. With an almost
superhuman effort, he unbuttoned his shirt, slipped his hand in
but did not have the strength to pull it out. Then he said in
a voice so faint I could hardly hear it, 'There's a packet in
there . . . it contains Sultana's ornaments and her twelve
hundred rupees . . . they were with a friend for safe
custody . . . I picked them up today and was going to return
them to her . . . these are bad times you know . . . I wanted
her to have her money and the ornaments . . . . Would you
please give them to her . . . tell her she should leave for a
safe place . . . but . . . please . . . look after yourself first!'"

Mumtaz fell silent, but I had the strange feeling that his
voice had become one with the dying voice of Sehai, lying on
the footpath in front of the J. J. Hospital; and together the
two voices had travelled to that distant blue point where sea
and sky met.

Mumtaz said, "I took the money and ornaments to Sultana,
who was one of Sehai's girls, and she started crying."

We stepped down the gangplank. Mumtaz was waving.

"Don't you have the feeling he is waving to Sehai?" I
asked Jugal.

"I wish I were Sehai," he said.

(Translated from the original in Urdu by Khalid Hasan)

19

SAADAT HASAN MANTO

*Xuda Ki Qasam**

THE COUNTRY HAD been divided. Hundreds of thousands of Muslims and Hindus were moving from India to Pakistan and from Pakistan to India in search of refuge. Camps had been set up to give them temporary shelter, but they were so overcrowded that it seemed quite impossible to push another human being into them, and yet more refugees were being brought in every day. There wasn't enough food to go round and basic facilities were almost non-existent. Epidemics and infections were common, but it didn't bother anybody. Such were the times.

The year 1948 had begun. Hundreds of volunteers had been assigned the task of recovering abducted women and children and restoring them to their families. They would go in groups to India from Pakistan and to Pakistan from India, to make their recoveries.

It always amused me to see that such enthusiastic efforts were being made to undo the effects of something which had been perpetrated by more or less the same people. Why were they trying to rehabilitate the women who had been raped and

* I Swear By God

taken away when they had let them be raped and taken away in the first place?

It was all very confusing, but one still admired the devotion of these volunteers.

It was not a simple task. The difficulties were enormous. The abductors were not easy to trace. To avoid discovery, they had devised various means of eluding their pursuers. They were constantly on the move, from this locality to that, from one city to another. One followed a tip and often found nothing at the end of the trail.

One heard strange stories. One liaison officer told me that in Saharanpur, two abducted Muslim girls had refused to return to their parents who were in Pakistan. Then there was this Muslim girl in Jullundar who was given a touching farewell by the abductor's family as if she was a daughter-in-law leaving on a long journey. Some girls had committed suicide on the way, afraid of facing their parents. Some had lost their mental balance as a result of their traumatic experiences. Others had become alcoholics and used abusive and vulgar language when spoken to.

When I thought about these abducted girls, I only saw their protruding bellies. What was going to happen to them and what they contained? Who would claim the end result? Pakistan or India?

And who would pay the women the wages for carrying those children in their wombs for nine months? Pakistan or India? Or would it all be put down in God's great ledger, if there were still any pages left?

The abducted women were being moved from this side to that, and that side to this, all the time.

Why were they being described as abducted women? I had always thought that when a woman ran away from home with her lover—the police always called it "abduction"—it was the most romantic act in the world. But these women had been taken against their will and violated.

They were strange, illogical times. I had boarded up all the doors and windows of my mind, shuttered them up. It was difficult to think straight.

Sometimes it seemed to me that the entire operation was being conducted like import-export trade.

One liaison officer said to me: "Why do you look lost?"

I didn't answer his question.

Then he told me a story.

"We were looking for abducted women from town to town, village to village, street to street, and days would go by sometimes before we would have any success.

"And almost every time I went across to what was now India, I would notice an old woman, the same old woman. The first time it was in the suburbs of Jullundar. She looked distracted, almost unaware of her surroundings. Her eyes had a desolate look, her clothes had turned to rags and her hair was coated with dust. The only thing that struck me about her was that she was looking for someone.

"I was told by one of the women volunteers that she had lost her mind because her only daughter had been abducted during the riots in Patiala. She said they had tried for months to find the girl but had failed. In all probability, she had been killed, but that was something the old woman was not prepared to believe.

"The next time I ran into her at Saharanpur. She was at the bus stop and she looked much worse than she had the first time I had seen her. Her lips were cracked and her hair looked matted. I spoke to her. I said she should abandon her futile search; and to induce her to follow my advice, I told her—it was brutal—that her daughter had probably been murdered.

"She looked at me. 'Murdered? No. No one can murder my daughter. No one can murder my daughter.'

"And she walked away.

"It set me thinking. Why was this crazy woman so

confident that no one could murder her daughter, that no sharp, deadly knife could slash her throat? Did she think her daughter was immortal or was it her motherhood which would not admit defeat, not entertain the possibility of death?

"On my third visit, I saw her again, in another town. She looked very old and ragged. Her clothes were now so threadbare that they hardly covered her frail body. I gave her a change of dress, but she didn't want it. I said to her: 'Old woman, I swear to you that your daughter was killed in Patiala.'

"You are lying," she said. There was steely conviction in her voice.

"To convince her, I said: 'I assure you I'm telling the truth. You've suffered enough. It's time to go to Pakistan. I'll take you.'

"She paid no attention to what I had said and began muttering to herself. 'No one can murder my daughter,' she suddenly declared in a strong, confident voice.

'Why?' I asked.

"'Because she's beautiful. She's so beautiful that no one can kill her. No one could even dream of hurting her,' she said in a low whisper.

"I wondered if her daughter was really as beautiful as she said. I thought: all children are beautiful to their mothers. It's also possible that the old woman is right. Who knows? But in this holocaust nothing has survived. This mad old woman is deceiving herself. There are so many ways of escape from unpleasant reality. Grief is like a roundabout which one intersects with an infinite number of roads.

"I made many other trips across the border to India, and almost every time I somehow ran into the old woman. She was no more than a bag of bones now. She could hardly see and tottered about like a blind person, a step at a time. Only one thing hadn't changed— her faith that her daughter was alive and that no one could kill her.

"One of the women volunteers said to me: 'Don't waste your time over her. She's raving mad. It would be good if you could take her to Pakistan with you and put her in an asylum.'

"Suddenly, I didn't want to do that. I didn't want to divest her of her only reason for living. As it was, she was in a vast asylum where nothing made any sense. I didn't wish to confine her within the four walls of a regular one.

"The last time I met her was in Amritsar. She looked so broken that it almost brought tears to my eyes. I decided that I would make one last effort to take her to Pakistan.

"There she stood in Farid Chowk, peering around with her half-blind eyes. I was talking to a shopkeeper about an abducted Muslim girl, who, we had been informed, was being kept in the house of a Hindu money-lender.

"After my exchange with the shopkeeper, I crossed the street, determined to persuade the old woman to come with me to Pakistan.

"I noticed a couple. The woman's face was partly covered by her white *chaddar*. The man was young and handsome— a Sikh.

"As they went past the old woman, the man suddenly stopped. He even fell back a step or two. Nervously, he caught hold of the woman's hand. I couldn't see her full face, but one glimpse had been enough to show that she was beautiful beyond words.

"'Your mother,' he said to her.

"The girl looked up, but only for a second. Then, covering her face with her *chaddar*, she grabbed her companion's arm and said: 'Let's get away from here.'

"They crossed the road, taking long, brisk steps.

"The old woman shouted: 'Bhagbari, Bhagbari.'

"I rushed towards her. 'What is the matter?' I asked.

"She was trembling. 'I have seen her . . . I have seen her.'

"Whom have you seen?' I asked.

'I have seen my daughter . . . I have seen Bhagbari.' Her eyes were like burnt-out lights.

'Your daughter is dead,' I said.

'You're lying,' she screamed.

'I swear on God your daughter is dead.'

'The old woman fell in a heap on the road."

(Translated from the original in Urdu by Khalid Hasan)

20

NARENDRA NATH MITRA

The Four-Poster

MAKBUL BROUGHT THE letter from the post office. He had
been to the Choudhurys' residence to deliver milk in his tiny
skiff. The village post office occupied a part of the building.
The Postmaster had handed the letter to him and he brought
it to Rajmohan Ray.

Rajmohan was hanging wet jute fibre on horizontal bamboo
poles in his courtyard. A servant and a maid were helping
him. The sight of the letter enraged him and he cursed, "Look
at what you have done, you son of a swine!"

"Why, what's wrong, master?" Makbul was surprised.
Rajmohan flared up again. "What's wrong? You want to
know what's wrong? Here, have a look at this letter. It's had
a good dip in the canal, hasn't it? Must you add water to
whatever you bring, as you dilute your milk, you rascal?"
Makbul looked grave. "Don't say that, master, I never add
water to milk. My boat needs a plank, master, that's why the
letter got wet. What can I do. You refused to give me a new
plank. I kept the letter near the bow, yet it got wet anyhow."

Rajmohan mimicked him sarcastically, "It got wet. Do
you think you'll get a plank out of me that way? You have
the brain of a devil, Makbul, I've never seen another one like

you. Oh, come now. You're not going already, are you? Take a little rest. Have a smoke before you go."

A tobacco box and an earthen bowl with live coals lay on the north verandah. A water pipe for the use of Muslims stood against a pillar. Grumbling to himself, Makbul went up there to take some tobacco.

Rajmohan finished hanging out the jute fibre and looked at the letter. He had recently undergone an operation and the cataract was removed. Without his glasses he could not read. "Kalu, bring my specs," he called to his servant. "They're over there next to the almanac on the table. Bring them to me."

He wiped the thick lenses of the nickel framed spectacles with care and put them on cautiously. As he looked at the envelope he broke into a smile. "It's my daughter-in-law's handwriting. She's written the address. The *babu* has no time to write. She can write better than he does anyway. Who'd guess this was written by a woman? Look at the letters, Kalu, they're wonderful, just like a man's. Look, Kalu, look for yourself."

Kalu, the fourteen-year-old servant, was illiterate. Still he peered at the English letters on the envelope and murmured in appreciation, "Right you are, master. The lady writes real nice. She looks dainty as she writes dainty, and she talks just as daintily. When she came last time, she gave me two rupees. Of course, I wouldn't take them but would she listen? This is how a respectable lady of your caste behaves, master, so different from us."

Kalu, was certainly tactful for his age. His comments seemed to please Rajmohan. Beaming, he said, "Caste isn't all there is to it, you silly boy. Think of the ancestral heritage, the family. Don't you see? The granddaughter of the famous Ambika Bose of Chandipur. What a man he was—in learning and wisdom he was without an equal around here. A daughter from that family—I didn't just pick anybody for my daughter-in-law."

He tore open the envelope and started reading the letter aloud. "You saw the handwriting Kalu, now mark the language. Do you think a lawyer could write better than this?"

He called Makbul too. "Come here, Makbul, listen to this."

Curious, the pipe and stand in hand, Makbul drew close. Rajmohan began,

"'Respected father,

"'It has been a long time since we heard from you. It worries us when we don't hear from you. When we think of you living there all alone with just a few servants, our hearts grow heavy with sadness. We are not near to look after you in your old age—the thought simply makes me miserable. But it can't be helped. You did not listen to us. You refused to leave Pakistan. All the neighbours have long ago sold their houses and property and moved here. The Banerjees, the Mukherjees, the Rahas, the Sahas, the Kundus, the Nandis— all of them have migrated to this part of the world. The village is practically deserted. Still, you preferred to stay alone, neither did you think of the future. But your friends and neighbours made some money while the going was good. They are men of means here. But you did nothing.

"It has come to our knowledge that you boast that you are not going to sell an inch of land or even a stick from what belongs to you. You would rather see the Muslims grab your property, loot your belongings, than sell them. Well, the property is yours, we have no right to say anything. You are perfectly entitled to do what you please.

"I am writing this letter today to request you to do me a favour. You know how damp and unhealthy our flat in Beleghata is. The children have to sleep on the floor. Your beloved Kanu, Tenu, Rina, Meena are laid up with fever. The medical bill is going up every month. When I ask your son to buy cots he says he is short of money. That is why I have this request to make. Please sell our four-poster bed, the

- 173 -

wedding gift from my grandfather. If you send that money we can try to get decent cots and beds for the children. I cannot bear to see their suffering.

"You cannot possibly object to this. The four-poster doesn't belong to you, really. It was part of my dowry. If you sell that it won't hurt your prestige. You can tell others that I'm selling it. This is the jute season, the right time. The Muslims have got plenty of money. Besides, there is no one to sleep on the bed. So is there any sense in keeping it? It is better to sell it than have it eaten by termites. The money will be of good use to the children. Your son agrees with me.

"We are all well. Your son is very busy. He will write when he finds time. Please arrange to sell the bed immediately. Do write to us. With deepest regards.

Your loving
Asima."

Suren, his son, added a line to endorse what Asima wrote. "I think you won't object to what Asima has asked for."

"No, no, no objection, no objection. Let them do what they wish."

Rajmohan threw the letter away as he called his servant, "You there, Kalu. Go get that four-poster bed from the east room. I'll see to it that this piece of furniture is removed from the room and goes to rack and ruin. She isn't pleased with taking away whatever belonged to her, now she must have the four-poster. I'm not going to keep it anymore. And look at that henpecked husband, I mean that son of mine . . . 'I don't think you should have any objection' . . . Why should I? I am not going to rest in peace till I throw that confounded bed out of my sight. Go, move that bed, Kalu."

Kalu tried to stop him, "Listen to me, master."

"No, no I'm not going to listen to anyone, Kalu. My word

is final. That bed is as good as a urinal to me. No, Kalu, that bed must be removed. The sight of it sets my whole body burning."

Rajmohan threw open the door leading to the east room and went in. Suren and Asima used this room whenever they came home on holidays. Their last visit was a year ago. Placed close to the two southern windows, the bed was carefully covered with dustsheets. Rajmohan would come in every day to see if it was safe from termites. He would dust it himself with the towel he carried on his shoulder. A picture of the couple hung from the wall on the east. Bunches of dry jute and paddy lay heaped on the floor.

Makbul had followed him to the door. Rajmohan said, "Come in, Makbul, take that stuff away."

"Are you serious about selling it? Do you really want to sell it, master?" asked Makbul.

Rajmohan was positive. "Yes, I do. If I find ready cash. I would sell it and send a money order to Calcutta right away."

The room had no image of gods or pitchers of drinking water—nothing in fact to stop the low caste labourers from entering the room now. So Makbul got through the doors to the room.

He looked greedily at the beautiful teak four-poster bed, with tigers' paws for its legs. Elegantly elaborate designs flanked the sides with a row of tiny elephants in between.

"Would you sell this, master?" Makbul asked again. "But of course you should, after this insulting letter from the daughter-in-law, a self-respecting man like you should never keep it. I'll tell you something. Why don't you give it to me?"

Rajmohan stared at him. "To you?" he said.

"Why not, master," Makbul continued. "Of course, I wouldn't take it free. I'll pay for it, as much as I can. You just wanted to throw it away. The dump and my house would be the same thing to you. Please let me have it, master."

Still smouldering inside, Rajmohan thought it over. Makbul was right, he concluded. Mean as his daughter-in-law was, this would serve her right. This is the proper place for it, the home of a common labourer. He accepted the offer.

Looking at Makbul, he enquired, "If you have the cash ready then take it—clear my room of this dirt at once."

"All right, master, please have it dismantled while I go home and get the money." Makbul strode towards his house in hot haste.

To the south of Rajmohan's home an abandoned building lay in ruins. There was a narrow ditch beyond, which was filled up during rains but was dry in summer. Over this ditch Makbul ran, balancing on the single bamboo pole which served as a bridge. There was another pole higher up to be used as a railing and hand-rest. This bamboo stretched from a mango tree on the deserted ground to the trunk of a tamarind tree on the other side. Under this tamarind tree was a hut with a rusty, corrugated iron roof. This was Makbul's home. The walls were made of woven twigs of bamboo, and jute strips. Puddles of water formed near the walls, a few earthworms dug their shelter through them. The small yard in front was wet and slushy. The water from the canal almost touched the foundations. A handsome young woman of twenty-two wearing a blue *sari* sat cutting watercress. Two thin and famished children played around with water weeds. A string round the waist from which dangled a single coin was all each had on. Along the east side of the yard, jute sticks were hung up to dry, to serve as fuel later, as well as building material. Partly hidden from sight was an emaciated cow munching hay and occasionally flapping its tail.

Breathless from running, Makbul approached his wife, "Get up, Fati, get up. Get some money, quick."

Fatima stared at her husband, her big eyes wide with amazement. Throwing the end of her *sari* on her head, she said, "Say, who are you talking to? Where do I get the money from?"

Makbul smiled mysteriously, "You'll see." Then he told her about the secret store, where in a hollowed bamboo branch, he had saved a few currency notes, procured bit by bit, selling jute and milk, occasionally a couple of trees.

But Fatima was reluctant to part with it. "Didn't you promise to buy a cow, don't you know the house needs repair, besides, what about the jewellery you said you'd buy for me with that money? Kill me first, before you take that money from me."

Her outburst amused Makbul. But he said with affection, "It's more than a piece of jewellery, Fati, you haven't seen the like of it, neither have I."

Then he went into all the details about what a bargain it was, that they should not let this chance of a lifetime slip through their fingers. Once the master relents, the offer would be gone. So they must act quickly, before somebody else gets it. When the Hindus left their furniture, their utensils were practically sold for a song. But Makbul never had any money, he could never touch anything. Now when chance had brought a valuable bed to his door, why not have it. He should have at least one object worth having.

"But where would you keep that princely possession in this shabby hut?" Fatima was sceptical.

Makbul lifted her chin towards him, "If my hut is good for the light of my heart, it will be good enough for the bed," he said.

He took fifty rupees out of their bamboo box and then rushed back. Around the decrepit old house, Yakub, the watchman, was searching for creepers for making fishing rods. He saw Makbul hurrying by. "What's the haste for, man?" he shouted after him. "Who is it? Oh, Yakub! Would you come with me for a minute, Come on quick. I'll make you a fishing rod later; hurry now."

Makbul held his hand and resumed running.

When he arrived at Rajmohan's house the old man had brought the bed out in the yard. Makbul put the money near his feet. "Here you are, master," he said. "Here's your money."

"What do I want money for? Take the bed and throw it into the river. I have got nothing to do with it," said Rajmohan.

Makbul replied, "If it had been your own, I would have asked for it. Since this belongs to the mistress, being a gift from her parents, I must pay for it. Please take the money on her behalf and send it to her, master."

His words struck the old man like an arrow. True it wasn't his property. Asima had made that quite clear in her letter, every line of which stung him like a poisonous snake.

"All right, all right," he shouted, "that daughter of a bitch is after money, she'll have it, you take this out of my sight, Makbul. It is not a bed, it's my funeral pyre. Take it away."

With assistance from Yakub, Makbul crossed the canal on a boat, taking the bed.

Yakub said, "It was quite a bargain, brother. This bed would have fetched at least two hundred, I tell you."

Makbul evaded the question of price. He said, "That old miser! So many of the Hindus left, but would he budge a step from here. He stays, keeping guard on all he has—the wicked old miser. We can't touch a single fruit of his orchard. Who would live in that house when he dies—but us? I'll be damned if Suren comes back."

"You are right there," admitted Yakub. "He has gone for good. Won't dare come to Pakistan."

Makbul went on, "Let him close his eyes, then I'll make that home of his a true piece of Pakistan. My family would walk on those cement floors. You say I had a bargain, but I tell you what. This was a dead loss. I would have got this for nothing—it was just a matter of waiting."

But as he thought over the blissful prospect, he seemed to change his mind. "No, brother, I didn't mean that really. It's much better to pay for something rather than snatch it. People won't talk then. Isn't that right?"

"Right, brother," said Yakub.

News soon spread through the village. People of means crowded to Rajmohan to verify if he had really sold that beautiful piece of furniture for a mere fifty rupees. It was unbelievable. Rajmohan had never sold as much as a bunch of hay before.

Said Sarat, "Have you gone off your head, master? I would have given you a hundred and fifty—easy."

Gedu Munshi went a step ahead. "What is all this nonsense. I would have paid two hundred and fifty; why didn't you ask me, sir?"

Rajmohan was suddenly angry. "Get out, all of you. I didn't sell it, I threw it away. Now go away."

Before they went, one of them stayed back to make a final request. He was Chandan Mridha, a wealthy and respectable Muslim farmer. "If you ever decide to sell chairs, tables, trunks or anything—please let me know first. I'll pay the right price, I wouldn't cheat you, master."

Rajmohan chased him out of the house. "Will you be off, Mridha. Take whatever I have when I die. I haven't sold anything yet and I am not going to sell a single thing as long as I am alive."

They slunk away, intimidated. The old master has gone off his head, they whispered among themselves. Imagine living in this deserted house without children and grandchildren; no wonder he has come to this end.

When they went away, Rajmohan realised his foolishness. He had been cheated, there was no mistake about that. His own ill temper was responsible. He had eaten off the floor out of anger for the thief who took away his plates. What an utterly silly thing to do.

Finally, he made up his mind. "Kalu," he called the servant, "Get the boat ready. I'm going to Kumarpur."

Rajmohan used to draft documents in the office of the Registrar there. Kumarpur was about a mile and a half from Sonapur. Though now his services were no longer required by customers, Rajmohan insisted on spending some time at the office premises in the hope of procuring work.

When people asked him why he was troubling himself at this age, Rajmohan would say: "I have to lose my night's sleep otherwise."

Kalu took out the small boat, "Wouldn't you have some lunch, master?" he enquired.

"That won't be necessary, Kalu, you have had your meal, haven't you? That'll do." Then suddenly, he grasped his servant by the hands and broke down, "Oh, Kalu, what did I do, I ate mud with my own hands—Kalu."

"Didn't I tell you, master," Kalu stopped in some confusion. As he stared at the helpless old man he did not know how to comfort him. Then he spoke quietly, "Come on, master."

In his prime the master had been as handsome as a prince. He was undoubtedly the most handsome man in the village. The fair master they called him. Now at the ripe old age of sixty-five, his massive shoulders drooped, his skin was creased, his complexion had lost much of its glow. But in a way he was still the fair master.

From his hair down to his moustache and the hair on his chest, he was white as ripe jute through and through.

"Get in, master," said Kalu.

"Coming, coming." Worn out, with slippers in hand, Rajmohan got into the boat. His shirt was not too clean, his umbrella was patched. With sadness weighing heavy on him, Rajmohan went up the river.

When he came back at night the first thing he did was to enter the now empty east room where the bed had once stood. In the dim glow of the lantern, the sight shocked him. He hurried out, but the vision of emptiness kept haunting him. He felt as though with that bed he had given away his all.

Even at his night prayer the east room and the empty space came crowding into his head, making him forget his ritual.

He felt utterly alone and remembered the face of his wife who had died long ago. Though he had everybody yet nobody cared for him. He was alone in this big world.

Next morning he sent Kalu to fetch Makbul, but he did not come. He said he was busy then, he would see the master as soon as he found time.

Rajmohan gnashed his few remaining teeth in anger. "The son of a bitch! I called him and his lordship is busy. I'll see how busy he can be."

Kalu said sympathetically, "What can you do, master. This is their day, their government. The saplings are more stubborn than bamboos." Rajmohan only said "Hmm."

After a while, he limped towards Makbul's cottage, across the canal, past the wild bushes.

"Makbul, are you busy?" he called.

Makbul was just back after delivering milk. He was helping his wife make twine. Fatima went inside as she heard Rajmohan. Makbul showed him in.

But his diffidence was only too apparent. Still he offered him his own wooden seat and said, "I would have come to you, master, why did you trouble yourself?"

Rajmohan said, "Oh, just to visit you. To see how you were doing. Your new room has been built well I see, big enough for your family. But why did you put old iron sheets on the roof, pull them out and put new ones."

Makbul said, "I wish I could do it, master, but where is the money? I have been wanting to buy another cow and a new boat—but money is the problem."

Keeping his voice low, Rajmohan said, "I've brought you money."

Makbul stared at him, "What did you say?"

"I have things to talk over with you. Come with me." Rajmohan walked down to the courtyard.

But Makbul did not move. He said, "There is hardly a soul here. You can talk." Rajmohan did not listen to him. He almost dragged him out of the house.

The whole area was overgrown with wild shrubs. Canals surrounded it on three sides and the river on the other. Houses belonging to a few other Muslims stood like islands isolated by water. Rajmohan walked up to a bamboo grove in the south-east corner.

"What's the matter, master?" asked Makbul.

From the belt of his cloth Rajmohan took out the notes Makbul had given him the day before, and he had a new five rupee note. "Here, count these," he said. "There's fifty-five in all, and five rupees for buying sweets for the family—that's extra."

Makbul had understood his intention from the start. He kept his bloodshot eyes directed straight at Rajmohan. Tall, square and black as a tree, this young man with long bushy hair somehow looked ominous. The beard he wore made him look like an animal. Rajmohan felt uneasy. He moved back a few steps.

"Don't be scared, master," Makbul gave a short laugh. "I'm not going to hurt you. After all, you are an old man and a respectable person. I couldn't insult you, could I? But take your money back. My kids don't eat sweets, they get worms if they do. You go home, master, I'm not going to return that bed."

Rajmohan felt the tip of his hairy ears burning in shame and humiliation. He tucked the money back into his belt and said, "All right, all right. But remember Makbul Sheikh, winter is not over in a year, it will come back next December. You may have got your Pakistan, but that doesn't make all of you Governors."

When he was gone Fatima came out. "Why did the master shout so?" She was afraid.

"Oh, him!" Makbul answered. "He wants back the bed he sold me. Tried to tempt me with money."

"Good gracious," exclaimed his wife. "What did you tell him?" "I begged him to take away my wife instead," Makbul gave her a sly smile.

Fatima was surprised. She said bashfully, "You said that to the old man? Do you have no shame?" Makbul did not answer. He was enjoying his own joke.

Now Fatima realised that this was not the nature of the argument Makbul had had with the master, that he was only teasing her.

"Well, if your wife means so much to you then why are you gone crazy over this bed of his? Why don't you give it back to whom it belongs? He isn't a straightforward person. Who's going to stop him if he wants to do mischief? When I think of the children, I tremble with fear inside my heart," said Fatima.

Makbul looked at his wife's well-formed body and said, "Trembling heart! Let your heart tremble, that's when you look best, honey."

Fatima quickly covered her bosom with the end of her *sari*. "Is that a decent way to talk?" she said shyly. "You have the eyes of—" she could not find an apt comparison.

Makbul laughed and said, "They are the eyes of a young man, Fati, that's the way they are; they look at injustice and glow in anger, they glance at young and beautiful things and admire."

A couple of days later Makbul was called again to Rajmohan's house. In the spacious north verandah, two carpets were spread with smoking paraphernalia on the floor and two separate water pipes for Hindus and Muslims.

All the caste-Hindus having left the village, those who remained were low-born and dark—and most of them were obliged to Rajmohan. In some way or other, he had helped them in adversity. Among the Hindus were Sarat Sheel, Murari Mondal, Fatik Karmakar and Nibaran Rajak. The Muslims present were Chandan Mridha, Badan Sikdar and Gedu Munshi.

No sooner had Makbul arrived on the scene, Gedu Munshi began with an air of self-imposed superiority. "That wasn't quite fair, son of the Sheikh. All the Hindu gentlemen have left, but only the old master could not break our ties. He still loves us more than anything else. We still till his land, visit his house, come to him in need. You must restore what belongs to him."

"*Munshi Sahib*, please don't make such unjust requests. The master himself has sold the bed to me. He took money for it. Ask Yakub, the watchman, he was a witness. How can he ask for it now?"

Rajmohan sat glumly on a wooden seat. He turned up the wick of the lantern and raised his voice at the same time, "I took money? How can you say that? Do you think fifty rupees is any price for the bed?"

"That's what you asked then," said Makbul. "Besides, that was all I could pay. I could not possibly pay more. The price depends on one's power to pay—doesn't it?"

Sarat Sheel remarked, "That would hardly hold water, Makbul. You don't have the power to pay but somebody else has. So either hand him over another hundred or give back his stuff."

The Hindus nodded assent but the Muslims kept quiet. They smoked by turn and the problem did not come any nearer a solution.

"If that is what you call justice, I don't go by it," declared Makbul. You may go to the law court, I don't care."

"Shut up, you have got a big mouth, you mean fellow," said Gedu Munshi.

When Makbul left, the Muslims tried to pacify Rajmohan. "Don't you mind him, master," they said. "He is as stubborn as a mule; who doesn't know it? He doesn't listen to arguments. We'll see what we can do, master. What would he do with that bed? But you too have not acted very wisely. You've really left nothing for us to say."

They left one by one. Then Sarat said, "These Muslims are all one, master. Makbul has their secret support, or how could he have the cheek to defy us? You have to swallow it, master, there is no other way. The times are not good. You have lost a single bed. So many have given away their houses and lands, practically for nothing. What does it matter, really? They got their lives to live. You are not going to die for the loss of that bed, master. You can stack your room with five such beds if you wish, who doesn't know that? Now go to bed, master, it is late already."

Sarat smoked for a while, then he took his leave.

The lamp hurt his eyes. Rajmohan put the light out and sat in darkness. Kalu was already asleep on his matting. Not a soul stirred outside. Rajmohan once again measured the extent of his loneliness. He felt helpless against this onslaught of humiliation. Only if his son was here now, by his side, he would have felt so much stronger. But would he? Neither would Rajmohan ask him. Let him live happily where he is.

The father and son separated not because they had a quarrel. They simply did not understand each other. Suren did not care for the things his father valued more than anything—the ancestral home, the land, the paddy and jute fields, the village. He did not understand the country and her people. Books and books, that was all he was ever interested in. He left home long before Pakistan came into being. Now, the father and son were citizens of two different nations. They belonged to two different eras.

Wind stirred the leaves of the *deodar* tree—it had grown so tall. Rajmohan had planted it himself, it was of the same age as Suren, his son. At least the *deodar* did not desert him like Suren.

It seemed to Rajmohan that in his friendless world the *deodar* was all he had. It did not care for Hindustan or Pakistan, it did not change with a few years of education. It stood firm on the ancestral soil.

He had had offers for this tree also, even to the extent of twenty-one rupees. But Rajmohan had always been adamant as far as selling his property went. "I buy, I don't sell," he would say with pride.

Never in his life had he agreed to sell anything until now. Why did he do it? His heart ached. What madness had seized him? Would he ever be able to get it back? He had fought for and got back the property of so many and now when it came to something of his own, would he give up? No, he must get it back, by hook or by crook.

It was easier thought than done. Makbul was not his direct employee, nor did he borrow money. He could not very well bring false charges. Even if he tried, it would be difficult to fabricate evidence against a Muslim, now that it was Pakistan. It would serve no purpose except infuriate the big guns of the Muslim community.

As he could not devise ways to punish him, Rajmohan tried meaner tactics. He used to buy half a *seer* of milk from Makbul, now he stopped that. Instead, he asked Wahed for his daily supply. He even went to the extent of asking other labourers to work for him, boycotting Makbul as far as it was in his power to do.

Makbul was not a farmer in the proper sense, but worked as a hired hand for others occasionally. During the jute season he would wash jute fibre, in the paddy harvest he would join other labourers. When the harvest season was over he would cut firewood and do all sorts of small jobs. Rajmohan used to employ him for various errands but now he boycotted him completely. Ever since the Hindus left, Makbul had fallen on evil days. Most of the Muslim landlords would do the manual jobs themselves. Makbul was in a real fix.

Through Kalu all the news reached Rajmohan. While rowing to Kumarpur, Kalu said, "The son of the Sheikh has been served right. Now he'll starve to death. He thought he

could outwit you—what hopes! He doesn't have the sense
worth one of your teeth."

Rajmohan's hollow cheeks spread in a self-contented smile.
"If I had all my teeth, though."

"What you've got is enough, master," Kalu assured him.
"Your gums are strong enough to ruin him."

Makbul was really on the verge of ruin. He swore to his
wife viciously, "I'll wait for a couple of days more. Then I'm
going to rob him in front of his very eyes, and then I'm
going to cut his throat." Fatima got frightened. "Don't—I
won't have you think of such things."

"Why not," retorted her husband. "So I'll be hanged? All
right. But Rajmohan will be dead as well."

"But what about us," wailed his wife "We'll be left here,
what would happen to us? Don't you lose your temper. You
have a family now. You must not be headstrong. Feed your
children, that's how you prove your worth. That'll mean that
you are a real man."

Makbul gave a grunt.

"What do you mean by that?" Fatima went on. "It's very
easy to show off and threaten. What temper! Can you take
care of your children like a father should? That shows a man!
Have you ever cared to look at my little darlings, my Sabdul
and Manju, to see that they are not reduced to bones?" She
drew her two rickety children near her and caressed them, as
if love was any substitute for nourishment.

Casting angry eyes full upon his wife, Makbul shouted:
"Don't drive me crazy, don't you drive me to murder, woman."

Fatima held him by the hand. "Please, listen to me. Give
the master's bed back to him. What do we need such luxuries
for. If we can have rice twice every day, then our simple
matting would be good enough—we'll sleep in peace."

Makbul broke loose from his wife's grasp and said, "Shut
up, Fati, I'll break your big jaw if you keep on saying the
master's bed, the master's bed—it doesn't belong to him,

understand? Did I steal the bed? I paid good money to buy it. It's mine, mine. So keep your bloody mouth shut."

Makbul went inside the room and grabbed his proud possession by one of the posts as though it was going to be taken away from him.

A little later, he sharpened his axe and went out in search of work. But most of the villagers could not afford hired help. Makbul got no work. He went about with vengeance in mind, but did not have the guts to murder Rajmohan. Instead, he satisfied himself by stealing fruits from his garden. He took a couple of green coconuts, and a bunch of nuts.

In due course, this came to Rajmohan's knowledge. He cursed and threatened to call the police, then employed a local lad to watch over his garden.

But nuts and coconuts do not appease hunger. Makbul's hunt for food made him take leave of his senses. Usually the rainy season is a bad time for all labourers. The price of rice and cereals goes up, jobs become scarce. But this was the worst year of all. The jute season was over, the paddy season hadn't started. Houses were water-logged, nobody had a handful of rice.

Now that his small savings were gone in purchasing the four-poster, Makbul was absolutely broke. At home his wife constantly quarrelled, the children went wild. Fatima sometimes boiled bits of rice with wild roots or caught shrimps using her *sari* as a net.

One day Kalu came to visit. "Hello Makbul, how are you all?"

This made Makbul pucker his brow. "I'm all right. How are you, rich servant of the rich gentleman?"

Kalu lost no time in disclosing the purpose of his visit. "The master is now willing to pay you ten more, so why don't you come round, mister?"

Makbul almost sprang on him. "Get out, get out of my

house. If I find you again uttering such filthy words, I'll break your legs, I warn you."

Kalu left, but was soon followed by others. Chandan Mridha and Gedu Munshi came secretly, offering more money. The master wouldn't know, and why should Makbul care even if he heard?

The price went up to seventy-five. But Makbul was still not willing. He bought it for use, and he must use it.

Both the customers went away, flinging swear words at him. "Take your bed with you to the grave."

Even Fatima lost her temper. "What kind of man are you. If this had been a cow, a tree or a measure of land I would have understood, but what's the sense of keeping this dead junk which would neither yield crops nor bear fruit."

Makbul looked fondly at her, then said. "That's not for a woman like you to understand, Fatima. It's not a piece of dead wood, Fati, it means my price. The self-respect of a man."

"Self-respect," Fati pooh-poohed the notion. "If you are so self-respecting why don't you go out and seek some work. I hear this is Pakistan now, the Government of the Muslims. Why must we starve then?"

Makbul had tried all sources, but there was no job for a poor, illiterate man like him.

At his wife's remark he smiled sadly. "The poor like us have no Pakistan or Hindustan, Fati. The grave is the only place we have any right to claim."

Then he sold the cow. It had gone dry for want of fodder. Next he sold the skiff. With the money he bought an old ferry boat, the rest he gave to Fatima. For days he rowed his boat up to Kumarpur. If luck favoured he earned a rupee or so, but these were gloomy days when no passenger turned up. Sometimes he sailed away to far off villages. On those days he didn't return home but slept in the boat tied to the landing place.

It was one of those days when he had gone out, Fatima

sat lighting her stove and getting ready to cook. Rajmohan appeared. "Makbul, are you at home?"

Fatima hastily hid behind the hedges. She sent her son to tell the master that father was out and what was it that he wanted?

The son was shy and stupid for his five years. So Fatima had to speak. She spoke through the hedge. Rajmohan told her. "I have got a bad cough. I heard you have a *vasaka* tree, the juice is good for cough. May I pluck a few leaves?"

Fatima smiled, "Why, of course, master, let me get them for you." "No, no, don't bother. I will get them."

Rajmohan slowly ascended on to the verandah. As he cast a look inside the room, something in him snapped. Oh, his four-poster, his four-poster. He couldn't bear to look at the state it was in. Lime and grease stains ruined the beautiful carved legs. The rag of a mattress and a couple of oily pillows and quilts lay on it! What a shame. These people are not worthy of the four-poster. What do they know about taking care of such treasure!

Rajmohan talked for a while, then said, "If you don't mind, daughter, I'll tell you something. Talk some sense into your husband. I'll give him whatever price he wants, but he must give my bed back."

From the other side of the hedge Fatima answered politely, "No, master, I can't do that. You take your *vasaka* leaves and please don't broach this topic again." She went inside.

After this slap on the face, Rajmohan lost all desire to pluck the leaves. He still sat as long as he could, staring at his four-poster through the hedge. Then he plucked some leaves before he departed, the pretence had to be kept up.

Rajmohan went home, took his bath, and thus cleansed, entered the shrine and sat before the image of Radhagovinda. Looking at the smiling Govinda, he prayed, "O my dear God, please help me get rid of all earthly possessions. Take me to your Vrindaban of eternal happiness, let the red dust of its alleys hide all my shame."

For a time he felt purged, but the next day he once again felt an urgent need to visit Makbul for the vasaka leaves. To convince Kalu he had to feign a cough.

Fatima heard him coming. She was afraid lest the master should harp on the same subject and so she did not come before him. Rajmohan understood, still he went through the pretension of plucking *vasaka* leaves, then sat on the verandah and chatted with Makbul's son Sabdul, since nobody else was around. He peered through the wall at the bed. As days went by Makbul's *vasaka* tree grew leafless but Rajmohan's cough showed no sign of improvement.

Makbul was sceptical about those visits. One night when he came back from work he said to his wife, "What is this about the master coming over everyday? I hear he sits on the verandah?"

"Oh, yes," said Fatima, "He comes to get some leaves of the *vasaka* tree."

"Nonsense," Makbul smiled indulgently, "The old man has taken a fancy to you."

Fatima said angrily, "Of course not."

Makbul said, "Then come to the point."

"Point? Don't you know it?"

"Yes I do. But careful, if you are tempted by money to sell it back then I'm going to kill you, Fati."

"Are you mad?" said Fatima. "I avoid him precisely for that reason. But the old man keeps eyeing the bed. I don't like it a bit. His curse might poison our whole family. I am so scared."

Makbul assured her, "Oh come on. He is a snake that has lost its venom. It won't do us harm. Don't you worry. I'll tell him tomorrow that if he steps into my house again I'm going to break his leg in two."

But before the threat could be conveyed to him Rajmohan

was down with high fever and blood-dysentery. The village doctor said that his son should be informed. "It doesn't look good to me, sir," he said. "After all, you have your age to consider."

But Rajmohan shook his head as he rejected the notion. "No, doctor, not now. If the time comes I myself will let him know. I hear a promotion is due at his office. I don't want him to lose it by coming away."

He had sent two hundred rupees to his daughter-in-law. She might not believe that the bed was sold for fifty. In the meantime Rajmohan's health grew worse. The doctor came everyday.

Misfortunes piled on Makbul. His boat was stolen in Naopara. He knew perfectly well who the culprits were. The village was notorious for thieves, and Gedu Munshi was friendly with those characters. Makbul managed to catch a boat home. But with his cow and the boat gone, his luck also ran out and it was worse than ever. Now only the house and the bed were left for him to sell.

Rajmohan heard it all. Sarat Sheel remarked, "This serves him right. This is the result of daring to disobey you." A couple of days later, Kalu brought another bit of news.

"Have you heard, master?"

Rajmohan answered slowly, "Heard what?"

"This Makbul is going to sell the bed to Atajaddi of village Talkanda. Atajaddi will furnish his new home with it."

"Let him," Rajmohan was disinterested.

"He has offered one hundred and fifty."

"I see."

"Atajaddi is coming over with the money this evening."

"I see." Rajmohan said and turned over on his other side.

Kalu went to see a play in the neighbouring village that afternoon. He left early, to get good seats. The maid brought a bowl of soup. Rajmohan did not touch it. He stirred restlessly in the bed as the night grew dark and quiet outside. Suddenly, he got up, and in the darkness he groped for his walking stick. He could not walk very well, still he came out, locking the room.

There was a drizzle outside, but he took neither a lantern nor an umbrella. Groping and tottering, he made his way towards Makbul's house.

Fifteen minutes later he was standing in Makbul's yard. "Makbul, you son of a bitch, come out," he called in a voice faint with weakness.

Makbul came out, "Who is it? Is it the master?" Rajmohan's answer did not rise beyond a whisper. "Yes, it's me. So you sold the bed, you rascal! And you did not even tell me."

Makbul stood speechless in the dark. Then he said quietly, "Who told you?"

"Things like this can't be hidden."

"But how did you come in this darkness and rain, how did you cross the ditch?"

"I walked on the mud bank."

"Good God! Come in, master."

"I'm not going to enter your house now, you have done the worst.

"No master, I haven't yet," Makbul said. "Come and see for yourself."

He took the sick old man gently into the room, his bare body burning with fever. He was without even his spectacles.

Makbul woke his wife. "Light a lamp, quick."

Fatima was lying almost unconscious on the bed. She woke with a start, then got down from the bed.

She tried to cover her face with the torn end of her *sari*, as she lifted the kerosene lamp with the other hand. The two children lay like two corpses on the bed.

Rajmohan said, "So it is still there. It hasn't been sold."

"It is here, master."

"Didn't Atajaddi come?"

"He came, he offered ten more. I asked for time. We

haven't had any food for the last two days. Still I refused him, master. The wife kept crying, hunger was hurting so. Master, do you know what I told her? I told her—give me one night's time, woman, just this night. Hold your stomach tight and let me keep my pride just for this night, just for tonight."

Rajmohan said, "Makbul."

Makbul replied, "Master."

They did not utter a word. Fatima held the lamp before them. In that pale smoky light, the two men faced each other across the barriers of age, race and faith with the same passion for beauty in their heart.

After a while, Makbul told his wife, "Fati, get the kids down. I'll dismantle the bed."

"Makbul, what did you say?" Rajmohan asked.

"Yes, master, take it back. I've kept it till today. Who knows about tomorrow?"

Makbul was going to wake his children, but Rajmohan stopped him. "Don't," he said. And he continued as if speaking to himself, "I used to come to look at the bed. But what I saw was just an empty pedestal. Today I have seen my Radha and Govinda on it. My God has returned. Makbul, take me home."

Taking the lamp from his wife Makbul said, "Come along, master."

(Translated from the original in Bengali by Enakshi Chatterjee)

21

GIANI GURMUKH SINGH MUSAFIR

The Broken Shoes

THIS WAS WHEN the shoes were not broken. Wherever Vairag went, people noticed them. Those who knew him made endless enquiries; even strangers had the temptation of asking him about his shoes. Vairag had hardly a friend who had not requested him at least once to get for him the like of his shoes. "I say, Vairag where did you get this pair of shoes from? When? How much did it cost? Who got it for you?" Every time someone asked him about his shoes, he felt happy. He was never put off. He seemed to enjoy it. In fact, if someone ignored his shoes, it made him unhappy. Vairag met with a number of minor accidents and at least two serious ones because of his shoes. Rather than looking ahead, he would start gazing at his shoes. When he looked at his shoes, it was not the shoes alone he saw—his memory took him far, far away.

Memories know no barriers of national frontiers. Memories disregard passports and visas. Vairag remembered the corner of the hut where the shoes were made, the tools that made them, the hands which stitched and washed the leather, the knees placed upon which, they came to be born. All this moved before Vairag's eyes like a film. He had enjoyed

wearing shoes made by those hands all his life. The moment
a pair was slightly worn, he would give it away to a servant
and obtain for himself a new pair. Repeated orders for shoes
gave Vairag more frequent opportunities to visit the
shoemaker's *mohalla*. Requests for shoes from his friends and
acquaintances provided him with an excuse to go to the
mohalla every other day. Many a friend said, "My size is the
same as yours, get me a pair of shoes done by your cobbler."
When Vairag went to the shoemaker, he would shout from
outside the door, "*Salaam*, Seraj Uncle!" "Welcome, Shah,"
Seraj would reply, continuing to do his work. He would then
ask his daughter Nooro to bring a *peedhi* for him. Nooro would
bring a *peedhi* and sitting beside Vairag, start feeling his feet
with her hands as if she were measuring them. Seeing this
Seraj would say, "There couldn't be a change in his
measurements so soon. I know Shah's feet so well that if I
were to make his shoes with my eyes shut, they would fit
him comfortably." They would remain engaged in this small
talk for long in the tidy, mud-plastered *kutcha* hut of the
cobbler.

His present pair of shoes brought these sweet memories
back to Vairag and he would be lost in them for hours on end.

Vairag had been using his broken pair of shoes as slippers
for long. They were now so miserably torn that the openings
on either side of them let in dust and had also started hurting
his feet. Every time Vairag decided to go out, he had to get
the blisters on his feet dressed by his sister-in-law. "Why
don't you discard the broken shoes?" she would always start
an argument with him. "They hurt your feet badly every day."
At this Vairag would quote a verse from Hali, the renowned
Urdu poet—"It is the only memory of friends left with me.
May God, my wound never heals!" It was on such occasions
that Vairag's sister-in-law would reminded him about his
marriage. She would start recounting the names and describing
the various girls she had in view. "*Bhabi*, you are not much

educated, but you can be an excellent painter. Even beat
Amrita Shergill if you had a brush in your hand," Vairag
would try to confound the issue. "If you remain unmarried a
little longer, no one will ever marry his daughter to you,"
his sister-in-law would remind him. "You will then have to
remain a stag all your life. People don't even let their
houses to bachelors." "Marriage is not the only thing one
has to do in life. Mothers and sisters-in-law are
unnecessarily worried about it." Vairag would reply, and
then recall a number of bachelors in the country who
had earned a great name—the Chief Minister of West
Bengal, Dr B.C. Roy; the Chief Minister of UP,
Shri C.B. Gupta; the Chief Minister of Tamil Nadu,
Mr Kamraj Nadar; India's Defence Minister, Mr Krishna
Menon, and so on. "Are all of them good for nothing?
Couldn't they get girls to marry them if they had only
cared?" Vairag would ask. And he would remind her of a
number of people in the Punjab itself who were not married
but were doing excellent social work, service to the country
being dear to their heart.

"I refuse to hear this idle talk. I am going to throw these
broken shoes into the litter dump tomorrow. They make the
house untidy wherever you go wearing them."

"But what has marriage to do with the broken shoes?"
Vairag protested. He never took his sister-in-law seriously.
She, too, was hardly ever serious with him.

Vairag understood the language of his *Bhabi's* eyes and
the smile on her lips. His sister-in-law also kept on gauging
the depth of his sentiments and the extent of his infatuation.

Then, one evening, she actually threw the broken shoes
out on the litter dump for the scavenger to take them away.
She was amused to find them again lying outside the drawing-
room the next morning! She thought that she would throw
them back but then she forgot all about it.

"*Bhabi*, do you believe that when something gets old

it should immediately be replaced by new?" Vairag asked
his sister-in-law one day.

"I am aware of what you are driving at. But what do you
think of a man who uses the old along with the new?"

Vairag didn't know how to continue the argument.

"I wish I had not brought these shoes from Lahore when
I was last visiting Pakistan."

It was a strange coincidence. When Vairag's sister-in-law
went on the annual *Jor Mela* pilgrimage to Lahore, she came
across Seraj, the cobbler. He had brought the shoes to be sent
to India for Vairag with a pilgrim.

"But then what is wrong with that?"

"There is nothing wrong. Only when I told you what
Seraj had said—Nooro has now become Noor. She made this
pair herself with her own hands. And then she insisted on my
taking the pair to Lahore at the time of the *Jor Mela*
pilgrimage to be sent to India with a visiting pilgrim. How
you blushed! Your face was wreathed in smiles!"

"I didn't attach any importance to it at that time," Vairag's
sister-in-law continued after a little pause. "But now I wish I
had rather not brought this pair of shoes. I am amazed at your
obsession with the broken shoes."

"*Bhabi*, you are magnifying the issue too much, needlessly,"
Vairag said as if it hurt him.

"You think it is any secret? Your brother knows all
about it. Don't you forget, you had once gone and eaten at
Seraj's house. The village folk naturally objected to a Hindu
eating at a Muslim's house! It is never done. They took your
brother to task for it. He asked Seraj. He would not admit it
first. Then he said, 'Yes, but Nooro had the *chapatis* baked in
milk, not water. It's water that gets polluted for Hindus if
touched by a Muslim hand, not milk.' And as far as I
remember, you had yourself confessed to having eaten at a
Muslim's house."

Vairag remained silent. He was lost in old memories.

Then teasing him indulgently, she continued, "Incidentally when Seraj told me that the pair of shoes was the last gift from him, that he had grown too old and Nooro had become Noor Bhari, I gave him one of the new silk suits that I was carrying with me to present to her at the time of her wedding."

"Times have changed. Nobody now bothers about Hindus and Muslims eating together," Vairag answered, feeling a little relaxed after hearing what his sister-in-law had told him. "I believe, we have left those prejudices far behind."

"But at what price?" said his sister-in-law. "We have got over the prejudices in respect of eating and drinking but have become victims of the most heartless restrictions of borders and boundaries, passports and visas. One cannot go even to one's place of birth freely anymore. How I wish we could go on a pilgrimage to Punja Sahib this year!"

Vairag made a mental note of it, and apparently to meet the wishes of his sister-in-law, made arrangements to visit Punja Sahib on the holy festival of *Baisakhi*.

A day before the *Baisakhi* festival when they arrived at Rawalpindi railway station, they were delighted to find Seraj and Noor Bhari come to meet them. Noor Bhari had a baby in her arms. *Bhabi* took him over from Noor and started fondling him. Then, looking at the baby's face, she said all of a sudden—"He is the image of Vairag!" Noor Bhari heard it and sweated through and through. This is exactly what one of her neighbours had also told her.

Seraj pulled a pair of shoes and offered it to Vairag. "This was done for you by Noor before her marriage."

Noor Bhari's mother had died when she was a small child. She was always excited when Vairag visited them. She had also entertained him once with *chapatis* baked in milk. But just once. She dared not do it again. The village folk made such a fuss about it. When Nooro came of age, it so happened once that Vairag came to visit them when she was all alone at home. She didn't open the door but shouted from within, "You must come again when Abba is at home. You must, otherwise I'll never talk to you."

They travelled together, all of them—Vairag and Noor, Seraj and *Bhabi* and made their pilgrimage to Punja Sahib, the Temple of the Guru's Palm.

God alone knows if the *Bhabi* succeeded in getting her brother-in-law to marry. But they had a new pair of shoes and they talked about the broken shoes no longer.

(Translated from the original in Punjabi by K.S. Duggal)

22

SURAIYA QASIM

Where did She Belong?

MUNNI BAI WAS her name. Was it her cradle name? She did not know. Indeed, she did not know if she had had a cradle at all in the first instance. She hoped she had had one. After all, her parents could not have carried her about all the time.

But parents! Who were they? She did not know. All that she did know was that she must have had them. How else could she be in this world? But who on earth were her parents? She did not remember either of them.

What could her mother have been like? Was she beautiful or a repulsive creature? To go by her own looks, her mother, whoever she was, must have been at least attractive. Beauty rarely, if ever, comes out of an ugly womb.

But what about her father? What did he look like? What did he do for a living? And, come to think of it, to which community did he belong?

These were the questions Munni Bai never tired of asking herself. Not that she wanted to be prepared to answer them should someone ask. In the world in which she lived, parentage did not matter; looks and youth alone did. And Munni Bai was a ravishing beauty at a mere seventeen!

With her Venus-like face, conical breasts, slim waist, she

was acknowledged throughout not only Hira Mandi, but the city of Lahore, as the girl to be possessed. And possessing her was not difficult—anyone who could pay could possess her. She lived to be possessed—of course, at a price. Her wares were for sale.

This acknowledged princess of Hira Mandi did not like what she did. But there was nothing else she could do. Besides, what would "Ma" say if she refused to do what she was bidden?

Ma was a matronly figure who ran the brothel whose chief attraction was Munni Bai. Ma was alternately brutal and kind to her wards. There were six of them, including Munni Bai—the youngest and the loveliest of them all.

Ma treated Munni Bai with greater affection—real or simulated, for she was the chief source of her income—than she did anyone else. The birch was so sparingly used on Munni Bai that it seemed as though it was reserved for the others.

Munni Bai could recall only one occasion when Ma had thrashed her. That was when the girl had the audacity to ask forbidden questions. Finding Ma in a genial mood one day, Munni Bai had asked: "Ma, who are my parents? How did I come to be where I am? Why do I have to do what I do?"

Ma's face suddenly turned red. In a jiffy she picked up the birch which had lain hidden behind her and used it mercilessly on her "darling daughter"—as she herself used to address Munni Bai.

As the victim writhed in pain, Ma went on: "The answer to your first question, you bitch, is that I don't know who your parents are. You're a foundling. I found you crying and lying unattended on the road, the main road, mind you, equidistant from a mosque and a temple. Traffic was flowing by you, but no one had the heart to stop and attend to you, let alone pick you up, feed and fondle you.

"Fortunately for you, and unfortunately for me, I happened

to be passing that way at that time. I took pity on you that winter evening, picked you up, wrapped you in my shawl and brought you home where you still find yourself.

"Since your parents, pox on them whoever they were, had left you halfway between a mosque and a temple, I could not decide whether you were a Hindu or a Muslim, whether to give you a Hindu name or a Muslim name. Therefore, I gave you a name used by both Hindus and Muslims in our world.

"That, anyway, has always been immaterial in our house. On *Diwali*, as you know, we all burn earthen lamps and worship the Goddess Lakshmi with greater piety and fervour than most Hindus. And throughout the month of *Ramzan*, all inmates of this house observe the fast. So what difference does it make whether you are a Hindu or a Muslim? You are, in fact, better than both because you combine both in you."

Despite her bulk and stern exterior, Ma knew that age had begun to take its toll on her. No, she was not exactly old. Middle-aged, yes; but not old. She was just past fifty, but considering the sort of life she had led, had had to lead, she looked old and, worse, felt it.

Ma paused for breath before she could atone for her heartlessness by answering the other questions. "I have answered, you bitch, your second question also in the process of answering your first: the question how you came to be where you are. Your third question is why you have to do what you do. That is more easily answered. You eat during the day when you earn at night, and you've got to have something to eat if you want to stay alive."

Having thus explained everything, Ma strode back to her room and shut herself in. When one of the girls took food to her room, Ma refused to open the door from within, saying she was not hungry.

That night Munni Bai could not sleep. She lay tossing in

her bed. She could not lie on her back, which still ached. Now suppose some "customer" called! What would she do? What could she do?

She was the first choice of every customer, and her refusal to oblige might turn him away forever if he was a regular. After all, there were other *kothas* in Hira Mandi! Competition was stiff.

And Munni Bai could not afford to lose customers. No woman in her profession could. Plainly, it was a question of making hay while youth shone; and youth somehow did not seem to last even as long as the sun did. If the sun went down in the evening, it rose the next morning. But once youth sank into age, it was never to come out of it again.

Munni Bai hated even to think of it. Hadn't Ma said that she had to eat during the day what she earned at night? Munni Bai knew that a time was bound to come when the night would yield nothing to see her through the day.

Contemplating the bleak prospects between the spasms of pain resulting from the caning she had received, Munni Bai switched off the light and lay in darkness. Suddenly, she felt that the door of her room was being opened surreptitiously, as though by a burglar.

Now she could distinctly hear advancing footfalls as someone entered her room. Who could it be? A burglar? What was there in the room for a burglar? Indeed, she herself had nothing which could be stolen. The elite of the society had already robbed her of the only precious thing she had ever possessed.

The soft tread sounded familiar. Yet Munni Bai did not move in her bed and kept her eyes closed. A figure approached her cot and sat down on the vacant side, adjacent to Munni Bai's back. A hand which was muscular enough to be masculine touched and then slowly lifted her unbuttoned blouse, unstrapped the loosely hung bodice and with the utmost care went over the lacerated back. An instant later

Munni Bai, with her eyes still shut, felt the sensation of some ointment being applied softly to bruises and spread over the rest of her back. The ointment smelled of sandalwood.

Munni Bai felt so relieved and so touched that she sat up, embraced Ma and cried like a child.

Days passed, and with each day Ma's establishment attracted more clients that any other in the whole of Hira Mandi. Everybody wanted Munni Bai and only Munni Bai. She, on her part, made herself available to as many of her customers as she could.

However, Munni Bai's heart was not in her profession. But she had to keep her heart beating, and the only way to do so was by overcoming the feeling of disgust and revulsion that often suffused her heart.

In the privacy of a closed room, she was totally at the mercy of the master of the moment. Some dealt with her brutally and she suffered in silence. With the passage of time her body became inured to every kind of treatment. But her soul still writhed and squirmed.

As she kept busy the best part of every night, Munni Bai had more hours to herself during the day than anyone else in the establishment. With nothing to do in those idle hours, she would lose herself in thought.

She would think in particular about two of her customers who also called themselves her lovers. They had come to her at different times, but they spoke the same language. They made love and talked hate. As she lay in the bed totally spent, Munni Bai would suddenly start hating them—hating them for the innate hatred they divulged so soon after making love to her.

Raj Kamal was about twenty-five and extremely virile. But since he had a wife at home, and a rich one at that, without whose benefactions he would be out on the streets begging, he had to divide his passions between Munni Bai and his wife. Thus he could not inject full ardour into his love-making with Munni Bai. So he made up vocally for what he lacked sexually.

He would often tell Munni Bai, in the gentle flow of amiability induced by satisfied lust, "These good-for-nothing fellows, the Muslims, who cannot live for a day without loans from us, are already living in a fool's paradise. They are already dreaming dreams of a country of their own from which non-Muslims like you and me would be expelled."

Munni Bai would invariably interrupt him: "What do you mean by saying 'non-Muslims like you and me?' How do you know that I am not a Muslim? And what if I am?"

"But that's impossible! A beauty like you can only be a Hindu," Raj Kamal would assure her with considerable vehemence.

His outbursts would amuse Munni Bai. She would tease him: "Still, what if I turn out to have been the child of Muslim parents? Would you have desisted from making love to me?"

"Don't talk rot," he would shout at that. "I have been making love to you because you are such a ravishing beauty, and a ravishing beauty can never be anything but a Hindu. I am convinced of it." But it was clear every time that he was a bit nettled.

"Raj, tell me one thing honestly. Suppose, for the sake of argument, that a Muslim country comes into being. Suppose also that I am then adjudged a Hindu and expelled from it as you too would be. Would you abide by me in whatever country we both happen to be?"

Munni Bai could not keep count of the number of times she had asked this question, but every time the answer was the same.

"What a silly question, Munni Bai!" Raj Kamal would scoff. "No force on earth can drive us from our homes and hearths. Lahore—Hira Mandi particularly—belongs as much to us as it does to the Muslims. Nobody can dislodge us from our city.", And he would pause a little before adding: "If, God forbid, that comes to pass, I shall be with you, although we are not married, till death do us part."

Munni Bai was not one to let it go at that. "What will you do with your rich wife? You can't commit bigamy, much less murder!"

Raj Kamal would leave her room at that point, saying, "We'll cross that bridge when we come to it."

Munni Bai's other lover was Jafar Khan, who claimed to be a thoroughbred Pathan. "Today you are not exclusively mine because rich *kafirs* are as attracted to you as I am and they can outbid me. But when Pakistan is formed and after we have driven out all the *kafirs* you, Munni Bai, will belong only to Jafar Khan." This was his most frequent boast.

Munni Bai would set him the same poser she did to Raj Kamal, and his reaction would be the same as that of his unknown rival. "I have been making love to you, Munni Bai, because you are a fairy, a *houri,* from *behisht* and a *houri* can only be a Muslim. I am sure of that," he would say.

Both Raj Kamal and Jafar Khan had their own convictions without either of them being able to reveal its source. Munni Bai would tell the latter: "Suppose your dream of a nation for the Muslims is fulfilled and then you discover that I am not a Muslim, what will you do?"

Jafar Khan would stare banefully at Munni Bai for a second or so and then say, "If, Allah forbid, it is discovered that you are a Hindu, I shall convert you to Islam and marry you."

Munni Bai treated this bravado with just as much contempt as she did Raj Kamal's boastings. If Raj Kamal was totally dependent on his rich wife, even for his meals, not to speak of his extravagances, Jafar Khan and his wife were both more or less equally poor. Munni Bai had it on good authority that every time Jafar Khan spent a night with her, smothering her with currency notes, he was afraid of being arrested the next morning for theft or burglary. Therefore, there was more fear than passion in his love-making.

Munni Bai would persist: "Tell me, honestly, Jafar Khan: would you find me less desirable if you discovered just now that I wasn't a Muslim? I really don't know whether I am a Muslim or a Hindu. I was found on a road halfway between a temple and a mosque. Maybe that is symbolic of the fact that I am part Hindu and part Muslim."

"How can anyone be part Hindu and part Muslim? I feel it in my bones that you cannot but be a Muslim," he would say decisively and also a bit testily.

Munni Bai had known too many men even in so short a life, not to be able to read Jafar Khan's thoughts. She knew that what he really felt in his bones was not that she was a Muslim, but that he who was finding it difficult to maintain one wife would not be able to assume the responsibility of taking care of another being.

Then began those memorable months of disgrace by the end of which the Hindus had won, the Muslims had won, but humanity had lost. As an area frequented by members of all communities, it had initially been presumed that Hira Mandi alone would be immune to destruction. But the hope proved false.

Professional jealousy which had festered for years found an outlet in communal frenzy. The rioters and arsonists were made to believe by frustrated denizens that Ma, like every other inmate of her establishment, was a Hindu. Consequently, the establishment had to be wound up before it could be burned down.

With her wards in tow, Ma fled Lahore before it was too late. Only Munni Bai seemed to wish to tarry a little. She kept looking even in the frenzied crowds with flaming torches for Raj Kamal and Jafar Khan, but there was no trace of either. Maybe Raj Kamal had managed to cross the border and was waiting for her on the other side, but whatever could have happened to Jafar Khan? And to think that both had promised to abide by her through thick and thin!

Finally, Ma and her wards reached the refugee camp in Delhi, tired but all in one piece. True, here they lacked the comforts to which they had got accustomed in Hira Mandi, but at least there was no danger to their lives.

They were grieved to see countless refugees mourning the loss of their kinsmen. But Ma and her group had no kinsmen, only clients. Therefore there was no sense of loss. They could not have cared less if all their clients had been done to death. They had rendered services for which they had been paid, and so they were quits. Human bonds are not forged in commercial transactions.

With the passage of time popular frenzy abated; murderers and arsonists had either tired of what they had been doing or had run out of objects of hate. It was not yet back to business; but the business of destruction was nearly over.

The authorities announced one day that such of the refugees as wanted to leave the camp and start life anew would be given all assistance. Munni Bai kept hoping that some day, somewhere, she would run into Raj Kamal and remind him of his promise to take care of her. Why, she would even remind him of his promise to marry her!

Munni Bai had seen brides and envied them. She had herself had bridal outfits made without ever being a bride. She wished to be one.

One day Ma returned from a round of the city of Delhi and announced to her flock that she had fixed up a house for them to live in. It sent a wave of jubilation through her companions. With their meagre belongings held close to their chests, they trooped out of the camp, engaged a *tonga* and got into it.

Ma gave an address to the *tongawalla* and after what seemed like an eternity, the vehicle stopped in front of a partly damaged house.

The *tongawalla* addressed Ma: "*Bibiji*, this is the house where Salma used to stay with . . . er . . . companions. What a beauty she was! Nawabs and rajas used to visit her frequently. She has now gone with her group to Hira Mandi in Lahore."

In no time at all, women giggling and joking appeared on the balconies of the surrounding houses. One look at them, and it was clear to Ma and her group that they were kindred spirits. Meanwhile, the *tongawalla* said, "*Bibiji*, this is known as G. B. Road."

It was then that the ugly reality of the situation dawned on Munni Bai. She turned to Ma and asked in a voice without emotion. "Ma, the Muslims asked for a Pakistan and they have got it. The Hindus wanted to see the back of Muslims and they now have a Hindustan and are happy. We asked for nothing. Why, then, have we got all this suffering?"

Ma did not answer the question; instead, she led her party into the room.

Within days the newcomers were accepted as part of the "community." Despite all her harrowing experiences, Munni Bai had managed to retain her charm. Word soon spread that an exceptional beauty had landed from Hira Mandi where her name had been on everybody's lips. But Ma, who knew all the tricks of the trade, also knew how to handle the publicity. She quickly spread the word that the beauty from Hira Mandi would be accessible only to the very rich.

Munni Bai's neighbour told her: "I am afraid Ma is going about it in the wrong way. Where are the very rich now? So many Hindus and Muslims have perished in the holocaust and so much property has been destroyed that I doubt if there is any rich man around, either a Hindu or a Muslim. Even the poor belonging to both communities have perished."

The same night, two limousines stopped in front of the house, one hour after another. The first disgorged a raja, who sent in his compliments ballasted with currency notes and expressed the desire to spend time with the fabled beauty from Hira Mandi. He was obliged. But no sooner had he left than another limousine arrived, disgorging a nawab who desired the same satisfaction, paid generously for the service rendered and departed.

Before retiring for the night Munni Bai asked Ma: "Ma, Pakistan has been formed but the nawabs are as rich in India as they ever were. The Hindu rajas have been shouting from housetops that such of them as have not been butchered have been pauperised. Yet they have so much money for one night's enjoyment. Then who lost and who died in the Partition?"

(Translated from the original in Urdu by Md. Vazeeruddin)

23

Mohan Rakesh

The Proprietor of the Debris

They were visiting Amritsar after seven and a half years. They had come from Lahore. The hockey match was merely an excuse. They were anxious to see the houses and streets that had once been theirs seven and a half years ago. Clusters of Muslims from Pakistan were on every road. Their eager eyes devoured everything around them. Amritsar was no ordinary town—it was something special to them.

Walking through congested streets, they were reminded of the old times and pointed out to one another: Look Fatehudin, there are no more as many sugar merchants as there used to be. . . . The corner, there, where that betel-seller is, Sukhi used to sit, parching grams, roasting and toasting them for the passers-by. . . . This is a salt market; every Hindu woman here had a crystal brightness in her complexion. . . .

It was after a long time that the people of Amritsar were seeing Jinnah and *karakuli* caps. Most of the visitors from Lahore were those who had been driven away from the town at the time of the Partition. Noticing the unmistakable change in the town in these seven and a half years they would, at times, be delighted while at others disappointed. The comment one most frequently heard was, "Amazing, how has the mosque remained unoccupied? Why have they not converted it into a *Gurdwara*?"

Wherever the Pakistani visitors went the local residents followed them. There were, of course, some who avoided them, but most of them would come forward and embrace each one of them. They asked the visitors about Lahore; is the Anarkali still as crowded as it used to be? Has Shahalmi Gate been raised afresh? Has there been any change in Krishna Nagar? Is it a fact that your *Rishvatpura* has been colonised mainly with graft money? It is said that the ladies in Pakistan no longer wear the veil? The way they made inquiries, it appeared that Lahore was no mere town, but a place of pilgrimage for people on this side of the border. They were anxious to know about its welfare. The visitors from Lahore were honoured guests whom it was a privilege to meet.

The Bansawala Bazaar used to be a neglected area in the pre-partition days. Only the poor Muslims used to reside there. There were bamboo and timber shops which were set on fire in the early days of the riots. The fire in this bazaar became so menacing at one time that it was feared it might engulf the whole town in it. In any case, it did succeed in doing damage to several Hindu houses in the neighbourhood. Some of them had been rebuilt in the last seven and a half years, while others continued to be piles of debris. It was a dismal sight to look at.

Most of the residents of Bansawala Bazaar had been exterminated along with their houses. Those who escaped dared not return. A lean, old Muslim evacuee came to the godforsaken bazaar that day and was completely lost. He wanted to get into the left-hand street, but his feet were paralysed. He was not sure if it was the same lane. There were a couple of children playing in the street and one could hear two women shouting at each other.

"Everything has changed but not the language of abuse,"

said the old man to himself as he leaned on his walking stick. His pyjama was worn out at the knees, his *sherwani* too had a number of patches. Suddenly, a child emerged out of the lane. He was crying. The old man offered to give him a coin with a view to pleasing him. As he was searching his pockets, a young girl came running and pulled the child away. The child began resisting. The young girl picked him up, telling him, "Don't you misbehave, otherwise the Muslim fellow will carry you away."

The old man who had taken out a coin for the child put it back in his pocket. He took off his cap, and scratching his head for a while, put the cap under his arm. His throat was parched. His legs were trembling. He leaned against a wall and put on his cap again. At the place where logs of wood used to be stored, a multi-storyed building had come up. Two kites had settled on the electric line running through the street. The electric poles seemed to be relishing the morning sun. For a while the old man watched the dust particles floating in the sunlight, "*Ya Allah!*" he said fervently.

A young boy came playing with a bunch of keys in his hands and seeing a stranger, asked: "Who are you looking for, Sheikh?"

The old man felt a sort of vibration in his body and looking at the boy carefully, said: "Son, is your name Manori?"

The young boy stopped playing with the bunch of keys. "How do you know my name?" he asked.

"Seven and a half years ago, you were a small child." Saying this the old man tried to smile.

"Have you come from Pakistan today?" asked Manori.

"Yes, but there was a time when we lived in this street. My son, Chiragh Din, was your master-tailor. Hardly six months before the Partition we had a new house built here."

"Oh, so you are Ghani Sheikh!" The youth recognised the old man.

"Yes, son! I am Ghani Sheikh. Since I can no longer

meet Chiragh and his family, I thought I would come and see the house at least." Saying this, he took off his cap again and started scratching his head. This was his way of trying to control his tears.

"They say you had left Amritsar much earlier," Manori tried to sound sympathetic.

"Yes, child, it was a misfortune that I did so. If I had stayed back I too would have been. . . ." Saying this he suddenly realised that he should not be talking like that. He left the sentence incomplete to fight back his tears.

"Forget about it, Ghani Sheikh. What use is it to scratch old sores?" And holding him by the arm, Manori urged, "Come, I'll show you your house."

Word had gone around in the street that there was a Muslim from Pakistan who was about to abduct Ramdasi's son. Luckily his sister had turned up on the scene and rescued the child. Hearing this, the womenfolk who were squatting outside their front doors, withdrew into their houses. They collected the children playing in the street and shut them in. So when Manori brought Ghani, there was hardly anyone left in the street except a chance vendor and Rakha, the wrestler, who was sleeping under the *peepal* tree by the side of the well. However, there were a number of faces trying to peep from behind the half-opened doors and windows. Seeing Ghani Sheikh enter the street, people started talking about him. Despite the fact that he had gone completely gray, they could still recognise him. He was no other than the father of Chiragh Din.

"This was your house!" Manori pointed to a heap of debris. For a moment Ghani Sheikh didn't believe his eyes. He had known about the slaughter of his son and his family, but he was not aware of the fate of his house. He was thunderstruck, as it were. His throat went dry and his knees trembled feverishly.

"That rubble?" He could not believe his eyes.

Manori offered him his arm for support and told him discreetly, "Your house was burnt down during the riots itself."

Ghani Sheikh, somehow, reached the heap of debris with the help of his stick.

It was a mound of earth and shattered bricks. The wood and iron pieces had been removed, nobody knew when. The charred frame of the main door had escaped attention somehow. It was half-buried in the rubble. There were two almirahs at the back which were also charred. "This is what is left," muttered Ghani Sheikh looking at the debris. His knees seemed to collapse. He held the half-burnt frame of the door for support and sat down. After a little while, he began hitting his head against the door. He wailed, "Oh Chiragh Din, my darling son."

The charred frame of the door had withstood the ravages of time, but during the last seven and a half years its wood had softened. It seemed to give way when Ghani banged his head against it. The wood-dust spread all over Ghani's head and beard. Along with the wood-dust, an earthworm also came out of the frame and fell in the drain. It suddenly started moving and forging its way.

The number of faces peering through the windows had multiplied. They feared that something untoward would take place that day—Chiragh Din's father had turned up after seven and a half years. Everyone remembered the dastardly act that had been perpetrated in the street. People felt that the rubble of the house itself was tell-tale. No one need tell Ghani Sheikh that as evening fell on that fateful day, Rakha, the wrestler, had called Chiragh Din to come down to the street. Chiragh Din was eating his evening meal in the living room of the first floor. Those days Rakha styled himself as the virtual ruler of the street. Even the Hindus feared him. Chiragh Din was but a Muslim.

Chiragh came down without finishing his meal. His wife,

Zubaida, and his two daughters, Kishwar and Sultana, were watching him from the window. The moment Chiragh stepped out, the wrestler pulled him by the collar of his shirt and threw him on the ground and started stabbing him. Chiragh Din begged him again and again not to kill him. He shouted for his wife and children to help him. His wife came rushing down to the street, but before she could arrive he had been done to death.

All the windows of the houses looking on to the street were suddenly shut. As if no one had noticed the crime! Everyone washed his hands of the responsibility for it. However, they continued to hear the screaming of Zubaida and her two daughters, Kishwar and Sultana. Rakha and his band of toughs killed Chiragh Din's wife and daughters the same night. But they were subjected to a different ordeal. Their dead bodies were found in the canal the next morning.

The *goondas* continued to ransack Chiragh Din's house for two days. After the house had been swept clean, someone set it on fire. Rakha, the wrestler, had pledged that he would bury the man who had burnt the house. He had taken a fancy to the house and it was to possess the house that he had slaughtered Chiragh Din and his family. So keen was he to possess the house that he had even purchased the ingredients for the purifying ceremony of the house. He tried his best but could not find out who had set the house on fire. He then laid claim to the debris. For the past seven and a half years he would not allow even the street cattle to be tied there, much less a street vendor to install himself on the premises. No one dare remove a broken brick from the rubble without his permission.

People seemed to believe that the entire story would somehow be communicated to Ghani Sheikh. Meanwhile, the old man was digging in the debris and wailing for his son, his daughter-in-law and his granddaughters. "Why have you left poor me behind?" he was crying out again and again.

No one knows whether someone had woken him or he woke up of his own accord. Rakha was sleeping under the *peepal* tree near the well. Learning that Ghani Sheikh had come from Pakistan and that he was sitting over the debris of his house, Rakha suddenly flared up. But he subdued his anger soon thereafter. He looked at the debris with fierce eyes.

"Ghani is sitting on the debris," his companion Lachha told him.

"The debris is ours. How does it belong to him?" The wrestler's voice seemed to be choked with anger.

"But he is squatting there," Lachha repeated meaningfully.

"If he sits there, let him do so. Get me my *chillum*," said the wrestler. For a while he scratched his legs.

"If Manori tells him anything . . ." Lachha muttered to himself as he rose to get a *chillum* for Rakha.

"I'll teach Manori a lesson," said Rakha.

After Lachha had gone, Rakha picked up the dry *peepal* leaves strewn around and started crushing them in his fist. When Lachha returned with the *chillum,* Rakha said, "I hope no one else has talked to Ghani."

"No one."

Rakha handed over the *chillum* to Lachha after a pull or two. They saw that Manori was escorting Ghani Sheikh towards the well, holding him by his arm. Lachha was now taking deep pulls at the *chillum,* viewing Rakha and Ghani alternatively.

Manori was holding Ghani's arm and trying to lead him so that he might not have to encounter Rakha sitting near the well. But the way Rakha was sitting, Ghani could see him from a distance. Before he reached the well, Ghani stretched both his arms out and said, "Rakha!"

Rakha looked at him straining his eyes as if he were finding it difficult to recognise him. Evidently he felt embarrassed.

"Rakha, don't you recognise me? I am Ghani, Abdul Ghani, the father of Chiragh Din."

The wrestler looked at him with suspicious eyes. Abdul Ghani's eyes had suddenly brightened at seeing him. The wrinkles beneath his beard had deepened. Rakha's lower lip trembled a little and he spoke in his guttural voice, "Yes, I heard about you."

Hearing this, Ghani's arms fell listless by his sides. He sat down reclining against the *peepal's* trunk.

The people in the street watching from their doors and windows started commenting on the situation: Now that Rakha and Ghani have encountered each other, the truth must come out. Maybe they will start abusing each other. Rakha dare not harm Ghani now—the times have changed. How he laid his claim to the debris! The fact of the matter is that the debris belongs neither to Rakha nor to Ghani. It belongs to the Government. That Rakha—he would not allow even stray cattle to saunter there. Manori is also a coward: why has he not told Ghani that it was Rakha who killed his son and his family. There is no kindness in Rakha, he loiters about the street like a bull the whole day. Poor Ghani! How weak he has grown. And his beard is all grey.

Ghani now came and sat down on the platform of the well and started talking to Rakha. "What I left, and what do I see now? A mound of earth and a pile of debris. This is what it is. If you were to ask me the truth, Rakha, I would not like to part even with this." Saying this, his eyes filled with tears.

The wrestler suddenly sat upright, putting an *angochha* on his shoulder. Lachha pressed the *chillum* into his hands and he started taking quick pulls at it.

"Rakha, you would know—how did all this happen?" Ghani asked the wrestler, wiping his tears. "If he wanted, couldn't he find shelter in one of your houses. Did it not occur to him?"

"Yes," said Rakha. He himself realised that he sounded unnatural. His lips were slimy. There were drops of perspiration beneath his moustache. He felt a tension in his forehead. His backbone ached for support.

"What is it like in Pakistan?" Rakha asked casually. There was a congestion in his throat. He wiped the sweat from beneath his armpits.

"How would I know it, Rakha?" said Ghani, putting all his weight on the stick in his hand. "I am a ruined person. God alone knows how miserable I am. It would have been different if my Chiragh had been alive. Rakha, I pleaded with him again and again to accompany me. But he would not listen to me. He would say: 'How can I leave my newly built house unprotected? It is our own street. Everyone here knows us. There is no fear of any harm coming to us.' The poor dove did not know that if no one would harm him from among his neighbours, who was there to prevent intruders from other parts of the town? All four of them gave their lives protecting their home. Rakha! he had great faith in you. Every time he would say, 'As long as Rakha, the wrestler, is there, nobody dare look at us.' But when the time came, no one, not even you, Rakha, could help him."

Rakha's spine was aching. He tried to straighten his back. He felt a severe pain in his trunk and the joints of his legs. His intestines seemed to be contracting. His breathing became heavy. His entire body was bathed in sweat. The soles of his feet were burning. It seemed stars had descended from above and were swimming in front of his eyes. He felt as if there was a gulf between his tongue and his lips. He wiped the corner of his lips with his forefinger and muttered, "God is great."

Ghani noticed that the wrestler's lips were parched and the rings round his eyes had deepened. He put his hand on Rakha's shoulder and said: "Don't you take it to heart, brother. What's happened has happened. It can't be undone.

God's own grace on the good and may He forgive the wicked. If I have lost Chiragh, I have the whole lot of you. It is a great consolation that I have happy memories of my earlier days in all of you. Having met you, I have met Chiragh. May God give you long life and good health! May you be cheerful ever."

Rakha thanked him sheepishly. With his *angochha* tucked in between, he folded his hands. Looking at the street with a heavy heart, Ghani walked out of it.

People watching from the windows felt that Manori must tell Ghani all about it when they got out of the street. How Rakha was tongue-tied before Ghani! How dare he now stop anybody's cattle straying over the rubble! What a fine person Zubaida was! She never had a harsh word for anybody. Rakha, the accursed, has neither a mother nor a sister. He has little respect for anyone.

Before long, everyone came out in the street. The children started playing their games and two teenagers were heard quarrelling with each other.

Rakha remained sitting on the well platform till late in the evening. Some of the people passing by asked him, "Rakha! They say Ghani came from Pakistan today?"

"Yes, he did."

"Then what happened?"

"Nothing. What can happen? He came and went away."

As night fell the wrestler, along with his companions, came and installed himself as usual outside a shop in the street. Normally, he used to stop passers-by and give them tips about the stock market or on secrets of health. But today he was telling Lachha about his pilgrimage to Vaishno Devi— the pilgrimage he had undertaken fifteen years ago. It was after midnight, when Lachha had left, that he came and saw Loku Pandit's buffalo squatting at the foot of the mound of the debris. He drove her away.

Rakha, then, sat on a *charpoy* lying on the debris. The

street was desolate. There being no street light, it became dark the moment that night fell. The water in the gutter below the debris was running. Rakha heard queer sounds emanating from the debris in the quiet of the night—chu, chu . . . chik, chik . . . chir, chir. . . . Suddenly a crow came, God knows from where, and perched on the door frame jammed in the debris. As the crow came flying, a street dog saw it and began barking. The dog kept on a continuous howl. After howling for long and discovering there was no one in the street, the dog came and sat in a corner of the mound as if he were the proprietor of the debris.

(Translated from the original in Hindi by K. S. Duggal)

24

Bhisham Sahni

Pali

LIFE GOES ON and on. Its ends never meet. Neither in the mundane world of realities nor in fiction. We drag on drearily in the hope that some day these ends may meet. And sometimes we have the illusion that the ends have really joined.

Manohar Lal and his wife had also once lived under a similar illusion. They believed that a great calamity had at last passed over their heads. That the knots that had formed in their lives had been untied. But knots of life never get fully resolved even in stories, much less in one's life. No sooner is one knot untied then another knot forms in its place. The story thus never comes to an end.

One end of Manohar Lal and his family's life was left behind in a small town distantly situated across the border of Pakistan, a country newly carved out at the time of the partition. With their meagre belongings, the little that they could carry, Manohar Lal and his family had also joined the caravan of the countless uprooted people heading for India. The dust raised by their feet hung like a haze in the atmosphere. Like a big river forming into many channels on its onward sweep towards the sea, this vast concourse of unfortunate humanity also proceeded towards the boundary line demarcating the two countries.

Manohar Lal, his wife and two children—a little girl in her mother's arms and Pali, a boy of four, holding his father's finger—trudged along, carrying their bundles on their heads, their weary eyes searching their way through the haze, their ears pricked for any stray remark that might guide them on to the correct path. They were anxious to know the lay of the land and, more than that, what was in store for them.

On the last day, the refugee camp had started emptying out. Carrying their belongings on their heads, the refugees left the camp and proceeded towards the convoy of lorries, ranged one after the other along the road, which would carry them to the border. Holding his son's finger and carrying a heavy bundle on his head, Manohar Lal went towards the lorries, his wife, Kaushalya following close on his heels, her baby daughter nestled in her arms. Like her husband, she also carried a big bundle on her head. The refugees were frantically throwing their things into the lorries and storming their way into the vehicles, some of them wriggling in through the windows. Manohar Lal was struggling to push his way towards the entrance when he suddenly realised that his son, Pali, was not holding his finger. Kaushalya had already managed to enter the lorry. Manohar Lal showed no alarm, thinking that the child must be somewhere around. The sensation of the child's grip still lingered on his hand. Everybody was pushing forward madly from behind. There was a babble of sounds and the crowd got more and more frantic with the passing of every moment. The camp managers shouted at the top of their voices, urging the passengers to hurry up and get into the lorries. They had to cross the border before nightfall.

When Manohar Lal failed to find Pali around, he really got anxious. He rushed back crying, "Pali! Pali!" but failed to get any response. Getting alarmed, he raised his voice. His son's name, Pali, rang in the air above the pervading din.

Then he started running frantically alongside the lorries. The lorries had started leaving one by one. The lorry in which his wife was standing with her suckling child was jam-packed and its horn was blowing insistently, warning the people that it was ready to start. Manohar Lal's throat had gone dry shouting "Pali! Pali!" His legs shook and his head reeled. Such was the irony of the situation for this homeless man— he was shouting for his son on a road crowded with people, and yet he appeared to be shouting in a desert.

He was still searching for Pali when the lorry started moving. His wife's anxious eyes were fixed on her husband in the crowd and, to her horror, he suddenly disappeared from her view. Alarmed, she started wailing. Her locks of hair tumbled over her face, blinding her for a moment, and her child nearly slipped from her arms. She breathed heavily, her chest working like bellows.

"Stop! Stop! *Hai,* stop the lorry!"

But nobody listened to her. All of them had their own worries to contend with. They were all shouting and crying. Hers was not the only family being driven from its home. There were many of those whose only half luggage had been hoisted onto the lorry, the other half was lying scattered on the road. An old woman, apparently a grandmother, was having difficulty in climbing into the moving lorry. She was pushed from all sides, and struggled to keep her foot on the footboard. As the lorry moved forward, Kaushalya's eyes went wide with horror. In a daze, she searched for only one image in the crowd—her husband. Then she burst out crying, her plight like that of a bird whose nest was being destroyed before its very eyes.

She heard someone shouting, "Stop the lorry! Stop the lorry!" Other voices joined the cry. The lorry slowed down.

Kaushalya had thrown out one of her bundles and was going to hand down her wailing child to a man standing on the road when she saw Manohar Lal running up. But

their son was not with him. God only knew which whirlpool
had sucked in poor Pali.

Manohar Lal heard some voices being directed towards
his wife: "The child must be somewhere here." The people
gestured to Manohar Lal to come nearer. "Get in, get in!"
they advised him. "He must have got on to some other lorry."
There were other voices, loaded with venom and irritation,
"Will the lorry keep waiting for your child? If you want to
search for your child you'd better get down from the lorry."
The people had suddenly become callous. If they had not seen
Manohar Lal running up, perhaps Kaushalya would have got
down from the lorry, wailing, and they would have thrown
out her luggage after her. They were right. They must get
across the border before nightfall. So many lives were at
stake. Surely, the lorry could not keep waiting for one child.

The refugees' hearts had dried of all sentiments. The same
Pali had once got lost and the whole *mohalla* had gone out in
search of him. And here someone kept crying repeatedly, "Get
down, you! If you want to search for your child get down,
and let us proceed!"

The husband and wife could not decide whether to get
down from the lorry or proceed in it. Having failed to find
any trace of Pali, Manohar Lal and Kaushalya kept looking
out on the road. Slowly, the town was left behind and the
noise abated. Only Kaushalya kept wailing. The trees, the
fields full of greenery, swept past their gaze. Pali, lost
somewhere in the crowded small town, receded from his
parents. Kaushalya's wailing gradually changed into a whimper.
The mental anguish of the passengers expressed itself in the
moans of the insane and then changed into heart-rending cries
before petering out into an anguished silence. The lorries
moved on, lurching from side to side. Slowly, the morning
haze cleared up. Looking up at the vast expanse of the
impassive sky where one or two stars were still winking at
him, Manohar Lal tried to console his wife. "We may yet find

him," he said. "He can't get lost like this. Some kindly soul must have taken charge of him and pushed him into some other lorry." He looked at Kaushalya's abstracted gaze and, seeing the grief on her face, he said in utter desperation, "What can we do if we don't find him? God has been benign enough to spare a child for us. We must be thankful to him for that. You know Lekhraj's three children were killed before his very eyes. It's God's will. We must resign ourselves to it."

Kaushalya's empty eyes were still glued to the road. There was nothing strange about losing a child under these circumstances. There was no sense in creating so much hubbub over it. As time passed, the uprooted passengers fell to talking with one another. The women also followed their men's example. Here and there, they could also hear the sound of laughter.

The evening shadows lengthened as they neared the border. The convoy stopped for a short while at one point. Manohar Lal promptly got down from his lorry and ran past the lined up lorries, shouting, "Pali! Pali!" He peeped into all the lorries through their windows, but he got no response from any lorry. His voice seemed to be echoing back from the wilderness. He could not find Pali anywhere.

On reaching the border the refugees were transferred to other lorries which were parked there to receive them. The lorries raced through the darkness towards Amritsar. The sky studded with myriads of stars looked so mysterious. Overwhelmed by the immensity of the situation, the refugees had become very quiet and some of them had started dozing to the rhythmic jolts of the lorries. There were others who just sat there staring at nothing. Manohar Lal's wife had again started crying; its incoherent loudness made people think that she was going mad. Then her crying would change into moans and the onlookers would feel reassured that she was not mad yet. She must indeed be missing her child very much. At last, she rested her head against Manohar Lal's shoulder and fell asleep. Manohar Lal silently resolved that if he failed to find Pali he would go back to his old town in Pakistan and, following up certain clues, try to locate and bring him back home.

The convoy tore through the darkness on its way to Amritsar. Everyone was too absorbed in himself to think of what lay in store for him. Perhaps their minds had stopped thinking. Fate had thrown a black curtain across their eyes so that they could discern no ray of hope through it. There were only the joltings of the lorries and weariness. Their eyes had become glazed and their throats were parched, and above them were myriads of twinkling stars which seemed to mock at them.

That night, after crying for hours when Pali fell asleep at last, his head resting against Zenab's bosom, his sobs slowly dissolved in a sea of affection. A woman's bosom is the greatest shield against man's afflictions and the greatest source of love and affection. Zenab had, so to say, caught the child firmly within her citadel of love. For the first time in her life, Zenab was overwhelmed by a sense of joy which only a woman bereft of a child can experience. A tiny, delicate body was clinging to her, as if the child was specially made to fit into the contours of her body.

Her heart swelled up with maternal feeling. "Why don't you speak?" she asked the child.

Shakur, who had been lying in the courtyard in a cot adjacent to Zenab's, kept gazing at the sky sprinkled with millions of stars. It reminded him of Zenab's deep blue *chunri* in which she had first come to his house as a bride. Her *chunri* had glittered like stars. As he looked at her glowing face from behind her *chunri,* Shakur had felt as if the sun had descended into his courtyard.

Shakur made a living by selling chinaware. Carrying a big basket loaded with cups, saucers, plates and pots on his head, he would go from lane to lane and from street to street hawking his wares, waving a thin cane stick over his basket. He had been doing it for years together. That late afternoon, as the evening came down upon the small town, he had chanced upon a small boy who had been thrown to one side by the ebb and tide of the crowd. He was standing at the corner of the lane crying, *"Pitaji! Pitaji!"*

Shakur stopped on seeing the small boy. Then he sat down by the boy's side, uttering soothing words to him. He wiped the child's tears with the end of his *kurta* and the child stopped crying. "Come, I'll take you to your father," Shakur had said. "But where's your father?" Holding the child's hand, Shakur had taken him to the place from where the convoy of lorries had departed carrying the refugees. The lorries had left long ago and even the dust raised by them had long since settled down. The refugee camp was lying deserted. In the darkness of the night, when Shakur climbed the steps to his house, Pali was fast asleep, his head resting against Shakur's shoulder.

Shakur was a god-fearing man, timidly taking every step in life. When rioting started in the town he kept himself aloof from the trouble-makers. When the grain market was set on fire and there were stray cases of stabbing in the streets, Shakur had remarked, "It is God's anger visiting us." He would repeat this remark every time there was a violent occurrence.

"Why are you silent?" Shakur asked his wife.

"What's there to say?" Zenab said in a lazy voice, which trailed into silence. She was enjoying the feel of the child's small body. She felt for a moment as if all the obstructions had crumbled away from her path and her body was getting lighter. But she did not want to tell her husband that she had come upon a precious boon. Even the touch of that small unknown child as he clung to her, had sent a thrill through her body.

"All the Hindus and Sikhs have left their houses," Shakur said. "They have gone for good. The camp has emptied. Now nobody would dare venture this way."

Zenab gave no reply. The child mumbled in his sleep, heaved a deep sigh and, resting his head upon Zenab's bosom, fell asleep again.

Zenab looked up at the sky. It was looking so resplendent, as if auguring her good fortune. As if echoing Shakur's thoughts, she said, "Leave him at the place from where you picked him up, lest some unfortunate curse should befall us."

"Why should any curse befall us? We are giving the child shelter," Shakur mumbled. "If we deliver him to the police station, they can't restore him to his parents."

They were trying to read each other's mind.

"What's his name?" Zenab asked, rubbing her cheek against the child's cheek.

"How do I know? When I asked him he said Pali. Pali."

"These Hindus have such queer names. What a funny name! Pali! If I had a son I would have named him Altaf."

They lay silent for a long time, lost in their own thoughts. If nobody came to claim the child, he would become hers. A child prancing about in her courtyard. She hoped nobody would turn up to enquire. The tailor, Mahmud, had kept a Hindu woman in his house and no one had bothered to investigate. Mir Zaman had ransacked the Hindu tailoring shop next to his and had kept the stolen things in his shop for all to see. Nobody had taken him to task for it. And as for her, she was only giving refuge to a child—a lost child whom her husband had picked up on finding him crying in the street. What was wrong with it? But Shakur's mind was sometimes filled with fear.

On waking up the next morning, when the child found himself among strangers he again started crying and repeating,

"*Pitaji, Pitaji!*" Zenab put a bowl of milk against his lips and kept fondling his head and caressing his back. But little Pali would not stop crying and broke into hiccups. Zenab's eyes went to the door lest someone should hear the child crying and force his way into her house. Yes, the child was there all right and, all said and done, it was a stolen child. What if someone got wind of it? She must keep the child hidden from prying eyes for some days.

Pali stopped crying at last. Now he sat in a corner, maintaining a grim silence and emptily staring this way and that. He kept sighing and Zenab sometimes felt that with the coming of the child, she had herself become rootless.

Shakur had thought that within a day or two, after becoming familiar with his environment, the child would start feeling at home. But he still had his misgivings. One never knew. His parents may be knocking about in search of their child and may track him down to this house. There were still a large number of refugees who had yet to migrate. He feared the police may come to know about the lost child and they may create serious trouble for him.

The first two days were nothing short of an ordeal. On the third day, the child became a little communicative. He saw a white cat sitting on the wall of the courtyard and beamed at it. The cat jumped down and sat on the floor. The child ran towards it, crying, "A cat! A cat!" Zenab felt so happy.

There was a knock on the door. It sounded loud and ominous. Zenab and Shakur looked towards the door in alarm, their hearts pounding hard.

"They have come," Zenab said apprehensively. "The people to whom the child belongs!" Fear streaked across her eyes.

"Could be the people from the police station!" Shakur said, his fear mounting moment by moment.

Another powerful blow. It was like a heavy *lathi* crashing against the door. "Open the door!" A voice invaded the house from across the door.

As Shakur proceeded to open the door, Zenab hurriedly moved into the inner room with the child.

It was neither the police *havildar* on the other side of the door nor the child's parents. It was the bearded *maulvi* of the neighbouring mosque standing there, holding a thick *lathi*. There were two men standing behind him, both armed with *lathis*.

"Is there a *kafir's* child in here?" the *maulvi* barked, stepping into the courtyard. "Who has brought him here?" The two men wielding *lathis* had also followed the *maulvi* into the courtyard.

"Are you hiding some other *kafir* also in your house?"

Shakur ran in and hurriedly returned carrying a *murha*.

"I swear by the Holy Quran we are not hiding any *kafir* in our house," Shakur said. "We have only given shelter to an orphan boy."

"Where's that orphan?"

"*Ji*, he's sleeping inside."

The *maulvi* cast a suspicious look at Shakur and then tapped the floor sharply with his *lathi*.

"Produce him before me! I want to see him."

Zenab came out carrying Pali in her arms.

"So you are giving refuge to a *kafir* child?"

"I've adopted the child, *Maulvi Sahib*. It's no sin to adopt a child," Zenab said in a firm, steady voice.

"Have you had him circumcised? Has he read the *kalma*?"

New life surged back into Zenab. The *maulvi* had not come to snatch away the child from her. He had come only to make him a Mussalman. Zenab stood silent before the *maulvi*.

"Why don't you speak? You give a *kafir's* polluted child a place in your lap. You give him your breast to suckle. Do you want to nurture a snake?"

The *maulvi's* argument had driven Zenab against the wall. No, she couldn't refute his argument. Why hadn't she thought of it before? But she had found nothing polluted about the boy nor did he look like the young one of a serpent. She was going to speak when the *maulvi* banged his *lathi* on the ground and said, "Bring this *kafir*'s son to the holy mosque. Early tomorrow morning. Or you must be prepared to face serious consequences!"

The *maulvi* dramatically took a full turn and walked off towards the door. As soon as the *maulvi* had gone, Zenab tossed her head happily and smiled. All that the *maulvi* wanted was that the boy should say the *kalma* and be circumcised. Why wait till tomorrow? She was prepared to do it right now. What was there to fear? He had not threatened to take away the child from her. He had not even hinted at it.

The circumcision was performed the very next morning. Little Pali, got terrified at the sight of the razor and clung to Zenab's legs.

The circumcision done, the *maulvi* petted and consoled little Pali ignoring the fact that all the time the child had kept uttering *"Pitaji! Pitaji!"* in great agony. The *maulvi* did not mind it at all. He just smiled indulgently. The neighbours came and felicitated Shakur and Zenab.

The *maulvi* gave the boy the gift of a red *Rumi* cap with a black tassel and himself placed it on the boy's head. Zenab gave him a brand new white muslin *kurta* to wear and helped him to put it on then and there. The *maulvi* then lifted the boy and placed him in Zenab's arms.

"Take him!" the *maulvi* said happily. "He's your own child, not a *kafir*'s. He belongs to the whole community."

The child was renamed Altaf—from Pali to Altaf. Carrying Altaf in her arms, Zenab went around distributing sweets in the *mohalla*.

Gradually, the child took to his new ways. Within a year little Pali, now crockery-seller Shakur Ahmed's son, Altaf Husain, became a familiar figure in the area. Now, he played in his courtyard hawking chinaware, aping his father's drawnout lusty cry. He would collect all the utensils from the kitchen and put them in a basket, which he carried on his head and trotted round the courtyard announcing like his father, the articles he had to offer for sale.

When the month of *Ramzan* came, he would plant himself in the middle of his courtyard and proclaim to the beat of an empty tin canister, "Get up, you pious Muslims! Wake up from your sleep! Keep your holy fast!"

Shakur and Zenab lost no time in putting Altaf in the school attached to the local mosque where, sitting on the brick platform outside the mosque, he memorised the Quran along with other boys, swaying his back rhythmically in consonance with the lines from the holy book.

Zenab and Shakur's lives started revolving on a new orbit with Altaf as its focal point. They wove their dreams around Altaf. One day Shakur would stop going around, hawking his wares from door to door. Instead, he would set up a regular shop where father and son would sit together conducting sales. They would not be at the mercy of others. They would be their own masters and sleep peacefully with not a care in the world. Zenab eagerly looked forward to the day when Altaf's bride would set foot in her house, wearing ceremonial ankle bells.

Two years passed happily in this manner. One day, the chinaware seller had gone on his rounds and little Altaf was at school. Only Zenab was at home. Sitting behind the tarpaulin curtain, she was grinding wheat.

There was a knock at the door. "My man is not at home," she replied from where she was sitting. "Come in the evening."

After a pause, a voice said, "There's a court summons in Shakur Ahmed's name. He has been asked to report himself at the police station."

Zenab stopped grinding the wheat. Adjusting her *palla* over her head she came and stood behind the tarpaulin curtain. A tremor of fear ran through her spine. "What's the matter, *ji*?" she asked.

"Send him to the police station tomorrow morning. It's urgent."

"What for, *ji*?" Zenab asked in a tremulous voice.

"They have come from Hindustan to claim the child. There is a letter to that effect."

Zenab again shook from head to foot.

"Send him to the police station tomorrow morning," the man repeated. "Don't forget."

She heard the man's retreating steps from behind the curtain.

There are some wounds which heal with the passage of time, leaving a mark on the mind. But there are certain griefs which slowly eat into the heart like termites, completely ravaging the body. There is nothing a man can do about it. When Kaushalya reached India with her husband, her lap was bereft of a child.

That day if the convoy of lorries had safely reached the border and Manohar Lal had gone across it with his wife and child, they would have forgotten about Pali's separation from them as time passed. But, unfortunately, it did not happen like that. They had just crossed the city limits when something untoward happened. The convoy was passing along the road when a mob suddenly emerged from the fields flanking the road, raising war cries. Rushing up, they blocked the road. They wore masks and brandished swords and spears and shouted filthy abuses. Most of the lorries had already passed but the last three could not escape the attention of the marauders. Those in the lorries heard the same heart-chilling sounds of the brandishing of swords and spears which Manohar Lal and Kaushalya had heard back in the town from where they were escaping. Kaushalya did not even know when she felt a heavy jolt and fell down. She only heard Manohar Lal's voice, "Here, give me the child." Then that sound also faded out as she got another powerful push from behind, which sent her crashing to the floor of the lorry. When she regained her senses she heard whistles blowing all round her in the darkness to the accompaniment of groans behind her. She felt something clammy on the floor under her hand. It could have been water, it could as well have been blood. The lorry suddenly started and, as she looked out, she felt as if the stars were also moving with the lorry. Her throat was parched and she felt desperately in need of water. Then the stars started revolving and she passed out.

Even on reaching Delhi Manohar Lal could not get over the feeling that he was still lying crushed under a heap of dead bodies. He feared that if he could not extricate himself from under this heap he would die under the weight of these dead bodies. While foot-slogging on the roads of Delhi along with his wife, bemoaning the loss of his children, he realised that if he did not turn his back on the calamities of the past he would perish on these very roads of Delhi. He hired a push-cart and set up shop on it in one of the bazaars of Delhi. When he returned home, late at night, tired and weary, and found his wife moaning as if she was on the verge of insanity, his courage would desert him. What if she really went mad? How would he take care of her with so many other problems on hand? The small spark of life that was still left in him would also be extinguished.

Taking her hand in his own, Manohar Lal assured Kaushalya it was not too late for them to have another child. But at the mention of children her condition would worsen; she would start trembling and sometimes she wailed in such a heart-rending manner that even Manohar Lal got jittery.

The government had set up big establishments to trace abducted women and lost children and retrieve stolen goods. Government officials made frequent trips to Pakistan in this connection. Manohar Lal took time off his work to visit these

government offices and meet influential people in order to
seek their help in tracing his child. But he was just a nobody
and no one took much notice of him. Month after month
passed, but he found no lead. It was not easy to trace a lost
child in a town swarming with people. When he had begun
the job he had hoped that he had only to visit the town and
identify the particular spot where Pali had got separated from
him. He may find Pali at the entrance of some lane, eagerly
looking out for his father. He would immediately pick up the
child in his arms and on returning to Delhi, put him in
Kaushalya's lap.

What vain hopes! Things were just the reverse of what he
had thought. Much less pick up a thread out of a tangled
mass and go where it led him, he didn't even know where the
thread was and where to start. For two full years Manohar
Lal's case kept hanging in the air. Then he was allowed to
accompany rescue parties consisting of government officials
and social workers that visited Pakistan from time to time.
Manohar Lal would pick up his small tin trunk and join them.
But each time he returned plucking his hair in despair.

After another two years, he at last got a definite clue to
his sons's whereabouts. He learnt that the boy was living in
his erstwhile home town with one Shakur Ahmed who owned
a chinaware shop. This time Manohar Lal was quite sanguine
that his trip would not prove abortive.

The first time the police *havildar* came with the summons
for Shakur, Zenab felt greatly upset, her condition being like
that of a fish that has been thrown out of water. Her dreams
were crumbling before her very eyes.

When Shakur came in the evening his face turned pale on
hearing the news. The news soon went round the *mohalla* and
many sympathisers dropped in to console Shakur. The *maulvi*
also came tapping his *lathi* on the ground.

"You need have no fears," the *maulvi* said. "How dare they touch the child? Now he has accepted Islam. We won't let him fall in the hands of *kafirs*."

Maulvi Sahib's words revived Zenab's drooping spirits. He was right. Now he was not the same child who had slept in Zenab's arms on the first night of his arrival in her house. If someone had come to claim him at that time she wouldn't have stood in his way. But now things were different.

The elders of the town went into a huddle and it was decided that Maulvi Sahib would himself deal with the police. Maulvi Sahib had an ingenious device up his sleeve. The police *havildar* would be tutored to report that he had not found Shakur at home and hence the summons could not be served on him. If the *havildar* persisted in making the calls Shakur and his wife would go away from the town for a few months and stay somewhere else with the child.

"The *havildar* be damned!" Maulvi Sahib said. "I know how to cut him down to size!" He went away tapping his *lathi* and feeling very important.

A strange game of hide-and-seek started thereafter. The high-ups in the governments make agreements but it is the petty government functionaries who execute these agreements. The orders would come from above to produce the boy before the authorities. Walking straight in line with his nose, a police constable from the police station would come to the right house. He would bang on the door, make threatening noises, pocket a rupee, write on the summons papers that he had found the house locked, and that on enquiry he had learnt that the inmates had gone away and there was no knowing when they would return.

This was not a question of a small bribe nor one of returning an adopted child. The matter was taking on a religious slant. By not sending away the child they were doing a service to religion—something which was considered to be a pious act.

Months passed and merged into years.

On one occasion, the entire rescue party descended upon Shakur Ahmed's house but found it locked. They had got news in advance and the family had disappeared before the arrival of the party. Shakur Ahmed, it transpired, had gone to Shekhupura to meet his brother and they had no information as to when he would return. As the party reached Shekhupura it learnt that Shakur Ahmed had left the place only a day earlier with his wife and child for Lyallpur. "Yes, there was a child with them. But we do not know the man's address. He didn't leave any address behind before going away."

In this game of hide-and-seek three years passed. Manohar Lal's face had started turning dark. His cheeks became deeply lined and his hair showed streaks of gray. All the time the dust of despair kept blowing before his eyes. He could not even distinguish between a truth and a lie. Life was mauling Manohar Lal with the same ferocity with which a hawk tears a bird apart with its beak.

Whether it was the result of Manohar Lal's determination or the effect of Kaushalya's sighs, after seven years Manohar Lal found himself sitting in Shakur Ahmed's courtyard. He had gone there with a government rescue party and a woman representative of a social service organisation. From the Pakistan side there were two police officers and a magistrate to conduct the proceedings. The meeting had become possible due to the intervention of a high Government of India official who had moved his counterpart in Pakistan.

At the meeting Manohar Lal was required to prove that the child was really his. There was a legal angle to it and he must conform to a set procedure and convince the officials as to his right to the child.

There was tension in the courtyard. The Maulvi Sahib was sitting a little part from the officials. A lot of people had gathered outside Shakur Ahmed's house. Zenab was sitting in the verandah behind a tarpaulin curtain. Her face looked pale, but her eyes were sharp and watchful like the eyes of an eagle guarding its nest. Altaf Husain sat leaning against her, looking tense and bewildered. Zenab squeezed his shoulder again and again.

Before the proceedings started, Maulvi Sahib came out with all sorts of threats, perhaps to intimidate Manohar Lal.

"Nobody can take away the child. No *kafir* can touch him," he kept muttering.

The man heading the Indian party requested the magistrate several times to ask the *maulvi* to keep quiet. He reminded the magistrate that if the *maulvi* did not stop interfering it would increase the tension.

After the partition of the country the blood on the roads and streets had long since dried but its stains were still faintly visible here and there. The fire that had engulfed the houses had died out long since but the charred frames were still standing. The mad frenzy of the partition had abated but its effects still lingered in the minds of the people.

"Call the child!" the magistrate said, starting the proceedings.

"We have not stolen anybody's child," Zenab's agitated voice came from behind the curtain. "Why should I send him out?"

"Produce the child before me," the magistrate repeated his orders. Shakur Ahmed went behind the curtain to fetch the child.

Manohar Lal's heart was pounding hard. The most decisive moment of his life had come. He was eager to have a look at his long lost child. At the same time his mind was assailed by doubts and fears.

The boy was made to stand before the magistrate. Seeing the crowd in the courtyard, he became nervous and clung to Shakur's legs. Putting his finger in his mouth, he looked around at the people as if stupefied.

"Son, come here," the magistrate said. "Look, who is

here. Do you know any of them?"

"Nobody should prompt the boy," the police officer said in a warning tone. "Let the child decide for himself."

Manohar Lal himself failed to recognise his own son. An eleven-year-old boy, a *Rumi* cap perched on his head, dressed in a muslin *kurta* and *salwar*. Manohar Lal's eyes were beginning to deceive him. He stared at the boy for a long time. Then the image of his own child flashed through his mind and his throat choked with emotion, "Pali!" he cried. "Pali, my son!" But the voice died in his throat. Even otherwise, he was not supposed to draw the boy's attention to himself.

The boy surveyed the people sitting in the courtyard. His expression recorded no change at the sight of Manohar Lal. He was looking scared as before—only a little more so. Manohar Lal watched him intently. He had grown quite tall and fair and handsome and healthy. Manohar Lal felt that the time of decision was gone. The dice seemed to be loaded against him. Shorn of all joys, his life would remain bare and empty like a sandy waste.

Breaking the silence, the *maulvi* said, "So you have seen it. The child has failed to recognise him. Had he been this man's child he would have dashed forward to him. And look at this man's audacity—he has come to demand another's child!"

The lady social worker was greatly annoyed. "Come here, son," she said. "Look, who's the man sitting in front of you?"

"No prompting please!" the police officer warned the social worker. "Leave the child alone. Let him find out for himself."

Zenab was sitting inside, holding her breath. She was feeling uncertain.

Addressing Shakur, the social worker said, "You've yourself admitted that he is not your child—that you've adopted him."

Before Shakur Ahmed could reply, the *maulvi* banged his *lathi* on the floor and said, "We don't deny that he is an adopted child. But how can one accept this man's contention that the boy is a Hindu child and belongs to him?"

The magistrate nodded his head as if he was in agreement with what the *maulvi* had said. He looked now at the child, now at Manohar Lal. Manohar Lal felt more and more depressed. His own child was standing before him and all he could do was to watch him listlessly. The opportunity had really slipped through his fingers.

"The child has become nervous," the lady social worker said.

"Please keep quiet!"

"What more do you want now?" the *maulvi* said. "Its already decided. You people may go."

The social worker turned to Manohar Lal, "Yes, now I remember," she said. "Where's the photograph you had shown me the other day?"

By way of proof Manohar Lal had not been able to bring anything except a small photograph. At Kaushalya's request he had got himself photographed along with her at the *Baisakhi* fair. Little Pali was sitting in his lap. But the photograph could serve no useful purpose. Pali had now grown quite big and bore no resemblance to the little Pali of the photograph. Manohar Lal took the photograph out of his pocket and passed it on to the magistrate.

"My son is there in this photograph. It's the same child. You can see for yourself."

Shakur Ahmed flared up. "*Janab,* this photograph proves nothing," he said to the magistrate. "I too have a photograph."

He went in and came back with a framed photograph. Wiping it with his sleeve, he handed it to the magistrate.

"It's the same child whom you see standing in front of you," he said indicating towards the boy in the photograph. "You can verify for yourself."

"Come here, child." The magistrate placed Manohar Lal's photograph in front of the boy without making any comment, convinced that he would not be able to recognise anybody in the photograph.

The boy looked intently at the photograph for some time. Then, lifting his hand, he placed his forefinger on Manohar Lal's image in the photograph and cried, *"Pitaji!"* Then his finger slowly moved towards the woman in the photograph. *"Mataji!"* he exclaimed.

The child's eyes remained fixed on the photograph. A strange restlessness seemed to have seized him.

Manohar Lal burst out crying. He thrust the end of his turban into his mouth to suppress his sobs.

The magistrate placed the other photograph in front of the child. The child beamed. *"Abbaji! Ammi!"* he exclaimed.

A wave of joy surged through Shakur Ahmed's mind. Zenab peeped out from behind the curtain. Her eyes were brimming with tears.

The *maulvi*'s face had remained taut all this time. But now his expression suddenly mellowed.

"Now he is a Mussalman's son, not a Hindu's. He has read the *kalma*," the *maulvi* said with an air of finality.

"Please be quiet!" the social worker cried.

"Why should I remain quiet? This man had thrown him away and disappeared. We brought him up!" The *maulvi*'s voice rose.

Hearing the *maulvi*'s loud and threatening voice, the boy ran and clung to Shakur's legs. Then he ran towards the verandah and hid behind the curtain.

They must have heard what was going on in the courtyard for, suddenly, slogans resounded outside Shakur's house, *"Allah-ho-Akbar!"*

The lady social worker and the two Indian officials put forward the plea stoutly that since the child had recognised his father he should forthwith be restored to him without further ado. But things seemed to be taking an ugly turn. The tension was mounting. While the child was sitting in Zenab's lap with his arms around her neck, the complexion of the problem was undergoing a change. It had become a Hindu-Muslim question. Questions like "Whose child is he? Who had brought him up?" seemed to have become extraneous to the situation.

Finding himself at the end of his tether, Manohar Lal had a brainwave. Getting up, he went and stood near the curtain. Folding his hands he said, "*Bahen*, I'm not begging you for my child. I'm begging you for my wife's life. She has lost both her children. She is missing Pali very much. His absence is driving her insane. Day and night she keeps thinking of him. Please have pity on her."

The space behind the tarpaulin curtain remained steeped in silence. The officials of both the countries watched the curtain intently. The *maulvi* rose to his feet. He had no doubt in his mind that Zenab would hurl the choicest abuses at Manohar Lal. Instead, they heard the sound of sobbing from behind the curtain. "Take away the child. I do not want an unfortunate woman's curse to fall upon me. How could I know you have lost both your children?"

Manohar Lal felt like going behind the curtain and falling at the woman's feet.

An hour later the child was given a send-off. Amidst tears, Zenab and Shakur helped the child to put on new clothes which had been specially made for the forthcoming *Id*. They put a new *Rumi* cap on his head. Then Zenab said, "I will part with the child on one condition. You must send him to us every year on the occasion of *Id* to stay with us for a month. Do you agree? Then give me your word."

Manohar Lal's body tingled. His hands still folded in supplication, he said, "He is your wealth, *bahen*. I give you my word. I'll remain indebted to you all my life."

The wheel of life started moving again. The same meandering paths, the same turnings, the same ups and downs. If things had ended there, the narration would have assumed the form of a story, holding something of interest for everybody. But nothing ever ends, nothing ever comes to its finality. The powers that be scored out one more name from the long list of the abducted and transferred that name to the list of the "Found."

The government jeep was travelling at great speed. By the side of the driver sat an armed guard and next to him the police officer. At the back of the jeep sat father and son, tightly set against each other, and opposite them the lady social worker. The child looked lost and forlorn. In contact with the boy's body, Manohar Lal's body had again started tingling warmly. The chords of affection which had snapped were again slowly joining together.

They crossed the border in the afternoon. Getting down from the Pakistani jeep they submitted their papers to the scrutiny of the Indian authorities stationed on the other side of the boundary line. Manohar Lal, his son and the others then drove off in another jeep towards Amritsar.

The jeep had not gone far when the lady social worker, as if acting on a sudden impulse, stretched out her right hand to whisk off the *Rumi* cap from the boy's head and flung it outside the jeep. The red, black tasselled cap, flying in the air, landed in the dust at the edge of the road.

"My cap!" the boy's hand went to his head. "*Hai,* my cap!"

The lady social worker leaned towards the boy. "You are a Hindu boy. Why should you wear a Muslim cap?"

Manohar Lal did not appreciate the brusque manner in which the cap had been removed from the boy's head and thrown away. "That must have hurt the boy's feelings. He doesn't know that it is a Muslim cap," Manohar Lal said to the social worker. "Why did you throw it away? Stop the jeep. I must retrieve the cap."

The boy had pulled a long face and was on the verge of tears. His hand resting over his head, he kept moaning over the loss of his cap. "Oh, my cap!" he cried again and again.

"He is still a child, ignorant of these things," Manohar Lal explained patiently. "See, he's still crying."

"Let him cry," the woman said. "Crying is not going to do him any harm. You're not going to give him a *Rumi* cap to wear, are you? He'll stop crying in a short while."

The jeep raced on, raising clouds of dust behind it.

Far away from the border, in a small town, where a lot of refugees had settled down, the news spread at the speed of lightning that Manohar Lal and Kaushalya's son had returned. The impossible had happened. God's mill, they said, grinds slow, but it grinds fine. The boy was returning after seven years. A lucky child indeed. The women kissed the child's head and bowed their heads in gratitude to God. "See, *bahen*, one who is ordained to live, lives long . . . . See, *bahen,* the child you were holding against your bosom was snatched away by death right from your arms, and the one who had strayed away from you and was knocking about lone and forlorn, has come back hale and hearty. Nobody can harm a person who has God's benign protection."

Back home, the child kept whimpering as he had done many years ago on the first two or three days of his arrival in Shakur's house. On the first day of his arrival he kept watching his mother, Kaushalya, from a distance. He saw nothing of those traits in her which he hazily remembered to have marked in her as a mother. The loss of her children seemed to have wrought havoc with her youth. Dim memories of the past were slowly reviving in the child's mind—hazy, nebulous, incoherent. He vaguely remembered his small sister lying in his mother's lap. And the buffalo that stood tethered outside their door and on whose back he used to have a joy ride. Also the wooden bed that was a permanent fixture outside their house. He could hear a babble of sounds rising higher and higher every moment. The identity of his mother had gradually started returning to his mind. But sometimes he still wondered that the boy who was standing before her, finger in mouth, and brazenly staring at her, was he really Pali? He would feel more and more confused.

Three or four days passed in this manner.

Then came Sunday. The *dholak* began beating in Manohar Lal's courtyard from early morning. The women of the *mohalla* gathered in the courtyard and sang in tune to the rhythmic beat of the drum. Two small cotton carpets had been spread in the courtyard and there were a few cane seats lined against the walls, and also some cots to sit on in case there was an overflow of guests. Kaushalya was looking her normal self; she was not silent or withdrawn as before. Now she even laughed sometimes. That morning she wore a red *chunri* bordered with threads of gold—a red *chunri,* a traditional Hindu symbol of matrimonial bliss and good fortune.

Manohar Lal was all attention to the guests. He was not tired of telling his friends that those people back in Pakistan had taken great care of his son. He could not match the attention and affection they had showered on him. He would indeed remain indebted to them all his life.

The narrow courtyard was filled with guests. Holding a big platter of *laddoos,* Manohar Lal was about to go round to distribute the sweets when Pali did something very strange. He had been sitting by the side of his mother, listening to the women playing the *dholak* and singing, when he got up abruptly and fetched a mat from inside. He spread it on the floor, sat down on it folding his legs under his thighs, and started saying his *namaz.*

The people sitting in the courtyard watched Pali with curiosity. But their curiosity soon changed into dismay.

"What's going on, Kaushalya?" a woman asked. "What's your son doing?"

Manohar Lal was feeling embarrassed at his son's strange antics in front of his guests. He should have anticipated this and done something to prevent it from happening. He apologetically said to the man standing by his side, "Every afternoon right at this hour he sits down to say his *namaz*. He instinctively comes to know that it's time for *namaz*."

"Don't you stop him?" a voice asked.

"He's still a child. He'll learn soon enough."

A man who was regarded as a big shot in the *mohalla* said in a loud voice for all to hear, "He must at once get rid of this nasty habit. We don't want to have a Muslim among us."

The boy continued with his *namaz* while the people around him watched with feelings of disgust.

Manohar Lal said as if in self defence, "You know those people didn't have a child of their own. And . . ."

"Manohar Lal!" the big shot who was regarded as the *Chaudhri* of the *mohalla*, cut Manohar Lal short, "You must know those people have foisted a Muslim convert on you and yet you have nothing but praise for them."

The boy was still sitting on his folded legs and, with his palms raised upwards, repeating his *namaz* prayers. the *Chaudhri* went and stood by the boy's side.

His *namaz* finished, the boy was wiping his face with both his hands when the *Chaudhri* caught him by the wrist and dragged him to the middle of the courtyard.

"What were you doing?" he asked the boy.

Pali got unnerved. "I was saying *namaz*," he said in a faint voice.

"We won't allow you to do such silly things in this house," the *Chaudhri* barked at Pali. "No *namaz* hereafter. Do you understand?" Turning round to the people standing around him, he remarked, "Those *Muslas* have planted the poison of fanaticism in his mind. And at such a tender age!"

He stood thinking for a while. "Better call a *pandit*," he said in a decisive tone to a friend. "And also a barber. We must perform the boy's *mundan*. And let him keep a proper tuft. Those rascals! They have planted a *Musla* on us."

Pali stood there looking utterly confused.

"What's your name, boy?"

Pali looked timidly at the massive build of the *Chaudhri* and mumbled in a subdued voice, "Altaf, Altaf Husain, son of Shakur Ahmed."

The *Chaudhri* glared at the boy. With great difficulty he restrained himself from slapping him. The boy felt that the pressure of the man's grip on his wrist had increased. He gave the man a terrified look.

"No, your name is Pali—Yashpal!"

The boy stood silent and then mumbled, "Altaf."

"Repeat that name again and see what happens. I'll pull out your tongue!"

"Have you seen these *Musla's* doings?" the *Chaudhri* said, turning to the people standing around him. "They call it conversion—religious conversion. Reform!"

The barber arrived, followed by the *pandit*. There was also a man accompanying the *pandit* carrying *ghee* and other ingredients for performing a *havan*.

The boy was again made to sit on a mat. The barber sharpened the razor on his palm and according to the directions given by the *pandit*, started shaving the boy's head. As long as the ceremony lasted the boy kept sobbing with bowed head. Once he got up in fright and crying "*Ammi, Ammi, Abbaji!*" ran towards the wall of the courtyard. Standing with his back against the wall, he looked at the *Chaudhri* like a deer at bay watching a hunter. At the suggestion of the *Chaudhri*, Manohar Lal went to fetch the boy. He held the boy's hand and gently brought him back to the mat.

A tuft of hair was left in the middle of his cropped head. Pali was bathed, given a brand new *dhoti* and *kurta* to wear. To the chanting of *mantras* he was given a sacred thread.

"Child, what's your name? Say five times, Pali, Pali, Pali . . . ."

Some time later, looking every inch a *brahmachari*, Yashpal (Pali) stood at the door with folded hands, seeing off the guests. The relatives and guests caressed his head and blessed him while departing. Manohar Lal distributed *laddoos*.

At that time, sitting in their lonely courtyard hundreds of miles away, Zenab and Shakur were making all sorts of conjectures. Zenab said, "He is gone and with him is gone all the gaiety of this house. At this time I used to go out into the street in search of him. He would try to hide from me, running into all nooks and corners. I would never know where to find him. Oh, it was such joy! Well, what do you think? Will he come to visit us for *Id*? Will those people send him here? I think they will."

"Oh, yes; you once told me you had a cousin living in Bareilly. We shall go and stay with him and meet our son. What do you think of that?"

She wiped her eyes again and again.

(Translated from the original in Hindi by the author)

25

GULZAR SINGH SANDHU

Gods on Trial

NOORA SAT QUIETLY under a mango tree by the tombs of the *Pirs*. He was absorbed in doing the homework given by his teacher. Rahmte, his sister, was cutting fodder from the Sikh Martyrs field, near the *Pirs'* graveyard.

The Martyrs' entombed near our field are supposed to possess miraculous powers transcending death, fire and time. We of the Sikh religion have profound faith in them. So much so that I was not allowed even to take the school examination unless I pledged an offering to them. My grandfather believed that it was only because of the Martyrs' kind intercession that I never once failed in any examination.

That summer day, I was also sitting with Noora under the mango tree. While Noora was engrossed in homework, I watched Rahmte, cutting fodder from our field. I liked her so much that I felt like talking about her to Noora.

"Of your two sisters whom do you like more? Rahmte or Jaina?" I asked.

"Jaina," he said, naming the elder one who had been married for four years then.

"Why don't you like Rahmte?" I asked, and was suddenly aware that I could be misunderstood.

"She beat me once, which Jaina never did," he said casually, to my satisfaction, and returned to his book. Assured that I was not misunderstood, I started watching the rhythmic movement of Rahmte's limbs operating the sickle.

Just then something startled a peacock on the Martyrs' *peepal* tree, and it shot off into the air flapping its large wings with a heavy, muffled thud-thud. One of the feathers came off and sailed down to the ground. I was then a keen collector of peacock feathers. As I saw one sailing down in its rich dazzling colours, I threw down my book and ran for it. But it never touched the ground. Rahmte had grabbed it from the air, before I could.

"Hand it to me," I said a little tensely.

"I got it first," she replied coldly.

"None of that!" I threatened, "You have to give it to me."

"Oh, I have to, have I?" she scoffed. "In that case, I shan't."

"Come on, hand it over and I'll never ask anything more from you." I tried to sound suggestive and grown up. She flushed.

"Take it, there," she said curtly throwing the feather away. She collected the fodder into a sheaf, picked it up and started to go home. I could not take my eyes off her slender figure, straining under the weight of the sheaf. I was left wondering whether I had really offended her.

Back in the graveyard I found Noora's father, the saintly Badru, saying his *namaz*. Noora stood by humbly. Both the father and the son had incongruous yellow scarves, the symbol of the Sikh religion, around their necks, for they, along with others, had recently agreed to "conversion." These were the days of communal riots and the yellow scarf guaranteed security to the Muslim minority in East Punjab.

The partition of the country had torn India into two parts and conversion had been made a condition by the Sikhs, for those Muslims staying on in India, in retaliation to a similar declaration by Muslims in Pakistan for any Hindus or Sikhs there. The majority, no doubt, in our area were Muslims, and that too of the orthodox sect of Sunnis. But what could they do? They were in India and whoever did not convert to Sikhism was killed.

After the invitation for conversion a huge number of steel bangles, wooden crescent combs and yellow scarves were procured for an elaborate conversion ceremony. Just when the *prasad* (the sanctified sweet) was being prepared for initiating the Muslims to the Sikh religion, a phlegmatic voice said:

"What good is this initiation, bound by outward symbols? These cannot deter them from continuing to be Muslims at heart!" It was Baba Phuman Singh, pausing to fling a pellet of opium into the hollow cavern of his mouth.

"What else do you advise us to do?"

"Feed them with pork," he said.

"Our own people have been made to eat beef on that side of the border," said another.

Everyone agreed to feed pork to the Muslims gathered for initiation. Four or five pigs were killed and cooked immediately. This ceremony had been carried out in a similar manner in neighbouring villages also.

The Muslims listened and watched with the resigned passivity and indifference of those who no longer cared whether they live or die.

"Our Gurus baptised with *prasad* only," my father whispered to *Baba-ji*, in mild protest.

"Keep your mouth shut, man. Nothing like silence," he said, and drifted towards the pots of meat to examine the quality.

In a little while all the Muslims were initiated into the Sikh religion. Wearing the five symbols of Sikhism they started swallowing the pieces of pork served to them.

"We have always been Hindus. Only that blasted Aurangzeb made us change," one of them said in a futile effort to seek justification for his acts. *Baba-ji*, and a few other village elders, sat a little separately from the rest, in their own superior elite group of *Sandhus*.

"The Maharaja of Patiala is a Sidhu," I heard him say. "Sidhu and Sandhu are equal. The only difference is that our *jagir* provides us only with opium while the maharaja's gives him all the luxury he can dream of." The talk did not interest me.

"Noora and his people are not being baptised?" I asked my father. "Hush!" my father silenced me, "I have delivered all the five symbols to them and they are wearing them. Noora's father is a saintly person and respects us. I wouldn't want him to feel disgraced in public. Maybe he does not want to take part."

When my grandfather asked about the baptism of Badru and his family, my father managed to convince him that Badru had taken pork in his very presence. To allay any remaining doubts, Father swore solemnly, and thus the whole of Badru's family was also counted among the baptised.

And where was the lie in it? That day when I had demanded the peacock feather from Rahmte, she was wearing a yellow *dupatta* on her head and a steel bangle on her wrist. Her father, Badru, and her brother, Noora too were wearing yellow scarves around their necks and steel bangles on their wrists. Both were performing the *namaz*. They would not have dared to pray the Muslim way had there been a witness. But then the only person present was myself and I was Badru's pupil. They knew well that I would not tell anyone in the village that they were praying the Muslim way. How could I, who till the third standard had done my sums with the help of Rahmte?

It is still all so clear before my eyes—that day, Rahmte carrying the sheaf of fodder, Badru and Noora praying. The long *henna*-dyed beard of the holy man touched the ground as he bowed in prayer. His loose Lucknowi shirt was a little dirty. I stood at some distance watching them all, when I heard sudden shouts of *"Boley so Nihal, Sat Sri Akal."* It was the Sikh cry and it sent us running for our lives in great terror. In the general panic Noora stumbled and fell on the ground. The galloping hoofs came to a stop and many a spear was jabbed viciously into his body. He lay there with his entrails hanging out. It was the last I saw of him.

I looked at the riders in yellow and blue and stood there dazed. They had already closed in on Badru. The saint pleaded with folded hands, flourishing his yellow scarf and the steel bangle on his wrist to show he was a Sikh. A *Nihang* Sikh with fox-tail moustaches, playfully struck the wrist which was raised to exhibit the bangle, and cut it clean from the elbow. When Badru raised his other hand in abject supplication, the tyrant struck that off too.

"Send this bug as well to Pakistan," someone shouted and ran towards me.

Sending one to Pakistan was a common phrase for killing a Muslim.

"He's a Sikh one, you fool," a voice checked him. It was the *Nihang* Sikh who had speared Noora.

From his saddle he lifted me up and put me in his lap.

I do not know what happened after that, for I lost consciousness.

When I came to my senses the next day I was lying in bed on the verandah. My mother's eyes were red and swollen with crying.

"He's saved, don't you worry. It was only shock. He is just a child after all." *Baba-ji* was talking to my mother.

"It was almost the end of him," my mother said wiping her tears and rubbing my limbs.

"What a dreadful shock for you, my son! God protect you, God bless you," she said, wiping my face with her *dupatta*.

"Bless and be blessed, afterwards, first give offerings to

the Martyrs who saved his life," said *Baba-ji*, and everyone agreed to this proposal. They started making preparations for the Martyrs.

Chokingly, I told my mother about Noora's death and asked her in a trembling voice if she knew anything about Rahmte. She told me in tears that Jaina and Rahmte were abducted by the crusading rioters along with other Muslim girls of the village. Many were murdered, about fifty of them. Whoever was seen with a new yellow scarf and bright steel bangle was killed.

Meanwhile, the whole of the village made ready to offer *prasad* to the Martyrs. Though it was a quiet evening, everyone was frightened. Baba Phuman Singh was absolutely stunned. He was almost out of his wits. Just a short while earlier he had been informed that his life-long friend Ghanshiam Das had also been killed by mistake. He had been carrying a yellow scarf to one of his Muslim friends out in the fields, when he was surprised by the rioters who killed him, taking him to be a new convert. They did not wait to check who was who. They were busy people. They had to visit and plunder other villages too. For them the sight of a yellow scarf was proof enough of "converts".

While praying at the Martyrs' Field, *Baba-ji* (my grandfather) was still thinking of Ghanshiam Das. Yes, true, he had to die some day. But this sudden and uncalled-for death had given a new uncertainty to people, including Baba-ji. It meant that anyone who was carrying a yellow scarf, even if he was a Sikh or a Hindu, would not be spared. Where then was the guarantee of safety to converts? In fact, those who had not accepted Sikhism were safer, for they were cautious, not caught so easily, and hence not killed. Thus, absurdly, avowed Muslims were escaping while Sikhs were being slaughtered!

Even though he was singing aloud the praises of Guru Gobind's sons, the Five Beloved Ones, and the Forty Martyrs,

Baba-ji's heart was crying over the calamitous riots. Towards the end, when he was reciting verses in honour of those who had shared their wealth, fought sinners, offered sacrifices for the faith, his legs suddenly buckled beneath him. The mention of "sacrifices for the faith' choked his throat. His *khunda* fell off on the ground. The rest of the prayer was completed by my father. Having finished the ceremony, my father told me to go and offer *prasad* to the Martyrs. As I placed it on their tombs, the crows from the *peepal* tree nearby came cawing and swooping and ate it up in no time. "Let the Martyrs remain hungry," I said to myself.

As my father distributed the *prasad* to everyone and was about to leave, *Baba-ji* came forward and held him there by his arm.

"Tell the boy to put some on the *Pirs'* tombs too," he said pointing towards the *Pirs'* graveyard. Looking in that direction I remembered Noora. The *peepal* in the field reminded me of Rahmte who had frowned at me under it. Had she done it in love or in hatred? I would never know now.

"What do you mean?" Father asked Baba-ji, a little puzzled—'on the *Pirs'* tombs'?"

"You remember the massacre," *Baba-ji* whispered to Father, after taking him beyond the boundary of the field. Perhaps he dared not say it within the Martyrs' domain, afraid of their curse on his unbelief.

"Yes, I remember," Father said bitterly.

"Those who were initiated have been killed, haven't they?"

"So what?" whispered my father still puzzled.

"Those who did not agree to initiation are saved, you know that."

"I don't understand," Father said, frowning perplexedly.

"Well, if you don't, I can't help it," snapped *Baba-ji*, a little irritated by my father's denseness.

"Listen," he tried again, whispering very low to prevent the Martyrs' overhearing, "Those who remained Muslims were saved, were they not? Well, who knows if tomorrow the *Pirs* don't turn out to be more powerful than our Martyrs?"

Suddenly enlightened, I ran and offered *prasad* at the *Pirs'* tombs. Father did not stop me.

Perhaps the insinuation in *Baba-ji's* remarks still escaped him.

(Translated from the original in Punjabi by Raj Gill)

26

M. S. SARNA

Savage Harvest

As HE BENT over the furnace stuffed with hard coal, Dina's iron black body seemed to be moulded in bronze, resembling some statue of a healthy labourer. The muscles of his well-exercised body rippled as he swung the hammer around himself and a great blow fell on the red-hot bits of iron.

The blows continued to fall and echo. Immersed in his work, Dina was lost to the world until the hot sun of late August, streaming in through the open window, began to lick at his very bones. With a jerk, he looked out of the window. Already the sun was at its height and his work was not even half done.

With the heat from the sun and the furnace, his body itself seemed to be on fire. Each pore of his body had become a wick and at any moment it seemed one of these wicks would catch fire and blow up his body like a huge firecracker.

Suddenly, he dropped his tools and went to the window. On the left, the ploughed furrows awaited the seed. The scent of the wet earth made him nostalgic and he wanted to jump out of the window. He wanted to roll in the fields and let the pores of his burning body soak in the moisture from the wet earth.

He loved the fields. During the sowing and harvesting, his blood would tingle and a strange freedom would come into his limbs. He was the village blacksmith, but there had not been much work for him.

Sickles, harvests, the sugarcane swaying gently in the moonlight. The call of the golden earth and the lilt in the songs born of this earth. He forgot for a moment that a torrid fire raged behind him and that for the last twenty days he had done nothing but mould metal into axes and spears.

What kind of an unholy mess was he in? Carrying, as it were, the entire responsibility of arming the fighters of newly born Pakistan. The fledgling country was already a reality, but to complete that reality it seemed necessary to kill all the Hindus and the Sikhs. He did not understand this fully, but this was what everybody said. From the village heads to the *Imams* of the mosques, all of them said so. And this *jihad* would succeed only if his furnace kept raging and kept spitting out fierce instruments of death.

He turned again to the fire. The sharp bit of metal was brighter than the coals. His head began to swim. A sharp, hot pain was piercing through his side. Hunger. Not a drop of water had he taken since the morning. And now hunger was picking at his insides and thirst had turned his lips into wood.

"Oh! Bashir's mother!" he shouted into the house, "give me water, quick."

A woman of about forty-five brought water in a jug. She wore a nose ring and her silver earrings swayed as she walked. She stared at her husband. He was panting with thirst. She had asked him about food and water thrice, since the morning. But he had not responded and had continued to blow at his fire. What had made him think of water now? She stared at the bright fire, she stared at the bits of iron scattered around the room. She stared at the pile of axes and spears, her gaze continually returning to her husband's face.

Dina drained the jug at a go.

"More," he panted.

She brought more water and watched him as he drank.

"That's all," he said.

The taut veins of his body and forehead relaxed. His breathing became easier. And then a shadow crossed his face.

"Why are you staring at me like that? Why don't you talk to me? And why do you stand away from me, as if I have the plague?"

She did not reply. Instead she went into the house and brought a plate of food.

"I'm talking to you," Dina shouted, shaking her by the shoulders. "Why don't you speak? Have you put rice to boil in your mouth that you can't speak? Not talking to me, just staring as if I was the very devil himself."

"Allah forbid," she said, "but it does seem so to me."

Dina's mouth fell open in surprise. He had lost all hope that Bashir's mother would ever speak, that she would break the stubborn silence of so many days.

When he had recovered from his surprise, he said—"I know what's on your mind, but what do I do? Your sons won't let me be. Now Bashir wants fifty axes ready by tomorrow night. He'll be at my neck if they aren't ready. I know that if I don't obey them they will cut me up. They will drink my blood."

"Are they your sons or someone else's?" she asked, a little ashamed of her own question. "Should they fear you, or should you fear them?"

"You talk as if you don't know your own sons, what demons they are. Can I say anything to them? Won't they skin me alive?" said Dina.

"They are my sons, too." His wife's tone was softer now. "You know they shout at me and curse me. But I don't go making axes for them."

"I only make axes," he replied. "I don't kill people with them."

"It's worse than killing," she said. "The killer kills one, two or at most fifty people. Each axe made by you kills several scores."

A tremor passed through Dina's spine. Then this trembling touched every pore of his body. For a long time he was silent. And then: "You are telling me! Why don't you talk to your sons, the great warriors who burn two villages every night!"

"Nobody listens to me." Her tone had grown even softer now. "What can I tell anyone? Each one will have to answer for his own sins. Why should I tell anyone?"

For some time, both of them stared at the floor, silently. Suddenly, the woman said: "And why don't you eat food? You want to starve?" She again put the plate in front of him.

A soft knock at the front door shook Dina. He stood up in fright. It must be Bashir or his companions. Yes, they had come to warn him. He hesitated with his hand on the latch and looked around. The fire in the furnace was raging. Everything was in place. He opened the door. Rusted with the rain, it screeched at the hinges.

He jumped back several steps in fear, just missing the fire. His wife's face was drained of blood and a scream escaped her lips. At the door stood the old wife of the brahmin of Thakurdwar. A net of wrinkles spread across the turmeric which was powdered on her face. Her snow-white hair was trembling. Their eyes filled with fear, Dina and his wife stared at the old woman.

At long last, Dina's wife took courage and spoke: "Aunt, you are still alive!"

The old woman did not reply. Dina's wife recalled that she had been hard of hearing. Perhaps the affliction had pursued her in death also. She went closer to the old woman and loudly repeated her question.

Understanding flashed in the old woman's eyes and she said: "Can't you see that I am alive? Seven days I have been racked with fever."

With a strange relief Dina and his wife exchanged looks. It was true that she was the brahmin's wife and not a ghost. The fever had saved her from the holocaust that had struck the village. Her deafness had prevented her from hearing of the great sorrow that had befallen the village on Friday night. She did not know till now that her village was now in Pakistan. She did not know that Pakistan was now in her village. That not one Hindu or Sikh was alive except for a few girls in the hands of the rioters. Suddenly, she asked: "Dina, have you seen my goat anywhere?"

Goat, thought Dina, her goat! In these days, when the rioters had finished off even the cattle, this old woman was bothered about a goat.

"I don't know where she has run off to," the old woman continued "and she's due to breed. I can't even look after myself now. I can't go looking for her and how can I hold her, anyway. If you see her anywhere, tie her up, God bless you. You know she's due. I hope she doesn't give birth somewhere outside."

Dina said: "Old woman, your goat is not there. She has been eaten up and people are burping on her." But the old woman heard nothing. He was going to repeat himself loudly but a look from his wife silenced him.

"And look at this," the old woman said, "this chain I found near the door of Thakurdwar. I don't know how this goat managed to loosen the chain. This link, where the chain is locked is as if eaten away. I thought I'll tell you to fix it for me."

For some time, Dina's wife had been looking at the old woman in a strange fashion.

She seemed to be wrestling with something. And then, having reached some sort of decision, she said:

"Aunt, why don't you stay here? You will be alone in Thakurdwar. And your fever has just gone. Cook your food here, bring your own utensils, since you are a Hindu. Let Tulsi return and you can go."

The old woman seemed to have grown even deafer. Maybe it was the effect of the fever. She only caught Tulsi's name.

"I'm telling you he's gone out of the village. He has gone with the betrothal party of the daughter of Ram Shah to Nawachak. On the first of next month, Preeto is to be married. I told the Shah to gift me a cow. It's not everyday that there are celebrations in the houses of the rich. And you know, Tulsi needs the milk and the curds."

Ignoring the old woman's talk, Dina's wife was looking at her husband. She could see that he wanted to say something, to discuss something. But before she could say anything, Dina was already speaking.

"I know what's on your mind, but we can't do it. I have no objection, but where can we hide her? Soon your sons will be here, their nostrils smelling out human flesh, and you won't be able to hide anything. They will know and what will they do to us then?"

"She is old," beseeched Dina's wife, "a god-fearing old woman. It's a matter of a few days. Let her son return and then we will send her to some other village."

"Which village will you send her to?" Dina was almost screaming now. "Which such village is left where she will be safe? And her son, he will never return. This time he has been sent from where he cannot return. All the Hindus of Nawachak have been killed. Not one of them is left."

His wife's face fell. She put a trembling finger to her lips, begging him to lower his tone. "Can't you speak softly? Or won't you be satisfied until she knows that her son has been murdered?"

Except for Dina's outburst, they had been talking in

whispers. But it was unnecessary, for even their loudest tones would not have reached the old woman through her deafness. She stared at them with her fevered eyes.

"What are you two going on about? And Dina, why don't you look at me? Repair it, I say. It's not that I'm asking for much."

"Come tomorrow," Dina shouted into the old woman's ear, "I don't have any time today. And go home now."

"All right," the old woman croaked, her hands on her knees. "I'll go. If you say tomorrow, then let it be so, but keep an eye out for my goat. I've told you, if you see her then tie her up. Wretched thing, God knows where she has run away to."

And before Dina's wife could stop her, the old woman had stumbled out into the lane.

How much time this old woman had wasted. He could have made five axes in this much time. And Bashir was not going to listen to any excuses. He would want his fifty.

But Dina could not put his heart into the work. Something began to gnaw at his heart. He could not dismiss the vision of fever-ridden eyes and snow-white hair. Those eyes were constantly burning holes in his mind. Most of all, it was her ignorance that bothered him. She knew nothing. That Tulsi was never to return, that Preeto was never to get married, that Preeto along with her rich father's estate had already been taken by Bashir.

This was a rotten thing that Bashir had done. The honour of women was not to be touched. Loss of one woman's honour meant the loss of all women's honour.

A horrible scene rose before his eyes. Preeto, wailing and clutching at her father's corpse. Bashir pulling her away by her hair. Imploring him, wailing and screaming, she had been dragged away. And then she had become silent, in an unholy silence, like the silence of the lamb just before its slaughter.

And he, Bashir's father, had watched this evil sight from the sidelines. He had not stopped Bashir, or pulled him by the scruff of his neck and thrown him on the ground. He had done nothing to save the honour of the girl.

The pale, child-like face of Preeto began to swim before his eyes and her plaintive cries echoed in his ears. He was seized by a trembling, a cold and uncontrollable trembling, that seemed a precursor to certain death. The trembling, he felt, could be stopped only if he picked up the red-hot iron from the fire and clasped it to his heart. But why was his head on fire? The entire blazing furnace seemed to have entered his head. He pressed his head with both hands and the fire came onto his palms.

He was going mad. He would end up doing something terrible. He must run away, far away from all this. He opened the window and jumped out.

For a long time he wandered aimlessly in the fields. It was evening. On the horizon, someone had murdered the sun. The blood of innocents had spread across the sky and had dissolved in the waters of the streams and rivers. Would anybody eat the sugarcane sprayed with blood? Or wear the cotton which had grown in blood? And what kind of a harvest would it be after this bloody season?

The shower of blood that had reddened everything had been caused by the axes that he had fashioned. This crop of bones and flesh had been sown by his spears. And he had just finished making axes for those few who were still left. They too would be gone by tomorrow night.

He was guilty. Heavily, deeply guilty. His wife had spoken the truth. At least, he should not let them lay their hands on the new axes. His sins would not vanish. But what else could he do?

And then he was running, like a man possessed, towards

the village. He wanted to reach home before Bashir's men. He wanted to throw the axes in some well from where they would never be found.

When he reached the village, it was dark. The indifferent light of a hazy moon was throwing shadows of the houses in the lane. Last night's rain had left a muddy slush in the lanes. Stepping into puddles, he walked quickly through the lanes. Suddenly he stopped. He could hear voices coming from a short distance, in fact from his house. Had they already come? He could hear Bashir's echoing laugh.

He stumbled against some heavy object near his house and fell on his face. He tried to get up but could not. An icy cold grip had clasped his feet. He tried to free them but the grip only seemed to get tighter. Suddenly, he was frightened, a terrible fear clutched at his heart and he broke into a sweat. With a strong desperate jerk, he turned to look back. He could see a thatch of snow-white hair in the dim moonlight. The wrinkled forehead of the old woman had a long cut from an axe. And there was a curse in the wide open frightened eyes. He looked at his feet. They were clasped by the chain that she held in her hands.

His scream tore the night and he fainted. That night he was gripped by a high fever. All night he tossed wildly on the bed, all night his delirious shouts echoed in the silence of the village.

"Don't kill me, don't kill me with axes! Take away this chain! Oh my daughter! Don't harm Preeto! Oh these chains! In Allah's name, don't kill me with axes! Don't kill me!"

(Translated from the original in Punjabi by Navtej Sarna)

27

QUDRAT ULLAH SHAHAB

Ya Khuda*

Part I

Lord of the East:
"In this world of Yours, condemned and helpless am I."

Mohammad Iqbal

"**D**AMN YOU! WHY the hell do you keep looking towards the west? A lover coming to see you from that direction?"

Amrik Singh tickled Dilshad's ribs with the point of the *kirpan*—the scimitar—and pinched and pulled her left cheek until her face turned eastward.

Dilshad smiled. This smile had become a very useful tool for her. In childhood, crying was her most successful weapon. A little whimpering enabled her to get anything, from the milk stored in her mother's breast to the sweets hidden in cupboard. Now, her youth had endowed her smile with the same power. She became aware of its magical power when Rahim Khan, enamoured of her smile, took a vow never to let

---

* O God

her out of his sight all through his life. He swore that even if she were taken away by celestial beings, he would jump across all distances between earth and sky and bring her back.

But Rahim Khan had done nothing of the kind. All of his promises had proved to be lies. Let alone any celestial beings, he had lost her to ordinary earthly creatures.

Whenever she was alone, Dilshad would sit facing the west, and in imagination bow her forehead before Him who bestowed all grace and blessings. Ka'aba, God's house, lay westward. Mere thought of that house lit up a resplendent lamp of hope and reality in Dilshad's heart. But the thought of west peeved Amrik Singh no end. In many other ways too, of late the Sikhs in this village had been reacting strangely. From midnight to noon, for the entire twelve hours, every young and old man in the village was tense like a taut bow, as though he had been touched by a live wire and electrified.

Amrik Singh's house was directly behind the mosque, and recently the mosque had become the focus of some strange beliefs. A rumour had started making the rounds of the village that early every evening, some unusual, scary screams and grunts could be heard coming from the well of the mosque, as though a number of goats were being slaughtered simultaneously.

"The damned bastard," Amrik Singh would say. "Even dead, he's bellowing like a bison. Throw down a few more pails of garbage into the well."

"Oh, forget it," his younger brother Tarlok Singh poked fun at the *mullah*. "He's not bellowing; he's calling the faithful to prayer."

"Yes, in the Sikh raj everyone is free to practise his religion," the sage Gyani Darbar Singh said and chortled.

But Amrik Singh's wife felt scared. At night, when the loud screaming emerged from the well of the mosque, her whole body would be drenched in sweat. The image of the *mullah*, the man called Ali Bakhsh, who lived in a cell inside the mosque, appeared before her eyes—the image of a weak, emaciated old man with a foot-and-a-half long white beard, thick glasses on his eyes, a loosely wrapped green muslin turban on the head, tremulous hands, and the veins in the neck swollen and sticking out. But when he stood on the raised platform inside the mosque five times a day to call the believers to prayer, the domes of the mosque echoed with his call, and his weak and tired vocal cords produced sounds that could match in force and firmness the sound of a dozen waterfalls.

The calls to prayer continued to agitate Amrik Singh's wife. It might have been all right if those calls were occasional happenings, but to have to listen to the same words five times a day, every day, was very perturbing. Also, she had heard from the elders that a call to prayer was black magic and young women hearing it could get hexed. If an unmarried girl heard it, she would become infertile; if a married woman heard it, she would have miscarriages. So there was a custom in Amrik Singh's house, practised over many generations, that as soon as the call to prayer came wafting on the air, the women in the house started banging spoons on metal bowls, hitting the griddle with tongs, plugging their ears with fingers, or running into the back rooms to hide. That was how this brave family had protected its women from black magic and kept them fruitful.

A hundred and twenty-five thousand Khalsas were growing up inside the womb of Amrik Singh's wife. That was how the counting of Sikhs was done, each Sikh considered to be equal to and as strong and formidable as a hundred and twenty-five thousand human beings. In the middle of the night, when the horrible screams emerged from the well of the mosque—at least that was what Amrik Singh's wife imagined was going on—the army of one hundred and twenty-five thousand Khalsas in her womb went berserk. Sometimes the screams echoed in her ears, or she imagined the gaping mouth of the well leaping at her. She was unable to shed the dread that Mullah Ali Bakhsh, holding on to the parapet, crawling along it, was going to climb out of the well some day and, standing erect on the rim of the well, was going to put the hex on her.

Amrik Singh's sister's womb hadn't been occupied by any Khalsa yet, as she was still single, but her heart had already been taken over by 125,000 beings. At night, lying in her bed, when she recalled the ticklish sensation that her lover's hungry, probing fingers had produced, when she was with him in the corn field earlier in the day, a swarm of desires invaded her breast and in imagination she allowed her body to be possessed by young and strong Khalsas. But then the heart-rending screams from the well of the mosque destroyed all her pleasurable fantasies, and she felt as if Mullah Ali Bakhsh was using his black magic even from the depth of the well to wipe out the future generations which were to issue from her womb.

Amrik Singh detested both his wife and sister for their cowardice. Mullah Ali Bakhsh had been long gone. Amrik Singh had himself stabbed him when he sat on the parapet of the well one day doing his ablutions. Tarlok Singh had cut him up with his scimitar, and Gyani Darbar Singh had hurled his blood-soaked, shaking body into the well. And it was not just Ali Bakhsh who was out of the way; the entire village of Chamkor had been cleansed. All those who called others to prayers as well as those who obeyed those calls had disappeared—some had run away, some had died, and some had had their throats cut by the holy *kirpans* of the Khalsas. But these superstitious, cowardly women were still fearful of the calls to the prayers and were protecting their wombs from them. Thus, whenever his wife and sister woke up in the middle of the night screaming and beating their breasts, in anger he would beat them with a pair of tongs until they bled, and his own arms got tired and numb with the exertion, and the veins swelled up in his arms. Shaking off the drops of perspiration from his thick beard, like a madman he would run off to Dilshad. Just as a perpetual sufferer from cold occasionally takes a pinch of snuff, in the same way the Khalsas of the village, exasperated by their superstitious wives and sisters, and to ease the tension in their veins, went over to Dilshad.

Dilshad had been kept in the main mosque because the roof of the cell, which was her house, had burnt down. Dilshad's most prized possession, even though she possessed a body and a soul as well, was her father's chain of beads, the *tasbih*. Her father's fingers had grown old telling its beads. Marks of his fingers seemed to have been etched on the small, round jade beads; the tears of devotion and penitence he shed every night, year after year, seemed to have been strung together like pearls in that chain. These were the last pearls to remain in the ravaged oyster-shell of Dilshad's life. During the day she wore the chain around her neck, hiding it under her shirt. In the evening she took it off and hid it safely away in some abandoned corner of the mosque, lest the tongues laced with alcohol and *bhang* touch and defile it and erase the marks made by her father's fingers.

In the middle of the night, she would clasp the parapet of the well and cry, her eyes beginning to smart from staring fixedly inside the well for any sign of her father, even a glimpse of his floating turban. Her ears tired of trying to listen for any sound from her father, even his last gasp. She waited to hear those terrible screams and groans that had frightened the women of the village out of their wits. But the well remained dark and quiet as a grave. Whenever a bat wandered into it and flapped its wings, sharp whiffs of foul and putrid air rose up to the top of the well because the hundred and twenty-five thousand braves of the village had dumped a cart-load of garbage into the well in order to keep Ali Bakhsh's mouth shut even after death.

Dilshad was like an asteroid wandering alone in the

endless expanse of the universe. Her universe had been destroyed; there were no suns or moons left any longer, nor any shining stars. She was cast adrift, alone and friendless, leaning against the door-jamb of the mosque, worried, scared and lost. But because of her the mosque had begun filling up once again. People took turns to get in. When the brave Khalsas sat under the arch of the mosque, opened their quarts of home brews and lustily feasted on the pleasures offered by Dilshad's youthful body, they felt proud of themselves for having taken the revenge for the thirteen hundred years of prayers and calls to prayers in their village.

The Chamkor mosque had in fact become more populated than the *gurdwara*. Gradually, the wed and unwed women of the village began getting irked by the thought that after Mullah Ali Bakhsh, it was his daughter who was now bent on ravaging their wombs. After receiving their beatings with tongs, they would, of course, go back to sleep holding on to their cots, but their brave Khalsas spent the rest of the night with Dilshad, trading away the fate of their future generations. Amrik Singh, his father, his brother—all the Khalsas, one after the other, whenever they got the chance, dropped in to pay their respects. They drank bucketfuls of whiskey and *bhang,* ate roasted liver and kidneys and frittered away in the courtyard of the mosque the seeds which their wives had tried painstakingly to keep for themselves, to bloom in their wombs. And one day it came to be known that Dilshad was pregnant. The news set the whole village on fire. The wives screamed their heads off; the unmarried girls cried themselves half blind and stopped their clandestine meetings with their lovers in the corn fields. The screams from the well became louder. Tongs and rulers began to be used more often in the houses. All hell broke loose. At first, the men decided to kill Dilshad and throw her body into the well before the child could be born, but then Amrik Singh thought of a more rewarding plan. So, one morning he seated Dilshad in his bullock cart, took her to the nearest police station and handed her over as proof of his efforts to recover and help repatriate abducted Muslim women.

The police inspector, Labbhu Ram praised Amrik Singh and assured him that he would receive a letter of thanks from the police department; the Inspector Sahib even promised a testimonial from the Deputy Commissioner. Then the Inspector Sahib put on his glasses to examine Dilshad. She was pleasant looking, young, if a little pale, but certainly supple. But when his eyes came down to her abdomen, his desires received a jolt. At first he hoped it was a matter of ten or fifteen days, and he would be able to keep her in the police station, but when Head Constable Daryodhan Singh made a rough calculation and informed him that it would take her at least three months to be "through," Inspector Labbhu Ram was deeply disappointed. Even then, after the meal that evening as he lay down on his cot, he called for Dilshad to massage his aching feet. He decided to get whatever he could, given the situation. The pain in his feet rose to the calves, then to the thighs and finally settled in the crotch area. He kept guiding Dilshad"s hands to the more painful parts of his body and receiving satisfaction. For Inspector Labbhu Ram, all desires called out for satisfaction; if you didn't get it one way, try another.

None of this was new for Dilshad. In the last few months her life had unfolded in such a way that she had become like a balm—a universal panacea for everybody's aching limbs, to be applied wherever and whenever anyone needed her. And every part of her body was able in minutes to relieve the agony of excited, panting, and restless human beings. But how sore she herself was and how much pain she was herself suffering, no one knew. She wished Rahim Khan was there to see her. Dilshad was now angry at herself why she had so many times denied any closeness to Rahim Khan. Once when he had forcibly tried to kiss her, she was so angry that she hit him on the head with her wrists. She had hit so hard that pieces of her glass bangles had sunk into his forehead.

Herself, she was remorseful the whole night, wondering how God and His Prophet would punish Rahim Khan for his transgression.

Fifteen days later, when the pain in Labbhu Ram's knees, thighs and hip subsided, she was let go and sent to Ambala Camp with Head Constable Daryodhan Singh. Along the way, Head Constable Daryodhan Singh also suffered many bouts of pain in his knees, thighs and back, but Dilshad went on alleviating the pain efficiently. In this manner they were able to safely cover a journey of ten hours in twelve days.

There were many girls in Ambala Camp, many women as well, young and beautiful but subdued, like faded stars that had lost their glow, as if someone had rubbed dirt over their radiance. Army trucks arrived every day, bringing in new girls and women into the Camp. These pearls of dignity and purity, scattered when the thread binding them was broken, were once again returning towards the centre. They hadn't yet thought of calling on their merciful and compassionate God for forgiveness but were still being treated to incantations from the *Granth Sahib*, the holy book of the Sikhs, by the Camp Commander, Major Preetam Singh and his youthful soldiers. In any case, Dilshad was enjoying a break of sorts. Obedient and loyal children are a blessing for the parents, but Dilshad already had a lot of faith in her unborn; it was looking after its helpless mother even before it was born.

The railway tracks were just behind the Ambala Camp. In the sunlight, the tracks shone like silver strings and disappeared far away, in the west, in the pleasant islands of dreams. Somewhere in those islands lay the boundary between hell and heaven. The women became ecstatic just touching those tracks, for they knew that the other end of the tracks was not in the East, but somewhere in the West Punjab. Just thinking of the west lit a tiny lamp of hope in Dilshad's mind. Ka'aba was in the west, and Ka'aba was God's house, but the other women in the Camp insisted there were many other things in the west as well—there were their brothers, sisters, parents, a life of dignity and comfort. Dilshad thought perhaps Rahim Khan might also be there. Thinking of him made her so agitated and restless that she wanted to have wings to fly to her beloved's land and to rub its prized, sacred dust on her tired, aching limbs.

A week, two weeks; a month, two months; days and nights passed, and the promising image of the west went on breeding hope in Dilshad's mind. The population of the Camp increased day by day, and, finally, when the appetites of Major Preetam Singh's muscular and healthy soldiers—the *jawaans*—were thoroughly sated, one day the train which had kept the women's hopes alive, did arrive. When she boarded it, Dilshad remembered her father. He too had taken the train to go on the pilgrimage: he was garlanded and perfumed, accompanied by a party of villagers who had brought him to the station playing music.

Every burst of speed of the train shook up the women. Every turn of the wheel undid another knot in their beings. Looking out of the windows and watching the lampposts race by, they were gradually becoming convinced that they were, indeed, going forward. Every inch of land they traversed took them away from East Punjab and closer to West Punjab. If the train stopped anywhere along the way, the whole universe held its breath. Time itself seemed to stop. They became afraid that huge boulders had suddenly grown in front of the train. Their hearts began beating only when the train started moving again, and their breasts were filled with hopes and dreams. Taking their hands out of the windows, they tried to touch the air that was coming from the west.

Ludhiana, Phillaur, Jullundar, . . . Amritsar. At every step the women felt a little less strained, a little more animated; hidden melodies in their beings became alive; they began humming, smiling, rubbing their eyes and looking at each other as if deliberately trying to forget a horrible nightmare.

One began combing her hair; another shaking the dust off her clothes; a third started singing lullabies to her children. Some huddled together to sing songs—sweet, mellifluous, enthralling, devotional songs.

When the train moved out of Amritsar, someone mentioned that only an hour-and-a-half of the journey remained. Sixty plus thirty minutes; ninety minutes in all. This unbelievable thought affected them like a shot of potent liquor. The feeling that they had come so close to their destination was so intense that they felt paralysed. The poisonous memory of the previous few terrible months welled up in their breasts. The horror of their past suddenly drowned the pleasant dreams of their future. They remembered their verdant villages, their young brothers, their ageing parents whose unburied carcasses had been left behind rotting in the streets, their unhappy sisters who sat in refugee camps waiting for angels to hide them in their luminous wings and take them away, far far away, towards the west. . . . They began crying, shedding copious tears, sobbing bitterly. Dilshad's tears gushed like water from a mountain spring. She cried and cried until a thick sheet of tears blinkered her eyelashes. She was overcome by a strange numbness, an intoxication. She felt as if she were sinking to the bottom of the sea, and numerous fishes were crawling on her body, crawling all over her. . . !

Part II

Lord of the West:
"And You are the Lord and Master of my world!"

Mohammad Iqbal

When she woke up, the train compartment was empty. The sweeper woman was washing the floor with water, and a tiny baby-girl lay on Dilshad's side. The morning was bathed in

the early light. Frisky sparrows jumped about in the trees.
Dew drops glistened on the grass. There was a lot of bustle
on the station. A worker at the tea-stall near the compartment
window was boiling milk on a stove. Dilshad got up and sat
down, her body leaning against the window. Weakly, she
asked the tea-stall attendant, "Is this the west, brother?"

"Why, you want to say your prayer at this time?" he said
and bared his ugly yellow teeth in a laugh.

When the sweeper woman had washed the compartment
floor, she asked Dilshad for a four-anna piece for all the work
she had put in, but getting nothing, she began swearing at her:
"The slut. Polluted the whole compartment; couldn't even
wait; gave birth right here. . . . "

Then the sweeper woman went and brought a sturdy male
co-worker with her. Together, the two of them threw Dilshad
out of the compartment.

A luggage cart stood on the platform. Dilshad sat down
leaning against it. The tea-stall was right in front of her.
Swirls of steam rose from the copper samovar full of boiling
tea, like a young lady's tresses blowing in the wind. Ahead of
the tea-stall was a fruit shop. Bananas, oranges, tangerines
were arranged in neat piles on coloured paper. A pomegranate
cut in half lay open in a basket. Bunches of grapes hung from
the canopied roof of the stall. Dilshad's throat was dry like a
thorn, her tongue crusted over with a thick, dirty layer of
saliva. Her stomach felt strangely feverish; pain stabbed her
back, and her whole body felt sore like a swollen boil.

Dilshad moved her dry tongue on her lips. Her tiny
daughter was clinging to her breast, avidly sucking milk.
Dilshad wasn't sure where she was; she thought she had
perhaps slept through the night and had passed by her wished-
for western destination. Then she thought perhaps Rahim
Khan was standing outside the tall building of the railway
station waiting for her, or maybe he was looking for her
among the milling crowds on the platform. She made an

effort to stand up and move closer to the crowd, but she staggered and her calves shook badly. Holding her head in her hands, she sat down once again leaning against the luggage cart.

Two good looking and well-dressed boys, holding hands, were making the rounds of the platform. One was smoking a cigarette, the other a cigar. Whenever they passed by Dilshad, they turned around to look at her and give her a long stare. Gradually, their rounds became shorter, until, finally, they came and stood right in front of her. Dilshad's heart began beating fast, stuck between the extremes of hope and despair. Back in the Chamkor mosque, if any man had stared at her like that, she would have, out of a sense of helplessness, let go of herself and sat down to wait for his next move because she knew what the beholder's hands were likely to do to her. But since making the train journey, she had begun building different kinds of expectations, inspired in her mind by her idea of the west. So she imagined these two handsome boys to be the brothers whose filial love had kept the women in Ambala Camp waiting and hoping. A wave of joy danced in her heart at that thought. She would even have smiled had she not been hurting so much all over. She tried but couldn't even fake a smile. Even then, she looked at them with whatever sweetness and love she could summon in her eyes.

One of the young men excitedly blew out his smoke in the other's face and said to him smiling, "Anwar!"

"Rashid," the other responded equally enthusiastically.

Anwar, Rashid. The names were like music to Dilshad's ears. She had been thirsting to hear such names. The Anwars, Rashids, Mahmoods, Nasims, Khalids, Javeds of her village had disappeared long ago; in their place, names like Shamshir Singh, Amrik Singh, Kartar Singh, Tarlok Singh, Punjab Singh, and Darbara Singh oscillated before her eyes like daggers. The poison of those names had permeated every fibre of her being. Their stink had affected every sinew. Their wild bursts of passion had settled in her bones like a permanent ache. Hearing names like Anwar and Rashid, she felt as if she was immersing herself in the elixir of life, the filth and stench of her life were being washed away and her body was being enveloped in the fragrance of rose and camphor. Her tired, bent neck suddenly acquired the elegance of pride. Rays of hope and joy emanated from her sad and pained breast. With her hand she beckoned the two young men towards herself.

"What city is it, brothers?" she asked them.

"Lahore," Anwar replied.

"Where do you want to go?" Rashid asked.

"Anywhere I'm taken," she said. Dilshad regarded all the land in the west as her home, and every young man in the west her brother.

"Wow!" Anwar whispered to Rashid.

"What a great sport," Rashid gave Anwar a wink.

"Then why don't you come with us?" the two said together.

When Dilshad stood up, holding on to the bars of the luggage cart, the two brothers had the first glimpse of their tiny niece.

"Eh?" Anwar jumped up with astonishment.

"What the devil is that?" Rashid asked.

"It's a girl," Dilshad said somewhat shyly and hesitantly.

"She's really small," Anwar observed.

"She's only a day old." Dilshad didn't know what more to tell her brothers.

"Oh, dear!" Anwar was nauseated.

"Oh, no," Rashid felt his stomach turn.

The two boys ran from there as if they were about to throw up. On the platform across they saw a beautiful woman clad in a gaudy *salwar-kameez*. A light green head-scarf thrown across her well-formed shoulders fluttered about in the air.

Rashid and Anwar jumped across the tracks and holding hands, went in pursuit of that beautiful woman. Ignorant brothers! There were so many butterflies in the park, each better than the other; how many were they going to run after?

As the day passed, the activity on the station subsided. The sunshine became warmer and the warmth of its merciful rays began massaging Dilshad's aching body. An Englishman sat on a bench on the platform with his wife, basking in the sun. His little boy was playing with his dog nearby. When he saw Dilshad's small baby lying in the sun kicking her tiny hands and feet in the air, his eyes opened wide with wonder. Screaming excitedly, he ran to his mother and dragged her back to show her what he had seen.

"How wonderful, Mommy! How wonderful!" he was saying again and again, his eyes popping out with amazement and pleasure.

Wrapped in a soiled sheet, Dilshad's daughter was busy hitting at the sky with her fists, her small feet kicking at everything that stood in her way. Watching her, the English boy danced and clapped, and time and again tried to swoop up that living toy. He even got a rebuke from his mother about touching things that belonged to other people, but he was adamant.

"We'll get a toy like this for you," the boy's father said to him trying to take his mind off the little girl.

"No, you're lying," the boy was crying.

"Of course, we will. We'll get you a toy like this one," the boy's mother also promised.

"When will you do that?" the boy asked for assurances.

"Soon. Very soon, son," the father answered looking at the round bulge under his wife's gown. His wife turned her face away shyly.

"Mom, give this toy some chocolate."

"No, darling, she can't eat chocolate."

"All right, then give her a nice set of clothes."

"Yes, my darling. We can do that."

"And money too, Mom?"

"Yes, money too, darling."

Being happy once again, the boy started jumping up and down and clapping. When he was tired of playing with her, his mother gave Dilshad a piece of woollen flannel and five rupees. When they were about to leave, Dilshad blessed the boy under her breath, for he had come into her life as an angel of mercy.

As soon as Dilshad got the five rupees, her contact with the world around her was re-established. A tea seller moved his cart near her and bawled: "Hot tea!" A meat and bread vendor brought his trolley close. And when she started to eat, a dog, his tongue hanging out, also installed himself right in front of her.

Two elderly men were sitting on a bench nearby, commenting on the situation. One's beard was white, the other's *henna*-dyed. They had for some time been observing with annoyance the actions of the Englishman, his wife and his son. When the Englishwoman gave Dilshad the woollen piece of clothing and five rupees, they felt as if she had shaken them by their beards, or hurled an insult at them.

"Good heavens!" one of them said. "These bastards still think we live off their scraps."

"No, brother, it's not their fault," the other declared. "Why did this wretched woman not refuse the petty alms being given her?"

"How disgusting! We got freedom but never gave up our taste for servitude."

"Why should we, brother, why should we? When we can get a free meal for our servitude, why should we carry the burden of work in freedom?"

"It is better for a bird to die than submit to commands which retard its flight," with much passion one intoned a couplet.

The other also recited a few lines of verse in praise of freedom and dignity. When Dilshad had filled her stomach with meat worth four annas, bread worth three annas, and a cup of tea worth two annas, the two worthies got up and walked to where she sat.

"Woman, are you a *mohajir*?" one inquired indignantly, addressing her as a *qazi*—a magistrate—from days gone by would have an adulteress.

"No sir, my name is Dilshad."

"Maybe it is. I did not ask that. We want to know where you are from, where you are going, and what you want here?" the other demanded.

Dilshad wished she knew the answers, or knew where she would find the clue to where she was going. In her imagination all the world in the west was her destination. She had come over to join a vast brotherhood of those who were like her, but everything and everybody here was intent on asking her who she was, why she was there, whether she had any money in her pocket, whether her body could still give pleasure . . . .

"You are a *mohajir*—a refugee," one of the two wise men gave the verdict. "You should go to the *Mohajir* Camp."

"Remember, the daughters of a free country do not live on charity."

"You are not a child; you should be ashamed. . . . "

Dilshad sat there a long time wondering whether *mohajir* was the name of some girl whom the two men were looking for, one who had run away from home after committing a serious crime. But by evening many others also had referred to her by the same name, and everybody had urged her to go to the *Mohajir* Camp.

Perhaps the *Mohajir* Camp was like a *serai* or an inn. Once when she had visited the city with her father, the two of them had stayed at Haji Musa's Inn. It had a number of small cubicles for the travellers to sleep in, and a woman sat there in front of a fire made of dung-cakes, cooking victuals. As Dilshad sat down next to her on the mat to eat, the woman gave her lentils with onions browned in a lot of heated *ghee*—clarified butter—, and hot *chapatis*—thin flat discs of wheat cooked on a griddle and slathered with butter. Later that night when Mullah Ali Bakhsh went to say his late-night prayer, the woman brought her cot near Dilshad's, and lying down, began telling her nice and wonderful stories. One story was about a king and his seven daughters, the other about the princess of fairies. The woman also talked about her husband. Many times she laughed and cried. Even today, whenever Dilshad thought of the city, she pictured Haji Musa's Inn and that woman who had laughed and cried many times during the night, and who had given her scoops of butter on her *chapatis*.

Perhaps the words *Mohajir* Camp were a corrupted form of the word *serai*—the villagers did mix up names; for instance, they called a hospital the post office—, but she didn't like the name *mohajir* for herself. It didn't sound nice. Dilshad was a lot more musical, and it reminded her of her father who had chosen it from the Quran as an auspicious name. It also reminded her of Rahim Khan's love: he used to compose couplets using words that rhymed with Dilshad.

When she reached the *Mohajir* Camp, it was already evening. The caretaker of the camp sat, an open register in front, under a canopy. Dilshad's turn came soon.

"Name?" the caretaker rattled on the questions like a parrot.

"Dilshad."

"Age?"

"Twenty years."

"Father's name?"

"Mullah Ali Bakhsh."

"Dead or alive?"

"He was killed."

"Village?"

"Chamkor."

"District?"

"Ambala."

"Married?"

"No, Sir."

The caretaker stopped writing, put the pen down, and glared at her: "Then whose child is that?"

"Oh, she's mine," Dilshad stammered. "I forgot. I'm sorry. I'm married."

His pen once again turned towards the ink-pot.

"Husband's name? Answer carefully now."

"Rahim Khan."

"Dead or alive?"

"Sir, . . . I don't know. I hope he's alive. May he live long."

The area of the *Mohajir* Camp was quite big—800 by 500 feet. It was a yard surrounded by barbed wire all around under an open sky, lit by the moon and the stars. In one corner of the yard was the kitchen. Food was being cooked in large cauldrons on fires burning in open pits. In the dark the flames leaped up; it seemed as if corpses were burning in the cremation grounds. The vast yard looked bearable in the light of the fire. It reminded one of the crimson clouds lighting up a graveyard on a gentle and peaceful evening. A sense of gloom hung in the air, and one could feel a very light, almost indistinct tremor, as if thousands of innocent, trembling hearts and shattered hopes and dreams were suspended in the air. There was also the apprehension that this magical quiet, this artificial peace could not last long, that some day soon a huge storm, a powerful quake, or a horrible scream would destroy everything between the earth and the sky.

Dilshad moved about carefully, holding her baby in her

arms. She walked as one does in a graveyard, watching every step one takes lest one bumps into or hits something sacrosanct. Some of the refugees had erected little huts for themselves by tying sheets on bamboo sticks, just as the well-to-do often build roofs to cover graves. Some sat under the open sky, uncovered and unprotected. One of them might have an odd sheet, another a blanket, a third one a quilt. Dilshad had nothing. She herself looked like a rag, a soiled old piece of clothing, only a reminder of her earlier, unviolated self. There were many like her in the Camp, all living in the hope that now that they had arrived, the sacred s oil of their beloved land would cure them of their bleeding ulcers; its water would wash away all their sores; the light of its sun and the beauty of its moon would mend the tears in their beings.

Finding an empty space, Dilshad stopped there. A few yards away from her an old man had pitched his tent. There were two children with him; Mahmood, a boy of eight or ten, and Zubeida, a girl, perhaps eleven or twelve. The three of them were leaning over a clay bowl, eating from it. Mahmood was asking his grandfather: "Why is there no meat in the curry?" His sister speaking for the grandfather was saying: "You should not eat meat everyday. You'll get an upset stomach and your teeth will begin to rot." But Mahmood remained unsatisfied by those answers. The grandfather coaxed him; his sister rebuked him: "What do you want then? That I hack pieces of my own flesh and cook them for you?" The little girl was reprimanding him like an elder in the family. Those who observed her felt that it was not the grandfather, but she who was the head of the family; that her consciousness was so alive and acute that she was acting simultaneously as a sister, a daughter and a mother.

"Come. Sit down here. Is there anyone else with you?" the old man asked Dilshad.

"No, there's no one else."

"Go get your food from the kitchen. Do you have a bowl?"

"No. I have no dishes."

The grandfather gave her his own empty bowl.

"It's also very cold, daughter. Do you have any bedding?"

"No, sir, I have nothing."

The grandfather cast a look of profound sympathy on one who looked so lost and devastated. He too had been like her when he had arrived there. "There's the clothes store near the kitchen. Ask for a blanket there." Then looking at the stars, he guessed the time and said, "It's nine. The store clerk may still be awake."

The cook gave her two *chapatis* and a bowlful of lentils. A lantern was weakly lit in the clothes store. Quilts lay in piles inside a tent; also black, red and brown blankets. In one corner there was a small heap of woollen clothing—sweaters, waistcoats, shawls. The store clerk lay on a cot wrapped in a patchwork quilt, humming strains of the poet Iqbal's poem "The Complaint to God": "All the favours are for their rivals; for the Muslims only bolts of lightning." His humming stopped abruptly as he saw Dilshad standing in the doorway of the tent. He stared at her angrily.

"The Office is closed. Come back tomorrow morning at eight."

"Sir, we have no warm clothes. We'll die of cold in the night."

"Nobody will die. Go away. Come back tomorrow. The store is closed at this time."

When Dilshad pleaded once again, the clerk got annoyed: "Go away, I say. I too am human. I'm not a machine. Come back at eight." Then he pulled the quilt over his head and resumed his humming of "The Complaint to God": "The lovers went away, promising to return; go, look for them now; find your way through the glow of your beautiful face."

As the night advanced, the cold started becoming unbearable, and gradually it began to seem as if the whole

- 287 -

universe was freezing up. Blasts of cold wind hit the body like arrows, and moisture in the ground pricked it like thorns. Grandfather had only one blanket. He had used half of it for Mahmood and Zubeida to sleep on, and had covered them with the other half. Himself wrapped in a thin bedsheet, he lay on the ground tossing and turning. Dilshad's teeth began chattering with cold. She sat holding the baby wrapped in the woollen flannel close to her breast. Sometimes she would lie down, then again sit up or begin walking about. But no matter what she did, the cold steadily crept into her bones. She was afraid the very next minute she would freeze like an ice cube and fall down.

A little ahead of her a young woman was trying by whatever means possible, to transfer the warmth of her body into the body of her four-year-old girl. They too had neither a quilt, nor a blanket, nor any sheet. The girl was breathing with difficulty. Her chest wheezed and whistled when she drew breath. As it became colder, her wheezing turned into a ringing of bells, as if the angels of life and death were locked in a mortal battle. Her mother felt helpless and lost; she stood up and looked around; darkness had enveloped the whole world and there was a thin cover of clouds in the sky. A rare star would be seen shining here and there; sometimes the moon would peep through the clouds only to hide its face again. The woman sat down, almost shrinking into herself. She looked around stealthily, like a thief, and then slowly, hesitatingly, took off her clothes and wrapped her sick girl in them. A shaft of lightning a while later showed the naked body of the young woman to the world, as if telling everyone, look, don't miss this extraordinary sight; you may have seen many secrets in heaven and earth, but you will not be able to forget the nakedness of this mother whose clothes were covering the body of her dying girl when it was bitter cold and there were piles of quilts and blankets lying in the store, and the store clerk himself was lying wrapped in a quilt singing "The Complaint to God." The bare body of that woman was the worst insult to all that had been achieved by mankind; it darkened the face of the night even more, as if neither the stars nor the moon dared look at that scene. The thin layers of clouds in the sky now gathered together and rain began to fall.

Raindrops fell accompanied by a hissing wind. In the yard of the camp, a weak wave of life stirred. Some children woke up; some women screamed; a few men rebuked them, and then there was silence again.

The raindrops kept hitting Dilshad's body like shots from an air gun. She felt as if the scimitars of Amrik Singh, Tarlok Singh, Surmukh Singh and Darbara Singh were piercing her body. Rain water had begun seeping through the flannel and the baby too had started shivering. Dilshad thought, if her daughter could lie in the blanket with Zubeida and Mahmood, she would be able to stay warm. She thought she would ask the grandfather. She shook him by his knee; he lay there wrapped in his soiled sheet. Dilshad shook him by the shoulders, then by the arms, then even by the neck. But grandfather had already gone beyond any concern for heat and cold. Blood had already frozen in his veins; his body was stiff like an iron rod.

In the early light of the day, a statue shone like marble in the yard of the *Mohajir* Camp. A young woman's naked body was seen clinging to the corpse of a young girl. They were like masterpieces carved from stone by a skilful sculptor. Raindrops glittered like pearls on the milky white, taut body of the woman, her thick hair spreading in coils over her shoulders. There was a thin film of moisture in her half-closed eyes, as though her tears too had frozen with her blood. Some camp sweepers came carrying a pile of blankets. They spread one blanket on the grandfather, one on the body of the woman, one on her girl, and so on. They kept covering the dead with those woollen shrouds. The living looked at the dead with envy; if death did not involve a fear of the unseen and the unknown, they would all have been willing to die at that moment. Their bodies would also be wrapped in blankets and their shivering flesh and bones too would receive some warmth, some peace, some comfort.

Mahmood wanted to know where they had taken the grandfather. Zubeida told him he had gone to bring back their parents and would return soon. Then he wanted to know where his parents had gone. "They have gone to see God, for a short while, and will bring back nice toys from Him—a glass top, a rubber ball, an automobile with a key that can be wound, new shoes, a cap with a golden fringe. . . ." His mind imagined newer, more difficult questions, and Zubeida had to cook up inventive answers to elude or bypass them. Only when he was busy in his play, turning her face away from him, she'd let out her own grief.

Life in the *Mohajir* Camp was like a marathon movie show. Hundreds of scenes, each different from the other, appeared on the screen during the day and vanished. Great and dignified lords and noblemen came there; so did important bureaucrats and officers, and ladies, clad in rustling silks and precious velvets, looking like buds in bloom, delighting in the knowledge of their own loveliness, smelling of roses and jasmine. They all placed their hands on the heads of the children in pity, talked sympathetically to the women, patted the young men and old on their backs to encourage them and give hope, and then their vain automobiles took them away from the camp. Some brought sweetmeats, others huge pots of *pilau* and meat, or clothes to distribute, and when someone went out of his way doing charity work, a glow of pride and joy spread on his cheeks. In his heart he thanked God for enabling him to do all that. Dilshad thought that when people listened to Mahmood and Zubeida's stories, they would shoot the store clerk for his callousness. She believed that when she told her own story to some of those noble and dignified men their blood would boil at the outrage. They would pick up their guns and go looking for Amrik Singh, Tarlok Singh, Kartar Singh and Darbara Singh. But none of that transpired. The story-tellers went on telling their stories, and the audience went on listening. Sweetmeats and *pilaus* went on being distributed during the day, and at night the chill went on taking its toll. The movie show of life in the Camp kept running—one scene after another, without a beginning or an end. It was a continuous flow of charity, a complicated, unending play of pity in which each man was eager to act God and was willing to use any stratagem, any ploy to surpass others in doing that.

One gentleman, Mr Mustafa Khan Simabi, was more magnanimous than others. He was clad in a handsome suit of clothes, had a cap sitting crooked on his head, wore gold-rimmed green glasses, had gold-capped front teeth, sported expensive sapphire and ruby rings on his fingers, and carried a pipe in his mouth. He would roam the grounds of the Camp for hours, listening attentively to everybody's story, doling out money to some, giving chocolate and sweets to others. He bestowed many favours on Dilshad. One day, he brought a beautiful red sweater for her daughter. The next day, he promised to look for Rahim Khan. And a few days later, when he brought the heartening news that he had discovered the whereabouts of Rahim Khan, the world became once again a lovely place in Dilshad's eyes. Rahim Khan was weak and unable to walk but still very much in love with Dilshad and waiting to be with her, she was told. All atremble, with longings in her heart, she came and sat down with Mustafa Khan Simabi in his car. The car slithered on the wavy streets of Lahore, rushing past Jinnah Gardens, the outer wall of Gulistan-e-Fatima, Queen Victoria's statue, colourful restaurants on the Mall, the Square of the Blue Dome, the Anarkali Street, the Church, the Mosque, finally coming to a stop in front of Mustafa Khan Simabi's exquisite bungalow.

Gramophone records were playing even in the servants' quarters: "Come, adorn yourself as much as you can today. . . . " Dilshad's heart beat loud and fast, but there was a new sort of ecstasy in her heartbeat. Sitting in the veranda, she wondered if Rahim Khan's feet had ever touched the grounds of that bungalow, and if the air around the bungalow had Rahim Khan's sweet breath mingled in it. In her believing eyes, the grounds of the bungalow had been transformed into the sacred dust from the holy cities of Mecca and Medina. Each brick of the bungalow became sacrosanct for her. A servant brought her a dish of *pilau*, one of meat and spinach, another of minced meat and peas, and a clay bowl full of rice pudding. She didn't know what she ate, how much of it and when. She was oblivious of the world around. For a long time now, for months upon months, her whole being had been nothing but a wait incarnate for Rahim Khan, while her body all along was being gnawed at by dogs.

In his nightgown, Mustafa Khan Simabi hovered around her like a hungry vulture. A bottle of scotch whiskey glittered on the table. His arms were wide open, in a gesture of embrace, and he was saying: "Come, my darling, come close to me; I know you are very unfortunate, very poor, but I'm a rich man; stay with me a few days; I'll make you my queen; I don't know where your Rahim Khan has wandered off to; he may be lying dead in some wretched place; don't waste your youth waiting for that imaginary person; come, be my love; now you're in an independent country; you have nothing to fear; this is OUR country, our independent country; long live Pakistan." Mullah Ali Bakhsh's chain was hanging around Dilshad's neck. When Mustafa Khan Simabi's tongue leapt forward to lick its beads, Dilshad felt as if a Muslim brother of hers was trying to kiss the black stone in the Ka'aba.

A few days later, after Mustafa Khan Simabi had gone through the various stages of his "pilgrimage", Dilshad came back to the Camp. Mahmood sat there playing with a glass top. Clapping his hands and lisping, he told Dilshad that his sister, Zubeida too had gone in a car to visit their grandfather and that grandfather had sent him the glass top and a rubber ball and those colourful sweets. Today, she had again gone to see the grandfather. The car honked many times when it left. Today again, she will bring money from grandfather, and new shoes and a cap with a gold fringe. . . .

Lahore was not Lahore but Medina; its inhabitants not its usual citizens, but the warm-hearted, hospitable residents— the *ansaar*—of Medina. In this city, a new Rahim Khan came into being for Dilshad every day, a new grandfather for Zubeida. There were new fathers here for daughters, new brothers for sisters, bodies meeting bodies, blood mingling with blood . . . .

Part III

Lord of all the Worlds:
"Why should I care? The worlds are yours, not mine."

Mohammad Iqbal

Karachi.
Dilshad looked out of the train window. There was a lot of bustle at the Cantonment Station. All creatures from the Refugee Special were coming out of the train and assembling on the platform. The platform was jampacked. But it took only a few minutes for the crowd to disperse; only a few coolies, a few departing passengers and some ticket collectors remained. The incoming wave of refugees had merged with the crowds of Karachi. It seemed as if the sea had washed it away, as intoxication dissipates all fears lurking in the heart, or as the stench of a rotting corpse eclipses the smell of jasmine and roses.

Karachi! Manora Island glittering in bright lights; Clifton beach bathed in the light of the full moon; the waves lapping the shore and singing a gentle melody; waves hitting the reef, jumping up and forming fountains of mist. A very gentle chill in the air and a subtle agreeableness. The sweet urge to live and to enjoy acting itself out on the beach. . . .

Four young men sat on the beach mixing soda-water in their whiskies, reciting verses and waxing nostalgic for Delhi, the city they had left behind. One of them bemoaned the lost love of a prostitute—a singer, dancer and entertainer—the love that he forsook in the migration. They rolled about in the cool sand dreaming about their lost paradises.

Some distance away from this group an elderly man, sporting a proper cut beard and dressed in the orthodox manner prescribed by religion, sat chewing a *paan*. A few devotees sat facing him.

"We lost Delhi, its citizens, everything; yet we lost nothing. Bring some more *paan* for me."

It was dutifully presented to him.

"Good tobacco," the bearded man gave his opinion. "Where did you get it from?"

Somebody said that it had been purchased from Lucknow for twenty-nine rupees a *seer*.

"So, as I was saying, we lost Delhi," the bearded man picked up the broken train of his argument. "We lost the inhabitants of Delhi. Why? Do you know why?"

The devotees began thinking about the reasons. Their faces became question marks.

The bearded man answered his own question: "The Red Fort, the Jamia Mosque, the Qutab Minaret, the graves of the illustrious dead—of the poet Ghalib, the saint Nizamuddin Aulia, we lost all that not because we were unfortunate; it was because of our evil deeds. Bring more *paan*."

Among the party of four, one began arguing with the other. He insisted that Chand Jaan, the singer, loved him and not the other claimant. The remaining two were busy doing acrobatics: one was trying to stand on the other's head. A Parsi girl sitting nearby was laughing at their antics. She had a colourful bikini on. The bearded man was asking for more *paan*.

A bronze statue of Mahatma Gandhi stands between the Chief Court and the Assembly Hall, keeping, as it were, justice and politics safely away from each other. Two bicycle riders stopped to look at the statue. One tried to pull the staff away from its hand; the other tried to remove its glasses. When they failed to do either, one of them put his fez on its head and moved happily away from there. They had quietly Islamised the statue.

A Hindu family is migrating to India. Their baggage—steel trunks, leather suitcases, wooden chests—has been loaded on four camel carts which stand outside their beautiful bungalow. There is also a parrot cage there. The parrot is eating peas from pods. Whenever anybody passes him by, the parrot observes him through his half-open eyes. The look on his face seems to say: "Now I'm leaving too, you buggers; I'd like to see how you make your Pakistan work."

The orchestra was playing on the floor of the Qaiseria Hotel. The hotel manager came on the stage and announced that half of that evening's income would be donated to the Qaid-e-Azam Relief Fund. People clapped enthusiastically.

A pretty lady raised a glass of sherry to her lips and said to her partner: "I'm tired of Karachi, really. Let's go to Bombay for a few days."

Her companion was sipping champagne. He answered: "Now even Bombay is going to be a lost cause. The bloody Congress is bent on transforming this mini-Paris into a monastery. No whiskey, no gin, no champagne. Now I hear they are conspiring to disallow horse-racing as well."

"Oh, yes," the lady suddenly remembered. She said to her companion, "Professor Ghanshyam's letter came the other day. The poor fellow is feeling really helpless because of the prohibition. He wants you to send him a case of whiskey. Please do it, somehow."

A secretary of a foreign embassy was confessing to a secretary of another foreign embassy: "I like two things in Karachi."

"I like three," the other said.

"Parsi girls and veils of Muslim women."

"I also like those inside the veils."

"How uncultured! Who could love those tubercular women?"

"I could and do. By Jesus, I love pale beauty. Blue veins on pale skin, and the rouge on top. I swear, I've never seen such an admirable combination before. The veiled women are something else! Boy, bring us two whiskey sodas."

"This round's on me," the first one insisted.

"Doesn't matter who buys. The objectives of our brave countries are the same. We'll make our partnership last long. To your health!"

A Muslim news editor was quenching his thirst with lemon squash. Getting the chance, he cornered an important liquor and cloth merchant.

"Sir, I've heard that the consumption of liquor has tripled in Lahore and Karachi ever since Pakistan came into being?" he asked, beginning to gather material for his next editorial.

"Absolute bull!" the merchant denied the report vehemently. "Where do you pick up such nonsense from? Tripled? We'd be lucky if it's even doubled."

"How sad! Isn't this fact rather shameful for this Islamic country?"

"You should know, my dear fellow, that Pakistan is the fifth largest country in the world, and among Muslim countries, it's the largest," the merchant tried to add to the editor's knowledge.

"O.K. Isn't this fact rather shameful for this biggest Muslim country in the world?"

"My dear fellow," the merchant took a long sip of his scotch and said, "We are running a country here, not building a mosque."

The secretary of the second foreign country was saying to the secretary of the first foreign country, "Ah! Those black veils; those green and red rustling silken veils; those pale and red faces peering through the veils; those graceful arms, those shapely, conical hands! I swear by the Virgin Mary's Son, when I watch those sparks fly on the green of the Gandhi Garden, or when I see those veiled beauties in the stores on Elphinstone Street, I want to fall down at their feet and stay there, even if they walk all over me. . . . "

"Boy, two whiskies and soda," the first one called.

"This one's on me," the second one repeated the order.

"Doesn't matter who buys. Our brave countries share the same objectives. We shall both help the displaced refugees of Pakistan."

"This two-anna piece is counterfeit," the bus conductor told the passenger curtly. "Replace it."

"I didn't make this two-anna piece myself," the passenger answered equally insolently. "Nor did I bring it back with me from Delhi or Lucknow. I'm not going to replace it."

The conductor asked the driver to stop the bus. "The bus is going nowhere if you don't give me another two-anna piece," he said to the passenger.

A few Punjabis swore at the bus conductor: "Bloody

Sindhis. Got the country without any effort. We'll yet teach you a few things!"

The driver and the conductor walked out of the bus and stood by the roadside. "The bloody Punjabis. What do the bastards think of themselves? Damn their cheek. Think they're here for a family reunion!"

A Hindu passer-by heard this panegyric and stopped. In appreciation, he offered the driver and the conductor *bidis* to smoke.

Two Bengalis came out of the bus. One of them asked the other how far he thought Lawrence Road was. The other answered: "Oh, about a couple of furlongs."

"Let's take a walk there."

When they were at a safe distance from the bus, they commented on the two-anna piece frankly. "Let the Punjabi and Sindhi buggers fight it out. They claim Pakistan's national language is going to be Urdu. As if Bengali is a dead language. . . . "

In the Cantonment Square, an Irani restaurant owner was roaring at a fruit-seller: "I'm warning you. Don't keep these dirty bananas in your wicker basket; flies gather and come into my restaurant."

The fruit-seller was arguing with him stubbornly: "Do you think you own this bloody sidewalk?"

The Irani came forward and kicked the basket, sending the fruit flying all over the street. The fruit-seller jumped up and in an effort to pull him down clung to the Irani's legs.

A police constable arrived on the scene and gave the fruit-seller a resounding slap on the face. "You bastard. You have been told so many times not to sell anything on the sidewalk, but do you ever listen? Get up, and come with me to the police station."

The owner of the wicker basket made many appeals to the Constable. He cried and begged: "Sir, I'm from the holy city of Ajmer. I lost everything there in the riots. I've a blind sister with me. Please let me go this time. I swear I'll never sell anything here." But the law is the law. It does not make a distinction between the resident of Ajmer and of Lahore, nor between a blind sister and one with good eyes. The Constable performed his duty creditably and took the fruit-seller to the police station. However, when the Inspector heard about the blind sister, he was enraged by the Constable's stupidity. Why did the fool not bring the girl along?

"Two plus two equals four; four plus three is seven; seven plus nine—how much does that come to?" Chela Ram, the pimp, asked Khushi Mohammad, the pimp.

Khushi Mohammad had just spooned a fly out of his cup of tea. Shaking it off the spoon onto the floor, he took a long sip from his teacup.

"Seven plus nine makes sixteen," Chela Ram finished the calculation himself. Then he added, "It wasn't a bad season, eh?"

Khushi Mohammad's lower lip drooped a little further, and he took another long sip from his cup.

"Actually, if truth be told, it was an excellent season," Chela Ram said, his cheeks glowing with pride and pleasure. "Sixteen girls in one season! I haven't done such business in my whole life."

To show his satisfaction, Chela Ram took off his Jinnah cap and rubbed his hand on his pate.

Khushi Mohammad's lower lip drooped as low as it could get. He took another sip of tea and said, "Well, you were lucky. You had so many of them. I could get only three, and with difficulty."

"Ha! Just three," Chela Ram said sarcastically and shot out a big gob of phlegm onto the floor. "And tawny easterners at that! No one would even look at them; I had some rare pieces. Hot and hard-bodied Punjabi girls; slim and delicate ones from Delhi, and that farm-girl from Patiala—boy, she was an absolute gem!" He broke a salt cracker between his fingers. "That bastard Brown took her away to Port Said. He said she'd work well there. Eh, where's this Port Said anyway, Khushi Mohammad?"

"Must be around here somewhere," he replied. He was worried about his own sluggish business. "Get another cup of tea for me. No refugee trains coming in either!"

With the hot cup of tea, the two of them were once again lost in their thoughts. Chela Ram was thinking about all the girls who had gone through his hands. He was wondering where they were now. Cairo, London, Port Said, . . . He felt like going to Port Said, throwing his five hundred and seventy rupees back in that bastard Brown's face, and bringing the farm-girl back.

There was nothing but anger and misery in Khushi Mohammad's heart. Until recently there had been those train and shiploads of refugees coming in; what had gone wrong now? He read in the papers about bloodshed and riots, in Delhi, in Kanpur, in Calcutta, in Ahmedabad, in Ajmer, but out of this stream of blood not one refugee train had got into Karachi. Enough to make him fretful and depressed. Nonetheless, hoping for a turnaround in his affairs, he spent some more money and bought the day's newspaper. Avariciously he went over the headlines. The newspaper-hawker boy, his mouth open wide, was screaming loudly: "War in Kashmir. Thousands of Muslims massacred in Jammu . . . . "

Khushi Mohammad read the paper avidly. So, now the fires of hell were burning in the heaven of Kashmir as well! Instead of the morning breeze, it was the swords of the Dogra and Sikh soldiers that were sweeping through the valley now. Thousands had been killed; thousands were dying; thousands were trying to crawl out of that hell like mice or frogs.

Khushi Mohammad slapped Chela Ram's thigh hard and

said, "Did you see, my friend, the fire is raging in Kashmir now."

Chela Ram was still dreaming about Port Said. "Apples are going to cost more this year, I guess," he said casually.

But Khushi Mohammad was waxing poetic. Smacking his lips, he talked about the beautiful, luscious women of Kashmir, about their eyes, their lips, their cheeks, their breasts, until Chela Ram began to drool. Khushi Mohammad ordered another cup of tea for Chela Ram, and then the two of them went into a huddle and talked about their dreams, hopes and expectations.

The wind flapped the sails. Waves hit the boat, shaking it a little. The girl was frightened. She moved away from Seth Qayem Ali Dayem Ali's side.

The Seth shot out the *paan* spittle that had been collecting in his mouth and burst out laughing.

The old oarsman lit a *bidi* and smiled. He said, "She's from Kashmir, Seth. She's blind. A little timid, she is. Where do you want me to take the two of you? To Paris or Venice?"

Seth Qayem Ali Dayem Ali's firm had a sub office in Paris. Besides that too, he had heard a lot about that enchanting city. But right now, in that small boat, he was not ready to undertake a long voyage to Paris. The oarsman's offer, therefore, confused him.

The shrewd oarsman enjoyed the Seth's discomfiture. He smiled and said, "Don't worry, Seth, I won't take you far. Oh, what a fine place Paris is! You'll simply die when you see it."

There was a lot going on at the Kemari port. People were walking about enjoying their Sunday off. Some were leaving for Manora, some for Sandpit Island. One ship was ready to sail for Bombay. The colourful *saris* of hundreds of women could be seen fluttering on the deck. The passengers were taking a parting look at Karachi through their binoculars. As the ship slid away from the dock, they tossed their Jinnah caps into the sea and raising their clenched fists in the air shouted, *"Jai Hind!"*

Seth Qayem Ali Dayem Ali's blind girl sat clinging to his side. Whenever the boat rocked on the waves, she remembered her light dinghy which used to rock gently on the waves of the Dal and Wular lakes. The first time she drank a handful of sea water, she felt like throwing up. How bitter it was! The water of the Dal was sweet like fresh milk. And that of Shahi Spring? It was like drinking ice-cold, buttery and honeyed milk. She yearned once to be able to see the colour of the sea water, whether it was black or red, blue or green. But her eyes! Once she had had the blue of the Wular in her gentle eyes, and the delicacy of green almonds, but now there were only two big gashes; her eyes had become like two dark, deep and empty wells. The bayonet of a brave Dogra soldier had wrecked the magic castles in her eyes. . . .

Away from the noise and activity of the shore, a container ship had weighed anchor. It stood all alone. A warning in red lettering could be seen clearly on the port side of the ship: it was loaded with dynamite and ammunition. When the boat passed by that ship, Seth Qayem Ali Dayem Ali let go of the girl's hand. He was afraid the ship might suddenly blow up. But when the boat was at a safe distance from the ship, he took hold of both her hands and placed them on his pot-belly.

The boat came to a small island. There was nothing there except a few fishermen's huts. The oarsman told him that that "pleasure palace" was called Paris. There were also a few other islands like that one around, and an odd boat was moored on their shores as well. One of those islands was called Venice, the other Rome, the third one Naples. . . .

As soon as his two passengers were off the boat, the oarsman unfurled the sail, making a sort of canopy over his head. He winked to Seth Qayem Ali Dayem Ali and said, "All right, Seth. I'm off to do some fishing. You go and have fun. Enjoy your Kashmir holiday."

A fair is in progress at the *Eidgah* grounds. Here, a fair seems to be in progress every day, and every night some festivity is going on. In small huts fashioned from sackcloth, tiny lamps are lit. Cooked food, stitched clothes, second-hand shoes, fresh fruit, iron nails, wooden chests, cowhide chairs, cooking oil, pickled vegetables, soap—a strange assortment of goods and objects, keeps these homeless people propped up. A curious sense of satisfaction pervades the air, and life here has a certain perpetuity and endlessness about it. Watching this place one feels that the caravan that had lost its way has finally reached its destination.

One hut had been partitioned by means of a sackcloth. In the front portion Dilshad sat frying gram flour pastry in oil; in the back Zubeida sold yogurt dumplings. A Pathan—a northerner—sat cross-legged facing Dilshad.

"Hot pastry for you, Khan? For how much?" she asked.

"Is it soft? Is it really hot?" he asked, giving her a wink.

"Yes, Khan, it's hot and nice," she answered smiling, the spatula in front of her lips to hide her smile.

There was a strange magic in her smile. Seeing her smile, Rahim Khan had once taken a vow that even if it's the sun, or the moon or the stars that take her away, he would jump across the vast spaces between earth and sky and bring her back . . . .

The Pathan moved his tongue over his lips.

"One rupee?"

"No, Khan, five rupees."

"Come on, two and a half then?"

"No, Khan, nothing less than five."

Khan took whatever money he had out of his pocket and counted it. He had three rupees and four annas. He tried to ask for a credit for one rupee and twelve annas, the amount by which he was short, but Dilshad refused. "Credit acts like scissors for love," she told him. She promised to deliver nice and hot pastry if Khan brought the sum she had asked for.

The Pathan was disappointed. He went to the other side. There he bargained for yogurt dumplings. Zubeida was still young and ignorant. She agreed to give Khan credit for a rupee and twelve annas. She said to Dilshad over the partition, "Sister, watch my place for a while. Mahmood is sleeping. I'm going with Khan to buy some yogurt."

In the same way, when Dilshad goes with a client to buy gram flour for her pastry, she asks Zubeida to look after her daughter. From this mixture of yogurt and gram flour, the future of the biggest Muslim country in the world is being shaped. When Dilshad's daughter grows up, raised on hot and tender pastry, and when Zubeida's Mahmood matures, fed on yogurt dumplings, two valuable members will be added to the Muslim community—a strong brother and a beautiful sister. . . . Physical strength and physical beauty: these are the materials—the bricks and kneaded clay—with which brave nations are built. Strength and beauty of the body—these are the blessings given you by your God, by the Merciful and Compassionate God, the Lord of the East and the West, who grows dates and pomegranates on trees, pearls within oyster-shells, who is the Master of both heaven and hell.

So, which of your Lord's blessings will you deny?

(Translated from the original in Urdu by Faruq Hassan)

28

BAPSI SIDHWA

Defend Yourself Against Me

"THEY ARE MY grandparents," says Kishen. I peer at the incongruous pair mounted in an old gold frame holding an era captive in the faded brown and gray photograph. I marvel. The heavy portrait has been transported across the seven seas; from the Deccan plateau in India to the flat, glass and aluminium-pierced horizons of Houston in Texas. The tiny *sari*-clad bride, her nervous eyes wide, her lips slightly ajar, barely clears the middle-aged bridegroom's ribs.

"Your grandfather was exceptionally tall," I remark, expressing surprise; Kishen is short and stocky. But distracted partly by the querulous cries of his excited children, and partly by his cares as a host, Kishen nods so perfunctorily that I surmise his grandfather's height cannot have been significant. His grandmother was either exceedingly short or not yet full-grown. I hazard a guess. She could be ten; she could be eighteen. Marketable Indian brides—in those days at least—wore the uniformly bewildered countenances of lambs to the slaughter and looked alike irrespective of age.

We hear a car purr up the drive and the muted thud of Buick doors. The other guests have arrived. Kishen, natty in a white shark-skin suit, tan tie and matching silk handkerchief, darts out of the room to welcome his guests loudly and hospitably. "*Aiiay! Aiiay! Arrey bhai*, we've been waiting for you! *Kitni der laga di*," he bellows in the curious mix of Urdu and English that enriches communication between the inheritors of the British Raj, Indians and Pakistanis alike. "I have a wonderful surprise for you," I hear him shout as he ushers his guests inside. "I have a lady friend from Pakistan I want you to meet!"

I move hesitantly to the living-room door and peer into the hall. Flinging out a gleaming shark-skinned arm in a grand gesture of introduction, Kishen announces: "Here she is! Meet Mrs Jacobs." And turning on me his large, intelligent eyes, beaming handsomely, he says, "Sikander Khan is also from Pakistan."

Mr Sikander Khan, blue-suited and black-booted, his wife and her three sisters in satin *salwar-kameezes* and heavy gold jewellery, and a number of knee-high children stream into the living room. We shake hands all round and recline in varying attitudes of stiff discomfiture in the deep chairs and sofas covered, *desi* style, with printed bedspreads to camouflage the stains and wear of a house inhabited by an extended Hindu family.

Kishen's diminutive mother, fluffed out in a starched white cotton *sari*, smiles anxiously at me across a lumpy expanse of sofa and his two younger brothers, unsmiling and bored, slouch on straight-backed dining room chairs to one side, their legs crossed at the ankles and stretched right out in front. Suzanne, Kishen's statuesque American wife, her brown hair falling in straight strands down her shoulders and back, flits to and fro in the kitchen. As comfortable in a pink silk *sari* with a gold border as if she were born to it, she pads barefoot into the room, the skin on her toes twinkling whitely, bearing a tray of potato *samosas*, fruit juices and coke, the very image of dutiful brahmin-wifedom. A vermilion caste mark spreads prettily between her large and limpid brown eyes.

I know her well. Her other-worldly calm and docility are due equally to her close association with her demanding and rambunctious Indian family, and the more private rigours of her job as a computer programmer in an oil corporation.

I make polite conversation with Mrs Khan's sisters in hesitant Punjabi. They have just emigrated. The differences from our past remain: I, an English-speaking scion of Anglican Protestants from Lahore; they, village belles accustomed to draw water to the rhythm of Punjabi lore. They know very little English. Tart and shifty-eyed, their jewellery glinting like armour, they are on the defensive; blindly battling their way through cultural shock-waves in an attempt to adapt to a new environment as different from theirs as only a hamburger at McDonald's can be from a leisurely meal of spicy greens eaten in steamy village courtyards redolent of buffalo dung and dust-caked naked children.

Observing their bristling discomfiture and the desultory nature of the conversation, Sikander Khan moves closer to me. He is completely at ease. Acclimatised. Americanised.

Our conversation follows the usual ritual of discourse between Pakistanis who meet for the first time on European or American soil. He moved from Pakistan eleven years ago, I two. He has a Pakistani and Indian spice shop on Richmond uptown, I teach English at the University of Houston downtown. Does he have US citizenship? Yes. Do I? No, but I should have a green card by December. Mr Khan filed his mother's immigration papers two years ago: they should be through any day. One of his brothers-in-law will bring *Ammijee*. It will be his mother's, *Ammijee's*, first visit to America.

Mr Khan speaks English with a broad Pakistani accent that is pleasant to my ears. "I went to the Dyal Singh College in Lahore," he says courteously when he learns I'm from Lahore. "It is a beautiful, historical old city."

All at once, without any apparent reason, my eyes prickle with a fine mist, and I become entangled in a web of nostalgia so intense that I lose my breath. I quickly lower my lids, and the demeanour of half a lifetime standing me in good stead, I maintain a slight smile of polite attention while the grip of sensations from the past hauls me back through the years to Lahore, to our bungalow on Race Course Road.

I am a little child playing hop-scotch outside the kitchen window. The autumn afternoon is overcast with shadows from the mighty *sheesham* trees in the front lawn. There is a brick wall to my right, a little crooked and bulging in places, and the clay cement in the grooves is eroded. I keep glancing at the wall, suppressing a great excitement.

Spellbound, I sit still on Kishen's lumpy sofa, my pulse racing at the memory. Then, clearly, as if she were in the room, I hear Mother shout: "Joy, come inside and put on your cardigan."

Startled by the images, I snap out of my reverie. I search Mr Khan's face so confusedly that he turns from me to Kishen's mother and awkwardly inquires of her how she is.

I have not recalled this part of my childhood in years. Certainly not since I moved to the USA. Too enamoured of the dazzling shopping malls and technical opulence of the smoothly operating country of my adoption, too frequent a visitor to Pakistan, I have not yet missed it, or given thought to the past. Perhaps it is this house, so comfortably possessed by its occupants and their Indian bric-a-brac. It takes an effort of will to remember that we are in the greenly-shaven suburbs of an American city in the heart of Texas.

Bending forward with the tray, smiling at my abstraction, Suzanne abruptly brings me to earth. "Joy," she asks, "would you like some wine?"

"I prefer this, thanks," I say, reaching apologetically for a glass of coke.

"I used to know a Joy . . . long, long ago," says Mr Khan. "I spent one or two years in Lahore when I was a child."

Suzanne has shifted to Mr Khan. As his hand, hesitant

with the burden of choice, wavers among the glasses, I watch it compulsively. It is a swarthy, well-made hand with dark hair growing between the knuckles and on the back. The skin, up to where it disappears beneath his white shirt sleeve, is smooth and unblemished.

There must be at least a million Sikanders in Pakistan, and several million Khans. The title "Khan" is indiscriminately tagged on by most Pakistanis in the USA who generally lack family names in the western tradition. The likelihood that this whole-limbed and assured man with his trim moustache and military bearing is the shy and misshapen playmate of my childhood is remote.

But that part of my mind which is still in the convoluted grip of nostalgia, with its uncanny accompaniment of sounds and images, is convinced.

Having selected a glass of orange juice, Sikander Khan leans forward to offer it to a small boy whimpering half-heartedly at his feet. I glance obliquely at the back of Mr Khan's head. It is as well formed as the rest of him and entirely covered with strong, short-sheared black hair.

My one-time playmate had a raw pit gouged out of his head that couldn't have grown hair in a hundred years! Still, the certainty with me remains and, not the least bit afraid of sounding presumptuous, I ask, "Was the girl you knew called Joy Joshwa? I was known as Joy Joshwa then."

Holding the glass to the child's lips, Sikander looks at me. My body casts a shadow across his face. His dark eyes on me are veiled with conjecture. "I don't remember the last name," he says, speaking in a considered manner. "But it could be."

"You are Sikander!" I announce in a voice that brooks no doubt or argument. "You lived next to us on Race Course Road. You were refugees . . . . Don't you remember me?" My eyes misty, my smile wide and twitching, I know the while how absurd it is to expect him to recall the sharp-featured and angular girl in the rounded contours and softened features of my middle-ageing womanhood.

"Was it Race Course Road?" says Sikander. He sits back and, turning his strong man's body to me, says, "I tried to locate the house when I was in Lahore . . . . But we moved to the farm land allotted to us in Sahiwal years ago . . . I forgot the address . . . . So, it was Race Course Road!" He beams fondly at me. "You used to have pimples the size of boils!"

"Yes," I reply, and then I don't know what to say. It is difficult to maintain poise when transported to the agonised and self-conscious persona of a boil-ridden and stringy child before a man who is, after all these years, a stranger.

Sitting opposite me—if he can ever be said to sit—Kishen comes to an explosive rescue. "You know each other? Imagine that! Childhood friends!"

Kishen has squirmed, crab-wise, clear across the huge sofa and is sitting so close to the edge that his weight is borne mostly by his thick legs. Half-way between sitting and squatting, quite at ease with the restless energy of his body, he is radiant with the wonder of it all.

"It is incredible," he booms with genial authority. "Incredible! After all these years you meet, not in Pakistan, but on the other side of the planet, in Houston!"

Triggered off by the fierce bout of nostalgia and the host of ghost-memories stirred by Sikander's unexpected presence, the scenes that have been floundering in the murky deeps of my subconscious come into luminous focus. I see a pattern emerge, and the jumble of half-remembered events and sensations already clamour to be recorded in a novel I have just begun about the Partition of India.

Turning to Sikander, smiling fondly back at him, I repeat, "You're quite right: I had horrible pimples."

Since childhood memories can only be accurately exhumed by the child, I will inhabit my childhood. As a writer, I am already practised in inhabiting different bodies; dwelling in rooms, gardens, bungalows and spaces from the past; zapping time.

Lahore: Autumn 1948. Pakistan is a little over a year old. The Partition riots, the arson and slaughter, have subsided. The flood of refugees—12 million Muslims, Hindus and Sikhs fleeing across borders that define India and Pakistan—has shrunk to a nervous trickle. Two gargantuan refugee camps have been set up on the outskirts of Lahore, at Walton and Badami Bagh. Bedraggled, carrying tin trunks, string-cots and cloth bundles on their heads, the refugees swamp the city looking for work, setting up house on sidewalks and in parks—or wherever they happen to be at sunset if they have wandered too far from the camps.

A young Christian couple, the Mangat Rais, live on one side of our house on Race Course Road; on the other side is the enormous bungalow of our Hindu neighbours. I don't know when they fled. My friends Sheila and Sam never even said goodbye. Their deserted house has been looted several times. First by men in carts, shouting slogans, then by whoever chose to saunter in to pick up the leavings. Doors, sinks, wooden cabinets, electric fixtures and wiring have all been ripped from their moorings and carried away. How swiftly the deserted house has decayed. The hedges are a spooky tangle, the garden full of weeds and white patches of caked mud.

It is still quite warm when I begin to notice signs of occupation. A window boarded up with cardboard, a diffused pallid gleam from another screened with jute sacking as candles or oil-lamps struggle to illuminate the darkness. The windows face my room across the wall that separates our houses. The possession is so subtle that it dawns on me only gradually; I have new neighbours. I know they are refugees, frightened, nervous of drawing attention to their furtive presence. I know this as children know many things without being told: but I have no way of telling if children dwell in the decaying recesses of the stolen bungalow.

Although the ominous roar of slogans shouted by distant mobs—that nauseating throb that had pulsed a continuous threat to my existence and the existence of all those I love—has at last ceased, terrible new sounds (and unaccountable silences) erupt about me. Sounds of lamentation magnified by the night—sudden unearthly shrieks—come from a nursery school hastily converted into a Recovered Women's Camp six houses away from ours. Tens of thousands of women have been kidnapped and hundreds of camps have been set up all over the Punjab to sort out and settle those who are rescued, or "recovered."

Yet we hear nothing—no sound of talking, children quarrelling or crying, of repairs being carried out—or any of the noises our refugee neighbours might be expected to make. It is eerie.

And then one afternoon, standing on my toes, I glimpse a small scruffy form through a gap in the wall (no more than a slit really) where the clay has worn away. I cannot tell if it's a boy or a girl or an apparition. The shadowy form appears to have such an attuned awareness that it senses my presence in advance, and I catch only a spectral glimpse as it dissolves at the far corner of my vision.

Impelled by curiosity—and by my loneliness now that even Sheila and Sam have gone—I peep into my new neighbour's compound through the crack in the wall, hoping to trap a potential playmate. A few days later, crouching slyly beneath the wall, I suddenly spring up to peer through the slit, and startle a canny pair of dark eyes staring straight at me.

I step back—look away nonchalantly—praying the eyes will stay. A stealthy glance reassures me. I pick up a sharp stone and quickly begin to sketch hop-scotch lines in the mud on our drive. I throw the stone in one square after another, enthusiastically playing against myself, aware I'm being observed. I am suddenly conscious of the short frock I have outgrown. The waist, pulled by sashes stitched to either side and tied at the back, squeezes my ribs. The seams hurt under my arms and when I bend the least bit I know my white cotton knickers, with dusty patches where I sit, are on embarrassing display. Never mind. If they offend the viewer, I'm sure my skipping skills won't. I skip rope, and turning round and round in one spot I breathlessly recite: "Teddy bear, Teddy bear, turn around: Teddy bear, Teddy bear, touch the ground."

And again, I sense I'm alone. I rush to the wall but my phantasmal neighbour's neglected compound is empty.

The next few days I play close to the damaged wall. Sometimes the eyes are there, sometimes not. I look towards the wall more frequently, and notice that my glance no longer scares the viewer away. Once in a rare while I even smile, careful to look away at once, my lids demurely lowered, my expression shy: trying with whatever wiles I can to detain, disarm and entice the invisible and elusive object of my fascination.

It is almost the end of October. The days are still warm but, as each day takes us closer to winter, the fresher air is exhilarating. People on the streets smile more readily, the *tonga* horses snort and shake their necks and appear to pull their loads more easily, and even the refugees, absorbed into the *gullies* and the more crowded areas of Lahore as the camps shrink, appear at last to be less visible.

One such heady afternoon, when the eyes blocking the crack suddenly disappear and I see a smudge of pale light instead, I dash to the wall and glue my eye to the hole. A small boy, so extremely thin he looks like a brittle skeleton, is squatting a few feet away, concentrating on striking a marble lying in a notch in the dust. His skull-like face has dry, flaky patches, and two deep lines between his eyebrows that I have never before seen on a child. He is wearing a threadbare *salwar* of thin cotton and the dirty cord tying the gathers round his waist trails in the mud. The sun-charred little body is covered with scabs and wounds. It is as if his tiny body has been carelessly carved and then stuck together again to form an ungainly puppet. I don't know how to react; I feel sorry for him and at the same time repulsed. He hits the marble he was aiming at, gets up to retrieve the marbles and as he turns away I see the improbable wound on the back of his cropped head. It is a raw and flaming scar, as if bone and flesh had been callously gouged out, and my compassion ties me to him.

Suzanne is in the kitchen and Kishen is flitting between the dining table and the kitchen filling stainless-steel glasses with water and arranging bowls containing a variety of pickles. He places a stack of silvery platters, their rims gleaming, next to the glasses. The smell of mango pickle is strong in the room and, seeing our eyes darting to the table, Kishen's mother says, "We have made only a vegetarian *thal* today." She sounds apologetic: as if their hospitality will not stand up to our expectations. I know how much trouble it is to prepare the different vegetables and lentils that add up to the *thal*. Glancing at his sisters-in-law, Sikander says, "The girls refused to eat lunch when they heard you were serving the *thal, Maajee*." The sisters-in-law solemnly nod. "I've been looking forward to the food all day," I also protest.

Turning from me to Kishen, who is folding cutlery in paper napkins, Mr Khan declares, "I say *yaar*, you're such a well trained husband!" and at that moment, involuntarily, my hand reaches out to lightly feel Mr Khan's hair. Startled by the unexpected touch, Sikander whips around. He notices my discomfiture—and the unusual position of my hand in the air—and passing a hand down the back of his head, dryly says, "I'm wearing a wig. The scar is still there."

"Oh, I'm sorry. I didn't mean to . . . " I say, almost incoherent with embarrassment. But Mr Khan grants me a smile of such indulgent complicity that acknowledging my childhood claim to his friendship, I am compelled to ask, "What about the other scars . . . are they still . . . ?"

Wordlessly opening the cuff button Sikander peels his shirt sleeve back. The scars are fainter, diminished, and on that strong brown arm, innocuous: not at all like the dangerous welts and scabs afflicting the pitiful creature I saw for the first time on that mellow afternoon through a slit in the compound wall. With one finger, gently, I touch the arm, and responding to the touch, Sikander twists it to show me the other scars.

"You want to see the back of my head?" he asks. I nod.

Sikander turns, and with a deft movement of his fingers lifts up part of the piece to show the scar. It has pale ridges of thick scar tissue, and the hair growing round it has given it the shape of a four-day-old crescent moon.

Sikander smooths down his hair and notices that, except for the children shouting as they play outside, the room has become quiet; even Kishen has come from the dining table to peer at his famous scalp.

"I think I'm out of cigarettes," Sikander says patting his empty pockets with the agitation of an addict desperately in need of a smoke. "I'll be back in ten minutes, *yaar*," he tells Kishen, getting up.

While Sikander is out, Kishen and his mother sit close to me, and Suzanne, drawn from the kitchen by the hushed tone of their voices, joins them in pressing me with information and plying me with questions. Could I tell them what Mr Khan looked like as a little boy? Do I know what happened to *Ammijee*? No? Well, they noticed Mr Khan's reticence on the subject and stopped asking questions . . . . But they

suspect she has been through something terrible . . . .
Except for Mr Khan, her entire family was killed during the
attack . . . . Do I remember her? Was she pretty?

The focus of interest appears to revolve round *Ammijee*.
They have known Sikander for a long time and his mother's
anticipated arrival has caused a stir. I search my memory. I
dimly perceive a thin, bent-over, squatting figure scrubbing
clothes, scouring tinny utensils with mud and ash, peeling
squashes and other cheap vegetables, kneading dough and
slapping it into *chapatis*. . . .

The ragged cotton *chaddar* always drawn forward over
her face, the colour of her form blended with the mud, the
ash, the utensils she washed, the pale seasonal vegetables she
peeled. This must be *Ammijee*: a figure bent perpetually to
accommodate the angle of drudgery and poverty. I don't recall
her face or the colour of her dusty bare feet: the shape of her
hands or whether she wore bangles.

All I knew as a child was that my little refugee friend's
village was attacked by the Sikhs.

I did not understand the complete significance of the word
"refugees" at the time. I thought, on the nebulous basis of my
understanding of the Hindu caste system, that the "refugees"
were a caste—like the brahmin or *achoot* castes—who were
suddenly pouring into Lahore, and it was in the nature of this
caste—much as the *achoots* or untouchables were born to
clean gutters and sweep toilets—to be inexorably poor, ragged,
homeless, forever looking for work and places to stay.

Sikander had described some of the details of the attack
and of his miraculous survival. His account of it, supplied in
little, suddenly recalled snatches—brought to mind by
chance associations while we played—was so jumbled, so full
of bizarre incident, that I accepted it as the baggage of
truth-enlivened-by-fantasy that every child carries within.
Although I realised the broader implications of what had
happened, that the British Raj had ended, that there were

religious riots between Hindus, Muslims and Sikhs, and the country was divided because of them, I was too young to understand the underlying combustibility of the events preceding Partition that had driven my friends away and turned a little boy's world into a nightmare.

But I had heard no mention at all of *Ammijee's* ordeal. Excited by my ignorance, and the spirit of instruction burning in us all to remedy this lack, Mrs Khan and her three sisters also move closer; those who can dragging their chairs forward, those who can't settling on the rug at my feet. The entire ensemble now combines to enlighten me in five languages: English, Punjabi and Urdu, which I understand, and Kannada and Marathi—contributed by Kishen's mother in earnest but brief fusillades—which I don't.

The boys and some of the men in the village, I am informed, were huddled in a dark room at the back of a barn when the Sikhs smote the door shouting: "Open up. Open up!"

And, when the door was opened, the hideous swish of long steel swords dazzling their eyes in the sunlight, severing first his father's head, then his uncle's, then his brother's. His own sliced at the back because he was only nine years old, and short. They left him for dead. How he survived, how he arrived in Pakistan, is another story.

"*Ammijee* says the village women ran towards the Chaudhrys' house," says Mrs Khan in assertive Punjabi. Being *Ammijee's* daughter-in-law she is permitted, for the moment at least, to hold centre stage. "They knew what the Sikhs would do to them . . . women are the spoils of war . . . no matter what you are—Hindu, Muslim, Sikh—women bear the brunt . . . .

"Rather than fall into the hands of the Sikhs, the poor women planned to burn themselves. They had stored kerosene . . . but when the attack came they had no time.

Thirty thousand men, mad with blood lust, waving swords and sten guns!"

Mrs Khan casts her eyes about in a way that makes us draw closer, and having ascertained that Mr Khan is still absent, whispers, "*Ammijee* says she went mad! She would have killed herself if she could. So would you: so would I . . . she heard her eleven-year-old daughter screaming and screaming . . . she heard the *mullah's* sixteen-year-old daughter scream: "Do anything you wish with me, but don't hurt me. For God's sake don't hurt me!"

We look away, the girls' tormented cries ringing unbearably in our ears. Suzanne and the youngest sister brush their eyes and, by the time we are able to talk again, Mrs Khan's moment is over. The medley of languages again asserts itself: "God knows how many women died . . . . " A helpless spreading of hands and deep sighs.

"Pregnant women were paraded naked, their stomachs slashed . . . . "

"Yes-*jee* and the babies were swung by their heels and dashed against wall."

Much shaking of heads. God's help and mercy evoked.

"God knows how many women were lifted . . . but, then, everybody carried women off. Sikhs and Hindus, Muslim women. Muslims, Sikh and Hindu women."

A general clucking of tongues: an air of commiseration.

"Allah have mercy on us," says Mrs Khan, and in resounding Punjabi again asserts her authority as chief speaker. "His mother had a bad experience. Very bad. *Ammijee* never talks about it, but those who knew her when she was recovered, say . . . . "

Mrs Khan stops short. Having second thoughts about disclosing what her mother-in-law never talks about, she makes a deft switch and in a banal, rhetorical tone of voice says, "She saw horrible things. Horrible. Babies tossed into boiling oil . . . . "

Sikander Khan, having bought his pack and smoked his cigarette outside, quietly joins us.

Half-way through dinner two handsome, broad-shouldered Sikhs in gray shirts join us. I gather they are cousins. Their long hair is tucked away in blue turbans, and their beards tied in neat rolls beneath their chins. Again there is an explosion of welcome: a flurry to feed the late-comers and a great deal of hand-slapping and embracing among the men. Considering what I heard just a few moments ago, I am a little surprised at the cordiality between Sikander Khan and the young Sikhs. I hear one of the men say in Urdu, "Any further news about your *Ammijee's* arrival?"

His back is to me: but the sudden switch from Punjabi to Urdu, the formality in his voice and his mode of address, catch my attention. There is no apparent change in the volume of noise in the room, yet I sense we have all shared a moment of unease: an incongruous solemnity.

And then the Sikhs move to greet the women from Mr Khan's family in Punjabi, inquire after their health and the health of their children and indulge in a little light-hearted teasing. The unease is so dispelled, I wonder if I have not imagined it.

"You haven't invited us to a meal in almost a month, *Bhabi*," says the stouter of the two men to Mrs Khan. "Look at poor Pratab: see how thin he's become?" He pulls back his cousin's arms the way poultry dealers hold back chicken wings and, standing him helpless and grinning in front of Mrs Khan, asks, "Have we offended you in some way?"

"No, no, Khushwant *Bhai*," says Mrs Khan, "It isn't anything like that . . . . ."

"She's concerned about your health, brother," pipes up the eldest of her three sisters, "You're too fat and fresh for your own good!" She must be in her mid-twenties.

Khushwant releases his cousin good-naturedly and the sisters, hiding their smiles in their *dupattas*, start giggling. They have perked up in the presence of these young men who speak their language and share their ways, their religious antagonisms dissipated on American soil.

On surer ground, the same sister says, "What about the picnic you promised us? You're the one who breaks promises, and you complain about our sister!" Her face animated, her large black eyes roguish, she is charming: and I suddenly notice how pretty the sisters are in their pleasantly plump Punjabi way.

"When would you like to go? Next Sunday?" asks Khushwant Singh gallantly.

"We'll know what's what when Sunday comes," says another sister, tossing her long plaited hair back in a half-bullying, half-mocking gesture. She has a small, full-lipped mouth and a diamond on one side of her pert nose.

"I'll take you to the ocean next Sunday. It's a promise," says Khushwant Singh, "But only if *Bhabi* makes *parathas* with her own hands."

"What's wrong with my hands?" the pert sister asks. "Or with Gulnar's hands?" she indicates their youngest sister who promptly buries her face in her *dupatta*. Gulnar is the only sister not yet married. I guess she is sixteen or seventeen.

"Have either of you given me occasion to praise your cooking?" Khushwant asks.

"They'll give you occasion on Sunday," intervenes Mrs Khan. "But, tell me brother," she says, "what will you feed us? Why don't you bring chicken *korma* to go with the *parathas*?"

"No chicken *korma* till you find me a wife."

"*Lo!*' says Mrs Khan. "As if you'll agree to our choice! There are plenty of pretty Sikh girls, but you fuss!"

"I want someone just like you, *Bhabi*," says the handsome Sikh, and turns slightly red. "A girl who knows our ways."

"That's what you say, but you'll end up marrying a white-washed *memsahib*!" At once realising her folly the pert sister springs up from her chair and, abandoning her dinner, hugging Suzanne and holding her cheek against hers, says, "Unless it is someone like our Sue *Bhabi*: She's one of us. Then we won't mind."

Suzanne takes it, as she accepts the smaller hazards of her marriage to Kishen, in her twinkle-toed and *sari*-clad stride. She told me about a year back, when we were just becoming friends, that she felt content and secure in her extended Indian family. She tried to describe to me her feeling of being firmly embedded in life—in the business and purpose of living—that she, as an only child, had never experienced. Suzanne comes from a small town in New England. Her father teaches history at a university. I haven't met her family but I gather they are unpretentious and gentle folk.

It is the Sunday of the picnic. Kishen and Suzanne give me a ride to Galveston beach. It is a massive affair. Innumerable kin have been added to the group that met for dinner at Kishen's. Mr Khan, in long white pants and a blue T-shirt, staggers across the hot sand with a stack of *parathas* wrapped in a metallic gray garbage bag. Khushwant Singh and Pratab have brought the food from a Pakistani restaurant on Hillcroft.

Later in the sultry afternoon, exhilarated from our splashing in the ocean and the sudden shelter of an overcast sky, we converge on the *durries* spread on the sand. Mrs Khan and her three sisters flop like exotic beetles on a striped *durrie*, their wet satin *salwars* and *kameezes* clinging to them in rich blobs of solid colour.

The *parathas* are delicious. Sikander heaps his plate with *haleem* and mutton curry and, crossing his legs like an inept yogi, sits down by me. I broach the subject that has been obsessing me: I would like to use his family's experiences during the Partition in my novel.

As we eat, sucking on our fingers, drinking coke out of cans, I ask Sikander about the attack on his village: trying, with whatever wiles I can, to penetrate the mystery surrounding *Ammijee*.

I gathered from the remarks Mrs Khan let slip on the night of the party that *Ammijee* was kidnapped. But I want to know what Mrs Khan was about to say when she checked herself. I feel the missing information will unravel the full magnitude of the tragedy to my understanding and, more importantly, to my imagination. Instinctively I choose Sikander Khan, and not Mrs Khan, to provide the knowledge. His emotions and perceptions will, I feel, charge my writing with the detail, emotion, and veracity I am striving for.

Sikander's replies to my questions are candid, recalled in remarkable detail, but he balks at any mention of *Ammijee*.

I don't remember now the question that unexpectedly penetrated his reserve; but Sikander planted in my mind a fearsome seed that waxed into an ugly tree of hideous possibility, when, in a voice that was indescribably harsh, he said: "*Ammijee* heard street vendors cry: "*Zanana* for sale! *Zanana* for sale!' as if they were selling vegetables and fish. They were selling women for 50, 20, and even 10 rupees!"

Later that evening, idling on our *durries* as we watch the spectacular crimson streaks on the horizon fade, I ask Sikander how he can be close friends with Khushwant and Pratab. In his place I would not even want to meet their eye! Isn't he furious with the Sikhs for what they did? Do the cousins know what happened in his village?

"I'm sure they know . . . everybody I meet seems to know. Why quarrel with Khushwant and Pratab? They weren't even born . . . . " And, his voice again taking on the hard, harsh edge he says, "We Muslims were no better . . . we did the same . . . Hindu, Muslim, Sikh, we are all evil bastards!"

Mr Khan calls. His mother has arrived from Pakistan. He has asked a few friends to dinner to meet her on Saturday. Can I dine with them? *Ammijee* remembers me as a little girl!

I get into the usual state of panic and put off looking at the map till the last hour. It is a major trauma—this business of finding my way from place to place—missing exits, getting out of the car to read road signs, aggravating—and often terrifying—motorists in front, behind and on either side. Thank God for alert American reflexes: for their chastising, wise, blasphemous tooting.

I find my way to Mr Khan's without getting irremediably lost. It is a large old frame house behind a narrow neglected yard on Harold, between Montrose and the Rothko Chapel.

Sikander ushers me into the house with elegant formality, uttering phrases in Urdu which translated into English sound like this: "We're honoured by your visit to our poor house. We can't treat you in the manner to which you are accustomed . . . " and presents me to his mother. She is a plump, buttery fleshed, kind faced old woman wearing a simple *salwar* and shirt and her dark hair, streaked with gray, is covered by a gray nylon *chaddar*. She strokes my arm several times and peering affectionately into my face, saying, "*Mashallah*, you've grown healthier. You were such a dry little thing," steers me to sit next to her on the sofa.

Through my polite, bashful-little-girl's smile, I search her face. There's no trace of bitterness. No melancholy. Nothing knowing or hard: just the open, acquiescent, hospitable face of a contented peasant woman who is happy to visit her son. It is difficult to believe this gentle woman was kidnapped, raped, sold.

The sisters line up opposite us on an assortment of dining

and patio chairs carried in for the party. The living room is typically furnished, Pakistani style: an assortment of small carved tables and tables with brass and ivory inlay, hand-woven Pakistani carpets scattered at angles, sofas and chairs showing a lot of carved wood, onyx ashtrays and plastic flowers in brass vases. The atmosphere is permeated with the sterile odour of careful disuse.

Kishen, his mother and Suzanne arrive. Suzanne looks languorous and sultry-eyed in a beautiful navy and gold *sari*. There is a loud exchange of pleasantries. Kishen notices me across the length of the entrance lobby. "You found your way O.K.?" he calls from the door, teasing. "Didn't land up in Mexico or something?"

"Not even once!" I yell back.

Some faces I recognise from the picnic arrive. A Kashmiri brahmin couple joins us. They are both short, fair, plump and smug. They talk exclusively to Suzanne (the only white American in the room), Kishen (husband of the status symbol) and Mr Khan. The sisters, condescended to a couple of times and then ignored, drift to the kitchen and disappear into the remote and mysterious recesses of the large house. I become aware of muted children's voices, quarrelsome, demanding and excited. The sisters return, quiet and sullen, and dragging their chairs huddle about a lamp standing in the corner.

Dinner is late. We are waiting for Khushwant and Pratab. Mr Khan says, "We will wait for fifteen minutes more. If they don't come, we'll start eating."

Hungry guests with growling stomachs, we nevertheless say, "Please don't worry on our account . . . we are in no hurry."

Conversation dwindles. The guests politely inquire after the health of those sitting next to them and the grades of their children. We hear the doorbell ring and Mr Khan gets up from his chair saying, "I think they've come."

Instead of the dapper Sikhs, I see two huge and hirsute

Indian *fakirs*. Their dishevelled hair, parted at the centre, bristles about their arms and shoulders and mingles with their spiky black beards. They are wearing white muslin *kurtas* over white singlets and their broad shoulders and thick muscles show brown beneath the fine muslin. I can't be sure from where I sit, but I think they have on loose cotton pyjamas. They look indescribably fierce. It is an impression, quickly formed, and I have barely glimpsed the visitors, when, abruptly, their knees appear to buckle and they fall forward.

Mr Khan steps back hastily and bends over the prostrate men. He says, "What's all this? What's all this?" The disconcerted tone of his voice, and the underpinning of perplexity and fear gets us all to our feet. Moving in a bunch, displacing the chairs and small tables and crumpling the carpets, we crowd our end of the lobby.

The *fakirs* lie face down across the threshold, half outside the door and half in the passage, their hands flat on the floor as if they are about to do pushups. Their faces are entirely hidden by hair. Suddenly, their voices moist and thick, they begin to cry, "*Maajee! Maajee!* Forgive us." The blubbering, coming as it does from these fierce men, is unexpected, shocking; incongruous and melodramatic in this pragmatic and oil-rich corner of the western world.

Sikander, in obvious confusion, looms over them, looking from one to the other. Then, squatting in front of them, he begins to stroke their prickly heads, making soothing noises as if he is cajoling children, "What's this? Tch, tch . . . . Come on! Stand up!"

"Get out of the way." An arm swings out in a threatening gesture and the *fakir* lifts his head. I see the pale, ash-smeared forehead, the large, thickly fringed brown eyes, the set curve of the wide, sensuous mouth and recognise Khushwant Singh. Next to him Pratab also raises his head. Sikander shuffles out of reach of Khushwant's arm and moving to one side, his back to the wall, watches the Sikhs with an expression of incredulity. It is unreal. I think it has occurred to all of us it might be a prank, an elaborate joke. But their red eyes, and the passion distorting their faces, are not pretended.

"Who are these men?"

The voice is demanding, abrasive. I look over my shoulder, wondering which of the women has spoken so harshly. The sisters look agitated; their dusky faces are flushed.

"Throw them out. They're *badmashes*! *Goondas*!"

Taken aback I realise the angry, fearful voice is Sikander's mother's.

Ammijee is standing behind me, barely visible among the agitated and excited sisters, and in her face I see more than just the traces of the emotions I had looked for earlier. It is as if her features have been parodied in a hideous mask. They are all there: the bitterness, the horror, the hate: the incarnation of that tree of ugly possibilities seeded in my mind when Sikander, in a cold fury, imitating the cries of the street vendors his mother had described, said, "*Zanana* for sale! *Zanana* for sale!"

I grew up overhearing fragments of whispered conversations about the sadism and bestiality women were subjected to during the Partition: what happened to so and so—someone's sister, daughter, sister-in-law—the women Mrs Khan categorised *the spoils of war*. The fruits of victory in the unremitting chain of wars that is man's relentless history. The vulnerability of mothers, daughters, granddaughters, and their metamorphosis into possessions; living objects on whose soft bodies victors and losers alike vent their wrath, enact fantastic vendettas, celebrate victory. All history, all these fears, all probabilities and injustices coalesce in *Ammijee's* terrible face and impart a dimension of tragedy that alchemises the melodrama. The behaviour of the Sikhs, so incongruous and flamboyant before, is now transcendentally essential, consequential, fitting.

The men on the floor have spotted *Ammijee*. "*Maajee*, forgive us: Forgive the wrongs of our fathers."

A sister behind me says, "Oh my God!" There is a buzz of questions and comments. I feel she has voiced exactly my awe of the moment—the rare, luminous instant in which two men transcend their historic intransigence to tender apologies on behalf of their species. Again she says, "Oh God!" and I realise she is afraid that the cousins, propelled forward by small movements of their shoulders and elbows like crocodiles, are resurrecting a past that is best left in whatever recesses of the mind *Ammijee* has chosen to bury it.

"Don't do this . . . please," protests Sikander. "You're our guests . . . !"

But the cousins, keeping their eyes on the floor say, "*Bhai*, let us be."

The whispered comments of the guests intensify around me.

"What's the matter?"

"They are begging her pardon . . . ."

"Who are these men?"

" . . . for what the Sikhs did to her in the riots . . . ."

"*Hai Ram*. What do they want?"

"God knows what she's been through; she never talks about it . . ."

"With their hair open like this they must remind her of the men who . . . ."

"You can't beat the Punjabis when it comes to drama," says the supercilious Kashmiri. His wife, standing next to me, says, "The Sikhs have a screw loose in the head." She rotates a stubby thumb on her temple as if she is tightening an imaginary screw.

I turn, frowning. The sisters are glaring at them: showering the backs of their heads with withering, hostile looks. And, in hushed tones of suitable gravity, Mrs Khan says, "*Ammijee*, they are asking for your forgiveness. Forgive them." Then, "She forgives you brothers!" says Mrs Khan loudly, on her mother-in-law's account. The other sisters repeat Mrs Khan's magnanimous gesture, and, with minor variations, also forgive Khushwant and Pratab on *Ammijee's* behalf.

"*Ammijee,* come here." Sikander sounds determined to put a stop to all this.

We shift, clearing a narrow passage for *Ammijee,* and Kishen's mother darts out instead looking like an agitated chick in her puffed cotton *sari.* She is about to say something—and judging from her expression it has to be something indeterminate and conciliatory—when Kishen, firmly taking hold of her arm, hauls her back.

Seeing his mother has not moved, Sikander shouts, "Send *Ammijee* here. For God's sake, finish it now."

Ammijee takes two or three staggering steps and stands a few paces before me. I suspect one of the sisters has nudged her forward. I cannot see *Ammijee's* face, but the head beneath the gray *chaddar* jerks as if she is trying to remove a crick from her neck.

All at once, her voice, an altered, fragile, high-pitched treble that bears no resemblance to the fierce voice that had demanded, "Who are these men?" *Ammijee* screeches, "I will never forgive your fathers! Or your grandfathers! Get out, *shaitans*! Sons and grandsons of *shaitans*! Never, never, never!"

She becomes absolutely still, as if she will remain there forever, rooted, the quintessence of indictment.

They advance, wiping their noses on their sleeves, tearing at their snarled hair, pleading, "We will lie at your door to our last breath! We are not fit to show our faces."

In a slow, deliberate gesture, *Ammijee* turns her face away and I observe her profile. Her eyes are clenched shut. The muscles in her cheeks and lower jaw are quivering in tiny, tight spasms as if charged by a current. No one dares say a word: it would be an intrusion. She has to contend with unearthed torments, private demons. The matter rests between her memories and the incarnation of the phantoms wriggling up to her.

The men reach out to touch the hem of her *salwar*. Grasping her ankles, they lay their heads at her feet in the ancient gesture of surrender demanded of warriors.

"Leave me! Let go!" *Ammijee* shrieks, in her shaky, altered voice. She raises her arms and moves them as if she is pushing away invisible insects. But she looks exhausted and, her knees giving way, she squats before the men. She buries her face in the *chaddar*.

At last, with slight actions that suggest she is ready to face the world, *Ammijee* wipes her face in the *chaddar* and rearranges it on her untidy head. She tucks the edges behind her ears and slowly, in a movement that is almost tender, places her shaking hands on the shaggy heads of the men who hold her feet captive. "My sons, I forgave your fathers long ago," she says in a flat, emotionless voice pitched so low that it takes some time for the words to register, "How else could I live?"

On my way home, hanging on to the red tail lights of the cars on the Katy Freeway, my thoughts tumble through a chaos of words and images: and then the words churn madly, throwing up fragments of verse by the Bolivian poet, Pedro Shimose. The words throb in an endless, circular rhythm:

Defend yourself against me
against my father and the father of my father
still living in me
Against my force and shouting in schools and cathedrals
Against my camera, against my pencil
against my TV-spots.

Defend yourself against me,
please, woman,
defend yourself!

29

Khushwant Singh

The Riot

The town lay etherised under the fresh spring twilight. The shops were closed and house-doors barred from the inside. Street lamps dimly lit the deserted roads. Only a few policemen walked about with steel helmets on their heads and rifles slung behind their backs. The sound of their hobnailed boots was all that broke the stillness of the town.

The twilight sank into darkness. A crescent moon lit the quiet streets. A soft breeze blew bits of newspaper from the pavements onto the road and back again. It was cool and smelled of the freshness of spring. Some dogs emerged from a dark lane and gathered round a lamppost. A couple of policemen strolled past them smiling. One of them mumbled something vulgar. The other pretended to pick up a stone and hurl it at the dogs. The dogs ran down the street in the opposite direction and resumed their courtship at a safer distance.

Rani was a pariah bitch whose litter populated the lanes and by-lanes of the town. She was a thin, scraggy specimen, typical of the pariahs of the town. Her white coat was mangy, showing patches of raw flesh. Her dried-up udders hung loosely from her ribs. Her tail was always tucked between her hind legs as she slunk about in fear and abject servility.

Rani would have died of starvation with her first litter of eight had it not been for the generosity of the Hindu shopkeeper, Ram Jawaya, in the corner of whose courtyard she had unloaded her womb. The shopkeeper's family fed her and played with her pups till they were old enough to run about the streets and steal food for themselves. The shopkeeper's generosity had put Rani in the habit of sponging. Every year when spring came she would find some excuse to loiter around the stall of Ramzan, the Muslim greengrocer. Beneath the wooden platform on which vegetables were displayed, lived the big, burly Moti. Early autumn, Rani presented the shopkeeper's household with half-a-dozen or more of Moti's offspring.

Moti was a cross between a Newfoundland and a Spaniel. His shaggy coat and sullen look was Ramzan's pride. Ramzan had lopped off Moti's tail and ears. He fed him till Moti grew big and strong and became the master of the town's canine population. Rani had many rivals. But year after year, with the advent of spring, Rani's fancy lightly turned to thoughts of Moti and she sauntered across to Ramzan's stall.

This time spring had come but the town was paralysed with fear of communal riots and curfews. In the daytime, people hung about the street corners in groups of tens and twenties, talking in whispers. No shops opened and long before curfew hours the streets were deserted, with only pariah dogs and policemen about.

Tonight even Moti was missing. In fact, ever since the curfew, Ramzan had kept him indoors tied to a cot. He was far more useful guarding Ramzan's house than loitering about the streets. Rani came to Ramzan's stall and sniffed around. Moti could not have been there for some days. She was disappointed. But spring came only once a year—and hardly ever did it come at a time when one could have the city to oneself with no curious children looking on—and no scandalised parents hurling stones at her. So Rani gave up Moti and ambled down the road toward Ram Jawaya's house. A train of suitors followed her.

Rani faced her many suitors in front of Ram Jawaya's doorstep. They snarled and snapped and fought with each other. Rani stood impassively, waiting for the decision. In a few minutes a lanky black dog, one of Rani's own progeny, won the honours. The others slunk away.

In Ramzan's house, Moti sat pensively eyeing his master from underneath his *charpoy*. For some days the spring air had made him restive. He heard the snarling in the street and smelled Rani in the air. But Ramzan would not let him go. He tugged at the rope—then gave it up and began to whine. Ramzan's heavy hand struck him. A little later he began to whine again. Ramzan had had several sleepless nights keeping watch and was heavy with sleep. He began to snore. Moti whined louder and then sent up a pitiful howl to his unfaithful mistress. He tugged and strained at the leash and began to bark. Ramzan got up angrily from his *charpoy* to beat him. Moti made a dash toward the door, dragging the lightened string cot behind him. He nosed open the door and rushed out. The *charpoy* stuck in the doorway and the rope tightened round his neck. He gave a savage wrench, the rope gave way, and he leapt across the road. Ramzan ran back to his room, slipped a knife under his shirt, and went after Moti.

Outside Ram Jawaya's house, the illicit liaison of Rani and the black pariah was being consummated. Suddenly the burly form of Moti came into view. With an angry growl Moti leapt at Rani's lover. Other dogs joined the melee, tearing and snapping wildly.

Ram Jawaya had also spent several sleepless nights keeping watch and yelling back war cries to the Muslims. At last fatigue and sleep overcame his newly-acquired martial spirit. He slept soundly with a heap of stones under his *charpoy* and an imposing array of soda-water bottles filled with acid close at hand. The noise outside woke him. The shopkeeper picked up a big stone and opened the door. With a loud oath he sent the missile flying at the dogs. Suddenly, a human being emerged from the corner and the stone caught him squarely in the solar plexus.

The stone did not cause much damage to Ramzan but the suddenness of the assault took him aback. He yelled "Murder!" and produced his knife from under his shirt. The shopkeeper and the grocer eyed each other for a brief moment and then ran back to their houses shouting. The petrified town came to life. There was more shouting. The drum at the Sikh temple beat a loud tattoo—the air was rent with war cries.

Men emerged from their houses making hasty enquiries. A Muslim or a Hindu, it was said, had been attacked. Someone had been kidnapped and was being butchered. A party of *goondas* were going to attack, but the dogs had started barking. They had actually assaulted a woman and killed her children. There must be resistance. There was. Groups of five joined others of ten. Tens joined twenties till a few hundred, armed with knives, spears, hatchets, and kerosene oil cans proceeded to Ram Jawaya's house. They were met with a fusillade of stones, soda-water bottles and acid. They hit back blindly. Tins of kerosene oil were emptied indiscriminately and lighted. Flames shot up in the sky enveloping Ram Jawaya's home and the entire neighbourhood, Hindu, Muslim and Sikh alike.

The police rushed to the scene and opened fire. Fire engines clanged their way in and sent jets of water flying into the sky. But fires had been started in other parts of the town and there were not enough fire engines to go round.

All night and all the next day the fires burnt—and houses fell and people were killed. Ram Jawaya's home was burnt and he barely escaped with his life. For several days smoke rose from the ruins. What had once been a busy town was a heap of charred masonry.

Some months later when peace was restored, Ram Jawaya came to inspect the site of his old home. It was all in shambles with the bricks lying in a mountainous pile. In the corner of what had once been his courtyard there was a little clearing. There lay Rani with her litter nuzzling into her dried udders. Beside her stood Moti guarding his bastard brood.

30

KRISHNA SOBTI

Where Is My Mother?

WHEN YUNUS KHAN of the Baluch Regiment scanned the sky, the moon had traversed half its nightly journey. He had found time to gaze at the sky and the stars after a good many days. Where was he all this while? Deep down in a cavernous ditch that had now started overflowing with blood. But he was no miscreant. He was fighting for the land of his dreams. One can sacrifice anything to gain one's goal. These four days he had been all over Gujaranwala, Wazirabad and Gujarat. He and his dashing truck. Far and distant. What for? For Pakistan. For the brotherhood of Islam. He had no selfish interest of his own.

Was it the fire raging in the far-off hills that Yunus Khan was seeing while standing on the roadside? The screaming of the helpless victims was nothing new to him. His ears were used to the sound of wailing women and crying children when he and his companions surrounded the villages and set them on fire. He had seen many a bonfire. Children roasted like piglets. Men and women burnt alive. He had witnessed charred bodies in hundreds after a street had blazed all night. He was not scared of dead bodies. Freedom cannot be had without bloodshed. Every revolution is accompanied by slaughter and incendiarism. And out of this holocaust, an enchanting new nation was going to be born. He had to sweat for it day and night.

His eyes were sleepy. But he had to reach Lahore. He must ensure that not one *kafir* was left alive. There was a nip in the air but the thought of liquidation of the non-believers sent a wave of new vigour through his body. The truck was racing once again.

As the truck headed towards Lahore, Yunus Khan saw many villages ransacked and razed to the ground. He saw dead bodies strewn in the crop-laden fields. At times he heard the rioters shout "*Allah-ho-Akbar*" followed by "*Har Har Mahadev*". Then there would be the panic-stricken cries of the helpless. Yunus Khan heard all this and remained undisturbed. He was visualising the birth of a new nation, greater than the Mughal Empire.

Now the moon appeared to be descending. The milk white moonlight was acquiring a bluish tinge. Maybe the bloodshed on the earth was being reflected in the sky.

"Stop it, stop the truck," Yunus asked the driver. There was a shadow of a sort on the roadside. A tiny shadow. No, it was a girl, a small child lying unconscious, covered by a blood-soaked scarf.

The Baluchi went towards her. Why did he stop his truck? He never bothered about dead bodies. It was a wounded child. So what? He had known mounds of massacred children. No, he must pick up the child. And if he could save her, he would do his best. But what for? Yunus Khan himself failed to understand it. He would not leave her alone. But what if she was a *kafir*?

He picked up the frail, unconscious child in his strong arms. He brought her to the truck and laid her down on the front seat. The girl's eyes were shut. Her head was spattered with blood. And her face, a pale yellow patch, had blood-stains all over.

Yunus Khan's fingers were moving through the child's hair, resting on the blood-soaked plaits. He was fondling the child. He had not known such sentiments before. Since when had he become so considerate? He failed to understand it. The girl lying unconscious did not know that the hands that had slaughtered her people were tending her in utter solicitude.

Yunus Khan no longer saw a helpless girl lying unconscious before him. His half-shut eyes viewed his own sister, Nooran, back in his home town in Quetta. It was a chilly evening. His mother, a widow, had died leaving her an orphan. And then she, too, died soon after.

Yunus Khan suddenly realised that he was losing time. He must hurry. The child was wounded. The truck was speeding again. He must get her attended to immediately. Perhaps she could be saved. The truck was going as fast as it ever did. But why must he save this child when he had massacred hundreds of them? There was a strange conflict in his heart. He silenced it somehow. What had this innocent girl to do with their struggle? What had she to do with freedom and the birth of Pakistan?

Lahore was approaching. The Grand Trunk Road was running parallel to the railway line. It was Shahdara. He must not take the child to Sir Ganga Ram Hospital. In a Hindu hospital it would be like restoring her back to her own people. He would admit her in Mayo Medical Institute.

"Do whatever you can to save this child," Yunus Khan pleaded again and again.

The doctor assured him that he would do his best.

The child was treated with the utmost care in the hospital. Yunus Khan continued performing his duties as a soldier, but he was restless. He was anxious and wanted to be by the child's bedside.

Lahore was still burning. He noticed a knot of Hindus,

helpless and scared, rescued by a Muslim military patrol. There were dead bodies dumped on a dunghill. There were naked women lying dead on the roadside. Yunus Khan, who was most active till yesterday, moved about listlessly today.

His footsteps suddenly became brisk in the evening. It seemed that it was his own home and not the hospital he was hastening to.

Why was he so anxious about this unknown child? She did not belong to his community. She was a Hindu—a *kafir!*

He imagined it was quite a distance from the hospital gate to her bed. He took long strides.

The girl lay on the bed, her head wrapped in bandages, her eyes still closed. The dreadful sight she had witnessed was still imprinted on her memory. She couldn't forget it.

How should he address her? His sister's name, Nooran came to his lips. He stretched his hands and held her head in them.

Suddenly the girl moved and started shouting: "It's camp . . . run, run for your life."

"There is nothing. Open your eyes, child," implored Yunus.

The girl opened her eyes. She saw the huge Baluchi standing close to her and she started screaming.

"Doctor, for God's sake do something to cure the child."

The doctor gazed at her with an experienced look. "There's not much you can do. She is scared of you because she is a *kafir.*"

The word *kafir* echoed and reached Yunus Khan's ears. A *kafir!* Why must he save her? No, he must. He would bring her up as his own sister.

Many days passed in this dilemma. Yunus Khan worked hard at his job during the day and in the evenings he walked the hospital corridors. He preferred seeing her when she was asleep or lying with her eyes closed.

And then she recovered completely. Yunus Khan came to the hospital in the evening to take her home.

The child looked at him with her big black eyes. There was terror and suspicion in them.

Yunus tried to coax her, but she remained mortally afraid. She feared he would choke her to death with his big brown hands. She was at her wits' end. She closed her eyes. What did she see? She saw that dreadful night imprinted on her mind. The night, and her brother. Her brother, whose head was chopped off with one stroke of the sharp-edged weapon.

Yunus Khan called to her with great tenderness. "You are now all right. We shall go home."

"No, no," the child screamed. "I have no home. I won't go with you—you'll kill me."

"Me, child?" he asked. He wanted to reclaim his sister Nooran. But this child was no Nooran. She was a stranger, a Hindu child who was mortally afraid of him.

"I don't want to go home," the girl pleaded. "Take me to the refugee camp. I want to go to the camp."

Yunus Khan dared not look into her eyes. He was at a loss to know what to do. He was helpless.

The soldier in him looked at the child with compassion and solicitude. He begged for understanding. "Don't you worry," he said, "I am your own."

"No, no," she cried. Sitting beside the Baluchi in his truck, she was convinced that he would take her to a lonely spot and kill her. Maybe with a gun or a dagger. The child held his hand. "Khan, you must not kill me. For God's sake, do not kill me."

Yunus Khan put his hand on the girl's head and vowed: "You need not be afraid. You have nothing to fear. I am here to protect you."

The child suddenly became violent. She tried to pounce upon him but he held her back. Thereafter she began screaming. "Take me to the refugee camp. I only want to go to the refugee camp. . . ."

The Baluchi explained to her patiently. "You need have

no fear. You don't have to go to a camp now. You will live with me like my own sister . . . in my house. You are like a little sister to me."

"No, no," the girl screamed and began beating the Baluchi on the chest with her small fists. "You are a Muslim . . . you'll kill me."

She then started wailing, "I want my mother. Where is my mother?"

(Translated from the original in Hindi by K.S. Duggal)

Biographical Notes

KHWAJA AHMAD ABBAS (1914-1987): Novelist, screenwriter and film producer, he was born in Panipat and educated at Aligarh Muslim University in U.P. He began freelancing for a number of papers and magazines. Among his numerous publications are his biographies of Krushchev, Nehru and Indira Gandhi. He is, however, best remembered for his short stories, his novella *Blood and Stones,* his political novel *Inqilab* and his moving autobiography *I am Not an Island.*

AZIZ AHMAD (1913-1978): Born in Bara Banki, India, he did his B.A. Hons. from the University of London in 1938 and joined Osmania University where he became a Professor of English. He emigrated to Pakistan in 1948 and joined as Director in the Department of Films and Publication with the Government of Pakistan. In 1957 he was appointed Lecturer in the London School of Oriental and African Studies. In 1962 he left for Canada as Professor of Islamic Studies at the University of Toronto. Author of six novels and five scholarly books in English on Islam, Muslim Culture and History, Islam in India, and Modernism, he was awarded an honorary D. Litt. by the University of London and was made a Fellow of the Royal Society of Canada.

'AJNEYA': S. H. VATSYAYAN (b. 1911): An eminent Hindi poet and fiction writer, he has won several awards including the Bharatiya Jnanpith Award and the National Academy of Letters Award. Author of some fifteen volumes of poetry in Hindi, he has also published a large body of fiction. Of these, the most notable are *Shekar, Nadi ke Dvipa* and *Apne-Apne Ajnabi.* He has also written numerous essays and travelogues, and his works have been translated into German, Swedish, Serbo-Croatian and English.

MULK RAJ ANAND (b. 1905): Born in Peshawar, he was educated at the Universities of Punjab and London. After earning his Ph.D in

Philosophy in 1929, Anand began writing notes for T. S. Eliot's *Criterion.* Success came to him with the publication of his first novel, *Untouchable*, in 1935. Since then he has written some thirty works of fiction, including seven volumes of short stories. Currently he is engaged in a monumental autobiographical novel entitled *The Seven Ages of Man.*

SAMARESH BASU (b. 1929): Born in Dhaka (Bangladesh), Mr Basu now lives in Calcutta. Self-taught, he writes in Bengali and has a massive volume of fiction to his credit. He has authored over 100 novels and 315 short stories. Winner of the 1980 Sahitya Akademi Award, his outstanding novels are *Prajapati* and *Samba.*

RAJINDER SINGH BEDI (1915-1984): Born in Lahore, he worked as a clerk in the local post office and earned for himself a considerable reputation as a short story writer in Urdu. In 1941 he joined the All India Radio in Lahore and wrote a number of successful plays, including *Khwaja Sara*, *Rakhshinda* and *Naql-i-Makani.* On Partition in 1947, he was witness to loot, arson and murder. After a short spell as Station Director of Radio Kashmir, Bedi joined films and became a successful producer and script writer. In 1965 he won the National Academy of Letters Award for his Urdu novel *Ek Chaadar Maili Si.*

KRISHAN CHANDER (1914-1976): A prolific short story writer in Urdu, he was Secretary-General of the Progressive Writers Association in India for a long time. As such, he left his mark on a whole generation of young writers—making them conscious of social reality. Among his better known collections of short stories are *Talism-i-Khyal, Nazzare, Anna Data, Zindigi ke Mod Par* and *Ajanta se Aage. Ham Wahshi Hain* is the title of his collection of short stories devoted exclusively to the theme of Partition. He also wrote novels and a large number of radio plays. Some of these radio plays have been collected in an anthology called *Ek Rupya Ek Phool.*

SAROS COWASJEE (b. 1931): Educated at the Universities of Agra and Leeds (U.K.), he is currently Professor of English at the University of Regina in Canada. Author of critical studies on Sean O' Casey and Mulk Raj Anand, he is best known for his fiction *Goodbye to Elsa, Suffer Little Children* and *Nude Therapy and Other Stories.*

KARTAR SINGH DUGGAL (b. 1917): Born in Dhaminal, Rawalpindi, in Pakistan, he has served as Director, All India Radio, Director, National Book Trust, India, and Adviser (Information), Planning Commission. His published works include collections of short stories, novels, full-length and short plays. Among his better known fictional works are *Twice Born Twice Dead, Come Back My Master* and *Death of a Song.* He is the recipient of a number of awards including the National Academy of Letters Award (1965), Ghalib Award (1976) and Soviet Land Nehru Award (1981).

ATTIA HOSAIN (b. 1913): Born in Lucknow, she graduated from Isabella Thorburn College—being the first woman from amongst the Taluqdars of Oudh to do so. She is the author of *Phoenix Fled and Other Stories* (1953), and a novel *Sunlight on a Broken Column* (1963) which is a requiem for a whole way of Muslim life that vanished with Indian Independence. She has also done broadcasting in India and the U.K., and acted in *The Bird of Time* at the Savoy Theatre, London.

INTIZAR HUSAIN (b. 1925): Born in Dibai (India), he received his education in Meerut. He migrated to Pakistan in 1947 and has been living in Lahore ever since. Creative writer, critic, columnist, and translator, he has published six highly acclaimed collection of short stories, three novels, a novella and a volume of critical essays. *Town,* an English translation of his novel *Basti,* which deals, in part, with the partition of India and the subsequent breakup of Pakistan in 1971, was recently published by HarperCollins (India).

KAMLESHWAR (b. 1932): A front rank short story writer in Hindi, he edited *Sarika,* a Hindi journal devoted to the short story, for several years. His published works include seven collections of short stories and eight novels. He has also written an analytical treatise on the short story as a genre and is acknowledged to have given a new direction to the contemporary Indian short story. Equally popular as a film writer, Kamleshwar is hailed as a trend setter who has helped to bring in new-wave film in India's massive film industry.

SAADAT HASAN MANTO (1912-1955): During his short life he achieved considerable fame and notoriety for his bold writings in Urdu. Born in Sambrala (Ludhiana District), he opted for Pakistan in 1947 and moved to Lahore. Here he edited a literary journal called *Nai Qadrin* for a while, but he is remembered most for his short stories. His best-known collections of short stories are *Namrood ke Khuda* and *Ganje Farishte. Syyah Hashiya* is a collection of mini stories devoted exclusively to the atrocities perpetrated during partition.

NARENDRA NATH MITRA (1916-1975): A graduate of Calcutta University, he served on the *Ananda Bazar Patrika,* a leading daily, for the greater part of his career. He was directly affected by Partition, having lost his household and landed property. He is particularly known for his short stories on Partition. He published 47 novels and over 400 short stories. Some of his short stories have been translated into various regional languages of India as well as into English, French, Italian and Russian.

GIANI GURMUKH SINGH MUSAFIR (1899-1976): A freedom fighter who rose to be the Chief Minister of Punjab in Independent India, Giani Gurmukh Singh 'Musafir' maintained that his first love was creative writing. Both a poet and short story writer, he reflects his rich experience of the man-of-the-masses who was in jail several times fighting the British during the freedom struggle. A trusted lieutenant of Jawaharlal Nehru, he accompanied him invariably during his visits to the refugee camps on both sides of the border in the Punjab immediately after the partition. He was awarded the National Academy of Letters Award for his collection of short stories entitled *Urwar Paar* (On This Side of the Shore and That) posthumously in 1977.

SURAIYA QASIM (b. 1945): Presently based in Chandigarh, she earned an M.A. degree before taking to journalism. She continues to be a free-lance writer, contributing articles to leading English newspapers in India. She also worked as a stringer for *Asia Week*

(Hong Kong); and one of her poems, "Singing Silence", was included in *Lyrical Voices: An International Poetry Anthology* (1979).

MOHAN RAKESH (1925-1972): After equipping himself with Master's degrees in both Hindi and Sanskrit, he had a short spell at teaching before taking to journalism. A playwright and a fiction writer, he was a trend setter in his time. *Ashad ka ek Din, Lehron ke Rajhans* and *Adhe Adhure* are his three full-length plays; *Andhere Band Kamre Mein* and *Antral* are his two novels. He has also three collections of short stories. A refugee from Pakistan, he suffered grievously on account of the partition.

BHISHAM SAHNI (b. 1915): distinguished novelist and short story writer, he was born in Rawalpindi (now in Pakistan). After taking his M.A. and Ph.D. degrees in English, he spent nearly seven years in the Soviet Union where he translated Russian and Soviet classics into Hindi. His own works have been translated into Russian, English and Malayalam. His novel *Tamas* is an outstanding contribution to Hindi literature for its artistic control, firm grasp of reality, excellence of characterisation, and its authenticity of experience.

GULZAR SINGH SANDHU (b. 1933): Currently chairman of the Department of Journalism of Punjabi University, Gulzar Singh Sandhu was Editor of the Punjabi Tribune, a prestigious daily paper of Punjab, for several years. A recipient of the Sahitya Akademi Award for short story, his important works are *Ik Sanjh Purani* (An Old Partnership) and *Amar Katha* (An Immortal Tale). He excels in the presentation of the Punjab rural scene.

MOHINDER SINGH SARNA (b. 1925): A senior officer of the Indian Audit & Accounts Service who retired recently, he is currently a full-time creative writer, devoted primarily to short fiction. He has about a dozen collections of short stories to his credit. His latest works are: *Nawen Yug de Waris* (The Successors of the New Age, 1992) and *Aurat Eman* (Woman—the Custodian of Truth, 1994). Apart from a number of literary awards that he has won, he has been honoured by both the Government of Punjab and the Delhi

Administration as a distinguished man-of-letters. A refugee from the West Punjab, he has been a witness to the holocaust of the partition.

SHAHAAB, QUDRAT ULLAH (1917-1986): Born in Gilgit, he attended schools at Chitral and Gilgit and went to Jammu for his college education. He obtained his M.A. in English from Government College, Lahore, and joined the Indian Civil Service in 1941. After the Partition he became Secretary to the President of Pakistan—a position he held with three successive Presidents. He also served as Pakistan's Ambassador to the Netherlands and later as Federal Education Secretary. He has published a novelette, *Ya Khuda* (1948); three collections of short stories, *Nafsaney* (1950), *Man Ji* (1968) and *Surkh Feeta* and an autobiography, *Shahaab Namah.*

BAPSI SIDHWA (b. 1938): Born in Karachi (Pakistan) she divides her time between Pakistan and the United States. Winner of the Lila Wallace Reader's Digest Writers' Award, and author of four novels, her *Ice-Candy Man* won the literature Prize in Germany and was named a Notable Book of 1991 by the *New York Times.* Her other books are *The Pakistani Bride, The Crow Eaters* and her most recent publication *An American Brat.* She has written several short stories and essays as well, and has been translated into French, Russian, Urdu and German.

KHUSHWANT SINGH (b 1915): Novelist, historian and journalist, he is possibly the most widely read columnist in India today. With some 60 books to his credit, Khushwant Singh first shot into fame with his award-winning bestseller *Train to Pakistan* (1955), which powerfully depicts the mass hysteria and senseless communal violence that followed the partitioning of the country. This novel was followed by *I Shall Not Hear the Nightingale* (1959), a short-story collection, *A Bride for the Sahib* (1967), and the non-fiction collection *Good People, Bad People* (1977). Khushwant Singh has also published a two-volume *History of the Sikhs,* which now, fully updated, is still considered the most authoritative writing on the subject. His recent bestsellers include *Delhi—a novel, Sex, Scotch and Scholarship* and *Need for a New Religion in India and other Essays.*

KRISHNA SOBTI (b. 1925): Born in West Punjab, she was directly affected by the Partition. She shot into prominence in Hindi literature with her first novel, *Mitro Marjani,* and since then she has successfully published several works of fiction. Her latest, a historical novel called *Zindginama,* has been acclaimed as the most significant writing on the pre-partition Punjab. She has also written literary essays and pen-portraits of a cross-section of people from the world of art and letters.

Glossary of Indian Words and Phrases

Abbaji	:	Father
Ammi; Ammijee	:	Mother
Acha, Achha	:	All right
Aadaab	:	A form of salutation
Ai Baisakhi	:	The festival of baisakhi is here
Alam	:	A banner; here, the spear-headed block banner of Imam Husain
Allah-ho-Akbar	:	God is Great. A Muslim slogan shouted during the communal riots
Angochha	:	Towel
Arre	:	Hey
Babaji	:	Term of respect for an elder
Babuji	:	A term of respect for a learned man.
Bahen	:	Sister
Baisakhi	:	A harvest festival
Bande Mataram	:	Salutation to the Motherland. A popular Hindu slogan during the communal riots
Behisht	:	Heaven
Beti	:	Daughter
Bhagwan	:	Hindu term for God
Bhang	:	An intoxicating drug
Bhabi	:	Sister-in-law
Bhai	:	Brother
Bibi	:	Wife
Bibijee	:	Term of respect for a Hindu Woman
Bidi	:	Indian cigarette wrapped in leaf
Jo Boley so Nihal, Sat Sri Akal	:	A Sikh Slogan — He who says God is truth will be blessed.
Brahmachari	:	A person given to purity of life, sexual restraint, celibacy
Bulbul	:	Bird of the thrush family, admired for its musical chirping
Burqa	:	Veil worn by orthodox Muslim women
Chacha	:	Uncle
Chaddar	:	Sheet used for covering one's body
Chapati	:	Unleavened bread, baked on a griddle
Charpoy	:	Light wooden string bed
Chaudhri	:	Village headman

Chillum	:	A clay bowl for smoking tobacco
Chihlam	:	The fortieth day, following the death of a relative; here, the martyrdom of Imam Husain
Chor	:	Thief
Choti	:	Tuft of hair worn by orthodox Hindus
Chaudhri	:	Headman
Chaudhrani	:	*Chaudhri*'s wife
Chunri	:	A scarf or headcloth worn by North Indian women
Dal	:	Lentil
Dalkhor	:	One who eats lentils. A term of derision used for vegetarians
Darvesh	:	Member of Muslim religious order
Desi	:	Indigenous
Devi	:	Goddess
Dholak	:	A kind of percussion instrument, like a drum
Diwali	:	Hindu festival of light
Dhoti	:	Loin cloth worn by Indian men
Dopiaza	:	A meat dish with excessive mixture of onion
Draupadi	:	Wife of the Pandavas sought to be dishonoured by the enemies
Dharti	:	Earth
Deputy Collator	:	Mispronunciation of Deputy Collector
Dupatta	:	A scarf or headcloth worn by women of north India
Durrie	:	Rug or carpet
Ekka	:	Open single-horse carriage
Eidgah	:	A place of assembly and prayer for Muslim festivals
Fakir	:	Indian holy man
Furlong	:	One eighth of a mile
Ghat	:	Pier
Ghee	:	Clarified butter
Goonda	:	A miscreant; a bad character
Gulal	:	Red powder used in Holi festival
Gully	:	Lane

Gurdwara	:	Sikh place of worship
Hai Allah	:	Oh God
Hai Rabba	:	Oh God
Halwa	:	A sweetmeat
Han	:	Yes
Har har Mahadev	:	Mahadev is God—a Hindu slogan
Haramzada	:	Bastard
Havan	:	A Hindu ceremonial for propitiation
Haveli	:	Mansion; big house
Hijrat	:	Spiritual experience of migration
Havildar	:	Junior police officer
Henna	:	A reddish orange dye or cosmetic made from the leaves of Lawsonia Inermis
Hookah	:	Hubble-bubble
Hoor; Houri	:	Fairy; a beauty
Huzoor; Hujoor	:	Sir
Id	:	Muslim religious festival
Imam	:	A Muslim head priest
Imam-bara	:	A building maintained by the Shia Muslims for observing the Muharram Ceremonies
Janab	:	Mister
Jai Bali Dev	:	Victory to Bali Dev —a Hindu God
Jai Hind	:	Victory to India — a popular Indian slogan
Jagirdar	:	Landlord
Jat	:	People widely distributed in north-west India, mostly Hindus, and given to cultivation.
Jemadar Sahib	:	Term of respect; term generally used for second class native officer in the army
Jhatka	:	Cutting the throat with one stroke
Ji	:	A term of respect
Jihad	:	Holy war of the Muslims against the infidels
Jinnis	:	Etherial spirit
Jo bole so nihal	:	He who utters this will be blessed
Kafir	:	Nonbeliever; a non-Muslim

Kaliyug	:	The sinful age according to Hindu belief—the present age
Kalma	:	A vowel of Muslim faith
Kameez	:	Shirt
Karakuli	:	A Muslim head dress
Kariyana	:	Grocery
Kebab	:	Meat dish
Kewra	:	Essence
Khunda	:	Blunt knife
Kikar	:	A tree of the Acacia family
Kirpan	:	Sword worn by Sikhs
Kissakhani	:	A bazaar in Peshawar
Korma	:	A spicy meat dish
Kotha	:	A quarter in the red light district
Kutcha	:	Unpaved; not concrete
Kurta	:	Indian style shirt
Kutchery	:	Court-chamber
Laddoo	:	A kind of sweetmeat
Lajwanti	:	A flower —Touch-me-not
Lalaji	:	A term of respect for a rich Hindu
Lambardar	:	Registered headman of a village
Lathi	:	Stick
Lota	:	Metal tumbler
Lungi	:	Loose sheet of cloth worn by menfolk
Maajee	:	Term of respect for an elderly woman
Mahshallah	:	God is great
Mahya	:	A Punjabi folksong
Mai-Bap	:	Mother–Father; protector
Maidan	:	Open space for public assembly
Malta	:	A variety of citrus fruit: orange
Mantra	:	Vedic text used as prayer or incantation
Mataji	:	Mother; grandmother
Maulvi	:	Muslim religious teacher
Memsahib	:	Madam; wife of a sahib
Mian	:	A term used for Muslim menfolk
Mohalla	:	Neighbourhood

Muezzin	:	Mohammedan crier who proclaims the hour of prayer
Mujahid	:	Crusader
Muharram	:	Muslim festival, the first month in Muslim calendar
Mullah	:	Muslim religious teacher
Mundan	:	Hindu ceremony similar to baptism
Munshi	:	A learned Hindu
Murabba	:	A measure of land devised by British rulers for grant in lieu of services rendered
Murha	:	A cane seat
Musla	:	A derogative term for a Muslim
Namaz	:	Muslim worship at the five specified time of the day
Nargis	:	An Indian flower, Narcissus
Neem tree	:	A tree belonging to the Azadivacta Indica family
Newar	:	Broad tape
Nihang	:	A class of orthodox Sikhs
Ni tun ki Karni hain	:	What are you doing?
Ni tun kithe hain	:	Where are you?
Paan	:	Betel leaves
Paanwala	:	Betel seller
Palla	:	End of the sari
Pandit	:	Hindu priest
Patiwala	:	Share holder
Paranthas	:	Indian pancake
Peepal	:	The Indian tree, Ficus religiqsa, or Botree
Peedhi; Peera	:	Low string seat
Pera	:	A sweetmeat
Pilau	:	Rice cooked with meat or vegetables
Pir	:	Muslim saint or holy man
Pitaji	:	Father
Prasad	:	Offerings to the temple god
Panja	:	An aggregate of five; here it refers to a hand with five fingers extended
Puri	:	A small-sized *chapati* fried in oil
Purdah	:	Women screening themselves from male strangers

Pushtu	:	Language spoken in the North-Western Frontier Province of Pakistan
Pyjama	:	Loose trousers worn in north India
Qaid-i-Azam	:	A popular title of Mohammed Ali Jinnah, founder of Pakistan
Ramzan	:	Muslim month of religious fasting
Rishvatpura	:	The colony of bribe-takers
Roti	:	Indian pancake; unleavened bread
Rumi	:	Persian poet
Samadhi	:	Yoga posture
Salaamed	:	Saluted
Salwar	:	Baggy trousers used mainly by women in north India
Sari	:	Indian female garment
Sandhus	:	A Jat caste
Sidhu	:	A Jat caste
Sindoor	:	Vermilion used by Hindu women in the parting of their hair to denote marital status
Saras	:	A bird
Sardarji	:	An honorific often used to address Sikhs
Samosas	:	An Indian snack
Satyagraha	:	Non-violent political agitation
Sat Sri Akal	:	God is Truth--a Sikh slogan
Ser, Seer	:	About a kilogram
Shaitani	:	Mischief
Shami Kebab	:	Meat dish
Sheikhji	:	An honorific often used to address Muslims
Sherwani	:	A long coat popular with upper-class Muslims in India and Pakistan
Shikar	:	Prey
Sobhan Allah	:	God be praised!
Suhagwanti	:	A woman in marital bliss
Tation	:	Mispronunciation of station
Tandoor	:	Clay oven for baking, popular in North India
Tehmed	:	Cloth worn by menfolk in North India

Thal	:	Large metal plate
Thana	:	Police station
Tola	:	An Indian weight measure
Tonga	:	A horse-drawn carriage
Tongawallah	:	One who drives a tonga
Tonta	:	Cripple
Trinjan	:	Where young girls assemble for knitting, sewing, song and dance
Turrah	:	End of turban left protruding out
Ussi, tussi, saadey, twhaadey:		We, you, our, your
Vedas	:	Ancient Hindu Scriptures
Vay jaja	:	Go away, you!
Wah	:	Hurrah!
Wahe Guru	:	The Guru is great
Wahi-i-Guru Ji ka Khalsa	:	The Khalsa belongs to God
Wahi-i-Guru di Fateh	:	The success must go to God
Ya Ali	:	Oh God
Ya Allah	:	Oh God
Yaar	:	Friend
Yekka	:	See *ekka*
Zalim	:	Cruel; also a term of endearment
Zamindar	:	Well-to-do landowner
Zindabad	:	Long live